SPECIAL DISTRICT:
HARBIN
DRAWING THE TIGER'S BONES

TIM STICKEL

Special District: Harbin

Copyright © 2022 by Tim Stickel. All rights reserved.

No portion of this book may be reproduced in any form without written permission from the publisher or author, except as permitted by U.S. copyright law.

DEDICATION

To Stelarus, for help polishing the rough edges

Let him be helped to read a single history wisely, to apply the principles of historical evidence to its statements, to trace the cause and effects of events, to penetrate into the motives of actions, to observe the workings of human nature in what is done and suffered, to judge impartially of action and character, to sympathize with what is noble, to detect the spirit of an age in different forms from our own... let him learn to read a single history thus, and he has learned to read all histories...

—William Ellery Channing,
"Elevation of the Laboring Class"

PROLOGUE

ALTHOUGH HARBIN WAS LOCATED in the middle of Manchuria, or the Three Provinces, she was like no other city in China or the world. She was the quintessential cosmopolitan city where Russian tailor shops sat side-by-side with Chinese dry goods stores, Korean restaurants, and Japanese brothels, each displaying a cacophony of languages in their signage. Chinese men in jangly-bright robes and Russian businessmen in dark suits shared the sidewalks. European and American businessmen and Soviet railway officials, always in a hurry, passed them by. But it wasn't just the dynamic tableau of different cultures and races that made it cosmopolitan, it was also the interplay between modernity and the traditional European empiricism and Asian spirituality. Recognizing its uniqueness, the Chinese government designated the city as a Special District with its own civil administration.

In the beginning, the Russians dominated, bringing the railroad and their unequal treaties and created the city of Harbin in 1898. When revolution and civil war brought down the Imperial Russian government, thousands of refugees from across the Russian Empire fled across the Chinese border to the city. The local Chinese took the reins of power in the city rather than let them fall into the hands of the Bolsheviks. Then there grew a balance of sorts between the staid White Russian community and the new Chinese elite from a shared interest in the health and future of the city. A Russian predilection for organization and the Chinese desire for harmony created a marriage of convenience. Russian-speaking Chinese policemen patrolled the sidewalks together with Chinese-speaking Russian policemen in matching black Special District police uniforms. Criminals and litigants faced Russian law in Chinese courts, defended by either Russian or Chinese lawyers.

But in May of 1929, the peace and harmony was broken. Acting on a tip, the Harbin police raided the local Soviet consulate for holding an illegal Comintern meeting and found documents there plotting the overthrow of the Chinese government. On July 10th, the local warlord, Chang Hsueh-liang, also known as the Young Marshal, used this evidence as an excuse to seize control of the Chinese Eastern Railway, or CER, away from his Soviet partner and arrest the entire Soviet leadership. The Harbin police shuttered the offices of all Soviet newspapers, political clubs, and enterprises in the city.

Those were heady times, and many residents were thrilled by the Young Marshal's blow against the Soviets and their subversive efforts to control the CER and the city. For all their righteous propaganda about fighting the imperialism of the capitalist nations, the Soviets had proven themselves no different than any of the other western imperialist powers. Even reports of a Soviet mobilization and troop buildups at the far western and eastern borders of Manchuria did not seem to deter popular enthusiasm for the Young Marshal's martial stand. Even as the Soviets responded with provocations and border raids instead of diplomacy in the following months, the city's spirits remained high and crowds at the Harbin central train station cheered

SPECIAL DISTRICT: HARBIN

trainload after trainload of Chang's troops as they headed west to the contested border.

But as the warm days of July merged into the swelter of August, the violence came to Harbin even though it sat hundreds of kilometers from the region's borders. Not content with saber-rattling by his armies, Stalin sought to deny Marshal Chang and the Nationalist government the use of the CER, both militarily and commercially. What Stalin couldn't control he then meant to deny to his former partner through sabotage. It began with the removal of rails outside the city limits, hoping to derail the trains that were the lifeblood of the city and the Marshal's forces and his many commercial enterprises. Then telegraph and telephone lines were cut, and even railroad equipment within the city was damaged.

The city was still full of Soviet railway workers, and some acted as agents of the GRU, Stalin's foreign intelligence agency, stirring up class struggle, sometimes fostering alliances across the races, other times dividing them. Rumors and propaganda were rampant; the truth didn't matter, only whether the message served to undermine people's trust in the civil authorities. The residents became withdrawn and suspicious because one no longer knew whether your neighbor or coworker held the same politics as you. Martial law was finally declared in the city on the 10th of August, but it didn't stop the vandalism or the propaganda and subterfuge. The harmony that had seemed enduring now seemed to shimmer like the air in the heat of summer. Yes, the city would remain, but what would it become?

PART ONE

CHAPTER ONE

NEXT TO THE WINDOW, Borya felt invisible. And being invisible gave him the freedom to be himself. The window glass separated him from the world outside and yet still allowed him to be part of that world. That world was the Pristan district of Harbin, and he was sitting behind the window at his private table at Mama Melnikov's Tea Room on a corner of Kataiskaya Street. He had picked the table because it provided a view of one of the major cross-streets of Pristan, or Daoli to the Chinese, and was reserved for him alone night or day, whether he showed up or not. Like many busy commercial districts in major cities around the world that summer of 1929, traffic was already beginning to stir. Swift motorcars and the occasional motor-coach dominated the inside lanes, weaving around plodding horse-carts and daredevil rickshaws.

But Borya was not invisible, and the occasional pedestrians would look his way through the glass, often seeing him bent over his books. Some saw the wavy dark brown hair that he inherited from his father and figured him another Russian Kharbintsy. Others looked closer and also saw his Korean mother's eyes and pegged him the product of one of Russia's central Asian provinces or maybe one of the city's "mongrels." But here, behind the glass wall, Borya would sometimes stare boldly back like he was the one on the outside and looking into a cage at a zoo and they were the animals on display. Many would look quickly away, but others matched him stare for stare until they walked out of sight. There were also those few that he knew or had grown accustomed to him that smiled his way, and then he would smile back. And if they were pretty girls, he might even smile at them first, startling them into glancing shyly away or erupting into muffled giggles. But if he had met any of them on the street, they would only see the mask that was his shield of unreadable features.

But lately all the passersby seemed distracted, their heads turning constantly as if sniffing the air for danger. The current "troubles" had everyone on edge, wondering whether the current chaos would pass or if it was a portent of major social and political shifts that would change their city forever. And no one seemed to have the answer.

Borya didn't rate his own table at the window of the tearoom because he was a Special District policeman but because the owner, "Mama" Melnikov, was his aunt. Not a real aunt—she was his father's cousin, but she insisted Borya call her *Tatushka*, Auntie, and she made her tearoom his home away from home. Following the untimely death of his father, Sergei Vladimiriovich, he had lost all of his Russian family ties in Harbin except for Auntie Melnikov, who had no children of her own. It was she who encouraged him to keep ties with the city's Russian community through his school and church activities. These activities were, of course, all in White Russian organizations, founded by the refugees who fled across the border to Harbin to escape Bolshevism.

So Borya stayed true to his father's legacy and continued to make the trek up the bluff to New Town and St. Nicolas Cathedral every Sunday for Mass with Auntie Melnikov. Here he found comfort in the old familiar rituals, and in the chants and the hymns he could hear again the timbre of his father's voice. He would remember times when the church was crowded, and he ended up sitting in some pew well behind his father but could always pick him out from the peculiar way his head sat low between hunched shoulders and the small pink bald patch on the crown of his head. The pink patch was the subject of a recurring family joke, as his father insisted on denying its existence since he could not see it for himself in the mirror.

This morning Borya had stopped at his aunt's tearoom at the end of his night shift of patrol duty to have a glass of tea and a roll before returning to the family's apartment to sleep and eat again until his next night shift. Outside, the morning sun found ingress between the two-and-three-storey buildings, and shadows from the spiderweb of overhead electrical and phone wires cast dark lines across the storefronts. As the sun rose, Borya watched the lines slowly crawl down the buildings toward the sidewalk. He knew he was putting off returning home to avoid the cramped apartment he shared with his mother and two sisters. Between customers, "Mama" Melnikov abandoned her cash register to come over and greet her nephew. Where Borya's father had been hunch-shouldered and square-built, his cousin was erect and round but moved lightly on her feet like a ballerina despite her considerable weight and sporting a halo of grey/brown hair and a smile that was never far from her lips. She stopped behind Borya's chair and rested her meaty hands on his shoulders.

"Busy night, Borya Sergeevich? It worries me when you're out on night duty these days."

"It's okay, Auntie, they keep us in pairs now."

The cash register called her back, but her question returned his thoughts back to the night's events, shutting out the clatter of plates and conversation and the smell of boiled cabbage. Borya had spent the previous night on duty at the southern-most guardhouse in Harbin's 8th District, his first assignment as a full-fledged officer. The 8th held the majority of the city's Korean and Japanese population as well as many Russian and Chinese railway workers, and he was a native speaker of both Russian and Korean as well as being fluent in Mandarin. He had shared the night duty with another young patrolman, a Han Chinese named He. That night, their neighborhood had been relatively quiet, and they spent the dark hours monitoring the phone that connected them to the Special District central police station. The phone had to be attended at all times, and they were given new orders not to leave the guardhouse alone, so they were stuck there until relief came at dawn. The phone link was important because the central police station was connected to every home and business in Harbin through an ingenious modern signal system that had been the pride of the new Chinese police leadership and a progressive civil administration. A switch in every home allowed the resident to send a signal to police headquarters, once for a robbery and twice for a fire, and would also illuminate a triangular lamp outside the front door. If it was a break-in or assault, then Police headquarters would telephone the nearest guardhouse to dispatch patrolmen to the identified house or business. Other times, officers patrolling the streets would see an illuminated lamp and respond even before a phone call came through. It had greatly increased police response times and reduced nightly crime, especially as the majority of Harbin residents did not own their own telephone.

But lately the system could not keep up with the reign of terror that was currently happening in the city.

At the end of his shift, he was given a message to report to his precinct commander. Commander Cho was a pinched-faced man of about fifty and missing half of his left ear. There had been a dozen stories among the men in the precinct about how he had lost his ear, but no one really knew for sure, but they all warned him not to stare at it. Cho greeted him in his office with his usual scowl, even though Borya was always careful not to stare at the stump of his ear. Borya was never sure if he was a source of personal displeasure to his superior or it was this how he treated all his lowly patrolmen. He suspected the former.

"Are you interested in a special assignment?"

Borya's brain froze. Special assignment? For a first-rank patrolman, that could mean anything from escorting convicts to cleaning the precinct's latrine. Cho's scowl indicated he was not going to give an explanation before an answer was expected, and answering 'no' would not put him into the commander's good graces, if such a thing existed. He also knew if he ever wanted to make second-rank and a pay raise, he had to show proper compliance.

"Well?"

"Yes, Commander."

"Good. That's all for now." Borya's mouth opened, but nothing came out. The explanation would apparently be coming later. He was left with no recourse but to back his way out of his commander's office.

Borya was pulled from his thoughts back to the present by movement outside his window, movement that his brain didn't register a part of the normal pedestrian patterns. A shabbily dressed Chinese boy whose age was anywhere between eight and twelve jostled a middle-aged European in a western suit. Without seeing more than the fastest flash of a hand, he knew the older man's wallet had been lifted undetected. Borya's body told him he was tired, that his long shift was over, and he was no longer on duty. He jumped up and ran out the entrance of the tearoom and caught up to the pickpocket halfway down the block, running silently so he startled the boy when he grabbed him up by the back of his shirt collar, eliciting a squeal of surprise.

"Give it up."

The boy began to struggle and protest until he saw Borya's eyes, and he went slack and slowly pulled the European's wallet from his own pocket and handed it over. The European had meanwhile turned back to watch this bit of street theater and then patted his empty pocket, and his eyes went wide. Borya waved him back, holding out the wallet to its owner.

"Many thanks, Officer," the man announced in a Great Russian accent. Borya sized up the man's baggy suit and pegged him one of the railroad's Soviet workers or managers, making him half-regret his intervention. "May I offer you a reward," he continued, pulling a one-yuan note from the wallet.

Borya looked long and hard at the banknote, knowing what it would mean to his family's meager budget.

"Give it to him," he finally replied, pointing to a one-eyed beggar sitting on a straw mat next to the outside wall of the tearoom. Surprised, the Russian put the note into the bowl of the equally surprised beggar. Then Borya, still holding the pickpocket by his collar, walked him by his tiptoes into the alley at the end of the block.

"Are you going to take me to jail?" the boy said in a small voice.

That wouldn't really solve anything, Borya thought to himself. "Not this time," is what he said out loud. "But don't let me catch you stealing in this neighborhood again. Even begging is a legal profession." He let go of the collar and sent him on his way with a boot to the backside that was more educational than painful.

Borya returned to the tearoom and his seat by the window. In his short absence, the waitress had refilled his tea glass, only now the handle of the glass holder was no longer at the four o'clock position relative to his chair, and he carefully corrected it. Then his attention was again interrupted, this time by the sight of a stocky, barrel-chested Chinese man wearing a dark western suit and hat coming down the sidewalk, a lit cigarette dangling from his mouth. He had a pronounced limp that caused him to sway from side to side as he navigated his way around the beggar. Even without the limp, Borya recognized Inspector Chinn of the Harbin detective squad out of the central police station in New Town. One of the most senior detectives, he had come to Harbin's Police Academy once to speak to Borya's cadet class about the workings of the detective squad and how it interfaced with the precincts and patrolmen. To Borya, he had seemed an iconic force of nature, and Chinn had reinforced that image by not suffering any "stupid" questions but tolerating a few "good" ones. From that day forward, Borya had aspired to someday become a detective and to solve major crimes.

Borya watched as the detective came by his window and was surprised when the grizzled, square face stared in through the glass directly at him. For just a fraction of a second, their eyes met, and Borya could not see the bottom to those black orbs. The eyes looked straight at his own but seemed focused beyond him like they were locked onto some distant place, and

Borya looked quickly away, feeling like he might be trespassing into the other man's innermost thoughts. He was surprised again when the older man stopped at the tearoom entrance and tossed aside his cigarette and entered and then stumped across the room directly towards him. Borya felt a sudden stab of fear—were those eyes sad because the older man was bearing a burden of pain, a pain that would become his? He had a sudden flashback to that evening years past when his father's Chinese manager had come to tell his mother of "a terrible accident," standing at their threshold and turning his hat over and over in his hands. Had something now happened to his mother? One of his sisters? His grandfather?

"Officer Melnikov, I was told I might find you here. I am Inspector Chinn. You have been temporarily assigned to me. You speak and read Mandarin as well as Russian?"

"Yes, Inspector. And Korean. And a little Japanese."

"Good. We are to report immediately to Superintendent Liu at Police Headquarters." Borya breathed again, erasing the cold chill that had arisen only seconds before. Assisting one of the Special District's top detectives! Chinn's voice was flat and unemotional, so he couldn't tell if the older man actually welcomed the idea of being assigned a lowly first-rank patrolman as an assistant, but it couldn't have dampened Borya's excitement at that moment. He left his tea glass on the table and followed the older man outside, stuffing his half-eaten roll into a pocket of his black uniform tunic. The fatigue from having just finished a full duty shift melted away.

CHAPTER TWO

OUTSIDE, BORYA'S SHORT LEGS easily kept pace with Inspector Chinn's uneven gait. His arms and torso were long and proportional like his father, but his legs were short, for which his mother would apologize like somehow it had been her oversight in his development. That left him average height except when everyone in the room was sitting down, when he was often the tallest.

The Inspector elected not to wait for the streetcar and its circuitous route through the city and instead led them on the direct climb on foot up the hill from Pristan to New Town and the central police station. The older man kept a steady pace despite his limp and did not slow even to shake a cigarette out from a half-empty pack and light it from a match he struck with a thick thumbnail. Typical of August in Harbin, it began to drizzle, increasing the already high humidity, and he bent his head forward to shield the glowing match with the brim of his hat. He seemed perfectly content to remain silent all the way to their destination, but Borya could not stand the silence any longer. Could this special assignment have something to do with the current Bolshevik agitation? He hoped so, if only so he could have some small part in putting things back to the way they had been before.

"Do you know what this new assignment is about?"

"Not yet."

"Maybe about the shooting in Pristan?" Only yesterday, a White Russian patrolman, barely older than himself, had been shot dead in the street. The gunman, likely a Soviet agitator, was still at large after having escaped in a waiting motorcar.

Chinn snorted smoke out his nose. "Most of the detective squad is already working that case. No, it is something else. We will find out soon enough."

The headquarters of Harbin's Special District police headquarters resided in the monolithic Municipal Office building. It was a four-storey stone structure that occupied a corner on Prospect Street and was like many of the city's modern municipal buildings built there in the last three decades by the Russians to service their new city in the wilderness of Manchuria. The corner of the building angled to face the intersection like the bow of a huge ship. A masonry cornice wrapped around the building between the third and fourth stories and outside columns set on either side of the entrances ran all the way to the roof and were topped with oblique globes. Borya loved the art deco style for its outspoken modernity. Superintendent Liu's office was on the second floor in an office that directly overlooked Prospect Street. A young Chinese police cadet sat behind a desk that guarded the door to the superintendent's office, and after announcing their arrival beyond that door, he ushered Inspector Chinn and Borya inside. Only months ago, before his advancement from cadet to first-

SPECIAL DISTRICT: HARBIN

rank officer, it might have been him at the outside desk, Borya thought. Superintendent Liu was seated behind his wood desk, facing a single stack of papers that looked like they had been carefully squared and a clean ashtray on one of the corners that faced visitors. Everything in the room looked tidy and orderly except for the woodblock print on the wall behind the desk that hung crooked by a good inch. Borya fought the urge to step over and straighten the picture.

The superintendent looked directly at Inspector Chinn, not turning his head or even his eyes to acknowledge Borya. Borya, who had never met Liu before, found him a thin, angular man in a crisp police uniform, and he judged him medium height, though this was a guess as he was sitting. His hair was cut short and was sprinkled with grey and the set of his jaw and piercing black eyes and a rigid posture hinted at a past of serious discipline and formality. Borya had heard Liu was a graduate of the prestigious Nankai school in Tianjin, which taught a western-style education and focused on providing a new generation of leaders dedicated to building a strong China. Borya also knew him to be a rising star among the city's Chinese administrative elite, clearly shown by his position as supervisor over the elite detective squad as well as other departments. There were two wooden chairs facing the desk, but the superintendent did not offer them a seat, and they remained standing.

"I received a phone call from the chief of railway security at Changchun," Liu began. "They have a body of an unidentified white man that they can't tie locally, so they want us to check to see if it is one of our Russians." Borya knew from the reference to Changchun that he was referring to the Japanese Railway police that administered the South Manchurian Railway zone, but like most of the Harbin civil government, Liu avoided gracing a Japanese counterpart with any better title than general "security" at the risk of acknowledging their legitimacy. The Japanese had "won" the Russian concession for the southern branch of the Manchurian rail system in the 1905 Russo-Japanese War, including Changchun, and like the Soviets in the Chinese Eastern Railway, they ran their own railway zone like it was a piece of their own sovereign territory carved out of the Chinese Northeastern provinces. Liu used the Mandarin word for "Russian," but Borya wondered if he would have used the more common term *laomaozi,* or "old hairy," if he had not been present.

"Which means they're hoping he isn't a Soviet railway worker that died inconveniently in their zone," Chinn observed drily. "That could be messy for them."

Japanese and Soviet relations had grown icy since Stalin had come to power and began pushing the export of communism to the Far East. And the Russian CER and Japanese SMR respective railway zones met at Changchun. Liu did not respond, his face motionless, and Borya took that as tacit agreement. Apparently, so did Chinn. "Did he say how or when the man died?"

"Just not of natural causes. I want you two to go to Changchun and see if you can identify him." Borya's heart fluttered though he kept his face in its blank mask. Changchun! Yes, he'd been out west on the Chinese Eastern Railway but never south further than the outskirts of the city where he'd been born. Liu continued, "Check our files here first for any white men missing in Harbin. Do not take custody of the body unless you can prove he is from Harbin and he didn't die in their zone. They will try and dump him and any problems on us. Railway security at Changchun station will be expecting you."

Liu turned his eyes on Borya for the first time. "Officer Melnikov, I can't spare any other detectives to accompany Inspector Chinn, so you will be assisting him. Your name was provided by your precinct commander." Then, turning back to Chinn, Liu continued. "Draw a voucher for expenses for three days, and do not be gone any longer than that. Two days should be sufficient. Then report directly to me when you return," and he handed a handwritten sheet of paper across his desk to Chinn. "Here is your authorization."

Chinn and Borya bowed their way out of the office. Once outside Liu's office in the corridor beyond, Chinn turned to Borya. "I will go draw the funds and paperwork before Liu changes his mind or gets overruled by the Chief Superintendent," and then lowered his voice to a whisper. "This could be a real mess for us instead of the *Eastern Dwarves* if the dead man turns out to be a Soviet railway worker and his death can be traced back to here. The Soviets would be very happy to blame us for the death of one of their citizens. You must follow my lead exactly."

"Of course, Inspector!" Borya replied, trying to put the right tone of sincerity in his reply.

"With what is going on in the city right now it could be a blessing to be in the south, even for just a couple days," Chinn mused. Borya doubted that Cho, his precinct commander, had recommended him for this assignment just to get him out of danger. More likely he had seen an opportunity to rid himself of another Russian from his precinct, even if it was temporary. But Borya didn't care what was the real reason, it was a unique opportunity to work under a veteran police detective.

Chinn continued, "Go down to the detective squad and make notes from all of the open missing persons files for Russians or foreign white men going back a year. Include any photos or sketches."

"Isn't a year going back a long time?" Borya asked. He knew that the detective squad clerks would complain about any extra work on their part. "If you don't mind me asking."

Chinn grunted. "Certainly ask any sensible questions, that is how one learns... Liu said the *Eastern Dwarves* didn't tell him how *long* he has been dead before he was found, only that it appeared to be foul play. And there is always the chance he might be some European that bandits have been holding for ransom for months and they just ran out of patience."

Borya nodded to this logic. Bandits were numerous in many of the rural or wilderness areas of the Three Provinces, especially in those areas where poor harvests had driven many to desperate measures. It wasn't uncommon for them to hold a foreigner or provincial official for ransom, though usually the ransom was paid and the captive released. Killing your captives sent a poor message if you're trying to solicit future ransoms, better to let them live to pay another day.

"I will check on your progress in a couple of hours," Chinn concluded.

Borya knew the way to the detective squad room, but he hesitated at the open doorway, recalling the mixed feelings of nervousness and elation he felt at school each time he entered a new level classroom for the first time. Did he belong here? Would they question his right to even be here? He peered through the doorway in almost reverent awe—here was where the elite of the police force resided, applying their investigative skills to solve the unsolved and ferret out the evidence needed to bring the worst criminal elements of the city to justice. The doorway opened into a small foyer where the public was separated from the inner sanctum by a long wood-paneled counter whose three openings were zealously guarded by hard-eyed clerks in identical white shirts and black ties. Beyond the counter was a large room, one side taken up with rows of wood filing cabinets and shelves stuffed with rolled maps and documents; the other side was crammed with identical wood desks pushed up against each other nose-to-nose beneath electric lights in suspended milky white glass fixtures. Half the desks were occupied and a low buzz of conversation and the clanging of several telephones filled the air, which was dense with cigarette smoke.

Borya could see the desks were bunched in clusters by department and labeled by signs in both Mandarin and Russian that hung from the ceiling: Vice, Robbery, Murder, etc. His eyes were automatically drawn to the six desks that marked the territory of the murder squad. This was the operating center of the detectives who addressed the worst crimes of the city—the taking of a human life. Here worked the men who fought against the worst impulses and acts of men, defending that bedrock contract between society and the individual—the sanctity of a human life. Of course, the murder squad did not investigate every murder that took place in Harbin, that would have been impossible. Borya knew from his morning patrols, especially when assigned to the Fujiadian district, that the alleys of the city were dumping grounds for junkies and beggars killed for the few fen they carried. Those killings pretty much went unsolved unless there was a witness or the killer was caught in the act. The cases referred to the murder squad usually involved a better class of victim and, of course, any foreigner. It wasn't a policy of callous disregard for the lowest classes, it was simply an issue of practicality and resources.

Borya hesitated before the counter, acutely aware that he was an outsider to this elevated level of police hierarchy, but finally resolved to be bold. After all, had not Inspector Chinn himself directed him here? From his position and posture he identified the chief clerk, a middle-aged and sour-faced Russian manning the middle entrance through the counter like he was defending a breach in a castle wall. The man looked past Borya as if first searching for someone more worthy than a first-rank patrolman of his time and attention until Borya explained he was there at the direction of Inspector Chinn. He explained his mission but modified Chinn's instructions to also include any missing mixed-blood *ermaozi* ("second hairy") males also. He was concerned that the Japanese might not have bothered in their report to make a distinction between a mixed-blood *ermaozi* and a full-blooded *laomaozi* white man, or maybe even failed to recognize the difference, thereby missing a possible match. Borya personally disliked the idiom, having heard it often enough applied to himself, many times in a derogatory way but just as often without an intended negative connotation, and so he had learned to accept it as popular usage.

The senior clerk still frowned his displeasure, but Borya was used to senior clerks who ruled their departments like their personal fiefdoms. He passed the task along to a more junior Chinese clerk as young as Borya to whom he had to repeat the instructions. He was kept waiting at the counter a full hour before the junior clerk showed up with seventeen identical brown file folders, and Borya asked him which desk belonged to Inspector Chinn.

"Oh, so you are the one they sent to help Xiao Kongzi," the junior clerk said with a smirk, casually pointing him to which was

Chinn's desk in the center of the corner reserved for the murder squad.

"Little Confucius?"

"You'll see," the clerk answered with a second smirk. Then Borya asked for some paper and a pen, and the smirk was replaced with a downward curl of the lip.

The frozen mask returned to Borya's face, and his nostrils flared. "If it's not too much trouble."

The smirk disappeared, and the clerk hurried away. While Borya waited, he made some working space on Chinn's desk by consolidating a loose pile of police reports into one neat stack to one side and emptying the over-flowing ash tray into a nearby wastebasket. He tried to look inconspicuous, but his long torso made him stand out among those seated in the room. After several minutes, the junior clerk returned with some sheets of blank paper but no pen. Apparently, he wasn't about to be trusted with one of their own pens. Fortunately, Borya had his own fountain pen with him and hoped it had enough ink in it to complete his assigned task.

Borya addressed the first task of prioritizing the folders with eagerness, silently crediting his father with implanting a love of organizing all things and applying order to all aspects of his life. The elder Melnikov had been the consummate engineer, applying logic and physics to all aspects of his life, including to the raising of his children. Breakfast time was measured by a stopwatch, and study and play times were carefully scheduled and compartmentalized. Borya's sisters bridled at the control, and his mother usually could ignore it, but Borya embraced it wholeheartedly, finding calm and reassurance in the structure it provided even after his father's passing.

He glanced through all seventeen folders first to ensure they all met the criteria. Four were boys that were twelve years of age or younger and whose height and weight in their descriptions he felt would have kept them from being confused with an adult. Another was actually a woman! Was the junior clerk just that sloppy or was it a test to see if he would complain? Borya decided it didn't matter which it was, he had twelve missing adult white or mixed-race males, and that would be enough to keep him busy for the next couple hours. Seven were residents of Harbin: five Russians, one German, and one Frenchman; four were Soviet railway workers of the Chinese Eastern Railway; and one was an American who was not a resident of Harbin but had been reported missing there anyway. Borya remembered the American from the newspapers because the local American consul-general had made a stink about it at the time, but after seven months of being gone without a trace, that story had grown old. Could the body found be his?

Next, he put them in order of most recent missing first and started going through them again one at a time. He copied down their names, ages, heights, weights, and other descriptions along with any listed clothing or personal effects like watches or rings or briefcases from when they had last been seen, each on their own separate sheet of paper. There were photographs for all of the foreign residents, as they all have their pictures taken for the identity papers required of them by Harbin police. Some of the other files had only sketches of the missing, and he took one copy of each of these and wrote their names on the back if it hadn't been done already. If it was the only copy of the photograph or sketch in the file he carefully wrote out a note giving his name, rank, the day's date, and what was borrowed and left it in the file. By then his stomach rumbled, and he remembered the half-eaten roll from the tearoom in his tunic pocket and took it out and ate it with his free hand while he kept writing with the other.

He was on the seventh file when Chinn showed up at the desk. He looked carefully through Borya's notes as completed so far.

"I see you included *ermaozi*," Chinn observed.

"I—I thought in case the Japanese didn't make the distinction . . ."

Chinn chuckled. "No, that is good. Carry on." Then he left Borya to continue his research and came back a few minutes later with some paperclips and a cardboard accordion folder. He paper-clipped the sketches and photos to the appropriate finished sheets of notes and then left again. In another few minutes he returned, this time with two cups of tea, handing Borya one with a heavy dose of sugar, Russian style. The tea was strong and warmly welcomed as Borya could feel his lack of sleep starting to weigh on him. Chinn then brought over another chair and sat down and waited patiently as Borya completed his copying, smoking cigarette after cigarette and refilling the ashtray. Once he offered his cigarette pack of Pearls, a local Mukden brand, to Borya, who declined.

"No, I can't afford to get started." Even the cheap cost of a pack of a local brand would mean taking money away from his mother's scant household income.

"A bad habit. Got started in the Army," Chinn said and returned the pack to his suit pocket.

The ink in Borya's fountain pen held out, and he indicated when he was finished. Chinn paper-clipped the photos and sketches to the remaining sheets of notes and placed all of them in the cardboard folder and handed the folder to Borya.

"Good. Hang onto these overnight. We have reservations for the 7:25 AM train to Changchun tomorrow morning. I'll meet you on the platform at 7:00. Wear your uniform, it usually helps whenever going outside Harbin—the Japanese love uniforms and no one can accuse you of being a spy. And bring an extra uniform. You can take the rest of the shift off to get yourself ready."

Borya smiled, not in appreciation at the intended kindness, but the irony that he was actually halfway into the second of back-to-back shifts and was mentally exhausted. But he was not about to bring this up for fear of making him sound ungrateful for what was an auspicious opportunity.

"Do I bring my revolver?" he asked as Chinn began to step away, not sure of the protocols outside the Harbin Special District.

"Yes, as I will be wearing my Mauser pistol," Chinn answered, and then turning back to him winked, "... *after all, beware a tiger with a smiling face.*"

Borya wasn't sure he had actually seen a wink coming from that serious countenance, but before he could think of a reply he was sitting alone. What had he meant? That the Japanese were the "tiger" and couldn't be trusted? And was his reciting of a traditional Chinese saying the reason the squad room clerk had called him "Little Confucius"? And too late he realized that Chinn had not offered to let him carry any of the money that had been allocated for the both of them.

CHAPTER THREE

BORYA WALKED THE MAIN avenue that led down from New Town into District 8, home to Harbin's largest Korean neighborhood and the family's apartment. There his Korean mother, Ji Woo, had moved the family from the Pristan district after the death of Borya's father, both to find a cheaper apartment and to be closer to her own father, Borya's grandfather, and his shop where his father and mother had first met. His mother always liked to be the one to tell the story of how they met, probably because, like most of her stories, she liked her own version the best. Her father, Jung Byung-chul, had started work in an herbal medicine shop in a medium-sized town near Hamhung, a city in northern Korea, where he was apprenticed to the owner and learning the trade. The owner did not pay well, barely enough to keep him, his wife, and Borya's mother in food and clothes, but he did let the little family use a backroom over the shop free of rent. The owner had no family of his own, and Borya's grandfather hoped one day to take over the shop.

But shortly after the conclusion of the Russo-Japanese War in 1905 in Japan's favor, Korea became a colony of Japan in all but name. When the harvests were bad, Japanese money-lenders seized the land of local Korean farmers and sold it to Japanese immigrants. Rice grown locally was shipped to Japan while the dispossessed farmers starved. Like many of his neighbors, Borya's grandfather joined the Ch'ondo-gyo sect, or Religion of the Heavenly Way, for its stance on peasant reforms and against increasing Japanese control. It didn't take long before the Ch'ondo-gyo were targeted by the Japanese and by their Korean supporters in the Ilchin-hoe party. Arrests were widespread and made for any reason, and unless you had the money to buy back your freedom, you remained a hostage in jail. Borya's grandfather learned he was being targeted because of his life-long studies of the Taekkyeon martial art, taught to him by a local master and fellow Ch'ondo-gyo member, which to the Japanese made him a threat. He also knew he did not have near enough money to pay the requisite bribes, so he packed his few belongings and meager savings and fled with Borya's grandmother and mother across the border into the neighboring Kando region of Manchuria, a home to many Korean refugees.

In the Kando they lived hand-to-mouth with Borya's grandfather and grandmother taking odd jobs as farm laborers from the more established Korean farmers there. It was a hard life, and his wife died of consumption, and he struggled to raise Borya's mother alone. Then word came to him from his old mentor, the owner of the herbal shop back in Korea. He had heard of a Korean herbal medicine shop in Harbin, far to the north, was for sale by its ailing owner. His old mentor even sent references and enough money for train fare to take them to that far-off city. The family arrived in Harbin in the bitter winter months and were directed to a shop in the middle of a Korean neighborhood in District 8, a section of the city sandwiched between the commercial Pristan and Chinese Fujiadian districts. They found it true that the elderly Korean owner was ailing and had no sons to take over the business. Impressed with his grandfather's references from the homeland, the elderly shopkeeper offered to sell the business to Borya's grandfather for a loan to be paid to the old man or to his surviving daughters.

Borya's grandfather could not believe his luck. Well-experienced in the traditional medicine practices from his apprenticeship, and starting with a fully-stocked shop, he was soon able to make a decent income even with the loan payments. He developed a reputation in the neighborhood as an expert in curatives and supplements and for his honesty among both the Korean and Chinese residents of the district. When his grandfather's younger sister back in Korea became widowed, he even sent her money to come with her daughter to live with them in Harbin. And it was there in the front window of the herbal shop that Borya's future mother was arranging displays when Borya's future father first saw her and was immediately smitten by sight of the slight, serious girl of seventeen.

Borya's father, Sergei Vladimirivich Melnikov, had already been in Harbin five years at this time, having come fresh from engineering school in Moscow to take a position with the burgeoning Chinese Eastern Railway, or CER, which despite its name was really a Russian state project linking Vladivostok in the Russian Far East with the rest of the Russian empire via a shortcut across Manchuria. After helping with the design and stocking of the locomotive repair shops in Harbin, the central hub of the whole railway, Sergei Vladimirivich at the young age of twenty-seven was made the supervisor over all locomotive repair and tooling in the city's vast rail yard and machine shops. At the time, he lived in the CER's bachelor quarters in New Town, and although he regularly walked the streets between there and the locomotive repair yard behind New Town, he seldom needed to walk through District 8. But one day he had been walking down by the riverside, hoping fresh air might help him forget a nagging toothache. It didn't, and a passing Russian told him there was a chemist shop nearby in District 8 where he could buy some aspirin. He hadn't found the chemist shop, but the smile of a pretty girl in the window drew him into a nearby herbal shop. Several minutes later, he walked out with herbal remedies for pain and tooth afflictions. In the weeks that followed, he found frequent needs to visit the shop, but only when the pretty daughter of the proprietor happened to be there. Later, Borya's mother confessed she found the shy railway engineer handsome but wondered if he was falling apart with all the health afflictions that he professed to have. Finally, Borya's father found it cheaper to ask her out to a movie than add another unopened remedy to his medicine cabinet.

By the time Borya reached his neighborhood it was past mid-day, and the sun had burnt away the clouds and heated the air. He could feel sweat starting to trickle down between his shoulder blades. Being mid-day, there wasn't any shade on either side of the street, and he would have liked to have unbuttoned his uniform tunic, but that would put him at risk of being spotted by a senior policeman and cited for appearing too casual in public. It had been only a few months since his promotion from cadet, and he was barely past that probationary period, so he could ill afford any bad marks, and there were enough Russian or Chinese policemen who wouldn't hesitate to put a young mixed-blood *ermaozi* in his place. Under his cap his head felt hot, and his hair was damp with sweat. Finally, he reached the block that held his family's apartment and was happy to remove his cap as he walked up the stairs of the wooden tenement to the second floor over a noodle shop. The air in the narrow hallway upstairs was stifling, and the floorboards under the threadbare carpet runner creaked under his now shuffling feet. First he visited the shared bathroom at the end of the hall, fortunately unoccupied, to use the toilet and splash cold water on his face. Then he returned to the hallway and pulled his key from his pocket and unlocked the door to #3, already unbuttoning his tunic with his free hand. Finally, the mask came away.

The air inside the apartment was barely cooler than the hallway. The windows overlooking the street were open to capture any breeze but the curtains did not stir. The front room was barely five meters by six meters and was crowded with furniture that had come from their former, larger apartment in Pristan. It was in this room that the family cooked, ate, and his mother and two sisters shared a large bed in one corner. The bed was separated from the rest of the room by a curtain of old bedsheets to give his mother and sister's a pretense of privacy to dress and sleep when Borya was home. The other oversized furniture became a daily obstacle course and made the room feel even smaller, but his mother insisted on hanging onto every piece. Sometimes it felt to Borya like the thin walls were closing in on him. There was also a small side room barely the size of a large closet that was where Borya slept.

The first voice he heard was that of his younger sister, Min, already home from school. "It's only Borya," she announced in a breezy imitation of their mother's voice. Min, only thirteen, was already a young beauty, the combination of her wavy brown hair and Asian features giving her an exotic Eurasian look. Her name meant clever and sharp, and she was boisterous and spoiled by her older siblings. Hei-rin, whose name meant grace and orchid, was seventeen and had her mother's dark hair and eyes and was no less pretty than her younger sister, but unlike Min, she was shy and soft-spoken outside the family apartment. The two sisters had Korean given names at their mother's insistence after she had lost that battle with their father over Borya, the first-born and a boy. But it hadn't hurt that the Russian "Borya" sounded close to the Korean boy's name "Bora."

It was still early for Hei-rin to be home from her part-time job at a Pristan clothing store, where her proficiency in Korean and Russian and the pidgin *Moia-tvoia* helped with serving the store's diverse clientele. Together Borya and Hei-rin added their salaries to their mother's own income from doing sewing jobs for neighbors to cover the family expenses.

Min's greeting was immediately followed by a more strident tone from their mother. "Borya, where have you been, I was so worried! A Russian policeman was shot in cold blood in the street yesterday in Pristan. I was afraid it had happened to you too!"

Borya immediately regretted not having told her that news yesterday. But he knew it would have worried her, so he had put it off a day, hoping that she wouldn't hear it first on the street or at the market. But, of course, that was big news, and he knew he had only been fooling himself to think she wouldn't hear it sooner rather than later.

"Yes, Mama, I know. Today all policemen must patrol in pairs and be armed. I was safe in the guardhouse by the railway tracks all night with another patrolman . . ."

"And the morning too? Are all patrolmen doing extra shifts now?" Her taut face shone up at him as she moved in front of the light from the window, her greying head barely reaching up to his chin.

"No, Mama. The most wonderful thing happened this morning. I was picked to assist a senior detective on a missing persons case. And tomorrow morning I am to go to Changchun on the train with him!"

His mother's mouth opened, but to Borya's amazement, no words came out. He couldn't remember the last time his normally animated mother was at a loss for words.

"Changchun!" Min cried out, filling the silence. "Will you bring me a present?" Although now a teenager, Min still slipped easily into her role of the spoiled youngest child. But Borya shared her excitement as neither he nor his sisters had ever been to another big city. There had to be many marvelous and different things to see in another city as big as Harbin.

"Yes, of course. For you and Hei-rin and Mama. Everyone!"

By now his mother had found her voice. "But the Japanese are in Changchun! They throw Russians and Koreans into prison!"

Borya forced a laugh, hoping to allay her fears. "No, it will be okay. It is the Japanese that have asked us to come. They want our help."

Now his mother looked dubious. "The *Eastern Dwarves* are asking you for help? When did they ever think they needed anyone else's help? It could be a trick!"

"Well, not *my* help exactly. Inspector Chinn's help. I am only assisting him." He knew now his mother was on a roll, and it could take hours to calm her down. Even with his father, she had never been the shy, demure type. She more than held her ground with her husband in arguments and family decisions, and Borya could remember many times seeing his father throw up his hands in surrender. But it hadn't stopped his father from loving her dearly and had never once said he regretted marrying her.

But now Borya had to interrupt his own story about his day. "I need to eat soon and get some sleep. I need to pack and be up early to meet the Inspector at the train." Borya's mother had fried noodles that morning in anticipation of his arrival after the end of his night shift. When he had not shown up, she and his sisters ate their share, and she put aside the largest portion for him, and now she reheated the remnants of that simple meal. Since Borya's father's passing, she had always reserved for him a larger portion than for herself and his sisters. He is bigger, she would tell his sisters, or he works hard in school, and now it was because he was the biggest breadwinner in the family. Sometimes Borya felt guilty and would not finish his portion, saying he was full and instead share it with his sisters, but today he was hungry, having eaten only that single roll from Auntie's tearoom since that morning, and he quickly wolfed the meal down. While he ate, he told his mother of the long boredom (and safety) of his night shift and then the exciting events that followed with Inspector Chinn and Superintendent Liu at the central police station. She listened intently with wide eyes, getting caught up in his excitement. Even Min listened closely without bothering to feign a lack of interest.

"And now I must sleep, Mama." With that, he retired to the tiny room that was his alone, another benefit of being the only son. Here there was barely room for a mattress on the floor and a bureau with a mirror. Borya made sure the one tiny window was fully open, willing to put up with the street sounds outside in exchange for any passing breeze. And anyway, he had grown accustomed to the outside noises of the city and could sleep through all but the loudest din. He undressed in tired motions but still was meticulous in how he draped his black uniform over the upright frame of the mirror that sat atop the bureau and carefully placed his police revolver in its holster in the top drawer.

Next to it, he placed his police notebook, his most treasured tool of all his police gear. Here he would dutifully record all his shifts and every arrest, call, and complaint that transpired during them. Each entry added to a framework of order and stability for him like adding bricks to a wall to hold out the chaos infecting the city. Now tomorrow, it would begin to be filled with the details of a real murder investigation and hopefully help to map out a path to an arrest and justice.

Finally, he pulled the chain to turn off the single, bare electric bulb that hung from the ceiling and lay down on the mattress. He lay still for many minutes, but the combination of being over-tired and the excitement from the morning's events kept him from falling asleep immediately. He tried watching dust motes float in the sunlight coming through the open window, but then his mind became occupied looking for patterns in their dance. Through the door he heard Hei-rin enter the apartment, and her mother shushing her into whispers. Finally, he initiated the breathing exercises Grandfather Jung had taught him, and he fell quickly into a deep sleep.

CHAPTER FOUR

JUST STANDING ON THE platform in the sprawling Harbin central train station gave Borya a tingle of excitement. He had not ridden a train out of Harbin for years, not since before his father's death. Those earlier trips had been family vacations to the west to what had seemed like wild and exotic places compared to cosmopolitan Harbin. What new and strange sites would a trip south bring?

True to his word, Inspector Chinn showed up in a black summer cotton police uniform that matched Borya's instead of his usual dark suit and fedora that was normal dress for detectives. The stars and bars of a sub-lieutenant were on his shoulder-boards, and he was gripping a canvas traveling case. He also wore the large holster of his Mauser pistol on his belt on the outside of his tunic rather in its customary concealment. The heavy automatic was not police issue, and Borya assumed it was a holdover from Chinn's army days.

Chinn and Borya boarded the southbound CER train without tickets, climbing into one of the second-class sleeper cars. This was the express train, which would get them to Changchun in six hours and was much faster than the slower mail trains. The Russian conductor gave them dirty looks, but Chinn ignored him. There had been on-going animosity between the CER administration and the Special District Police over whether the latter should be granted free train rides. This conductor didn't choose to argue the point, maybe because the police were helping guard his railway from the Bolshevik saboteurs in Harbin, and anyway they hadn't been so presumptuous as to try boarding a first-class car.

A single, narrow corridor opened onto the car's separate compartments, their doors all open. They found an empty compartment on their third try. It was a typical second-class compartment with four berths, two uppers and two lowers, as well as a one-legged table attached to the wall beneath the window, under which stood an enamelware spittoon. The compartment smelled of tobacco, and the floor was littered with discarded matches and the husks of sunflower seeds, and the spittoon was filled to the top with cigarette butts. Chinn and Borya each claimed a lower berth where they could comfortably sit across from each other, storing their sparse luggage on their bunks.

Other passengers, no doubt with tickets, stuck their heads into the compartment but hurried on when they saw their police uniforms. But finally the car was filling up, and they were joined by two men, a Chinese and a Russian, both in western dress and who seemed to know each other and claimed the empty upper berths. Either all the other compartments were now full or these two believed police protection was a boon rather than a disadvantage.

After fifteen minutes had passed, they heard the shouts of the conductors and the whistle from the locomotive and then their car clanged against its couplings and jerked into motion. Borya's heart took a leap as it did at the beginning of every train ride that led him to somewhere he had never been before, marking the beginning of a new adventure. He moved to the end of his berth next to the table to see out the window, but the glass was grimy with a brown tobacco film. He pulled a clean cloth handkerchief from his pocket and wiped the glass clean, or at least cleaner than it had been, before reluctantly returning his now dirty handkerchief to his pocket.

Chinn leaned back in his own berth and closed his eyes, letting the growing rocking of the train lull him to sleep. Once they were outside Harbin, Borya stared out the window at long fields of wheat that stretched away from the rail-bed, moving in waves from the wind generated by the passage of the train. After an hour, this became boring, and he took a slim volume from his travel case, a book of poems by Tyutchev that had been one of his father's few non-engineering books, and began reading. He didn't know when he had also fallen asleep but awoke to the sound of a porter ringing a bell outside their compartment announcing that the mid-day meal was available in the dining car. Chinn's eyes shot open.

"Ahh, shall we spend some of Superintendent Liu's money on lunch?"

They hurried down the corridor of their car and through the first class car beyond to reach the dining car, hoping to get a table before they all filled up. Other passengers were already spilling into the corridor in front and behind them. When they reached the dining car, the tables of four that lined both sides of middle aisle were already half-full, but they found seats at one of them that aligned with a window and took the two chairs next to it and across from each other, leaving the aisle seats for someone behind them. The tables were covered with white linen tablecloths and place settings just like Borya's aunt's tearoom at opening hours, except the linen napkins were folded into the empty water glasses like white tulips. Sure enough, the two aisle seats were soon taken by a middle-aged Chinese couple in well-appointed Qipao robes. A minute later, a waiter in a white uniform appeared. Chinn ordered tea for the both of them while he continued to peruse the menu. Borya decided to defer to Chinn on ordering, as he still didn't know how much money they had been given for expenses, and anyway, there were few foods he didn't like. When the waiter returned with their tea, Chinn ordered two oxtail soups and two dinners of pork cutlets but raised one eyebrow toward Borya to invite any objection. Borya nodded his agreement. There was already a sugar dispenser on the table, and Borya applied a generous portion to his own tea. Chinn lit a cigarette as did the husband of the Chinese couple who shared their table, as well as did many others at adjacent tables. Soon the ceiling of the car was filled with a cloud of smoke that slowly drifted toward the back of the car. It was like this in his aunt's tearoom, too, Borya thought to himself; one hardly needed to buy their own tobacco, as it was impossible to get away from cigarette smoke in today's modern society, even up here in northern Manchuria. They learned the Chinese couple were traveling to Dairen in the Japanese zone to visit an uncle with whom they shared a soybean oil export business. It was a trip they took twice a year, and they reluctantly confessed that the Japanese SMR trains were cleaner and ran closer to their time schedules.

Borya found the oxtail soup salty, but the pork cutlets delicious, as were the accompanying mashed potatoes and mixed vegetables. He couldn't help thinking his meal alone could have fed his whole family. Chinn lit a last cigarette and declined dessert for both of them. Borya thought of asking Chinn if he was going to finish his mashed potatoes when his companion stubbed out his cigarette in the small white mound. Oh well, and it reminded

Borya of a saying his father used to repeat at family meals: There are two kinds of people—the quick and the hungry. It had become an oft-repeated saying, but after the hundredth time, only his father and Borya's youngest sister still found it funny enough to laugh, while the rest of them would only groan and roll their eyes. Together Chinn and Borya bade the prosperous Chinese couple a good journey and returned to their car and compartment.

Over time, which related to distance, the wheat fields and open grass of the northern plains began to give way to fields of millet and kiaoliang. At Yaomen, their locomotive took on more water and fuel, and they crossed over the Sungari River where it curved southward beyond Harbin and now crossed their path. The river was narrower here than at Harbin, and this bridge was only about 800 meters long—long but much shorter than the majestic Sungari Bridge at Harbin. Meanwhile Chinn had joined in a card game with their companions of the upper berths, and Borya returned to his book of poetry, struggling to read in the dim light afforded by the single small electric light of their compartment and the sunlight from the window. Chinn smoked his cigarettes and the Russian a cigar until Borya's eyes began to sting from the thick smoke and he put his book back into his travel bag and lay down on his berth to take another nap.

It was mid-afternoon when Chinn and Borya stepped off the train onto the spacious platform of the Changchun train station, each clutching their traveling cases. The air was warm and humid here also and smelled of coal smoke and humanity. It had been only twenty minutes since they had passed through the nearby Kuancheng station, which was the southern terminus of the CER. A treaty between the two railway zones allowed the CER's trains, with its wider Russian gauge rails, to run the remaining distance south to Changchun station, and reciprocally, the SMR's standard gauge and American-built locomotives could continue as far north as Kuancheng. Yet another example of the inefficiency resulting from the patchwork of companies and treaties that created the disordered railroad network of the Northeast Provinces, Borya mused.

Grim-faced Japanese soldiers in khaki with rifles stood at intervals of several meters up and down the platform that serviced the CER trains coming from the north. Uniformed Japanese railway police stood at the steps of each car and eyed every passenger as they disembarked, pulling some aside to check their identity papers or passports. Here the railway guards were active-duty Japanese soldiers. This was the northern terminus of the South Manchurian Railway zone —a lease territory born of treaties imposed on the Chinese government after Russia's shameful defeat in the 1905 Russo-Japanese war. The Japanese had then created the Kwantung Government to administer their Leased Territory and ran it like it was their own colony within the Three Provinces. Only a decade later, they coerced the Chinese government into extending the lease into the next century. The whole Leased Territory included a wide swath of land stretching the entire 1100 kilometers of SMR railway lines that ran through southern Manchuria, swallowing numerous cities and towns, and comprising 250 square kilometers of Chinese land.

Chinn and Borya had barely stepped onto the platform when a Japanese policeman motioned them aside, but almost immediately two other uniformed Japanese approached them, their uniforms styled different from the railway guards and policemen. One stopped before Chinn and bowed slightly and held out his hand to shake.

"You are Inspector Chinn from the Harbin Special District Police?" His Mandarin was flawless though accented, and his uniform impeccable. He looked to be of comparable age with Chinn and had a high brow permanently lined with deep furrows that gave him the appearance of a man in a constant state of displeasure. He then gave the taller Borya a curious look, trying to classify him from his mixed Eurasian features. It was a look Borya was accustomed to receiving and returned it with the placid indifference of his expressionless mask.

Chinn shook the proffered hand and bowed at the same time. "Yes, and this is Officer Melnikov, my assistant." Typical Japanese thoroughness in that they had Chinn's name and rank already at hand, Borya thought.

"I am Inspector Ota, and this is my assistant, Inspector Akashi." More bows all around.

"And you are SMR Railway police?" Chinn enquired.

Inspector Ota tightened his lips into a slight frown. "No, we are actually consular police of the Kwantung civil government. As we have reason to suspect the deceased did not come from our zone, it was no longer an issue for the railway police. ... We have the body in a railway car at the other end of the station. I will take you there now if you are ready, or do you wish to use the facilities or take some refreshments first? You have had a long journey."

"No, we're fine," Chinn responded without looking at Borya. Borya eyed the Japanese assistant out of curiosity, but the man avoided his gaze.

"Very well then, follow me."

As soon as it was apparent that Chinn and Borya were guests of the civil police and not being detained by them, a small knot of Chinese porters swept forward, pushing dollies or small wheeled trolleys and loudly advertising their services despite the meagerness of the pair's luggage. That is all but one porter, neither young nor middle-aged, who hung back from the rest and stood staring warily at Chinn and Borya. When Borya stared back, the lone porter quickly looked away and pushed his dolly to the far end of the platform. Maybe he was someone who had been in trouble at Harbin sometime in the past and recognized his and Chinn's Special District uniforms? If so, Borya didn't recall having seen him before, but that meant nothing considering the teeming thousands that lived in or passed through Harbin every year.

Chinn shooed away the rest of the porters with a dismissive gesture, and together they followed the two Japanese off the platform and through the grand lobby of the station, a marble hall bisected by rows of wooden benches and vendor kiosks. Inside, they were greeted by a cacophony of sounds from the milling crowd that reverberated from the stone walls, but they were quickly led out again through a side-entrance. Here there were several rail side-spurs and loading docks where newly arrived freight cars were being unloaded and other cars being loaded with outbound cargo. A swarm of sweating Chinese stevedores raced around with dollies laden with crates or sacks higher than their heads, reminding Borya of a disturbed anthill. The inspector and his assistant led the way toward a single car sitting alone at the end of the loading docks, the crowd of yelling and cursing stevedores carefully parting around the two Japanese like waves from the bow of a menacing warship. As they drew nearer, Borya could see the railcar was a refrigerator car, its once bright white wooden exterior now soot-stained. A single Japanese railway policeman sat on the set of iron steps that led down from the front of the car but jumped up into rigid attention at the sight of their approaching party.

"I commandeered this refrigerator car to hold the body until your arrival," Ota explained. To the rigid policeman he barked "Open the car," and the policeman pulled a key from a tunic pocket and unlocked and removed a padlock from the tall door that bisected the side of the railcar, allowing the heavy wooden door to swing open on creaking hinges and releasing a small cloud of condensation and a refreshing wave of cool air. Ota led the way inside, stepping across the short span between the platform and the open doorway and into the frosty interior. Just inside the door was a carbide lantern that assistant inspector Akashi sparked to life and held aloft, illuminating the railcar's interior sides of wooden slats and metal louvers. The only object inside was a bulky shape covered by a blanket and resting on what looked like a typical canvas ambulance litter occupying the center of the floor. With all the flourish of a vaudeville magician, the Japanese inspector whipped off the blanket, evidently hoping for a shocked response from the two Harbin policemen. The sight was both unique and gruesome but neither Chinn nor Borya gave him satisfaction by showing any reaction other than one of professional curiosity.

Lying on the litter was what had once been a large man with definite Caucasian features, slightly balding with bushy eyebrows and a thick mustache, and clothed in a western-style suit. Only it was no longer a large man. First, there were no legs below the thighs, just frozen blackened stumps. And second, the exposed face and hands were like shrunken leather, making it appear more like an Egyptian mummy than a recently deceased foreign male. Borya had seen enough dead bodies lying in the alleys of Fujiadian during morning patrols, the anonymous victims of violence or illness or simple exposure, to have become inured to the presence of death. At those times, it could still bother him to see the empty husk that so recently harbored a life and a soul, but this body was different, so distant from its former term of life that he found it more a spectacle of curiosity than of tragedy.

Ota, Chinn, and Borya all kneeled down to get closer to the body while Akashi remained standing to better cast the lantern light from above. There was an unmistakable odor of decay, but Borya had no doubt it would have been overpowering without the refrigeration. He removed his notebook and fountain pen and expectantly opened to a fresh page.

"You found this body only recently?" Chinn asked incredulously.

"Five days ago now, alongside the rails just beyond the station. It was found in an area that is visited daily by our soldier patrols, and it hadn't been there the day before."

"So it must have been buried or stored somewhere and recently brought here?"

Ota smiled as though he was privy to a private joke. "Do not be deceived by the appearance of the skin. Our police surgeon examined the body and determined it had been treated with quicklime. He assumes this was done to slow the putrefaction, but quicklime also desiccates the skin. However, there were enough bodily fluids still leaking out that he believes that death was somewhere within the previous two or three weeks. The effects of the quicklime, of course, makes an exact estimate difficult." Borya was scribbling furiously in his notebook with his fountain pen, and Ota paused to let him catch up, a slight look of annoyance on his face.

"Did you find the legs?" Borya asked. Now the Japanese inspector looked clearly annoyed. Was it Borya's singular mixed-race presence or just his audacity to intrude on a discussion between superiors? No, maybe he was being paranoid—he noted Ota's assistant had not spoken a single word since their introductions. But Chinn nodded slightly as encouragement.

"No. The police surgeon said they were sawed off post-mortem. We surmised that it was done to fit him into a trunk or crate. That was one clue that led us to look outside of the SMR Zone. Another was that he is not a match to any foreigners currently missing here in Changchun or elsewhere in our Zone."

Now it was Chinn's turn. "That doesn't mean he came from Harbin. Were there any identity papers or personal effects on him?"

"Nothing was found in his clothing or in the vicinity that provided a clue to his identity. However his suit jacket does have the label of a Harbin tailor."

Chinn raised one eyebrow. "But many foreigners in the Northeast Provinces buy suits from Harbin. We have many good Russian and Jewish tailors. Did your surgeon determine a cause of death?"

The inspector moved aside some hair, stiff with frost, from the side of the dead man's head. "Gunshot to the side of the head at close range. No bullet recovered... in and out. Looks to have been a small caliber... probably a pistol rather than a rifle."

Borya was puzzled. If the SMR's police surgeon had examined the body thoroughly, why was it still dressed? Did he put the clothes back on the corpse? That wouldn't have been an easy task. "Did the surgeon do a full autopsy?" he asked after a moment's silence.

This elicited another frown, and Ota directed his answer toward Chinn. "When the body was found near the station in this condition, we immediately moved it into refrigerated storage after examining the scene and taking photographs. The police surgeon examined him here in the refrigerated car. When we concluded he came from outside our Zone, it was decided to leave any complete autopsy to whoever are the responsible authorities.

And with it being a white foreigner in a Harbin suit, I naturally called the Railway Guards in your zone."

But it had taken the usually efficient Japanese three entire days before they telephoned Harbin, Borya noted mentally—Ota had said the body had been found five days previous, allowing two days for the CER Guards to pass along the message and the responsibility to the Special District Police and Superintendent Liu, and then another day for he and Chinn to get to Changchun. Probably the Japanese authorities were sweating bullets when they thought he could be a Russian. Ever since hostilities had broken out between the Bolsheviks and the Young Marshal, the Japanese had made it plain that they considered the hostilities solely a matter between the Russians and Chinese. They had, in fact, been trying to keep a low political profile in the Northeast Provinces ever since the assassination of Marshal Chang Tso-lin, the Young Marshal's father, the previous year. Although Japan had blamed the death on local bandits, everyone knew it had really been the work of Japanese hotheads from the Kwantung Army.

Chinn snorted. "Yes, and meantime our own railway guards passed this mess on to us," half to himself and half to Ota. "Do you mind if I search his pockets?"

"No, go right ahead. The only thing I found was a single coin, which I returned to the pocket of his pants."

Chinn moved to his knees and began searching the pockets of the man's trousers and suit jacket, including the inside pocket. It was slow work as the fabric was stiff with the cold, and he had to roll the body on its side to check the rear trouser pockets. As Ota promised, there was only a single coin in his right front trousers pocket, which Chinn examined and then shrugged and handed wordlessly to Borya. Borya held it up to in the light of the lantern for a closer look—it was a one fen bronze coin of Manchurian issue identical to thousands currently in circulation. Borya handed it back to Chinn who returned it to the pocket where it was found. No sense in taking away any evidence before they had determined the body and case belonged to them, but Borya made a note of the coin in his notebook.

Chinn got to his feet slowly, leaning one hand on a knee to leverage himself up. "Well, Borya, let's see if we can match him to any of our own missing person reports."

Borya removed the cardboard folder of files he had brought from Harbin from his travel case. He then laid each file open one at a time upon the chest of the corpse below the macabre, shrunken face. The three men crowded around the litter to try and determine a match on each photo, sketch, or description. The sixth file had an identity photo that showed a heavy-set balding man with bushy eyebrows and mustache. Borya could immediately see a strong resemblance in the features despite the desiccation. The corpse's original weight, and certainly its height, were no longer measurable, but he found it believable that the body could have once matched the listed size and stature. Even the age, forty-eight, looked about right.

"Ahh!" Chinn and Ota said together. "Who is the man in this file?" Chinn asked.

Borya picked up the page of notes for that file that he had written back at Harbin police headquarters and read aloud: "Manfred Geiger, a German employee of the Binjiang Products British Import and Export Company. He was reported missing on August 6th, last seen by his employers on July 28th."

"Ahh, the Chicken and Duck Company in Fujiadian district," Chinn nodded his head. "I know it. They have had the occasional labor dispute."

"Well, the time of his disappearance fits the window for the estimated time of death provided by our police surgeon," Ota announced almost happily or as happy as he allowed himself in front of foreigners.

"Yes, but as you said, it's rough estimate because of the chemical reactions on the body," Chinn cautioned. "But I have to admit there is definitely a resemblance." Borya knew Chinn was calculating what Superintendent Liu's reaction would be if they brought the body and the case back to Harbin. It was more than just a "close" resemblance, but that still didn't reveal *where* the man had been murdered.

Just to leave no stone unturned, they went through the remaining six files, but none of these came even close to the match with the photograph of Herr Geiger.

"Would you like to see where the body was found?" Ota offered with a polite smile, rising to his feet.

"Yes, please," Chinn replied. "Herr Geiger" was once more covered with the blanket, and the inspector led the way back out of the railcar. Now that he was no longer singularly focused on examining and identifying the body and taking notes, Borya realized how cold he had become and actually welcomed the return to the warm summer temperature of the loading platform. Chinn produced his ubiquitous cigarette pack of Pearls and offered it to Ota and the Japanese assistant, not bothering to extend the offer to Borya. Ota took one and returned the favor by lighting both their cigarettes from a small silver lighter.

They returned to the vast lobby again and then the train platform where Borya and Chinn had arrived, and then Ota led them down some steps to a set of rails currently devoid of a train. They trudged along the railbed for maybe a quarter of a kilometer before Ota left the railbed and turned toward a small strip of red cotton fluttering from a stake in the ground poking up among the weeds.

"Here is where he was found," Ota announced, pointing to the red flag. Chinn examined the spot and then walked in widening circles around the flag with Borya following behind, but there was nothing remarkable to be seen except a lot of footprints and trampled weeds.

"Were there any fresh footprints or wheel tracks found when the body was first discovered?" Chinn finally asked.

"Yes, too many footprints. As I mentioned, this area is a regular route for our railway guard foot patrols," Ota replied.

Chinn looked back at the train platforms in the distance. "Still plenty visible from the station."

"Yes, but not at night. Why don't we go to my office here in the station and have some tea, and we can talk about our next steps," Ota announced effusively, still wearing his polite smile and waving his cigarette in an expansive gesture and looking like the cat that had eaten the canary.

CHAPTER FIVE

WHEN THEY RETURNED TO the station platform, Borya noticed the lone shy porter had again retreated to the far end of the platform. He was fidgeting and kept his face low by staring at the platform deck. Did that mean anything? Should he speak out or act on it or just ignore it? But if this guilty-looking porter was somehow tied to the body and Borya unearthed it, that could very well increase his esteem in Chinn's eyes. Of course, if he acted on it and he was wrong, he would appear inexperienced and impulsive. But then this was only a temporary assignment for him and thus afforded limited opportunities to stand out. Nothing ventured…

"Excuse me, I will be right back," Borya announced to Chinn and the two SMR men and headed in the direction of the toilets inside the station lobby. But once out of sight of the platform, he veered back toward another set of steps that led down to the empty rails they had just vacated. Being in uniform, no one nearby thought to challenge him. He walked quickly past the length of the platform and ascended a second stairway back up to the platform, coming up behind the shy porter who still stood watching Chinn and the SMR police from a distance. Borya stepped up behind him and put one hand on his shoulder and clamped the other around his opposite upper arm. The man actually jumped into the air in shocked surprise. Borya gripped him tightly but allowed him enough movement to turn and see his antagonist, which only increased the look of alarm on his face.

"Hello, esteemed porter. I would like to talk to you about a crate you received here about five days ago."

"I am sorry, sir, –I—I help with many crates."

"I am sure you do, but I am talking about a particularly smelly crate. I am sure you remember it."

"No!" the man wailed, "I do not know what you are talking about." The man now seemed practically hysterical with fright. It seemed out of proportion, but maybe the man was frightened by their proximity to the local Japanese police, with whom Borya had just been seen together. The Japanese police had more of a reputation for ruthlessness than he could likely muster as a lowly policeman far from his own jurisdiction. Still...

"Well, let's see if my Inspector and the policemen here, the ones you are so carefully avoiding, believe you." He pushed the man ahead of him down the platform while maintaining the grip on the man's arm and shoulder. As they got closer, they drew surprised looks from Chinn and the Kwantung policemen.

"I noticed this man was carefully avoiding us when we first arrived," Borya explained. "And now he seems to be extremely nervous. I asked him if he remembers moving a crate that came here five days ago, but apparently his memory doesn't go back that far."

Chinn raised one eyebrow, and the Japanese inspector gave Borya a thin-lipped smile and then turned that smile on the porter, but when he did, the smile left his eyes.

"Well, let's take him to our station office and see if we can help trigger his memory," the inspector said in a flat monotone. The porter sagged in Borya's grip.

They followed the inspector and his assistant down and beyond the train platforms to a set of offices accessed through a door off the station's grand lobby. Inside the door was a small lobby and desk, but the inspector led them beyond it and into a hallway and then into a small room that held a single wooden table and several wooden chairs. Borya sat the man down in one of the chairs and took a chair with the others opposite the cowering porter. With his long torso, Borya suddenly towered over everyone else except for the assistant Akashi, who remained standing directly behind the porter's chair. The porter sat shaking and wiped snot from his nose onto his sleeve. Nobody spoke.

"I told you... I move many crates every day—"

The Japanese inspector slammed his open hand down hard on the table, making the porter jump in his chair and startling Borya with its suddenness. "This crate would be as heavy as a large man and probably leaking body fluids. I cannot believe you would not remember that. I think you will have to stay here until you remember..." He let the rest of the sentence hang in the air, ripe with menace.

"Yes, yes, I did... do remember. But I didn't know what was in it—"

Borya breathed a silent sigh of relief. His hunch had been right.

The hand collided with the table again with a sharp crack.

"I... I didn't know it to begin with..."

"Who received the crate?"

"I don't know him. I have never seen him before. He did not tell me his name, I swear!"

"Where did he have you deliver it?"

"Uh, well, I didn't—" This time the inspector slapped the porter hard across his face. Borya jumped in his chair again, but

Chinn, sitting beside him, lay a warning hand on his thigh below the table. The porter wailed and more snot dribbled from his nose and was added to his sleeve. "He... he paid me three yuan to dump the crate anywhere outside the station. I took it out past the last platform by the fence. I... I knew I could get almost a yuan for the crate from a scrap merchant, so I forced it open and emptied it out... and that's when I saw the body. I didn't know what was inside until then! I swear!"

"Where is the crate now?" Chinn interjected, knowing there had to be markings and paperwork.

"I took it home but it smelled so bad I didn't think I could sell it. I broke it up and burned it for firewood..." He looked from face to face, looking for understanding but finding none.

"Why didn't you report this to the railway police?" the inspector demanded, his voice rising even louder.

"I was... was scared. I was afraid you would think that I had killed the man."

"I think you did!" the inspector replied coldly.

"No, no! I swear! I didn't!"

"What about the shipping documents? Tags?" Chinn interrupted.

"The man... the man who paid me tore it off the crate and threw it away."

"Threw it where?" Chinn persisted.

"Off the platform. Behind the freight office."

They kept at him, but there was not much more to be gained. His description of the mystery man who paid him to dump the crate was vague—a middle-aged Chinese man in worn western-style clothes, no distinguishing features or in his appearance except he had a "hard face." No, he hadn't seen him before or since. Yes, he could take them to where he had seen the mysterious Chinese man throw away the shipping tag.

The porter led the way to the freight office next to the station platform and behind it to where there was an open space filled with weeds and broken crates that extended ten meters to a barbed wire fence. "It was there, along the fence. He crumpled it up and threw it there." The porter swept a pointed finger along a wide stretch of the wire fence. "After I dumped the crate, I followed him to the corner of the building in case he was trying to avoid paying me. I don't think he saw me. After that, he came back and paid me." Low bushes grew along the fence, and the fence itself was dotted with garbage that had been snagged out of the wind.

"Has it rained here in the last week?" Chinn asked Ota, who looked up at the sky while he searched his memory, as if he would find the answer from the few clouds that dotted the sky. Chinn turned next to Akashi.

"Twice, but not a hard rain," the assistant inspector volunteered.

Ota kept a tight grip on the arm of the porter while the rest of them fanned out and began searching amongst the debris. Borya found waxed paper wrappers, cigarette and cigar butts, discarded tickets, and even a soiled cloth diaper before he retrieved a crumpled card from under a thorny bush. He flattened it out. It was a CER shipping document, which meant it was in both Russian and Chinese. The destination was Changchun, and it was dated eight days ago, which put it in the right timeframe to have made it to Changchun and the discovery of the body on August 13th. The stated weight corresponded to the number of kilos one would expect coming from most of a body and a wooden crate.

"I think I found it!" Borya declared. "It has a good date, destination, and weight." He brought it over and held it up to the porter's face. "Is this what he took off the crate?"

The porter squinted hard. "It looks like it. But I cannot read, so I am not sure." Ota surprised Borya by reaching out to snatch the form from his hand, but Borya pulled it back, and the Japanese caught his wrist instead. He had little chance of moving Borya off-balance with the latter's short legs and low center of gravity, and instinctively, Borya took a half-step forward anyway and "fed the Tiger," twisting his wrist and putting slight pressure at the base of the other man's thumb, easily breaking the grip before stepping back, still holding tightly onto the paper. The older man's eyes widened but saw only Borya's face set in its mask. Borya was no longer at the Changchun rail station but in his grandfather's basement in Harbin, practicing his disengagement moves over and over again.

Ota's face reddened, and he let go of the porter, and this time grabbed both of Borya's wrists in a savage grip, but Borya easily broke it with a downward twist of his arms before stepping back once more, still holding the paper, his face still in the mask. He fought to suppress his training that would normally lead him into one of the many throws afforded by the other man's momentary imbalance. Always use no more force than what the circumstances dictated, his grandfather had taught him. But this new passive resistance brought a fresh flush of anger to the Japanese inspector's face. Akashi, who had taken over the task of holding onto the porter, looked frozen in shock, his eyes wide. Japanese authorities were known to arrest Koreans in their Zone for simply knowing even these simple martial art "tricks" as they considered them symbols of resistance. He realized that right then he was very far from Harbin.

CHAPTER SIX

ALARM SHOWING ON HIS face, Chinn stepped in between them. "Esteemed Inspector, this paper could be important evidence to our case. You must relinquish it to us or else you can keep the foreigner's body and the SMR zone can provide the explanation for his death."

Ota turned his glare now upon Chinn, nostrils flaring, but made no further move to take the crumpled form away from Borya. He was obviously unused to being challenged by anyone except his own superiors and looked like he was fighting hard to control his temper.

"Very well, keep it," he finally managed after a long pause, his words coming out like a hiss between his teeth. "I do not believe this man died in our Zone, so the case is now yours. I will have the body re-crated, and you can take it back to Harbin. I will prepare papers giving you written authorization to take possession of the body and all evidence. Do you wish to take this turd also?" and he gestured toward the cringing porter.

"No, I believe he is telling us the truth," Chinn answered. "His only crimes—of not reporting the body and destroying evidence—happened here. So it is up to you whether to charge him or not." The porter looked hopefully at the two Japanese but did not find a reassuring response from either of them.

Ota led the whole party back to the railway police office again. There the inspector handed Chinn a large envelope that contained the photographs taken at the scene of discovery and a carbon copy of his own preliminary report and said he would have orders immediately typed up and signed. They would need to be counter-signed by Chinn to acknowledge he was taking possession of the body and the evidence and for the body to be crated and taken to the station shipping department. It would take a while to prepare the documents, so he let Borya and Chinn leave the office but insisted they not leave the station property.

Together, they returned to the station lobby and Chinn bought them tea and a roasted chicken from one of the lobby vendors. Sitting at a small table and chairs in a corner of the grand lobby, they were finally alone and able to talk freely.

"Next time... if there is a next time... do not play tug-of-war with a Japanese police official in their own Zone, otherwise we may never make it back to Harbin alive. We are lucky they are fixated on getting rid of the body and the blame." Borya heard the stern tone of his own father's voice in Chinn's words, and he felt the same sting as when he had been a boy and was being admonished for some childhood mischief or dereliction of his schoolwork. Borya felt his face redden and nodded. He wanted to argue that the case and the evidence clearly belonged to them anyway and not to the SMR, but he held his tongue. They were not under Russian laws and Chinese courts here—it wasn't a matter of being right—it was all about power and saving face. Also he very much wanted to continue supporting Chinn on the investigation.

Chinn slowly lit a cigarette before finally breaking the ensuing silence. "So, how did you know the porter had something to hide?"

Borya shrugged. "I didn't... not for sure. He just kept watching us so closely, and somehow it didn't look right. I can't really say why, I just took a chance..."

"Good... *You may be able to draw a tiger's skin, but it's much harder to draw it's bones.*" Chinn winked but Borya's eyes clouded. "You may see a person's face but not know what they're thinking," Chinn translated, "and seeing what's in a man's heart is the key to finding the our murderer."

"So how do you... draw their bones?"

Chinn paused, blowing out a cloud of smoke. "Always watch the eyes, then the mouth and any body movements. But the eyes cannot lie, and you will learn to be able to read a man's thoughts through his eyes.... Now show me the shipping document."

Borya laid it out on the table between them along with his notebook, trying to flatten out some of the creases in the form with his hand. Chinn looked at it long and hard before speaking, and one eyebrow steadily rose. "I agree the weight and dates all work out, but take a look at the place of origin."

Borya turned the paper around so it faced him. "Barim." Borya knew the town lay on the CER route in the mountains between Harbin and Hailar. He had even been there once as a youth.

"Yes, not Hailar or Harbin. And the name of Bolormaa for the sender." Then Chinn pointed to the open notebook, and Borya quickly entered those details.

"Mongolian or Manchu?"

"Mongolian I think," Chinn replied, drawing the words out and ending it in a thoughtful sigh. Next, he opened the envelope containing the police photos from the discovery scene. There wasn't room enough on the small table to spread them all out at once, so he laid them down one by one so they could view them together. Several photos were of the body from several angles, shown lying face down in a tangle of weeds. Other photos showed the vicinity of the rail tracks and fencing, and they both agreed it matched the location they had been shown. The carbon copy of the Japanese inspector's preliminary report was in Japanese and would have to await translation upon their return to Harbin. His cigarette finished, Chinn turned his attention to the roast chicken, and it was Borya's turn to break the silence.

"I suppose we have to consider that Geiger could have shot himself and whoever found his body just shipped it to Changchun just to get rid of it or to embarrass the Japanese."

Chinn grunted, then replied, "Hopefully, after a proper autopsy in Harbin, our own surgeon will have something more to say on that."

As Chinn was being forthcoming, Borya hoped this might be another opportunity to learn more of the skills and thought processes of an experienced detective and decided to press further.

"If he was murdered, what about a motive? Why do you think he was killed?"

Chinn grunted again. "Greed. It is almost always greed."

Borya wrote *Greed* into his notebook and underlined it. "Always greed? What about crimes of passion? Or politics?"

"Greed of power."

"Or love?"

"Love? Just greed of this," and Chinn pointed downward toward the crotch of his trousers. "It is either the greed of lust or to have power over another."

"But politics—"

Chinn waved it away with a sweep of his hand. "Always it is when men... or sometimes women... have lost their virtues and family values. Or maybe they just never had any. So now we need to find out who the greedy one is."

"How does one go about finding the greedy one, if I may ask?"

Chinn allowed a sly smile. "You must pull on the threads and see which one pulls apart the seam and disrobes the guilty one. Of course, you begin with the most colorful, the most obvious, threads first. If those don't reveal the guilty, then you pull on the smaller threads. Sometimes you think you have pulled on every thread, but it could mean you just haven't looked far enough... or it could mean you just haven't pulled hard enough. So, you fill your notebook up with threads and cross each one off when they don't pan out. Hopefully, there will come a point when there is only one left. Your notebook is your most important police tool, much more than your weapon. I have ended only two investigations with a drawn weapon, but almost every one came about by capturing clues and organizing my notes."

Borya pondered on this for a moment. "What are the chances we will catch the murderer?" Immediately after he said it, he regretted his use of "we" instead of "you." Even to himself, he sounded presumptuous—after all he was a helper, not a partner. But Chinn only smiled. Was the old inspector warming to him?

"You mean *if* he was murdered and it was not a covered up suicide by your theory?"

Borya blushed, "Well then—to catch whoever was responsible. I just threw that out as a consideration. How often are you successful at solving a murder, if I may ask?"

Chinn smiled again. Three smiles. "Yes, you may ask. Almost always... almost. But most cases are obvious and easy.

Others, like this one, are more complicated and take persistence. Persistence and patience. But eventually the truth and the guilty party are revealed. *No matter how big your hands might be, they can't cover the whole sky.*" He winked again.

Together they finished picking apart the chicken with their fingers and remarked on the grandeur of the Changchun station, comparing it to Harbin's Central Station and the pride of the CER. The architectures of the two stations were comparable in their eyes, but both had to admit the Changchun station was cleaner. But it also had a much greater presence of police and soldiers than Harbin's station had in peacetime. But then it wasn't peacetime in the North now, and the Harbin station under the Bolshevik reign of terror now had as many or more police and railway guards as here in the Kwantung Zone. There were, however, also a few vendors in the lobby selling trinkets, and Borya found one where he could buy three colorful silk scarves for his mother and sisters. Chinn also found some trinkets for his family and a cart where he could buy more Pearls cigarettes.

It would be more than five hours since their arrival, and it was dark outside before they finally watched the new crate being loaded onto a freight car of the northbound CER mail train. Unfortunately, there were no more express trains running until the next day. The cost of the crate and the price to ship it to Harbin were courtesy of the SMR. Inspector Ota and Akashi came to see them off, probably more to ensure that they and their scandalous cargo left Changchun and the SMR Zone than it was any kind of professional courtesy. Nevertheless, they all shook hands and exchanged bows. Ota even shook Borya's hand, but

Borya silently hoped that he would not have reason to meet the grim Japanese inspector again.

Borya and Chinn found seats in a second-class passenger car. Borya did not see the guilty porter back among the others on the station platform and pondered his fate. Yes, the man had been guilty of crimes, and it had been his responsibility to bring them to light, but he couldn't help feeling some sympathy for anyone that fell into the hands of the Japanese Zone's police, guilty or not. It had been a long day, and after everything that had happened, he had not had a single chance to see any of the great city of Changchun beyond the limits of its railway station and what little he had seen of it through train windows. Maybe next time... if there was a next time.

CHAPTER SEVEN

BORYA AWOKE FROM DOZING in his seat by the window in time to see the morning sun reflecting from the towering white limestone buildings of New Town as the train pulled into Harbin's central train station. His heart warmed. Back home! For all its imperfections and challenges, Harbin was *his* city. Not just because he had lived here all of his twenty years, but because their souls were somehow intertwined. With a Russian father and Korean mother, he felt he and the city were alike, a blend of logic and the mystical, the West and the Orient. He was like *Moia-tvoia*, the Russo-Chinese pidgin that was the language of Harbin's streets and commerce, a mix of the disparate elements of the city that came together to help create a collective soul, and Borya was like a microcosm of that soul. And, as his Korean grandfather had told him, his backgrounds gave him the vision to see into more than one world at a time. But that was both a blessing and a curse, as it sometimes left him with too many choices of which vision to believe and which to follow.

There are many different faces of Harbin—after all, you can't form a composite without having separate components. Outside New Town, with its White Russian and European bureaucrats and wealthy Chinese Christian converts, there were the mixed districts of commercial Pristan and the worker tenements of District 8. And then there was Chinese Fujiadian with its overcrowded neighborhoods, a few for rich merchants and the rest for the many poor. Each district had their own distinct neighborhoods and cultural associations. But despite his partly Slavic features and Russian accent, Borya didn't belong here in New Town or Pristan, and likewise, he felt an outsider in Chinese Fujiadian. So, rather than resign himself to being an outsider in any of the city's streets and neighborhoods, Borya had pledged his citizenship to the city as a whole and not its parts. And to his family, both the Russian and Korean parts.

In the lobby of the train station, he dutifully crossed himself toward the icon of St. Nicholas, still there by edict of the Chinese civil authorities. Never mind their real reason for blocking its removal by their atheistic Soviet "partners" was to spite them and not in a spirit of religious tolerance. But the end result was that this symbol of the "opiate of the masses" still greeted all arriving and departing travelers. Borya stood by while Chinn supervised the unloading and delivery of Geiger's re-crated body. It was late afternoon and, taking the chance that Superintendent Liu was still in his office, Chinn led the way there, Borya following behind and bearing the reports and forms and evidence they had gotten from the Japanese police in his now bulging cardboard folder. Indeed, the Superintendent was still there, and they were immediately ushered in. Liu looked like he hadn't seen much sleep in the two days they had been gone from Harbin. His shoulders were still erect but there were dark circles under his eyes. Borya tried not to look at the picture behind him that still hung crooked.

"Well?" was Liu's sole form of greeting. Chinn proceeded to detail their trip to Changchun, including the preliminary findings of the SMR police, the identification of the corpse, the interrogation of the porter, the recovery of the shipping document and its strange location and name of origin, and finally the custody of the body. He even gave Borya credit for unmasking the porter and finding the shipping form, but thankfully left out the confrontation with the SMR inspector over the recovered paper, allowing Borya to finally expel the breath he had been holding.

Superintendent Liu listened silently, upright in his chair. His eyes moved to Borya when Chinn talked about his discoveries and a frown to his lips when Chinn talked about bringing the body back to Harbin.

"So," Chinn concluded, "I believe that Herr Geiger was not killed in the Japanese zone based on the amount of decomposition that had already occurred when the body was found at the train station and, of course, the shipping document. And I believe that whoever killed him was trying to cover up the location of his murder. That, and the fact that he was reported missing in Harbin, is why I agreed to take possession of the body and the case."

Liu's eyes turned toward the ceiling without actually raising his head. "Unless he was killed in the Japanese zone and their railway police forged the shipping document to lead us to believe he wasn't killed there."

Chinn shook his head. "I do not believe so. We would never have known about the shipping document had not Officer Melnikov spotted the porter's suspicious actions. The SMR men did not lead us to the porter nor to the document."

Liu's eyes returned to Chinn. "All right... but if he was shipped from Barim to Changchun, then he only passed through

Harbin while in a crate. And if he was only reported missing here and not killed here, I am still not ready yet to accept that this case belongs in our jurisdiction. Go and talk to his employer . . ." one eyebrow raised up in query.

"The British Chicken and Duck Company," Chinn replied.

". . . and find out everything you can. Where was he supposed to be? When he was last seen? Talk to his family, if he has one, and search his house. And when you have all that and the autopsy report, come back and report to me again."

"Yes, sir," Chinn replied and Borya echoed it, and they bowed heads and made their way out.

They did not set out for the British Chicken and Duck Company at once as it was already late in the day. Chinn led the way back downstairs to the detective squad room where he gave one of the clerks who could read and write Japanese the preliminary report from Inspector Ota to translate and then he gave Borya the "honor" of composing their written report from his notes that would cover their time and results in Changchun. Borya wrote out three pages in Mandarin guessing Chinn would rather read it in his native tongue than in Russian. Chinn, in the meantime, made a couple of phone calls and read through the scribbled notes, memos, and reports that had accumulated on his desk in their absence, blindly tapping the ash off his cigarettes, and sometimes even hitting the ashtray.

By the time Borya had finished his writing, the clerk had completed his translation of Ota's report. Borya read it carefully. It tracked to what the Japanese inspector had told them verbally, and he found nothing in it that made him want to change his own report, and so he handed both reports to Chinn to review.

Chinn read through them, grunting once in a while, made a few minor changes to Borya's report, and then handed it off to yet another clerk for typing and filing. Then, to Borya's surprise, Chinn introduced him to the other murder squad detectives as his assigned assistant, or at least to the three that were there at their desks; the other two were out pursuing their own investigations. One was a Chinese named Yan Guowei, younger than Chinn but balding and clean shaven. The two Russians were Nika Sergeeva and Patya Frolov, Chinn skipping over their patronymic names. Both were older and sported goatees, but Frolov easily had a couple of centimeters and twenty kilos over Sergeeva. All three shook his hand and smiled, although Borya was sure they were just being deferential to Chinn. Borya thought he had seen Frolov before at services at St. Nicolas, but he showed no sign of recognition.

"I made an appointment for us with a Mr. MacKenzie at the Chicken and Duck Company for noon tomorrow," Chinn next informed Borya. "He is the one who filed the missing person report for Herr Geiger. It has been a long two days, so let's not meet back here until eleven o'clock tomorrow morning."

Borya was tired and more than happy to return to the family apartment. His mother, Hei-rin, and Min were happy with their gifts of scarves, although his sisters immediately traded theirs to get their favored colors, and his mother put hers carefully away in a drawer, still in its wrapping paper. Over dinner, they pressed Borya to disclose every detail of his trip—from what was eaten on the train to the weather in Changchun. They were disappointed that he saw nothing of the city outside the train station but hung on his every word as he described the "arrest" of the porter and the subsequent discovery of important clues. He did leave out the most gruesome details of the body and his tussle with

Inspector Ota. However, he was lavish with his praise of Chinn's knowledge and patience. In turn, his mother expressed her relief at his "escape" from the Japanese zone.

Borya found Chinn already at his desk ten minutes before eleven the following morning, the latter back in his usual uniform of business suit and fedora. "We are still early for our appointment and I am hungry," Chinn announced. "Let's pick up some lunch along the way." It was a declaration rather than a suggestion, but Borya eagerly nodded in agreement—he was hungry as well.

They set out on foot, the distance to the British Chicken and Duck Company not all that far from Police Headquarters, and the day's weather was relatively pleasant with high clouds and less humidity. It also saved them the streetcar fare, although Chinn's police identity card and Borya's uniform would probably have worked as their ticket anyway. They walked the street that paralleled the railway spur leading northeast from Harbin Central Station. This spur fed the industrial sites of District 8 and those few businesses that spilled over into the neighboring Chinese Fujiadian district, one being the British Chicken and Duck Company. Conveniently, several food stalls lined the street they followed. They found an elderly couple selling "deep fried devils," a fried corn cake, and ate their purchases standing up before continuing on their way. Borya wrapped three of his corn cakes in his handkerchief and put them in the pocket of his tunic. Chinn responded with a raised eyebrow.

"For my mother and sisters," Borya explained.

"Good...*good bamboo produces good bamboo shoots,*" the older man intoned, followed with a wink. Borya raised both his own eyebrows in confusion.

"It means you were raised by good parents."

"Yes. Yes, I was," Borya replied. He had heard Chinn cared for his own elderly father in a house with his family in Fujiadian near to the boundary with District 8.

A side road and railway branch line led directly into the compound of the Binjiang Products British Import and Export Company Limited, popularly known as the Chicken and Duck Company because of their start in the poultry market. But unlike the Municipal slaughterhouse up on the bluff beyond Newtown, this venture was solely for export. Borya learned the company had been started by British investors for exporting the plentiful local domestic ducks and chickens to the markets of Europe and the Americas through Vladivostok. In just a matter of a few years' time, their initial success, and the cheap prices of local livestock, led them to expand their processing to include pigs, cattle, and sheep. Soon they were buying livestock from all across Manchuria and even Inner Mongolia. He knew they employed several hundred Chinese workers from District 8 and Fujiadian but that the office staff and managers were all Europeans or Indians, but he had never been inside their large compound.

"Have you ever been inside?" he asked Chinn as they approached a huge gate and a guardhouse that blocked the road entrance. The entire compound was hidden behind tall wooden fencing topped with barbed wire like a fortress.

"Once, more than ten years ago. We responded to a labor dispute here that had gotten ugly. The Sikh guards wouldn't let the workers leave at the end of a workday and ended up shooting about a dozen workers. The workers, in turn, killed several of the guards. It was all over by the time we got there. But then that night the workers came back and ransacked the offices. The investigation was handled by the Binjiang provincial police —

this was about five years before Fujiadian was rolled into the Special District — and they, of course, found no fault with the company. That naturally pissed off the workers, and they took over the plant and shut it down for three days until the owners agreed to pay compensation and fire the Sikh guards. There have been other strikes since, but nothing like that one."

Now they were at the gate and a sentry in a khaki uniform with a rifle held loosely in his hands came out of the adjoining guardhouse. To Borya he looked Indian but did not wear the turban of a Sikh.

"We have a twelve o'clock appointment with Mr. MacKenzie," Chinn announced in Mandarin.

"Yes, I was told," the guard responded in accented Mandarin. Turning back to the guardhouse he yelled, "Ahmed, take these two policemen to see Mr. MacKenzie."

There was a clank of a metal latch, and a smaller door within the gate opened up and another Indian guard in khaki with a shouldered rifle gestured them through into the compound beyond. Inside was a graveled courtyard that was a beehive of activities; Chinese workers pushing carts with large wicker baskets full of cackling chickens and others were funneling huge, shrill pigs from a boxcar into chutes that led into one of the surrounding buildings. But what caught Borya's eye was the large British flag hanging from a flagpole in the middle of the courtyard like this place was somehow sovereign British territory. Huge brick buildings ranging from two to four stories fronted the courtyard and belched grey smoke from even taller chimneys. The clamor of machinery and the yelling of men was oppressive to the ears, but even more disquieting was the overwhelming stench always common to abattoirs, an odor he had sometimes smelled when the wind took it westward over District 8 and the rest of Harbin.

Ahmed led them across the courtyard to a two-storey brick building with large glass windows that Borya presumed held the company offices. Inside was a spacious lobby with a large reception desk facing the door, behind which sat a severe-looking white woman in her thirties with dark hair in a bun at the back of her head and wearing a smart European dress that Borya would expect to see in the window of one of the higher class dress shops of Pristan. Behind her, he could see through to another larger room occupied by straight ranks of wooden desks where clerks sat hunched over ledger books and stacks of paper. Most were European men, although there were a few Chinese and Indians in western dress. Ahmed led them directly to the woman at the reception desk.

"These policemen have an appointment with Mr. MacKenzie," the guard announced, this time in English.

"Yes, he is expecting you. Let me take you to his office," the woman said, smiling primly and rising to her feet. Her accent was not Russian nor British, and Borya guessed her to be from one of the many other ethnic groups that had found their way to Harbin in the years after the collapse of the Tsarist empire, maybe Armenian or Baltic? They trailed behind her and up a grand wooden staircase to the second floor, then down a long corridor of dark wood paneling lined with portraits of unsmiling older white men and pastoral paintings of English rural scenes. At the end of the corridor she opened an immense carved wooden door and leaned in.

"Mr. MacKenzie, your twelve o'clock appointment is here." Then she stood aside to let them enter the office beyond. The office was immense and covered with more wood paneling, except where tall windows looked out over the courtyard and the British flag. More paintings covered the walls here along with bookcases and curio cabinets filled with Chinese vases and figurines. Behind a large carved wooden desk sat an equally large white man of about sixty in a dark suit and patterned tie and sporting thick white hair with faint traces of yellow that hinted that it once had been blond. He sported a thick mustache and eyebrows, also white, and a florid complexion.

He rose to his feet and gestured to two green leather chairs that faced his desk. "Gentlemen, please be seated," he exclaimed in Russian in a booming voice and sat back down behind the desk. "I'm afraid my Mandarin is a bit spotty, but my Russian is tolerable unless, of course, your English is better than my Russian?"

"Russian will be just fine, thank you. I am Inspector Chinn, and this is Officer Melnikov of the Special District Police."

The large man smiled and nodded. "I understand you are here regarding the disappearance of our Herr Geiger? Have you found him?"

"Yes, we believe we have. Unfortunately, a body has been found in Changchun that closely matches the description and photograph of Herr Geiger. We are now investigating his death as a murder."

The smile changed into a frown, and the big man's shoulders seemed to sag inward. "Oh my! But then I was afraid that would be the outcome after so many days had passed. Changchun you say? A bit out of the way. We sent him on a buying trip out to Hailar, quite the opposite direction." Hailar was north and west of Harbin, almost to the Soviet border. It went into Borya's notebook.

"Well, yes," Chinn continued, "but we believe he might have been killed elsewhere and his body shipped to Changchun by rail. He was on a business trip to Hailar? Is that where he went missing? The missing person report wasn't specific."

MacKenzie frowned again. "Well, you see, we're not quite sure. He was *scheduled* to leave for Hailar on July 29th on a trip to buy cattle and sheep from the local merchants and auctions there, but we never heard back from him. We had a telegram from a wholesaler in Hailar who was supposed to meet with him there but said he never showed up for their appointment, plus there were no wires from the bank there saying any money had been drawn against our letters of credit. So I can't really say whether he actually *did* reach Hailar or for that matter even left Harbin. When we didn't hear anything for a week, we sent someone around to his house just in case he had fallen ill and hadn't left, but he wasn't there. After that, we filed the missing person report."

Chinn leaned forward in his chair. "Then Geiger was traveling to Hailar alone?"

MacKenzie now shook his head from side to side. "Well, no, he was to travel with one of our Chinese agents to do the interpreting and help with contacts there. But that chap appears to have disappeared also. We used to send three or four of our staff out there every year, but your rail rates have gotten so much higher that we've had to look closer at hand." A slight hint of displeasure had crept into his voice.

Chinn smiled politely. "We're the police, I'm afraid we have nothing to do with the CER rail rates."

"Did you file a missing person report for the Chinese agent?" Borya asked, looking up from his notebook.

MacKenzie seemed surprised when Borya spoke, but recovered. "Well, no. These Chinese agents aren't always the most reliable of employees. They quit or disappear for months at a time and then show back up and want you to pretend they were never gone. Very frustrating."

"So Herr Geiger position here was a buyer?" Chinn asked drily.

"Oh no. He was the manager of our cattle processing department. He had a great mechanical mind and a real gift for finding ways to improve our processes." And then the big man tapped a finger against his pink cheek. "Funny thing, he specifically asked to go on the Hailar trip. Said he wanted to see more of the country instead of always being stuck up here in Harbin." Borya and Chinn shared a quick glance. Another entry into Borya's notebook.

"Well, we will need to see your personnel files on Herr Geiger and this agent and the telegram from Hailar," Chinn continued. "And we would like to examine Geiger's office."

"Of course, of course," MacKenzie assured. "Anything we can do to bring this matter to justice. The staff here will all miss Herr Geiger immensely."

"So Herr Geiger was a popular man here? No enemies?" Chinn prompted.

Now the big head bobbed side to side. "Well, truthfully, Manfred could be a little standoffish. And he wasn't as close with the British staff as they are with each other, him being German and the War and all. Though I don't think he actually served in the War now that I think about it. But he got on well enough."

"And with the non-staff employees? The Chinese workers?"

"As well as any of the rest of the staff. There's always the occasional disgruntled employee or labor issue, but nothing that stands out to me."

"And did Herr Geiger have any business in Barim?"

The bushy eyebrows met in confusion. "Barim? Not that I'm aware of."

"Well, thank you for your time, Mr. MacKenzie. And we will keep you current on our investigation as we learn more," Chinn added, rising to his feet. "Who can take us to the personnel files and his office?"

"Mrs Esibov. She is the receptionist that brought you upstairs. And please, if there is any other way we can help, please let me know." MacKenzie rose also but made no effort to circle around his desk to shake their hands.

Borya followed Chinn to the door, but then he turned back to MacKenzie, who was already sitting back down.

"Oh, Mr. MacKenzie, one more thing. Did Herr Geiger have a family?"

MacKenzie looked up, showing for the first time an expression of annoyance. "Yes, he does … did, but they're all back in Germany."

They found Mrs Esibov waiting just outside the door in the corridor. She must have been listening in on their conversation because she smiled politely and led them back down the corridor. "I will take you directly to the personnel department," addressing them in English, "it is back downstairs." Borya wondered if she had been waiting just to escort them back downstairs or to ensure they were not left alone to wander the upper floor.

The personnel department was in a separate room of its own down a corridor from the lobby. Inside were two desks, a larger one behind which sat a pale blond man in his late twenties and a smaller desk occupied by a Chinese man of about the same age. Behind them was a long wall lined with a dozen tall wooden file cabinets. Here the walls were whitewashed, lacking the detailed woodwork of upstairs.

Addressing the pale blond man in her accented English, "Mr. Phillips, Mr. MacKenzie said to allow these two gentlemen from the police to see the personnel files of Mr. Geiger and the agent assigned to him for his trip to Hailar . . ." She looked to Mr. Phillips who in turn looked to the Chinese clerk at the desk next to his.

"Song Nikan," the Chinese clerk supplied.

"And a list of all employees in Geiger's department who were fired in the last year, please," Chinn added.

Mrs Esibov gave a small frown but nodded her assent, and then turning back to Chinn, "And when you're finished here, come back to the lobby, and I can have someone take you to Mr. Geiger's office in the cattle barn."

After she left the room, Borya turned to Chinn. "Would you like me to review the files while you examine the office?"

Chinn shook his head. "No, I think it may take our combined language skills to get through everything." Borya knew he meant he did not trust his own written English to tackle Geiger's papers alone. And what if Geiger kept his personal papers and correspondence in his native German? Borya's English skills were spotty, and his German almost non-existent, and he guessed Chinn's knowledge of those two languages was even more limited.

Meanwhile, Mr. Phillips had retrieved Geiger's personnel file from one of the filing cabinets, while the Chinese clerk pulled the file of Song Nikan from another. No doubt they kept the files of their European staff separated from the files of the Chinese workers. "You can use the table there while you examine them," Mr. Phillips offered, indicating a long low table and three chairs along one wall, above which two wall sconces added additional light to the overhead light fixtures. Chinn borrowed an ashtray from the Englishman that he brought with him over to the table.

Borya took Geiger's file, and Chinn took Song's, and they began reading and taking separate notes. The entries in Geiger's file were all in English, but Borya could follow the gist of it if he went slow. The front of Geiger's file primarily contained his personal and work history. Manfred Geiger had been born in Stuttgart, Germany, in 1881, which made him forty-eight years old. MacKenzie had been right, there was no record of Manfred having served in the German armed forces during the War even though he would have still been in his thirties then. His previous work history showed him working as a foreman in an abattoir in his native city beginning in 1903, and through and beyond the War, until 1921. Maybe he escaped the military draft because his job was considered essential or he had a medical condition that gave him a waiver? It probably didn't matter. In 1921, he took a position as a manager of an abattoir in Austria before taking a management job in Harbin with the Chicken and Duck Company in 1924, five years ago. He was married with two children; the date of the marriage and ages of the children were not listed, but her name and address in Germany were there. In five years' time, why hadn't he bothered to bring his family out to Harbin, Borya wondered. Had the wife been reluctant to leave Germany for the "wilds" of Manchuria? Or had Manfred planned to make his fortune here and return to Germany on an early retirement? Either way, the wife would need to be informed about his death through the German consulate by them or by the company, so Borya added the name and address to his notebook. Included was a photograph, a duplicate for the one that had been provided for the missing person report and that Borya had brought with them to Changchun.

The rest of the file covered his time at the Chicken and Duck Company. He had started as an assistant manager of pork operations and after two years was promoted to the overall manager of the cattle operations. His pay had increased yearly to a respectable salary for a white man in middle-management in Harbin—about what his father had made before he was sacked from the CER. His performance reports were positive but not outstanding, citing steady improvements in cost and profit in his department. Twice he had taken a three month leave to return to Germany to visit his family, once after a year's time and not again until two years later, and then not another time since. There were no disciplinary issues or unexplained absences, only the occasional sick day. If he had had to discipline or fire others, Borya supposed those reports would be in those men's respective personnel files or in the cattle department's files, which hopefully were in Geiger's office. His Harbin address was there, too, and Borya copied that down also—an address in New Town in a neighborhood which seemed upscale for a middle-level manager of a foreign firm that was also supporting a family back in Germany, but then again it could be a boarding house or a shared apartment. Nothing else stood out as remarkable or even particularly interesting.

There was a letter in the back of the file outlining his trip to Hailar: the itinerary, contacts, and money released for travel and hotel expenses. There was enough yuan to cover first class accommodations and certainly enough to catch the eye of a robber or the interest of a kidnaper. It was also not enough to buy herds of cattle and pigs, so Borya assumed the money for that would have come from the letters of credit with the banks in Hailar that MacKenzie had mentioned. He copied down the letter verbatim.

Chinn was already finished with his smaller file, much of which was in Mandarin. Apparently the Englishman kept the staff records and the Chinese clerk those of the workers and agents. They exchanged their respective notes and read quickly through them. Song Nikan had been a part-time employee of the company, hired specifically to support livestock buying trips in the west because of his contacts with merchants in Hailar and beyond in Inner Mongolia. There wasn't much there of his background or even age. The given name Nikan was one common among Manchus, and it was not unusual in these times for a Manchu to have also taken a Han family name like Song. He was recorded as a merchant in both Harbin and Hailar, with an address and a wife listed in both locations, the former location being a house in Fujiadian district. There was also a photo, showing the face of a man of about fifty with Manchu features, a scraggly beard, and hair showing streaks of both black and grey, and a drooping left eye.

"He looks shady," Borya remarked.

Chinn frowned. "And you can tell that by just looking at his photograph?"

"Well, no, I guess . . ."

"I find it hard to detect a guilty man...or woman...by their appearance in a photograph alone," Chinn admonished. Borya held his tongue.

They returned the files to Mr. Phillips, who nodded slightly in response.

"May we keep the photographs from the files? We will return them at the end of our investigation," Chinn asked.

"You may keep them," the Englishman replied magnanimously. "We have the negatives and can make more." And he handed Chinn a piece of paper, ". . . and here is the list of employees under Geiger that were let go in the last twelve months." Borya looked over to see a list of a dozen or so names in Chinese.

They retraced their steps to the lobby and found Mrs Esibov once more seated imperiously behind her reception desk. Standing beside her was a young Russian dressed in the identical white shirt and tie worn by the rows of clerks in the room beyond the lobby. Borya immediately recognized him as a student from his class at the Commercial High School where he studied before leaving to become a police cadet. It was not all that surprising, as there weren't that many secondary schools in Harbin. Borya remembered the boy's father had also worked for the CER but had been one of those who took Soviet citizenship to keep his job. But Borya couldn't blame the son for the betrayal of his father. What was his name?... ah yes, Boris Gregorovich Mishchenko. Borya smiled but Boris' eyes moved side to side in a discrete signal to keep his recognition unspoken.

"We are ready to see Herr Geiger's office now," Chinn proclaimed.

"Mr. Mischenko will take you there," she replied with a flutter of her hand before she returned her gaze back to her typewriter.

Boris led the way out to the courtyard, where he turned back to walk beside Borya. Chinn raised one eyebrow, apparently also having caught the silent signal. Was it a sign of amusement or another silent signal warning Borya to be careful? But the older man slowed his pace to follow behind the two younger men to allow them to walk side by side.

"Borya Sergeevich, it's been probably a year since I saw you last! Was it at graduation? I had heard you had joined the Police department."

"Yes, Boris Gregorovich, I think it was at your graduation." Never mind that it should have been his own graduation too. But he had gone to the ceremony anyway to see a few of his friends graduate. "How long have you worked for the Chicken and Duck Company? Do you like it here? What do you do?"

"I've been here about nine months. I work on filling out paperwork for export orders and I am learning about contracts. It's okay, better than working in the rail yards, but I had to get a whole lot better on my English rather quickly." Then he dropped his voice to a conspiratorial tone. "Sorry about the signal in there. Mrs. 'Taught Ship' told me to stick close to you two while you searched Geiger's office to make sure you didn't take anything without asking—not that you would. But if she knew we knew each other, she would probably have assigned someone else, and then I wouldn't have had the chance to talk to you." Borya allowed a smile.

"Oh, and I'm engaged!" Boris added.

"Great! Do I know the lucky girl?"

"I don't know if you do. Her name is Tanya Vladimirovna Novikof. Her brother Ilya Vladimirovich was in the year ahead of us." Borya remembered the brother and also recalled a petite girl with long brown hair and big, soulful eyes.

"Yes, I remember her. I think you are the lucky one!"

Boris laughed. "Yes, I am! The wedding won't be until after the New Year, but I will send you a wedding invitation. Do you still live in District 8?"

"Yes, still living with my mother and sisters," Borya admitted with an awkward half-smile. Silently, he wondered at Boris' effusive tone of friendship. Boris had not been among those Russian students who outwardly shunned him, but neither had he been a friend. Most shunned him, feeling superior in their "pure" Russian lineage, and the divide only became wider after Borya's family could no longer pay the tuition, and he was forced to apply for one of the municipal tuition waivers. Not that Borya had fared any better with the Chinese students, many of whom came from among the elite Chinese families of the city. Having a Russian father counted against his "Asian-ness" as much as his Korean mother had counted against him with the Russian students. Even the few Korean students found his Russian name and his half-Caucasian features cause for suspicion, like any friendship to him would further marginalize their own minority standing in the school population. And, of course, with no friends, there was little opportunity to meet their sisters and other girls.

Consequently, Borya ended up a loner in school, and in time it just became easier to distance himself first from the other students before they had a chance to shun him. He had withdrawn into his studies at school, into his family, and to the Church, which together gave him a small but solid world of his own choosing. His only consolation was the appreciation of his studious nature by a few of his instructors. But that part of his world abruptly ended when he left school to secure another income for the family. But then his world widened up a bit when he became a part of the Special District police force. Yes, there were just as many factions within the Special District police as there had been at school, but by now Borya was used to dealing with factions and had learned the skills necessary to avoid becoming trapped into one of them. At least so far.

By then they had reached the cattle barn, a tall brick building at the far end of the courtyard. "Hold your nose!" Boris warned them with a laugh and led the way into the structure. A glance at Chinn found the older man seemingly unperturbed, lighting a fresh cigarette and then offering the pack to Borya. "It helps somewhat with the smell." Borya only shook his head and began breathing only through his mouth. They were immediately enveloped by a much stronger dose of the smells and louder clatter of machinery than what had accosted them in the courtyard outside. While the courtyard seemed like a noisy beehive, the inside of the cattle barn was a clockwork of modern automation. Dripping carcasses of dead cattle hung from hooks that moved along overhead steel rails while Chinese workers in rubberized aprons hacked away with knives in blurs of motion. Streams of water from hoses sluiced the blood and detritus across the floor. The workers hardly looked in their direction, fixated upon their bloody tasks. Only one tall Chinese stared at them with cold eyes, probably the foreman who likely resented any intrusion into his little kingdom. As a city boy, Borya was used to seeing his beef displayed as cuts hanging up in the market or cooked on a plate, and seeing this much carnage in one place, on top of the stench and clamor, he found all a little disquieting.

Boris did not try to compete with the noise level in any more conversation, simply beckoning them to a set of wooden stairs that led up to a loft of three glass-windowed offices overlooking the factory floor. At the top, there was a gangway that led to a corridor that ran behind the offices, each office having doors and more windows off of the corridor. Boris led them past the first two offices, each occupied by a European male seated at a desk that looked up briefly as they passed, continuing all the way to the third and largest office where he unlocked the door with a key and led them inside. In here, the smell and noise had not gone away but were considerably reduced.

"This is Geiger's office," Boris announced. "I was told you can see anything you want, but if you want to take anything with you, I'm to get permission from Mr. MacKenzie."

"That's fine," Chinn replied, and then turned to Borya, "I'll start on his desk and you look in the files," pointing to two wooden file cabinets opposite the desk along the one sidewall that had no windows. Boris sat on a stool near the windows overlooking the factory floor, staring out at the activity below with only mild interest. No doubt he had seen it all before.

Borya opened the top drawer and began examining the files. They were in English and appeared to be production figures and future estimates in output and the like. While he skimmed through each file, he spoke loudly for Boris to hear him.

"Did you know Geiger well?"

There was a thoughtful pause. "I wouldn't say that… I mean, I talked with him here or in the headquarters on the odd occasion like when we were having trouble filling an order or we got complaints from the customers on quality issues. He didn't take kindly to the complaints, like he considered them all as a personal insult. He would get huffy but not like yelling or swearing," and then he laughed, "except sometimes he would fall back into German, and he could have been swearing then for all I know."

Another drawer. This one held files of machinery instruction sheets, tool expenses, repairs, warranties, etc. "Was he well-liked by his employees?"

"Well, he had no patience or sympathy at all for the workers on the floor. If they were ill or injured or just slow, he wanted to immediately get rid of them and bring in others. He didn't talk to the workers directly, he didn't speak any Chinese, so he would speak to them through the foreman."

Another drawer. "How was he with the other staff?"

Another pause. "He was a bit pompous… no, a lot pompous. He didn't think anyone was as smart or as capable as he was. Thought he was a regular brilliant scientist. He got along well enough with the Brits and the other Europeans, but he didn't have the time of day for us *kharbinsty*. I don't think he socialized much with anybody from the Company except for formal events," and then he laughed again, "but somebody did tell me he wasn't too keen on celebrating Remembrance Day, what with being German and the owners all Brits. And hey, this is just between us here, right?"

Another drawer. Trade studies and articles from professional magazines about livestock health and abattoir practices, some in German and most in English.

"Of course," Borya reassured. "How about any enemies?"

No pause this time. "Well, probably every Chinese worker he ever fired because he didn't believe in giving anyone a second chance. I know MacKenzie himself transferred some of his workers to another department rather than letting him fire them all to avoid a labor issue, but that happened before I was here. But I can't think of anyone on the staff that really had it out for him, but there were plenty that disliked him. And outside work, I couldn't really say. Did I hear right, that somebody actually murdered him?"

"We're treating it as a murder at this time," Chinn interjected, without looking up from his own search of the desk drawers.

"Yes, sure. Wow . . ."

More rummaging.

"Did you know the company agent, Song Nikan, who was traveling with Geiger?" Borya asked.

"Sorry, no. He would have been dealt with by the buyers. Not my area."

There was a rattle as Chinn tossed a small enameled pin with the letters "DVP" onto the top of the desk. "Mean anything to you?" he queried, looking at both Boris and Borya, who both shook their heads in the negative.

In the bottom drawer of the filing cabinet, Borya found files of disciplinary reports, thankfully in English and not German. In these reports, there might be disgruntled workers in the cattle barn who were disciplined but had not been dismissed, and so would be in addition to the list of those fired they got from the personnel staff. Borya showed them to Chinn, who had finished his search of the desk.

"We would like to take these with us," Chinn said, holding them up to Boris.

"Of course, I will ask immediately," and Boris scooped them up and left the office. Now alone, Chinn put the enameled pin in the inside pocket of his suit jacket and smiled at Borya. There was nothing else of note in the second filing cabinet, which was almost empty save for five pornographic postcards of half-dressed German women stuffed in the back of one of the drawers. These also went into Chinn's suit pocket. There was little else in the office: a coat stand, two chairs, a stool, and a blurry watercolor of a European pastoral scene on the wall by an artist Borya did not recognize. No secret envelopes under the desk drawers or behind the painting. Oh well, that was for cheap mystery novels, not real life.

Boris was back in fifteen minutes with the files, which he handed to Borya. "Mr. MacKenzie said it was okay to take these, as there should be carbon copies in the personnel file room. Just bring them back when your investigation is over."

Chinn thanked him. "And Herr Geiger had assistants?" pointing a finger in the direction of the other two offices they had passed on their way to Geiger's.

"One actually. In the office next door. Peter Entworp. English. The first office belongs to the head veterinarian, who doesn't ... didn't report directly to Geiger."

"We will need to speak with Mr. Entworp."

"Certainly."

They backtracked to the office next door, and Boris tapped on the glass of its door. When they heard a trite "Come in" in English, they all trooped into the small office. It was smaller than Geiger's office, with a smaller desk, only one chair and one filing cabinet. Entworp was a slightly built man of around forty with a pink complexion, receding hairline, and clean-shaven face.

Boris made the introductions all around. "They are here investigating the ... death of Geiger." Entworp stood and reached across his desk to shake hands with both Chinn and Borya, his gaze steady and assured. Too steady?

"Yes, just heard ... dreadful business ... anything I can do to help . . ." he proffered in English.

"Do you speak Russian?" Chinn enquired.

"Yes, of course," he replied in that language but still with an English accent. Entworp explained he had only worked under Geiger for the last seven months. He also knew of no obvious enemies, nor friends for that matter. Knew nothing of his life outside the job, and had never been to his home. No, he had not been acting strangely or different in the days before his disappearance, except saying he was looking forward to his trip to Hailar where he could finally "see some of the local color" instead of always being "cooped up in Harbin." No, he had never actually met the company agent, Song, although he had seen him once in Geiger's office right before they had left, supposedly planning out their trip.

When Chinn ran out of questions, Borya asked one of his own. "So when was the last time you saw Herr Geiger?"

"Well, here in my office the night before he was leaving on his trip. He said he was leaving early to finish packing at home and said he would see me again in a week's time and to 'hold the fort' in the meantime."

"And how well did you and Geiger get along?"

Entworp lips formed a thin smile. "Well enough."

They thanked Entworp for his help, and Boris escorted them back down to the factory floor where Borya felt the foreman's cold eyes on them again. From there, it was out to the courtyard and back to the Headquarters building. There Mrs Esibov had prepared a typewritten copy of the telegram from the Hailar wholesaler that had detailed the missed appointment and included the wholesaler's name and address. There was also a form for Chinn to sign, acknowledging his possession of Geiger's files and promising not to share their "proprietary" contents outside of police circles and ensuring their eventual return to the Company. They were finally free to take their leave, and Boris followed them to the gate to see them off and usher them past the Indian guards.

"Remember, save some free time in the new year to come to my wedding," Boris called after Borya.

"Yes, Boris Gregorovich, I certainly will."

CHAPTER EIGHT

BY THE TIME THEY exited the abattoir's gate, it was middle of the afternoon, and rain clouds had moved in, so they elected to take the streetcar on their way back to police headquarters, or rather Chinn elected it, and Borya went along. Back at the squad room, Borya wrote out his notes from the day's discoveries at the Chicken and Duck Company while Chinn attacked the fresh paperwork that had appeared on his desk in the hours they had been gone.

After Chinn had read through "their" report, he put it in a desk drawer.

"First thing tomorrow morning, we will go to Geiger's residence and see what we can find. Hopefully, there will be some paperwork to show where he banks, and we can check out his finances, though if he was having serious money troubles, I would have expected his company would have seen a few bank drafts drawn in Hailar. Meanwhile, I have business to attend to at the New Town precinct, so I'll leave you to go through the personnel files of those fired or reprimanded workers to see if any of them have a criminal record here. We also need to find our missing Manchu agent that was supposed to be traveling with Geiger.

Check him also for a police record. Hopefully, by the time we finish those tasks, the doctor will have completed his autopsy."

Borya was not deterred by the thought of slogging through the voluminous Harbin police records to try and find a match with the lists of dismissed and disciplined workers. He found comfort in the orderly framework and organization that the thousands of files represented. They were something that you could actually hold in your hands that could take you back to the exact time and place of any arrest or crime. Like all police cadets, he had had to take his turn in the records room, but he was probably the only one who enjoyed the assignment. He also remembered that persistence had been one of Chinn's stated tools of success and another reason to look forward to the task.

The police records room was filled with row upon row of wooden filing cabinets and smelled of dust. One could have easily felt trapped in a maze, but Borya was tall enough to peer over the tops of the cabinets and see the walls. The list of dismissed employees from the abattoir personnel office included eleven names, all Han Chinese. All eleven were also included in the records from Geiger's office, but those files contained an additional four names of workers disciplined or warned but not fired, leaving fifteen names in all. Borya read each file in turn, to find the reasons for firing or discipline. They were mercifully short, but it was still no easy task because, besides being in English, they suffered from Geiger's liberal application of German grammatical rules, forcing Borya to rearrange the sentences in his head. The most commonly recorded bad mark was for being too slow, although a few were labeled accident-prone, which Borya could easily understand having seen the frenzied knife work during his visit to the cattle barn. A couple were cited for "lying" or "stealing," but didn't include what were the lies or what was stolen. Then he looked for each of their names in the police files, which took another long while because of the different spellings applied to Chinese names by the investigating officers. He found files on five of them, but nothing particularly serious: three had petty theft convictions, one had been skipping out on his debts, and one had been arrested for drunken brawling, and none with any repeat arrests. Nevertheless, Borya dutifully made notes on all five in his notebook to share with Chinn in the morning. There had been no file on the Manchu agent, Song Nikan.

He left the windowless room to discover it had grown dark outside in the meantime. Hours had passed since he had started his arduous research, and his neck ached, and his shoulders felt stiff. He left the station, now depleted of the greater numbers that occupied it during the day. Outside, he was somewhat reinvigorated by the fresh outside air and followed the street lights downhill to the family apartment. At the family dinner that night, Borya was happy to let the dull description of his day take second-place to Hei-rin's large sale of high-end clothing to a French businessman. Their mother and Min, in turn, provided gossip from the neighborhood and schoolyard.

Borya arrived early the next morning and found Inspector Chinn already at his desk in the detective squad room, lighting a cigarette from the burning stub of another. "What luck did you have with the lists of abattoir workers?"

"Nothing much, just five petty offenses and no repeat arrests, and nothing on Song Nikan," and Borya briefly described the details.

"Good, good," Chinn nodded.

"Good?" Borya echoed, puzzled.

"Yes. Eliminating suspects only helps us to focus on the real suspect. After all, *failure is the mother of success.*" Wink. "Come, I want to visit Geiger's residence and talk to his neighbors. I only hope his extended absence has not already generated a break-in and ransacking of possible evidence. After we got his address from his employee files yesterday, I checked with the New Town precinct commander. He had no reports of any break-ins there but would send an officer to check the address anyway. The patrolman will meet us there."

Geiger's residence was in a modest neighborhood of a prosperous uptown district of New Town. Besides being home to the headquarters of the railway and the civil administration, New Town's residential area contained the lavish houses of the city's elite; the Russian, European, and Chinese business elite; top municipal and railway administrators; and foreign consuls. After crossing busy Prospect Street and being honked at by a speeding taxicab, Chinn and Borya entered another world, one far removed from Borya's District 8 tenement below the bluff, even far from the upscale apartment in Pristan where Borya had lived up until his father's accident. Here Russian-style mansions in brick or clapboard siding with tile roofs slowly gave way to smaller one and two-story versions the farther they got from Prospect Street. Along the way, they drew stares from the well-dressed passersby. Chinn appeared oblivious and Borya felt protected by the authority lent by his police uniform.

Two of Chinn's cigarettes later, they reached Geiger's residence, which was a two-story clapboard house painted a bright turquoise blue with a typical hipped roof of grey tiles. A picket fence separated the front garden from the sidewalk, with an open gate and gravel walkway that led to a covered porch, where stood another first-rank police officer awaiting their arrival. He was a young Russian who had been a police cadet at the same time as Borya but had been posted to the New Town precinct while Borya had been sent to District 8. Borya couldn't remember either his first or patronymic names.

"Inspector Chinn, I am Officer Galen. I was told to expect you." He gave Chinn a short bow and Borya a polite smile.

"Is the house secure?" Chinn asked.

"All the doors and the first floor windows are locked. I saw no signs of forced entry. I knocked at both the front and back, but no one answered."

"Good, good," Chinn replied. "You two wait here." The two young officers wondered but said nothing while Chinn stumped around the side of the house towards the backyard. Five minutes later, they heard footsteps inside approaching the front door and then the lock being turned and the door swung open, revealing Chinn framed by the dim light from the back entry beyond. "It looks like someone's been in here and taken some things, so they must have had a key to lock the door behind them," he announced.

Borya and Officer Galen stepped inside and entered the hallway beyond. Chinn led the way to the right into a large parlor with a high ceiling and ornate crown molding, snapping on the wall switch that illuminated the single electric light fixture hanging from the ceiling. A glass-fronted curio cabinet along one wall was empty and its door ajar. Borya examined the empty ornate plaster mantle to the room's fireplace and found spots in the dust that hinted there had previously been objects there also. A large landscape painting of some alpine scene, however, still hung on the wall and matching red velvet armchairs and a sofa faced each other across a floral rug.

"Whoever it was just took the smaller valuables that are the easiest to pack up and carry out," Chinn observed, then turned to the Russian. "Officer? . . ."

". . . Galen, Inspector."

"Yes, sorry, Officer Galen. Please check the rooms upstairs. Officer Melnikov, check out the library across the hall, and I'll check the rooms in back. Look for important papers or financial records or correspondence, or anything out of the ordinary."

The library was a smaller room, but had the same high ceiling and a distinct smell of stale cigar smoke. The furniture included a pair of brown leather armchairs, a modest bookcase filled with German books, and a secretary-style desk with the hinged desktop surface opened flat. Papers were strewn across the desk's surface and the small drawers pulled open. Some papers had even fallen to the floor and left there as though from a hasty search for money or more valuables. Borya sat in the wooden chair before the desk and started looking through the papers and the drawers and cubbyholes of the desk's interior. Most were letters or bills for purchases or services. More papers and letters were in the larger drawers below the desktop. Atop the desktop, one small red card caught his eye, and he picked it up. It was a CER rail pass, pink on one side with Geiger's name and the pass number, and his photograph overlaid with the railway's stamp on the other side. The man in this photograph matched the photograph from Geiger's company personnel file.

Borya heard footsteps behind him and saw Chinn enter the room. "Find anything?" the older man asked.

"Lots of financial papers and what looks like letters from his wife or family, but they're all in German. And take a look at this," handing the rail pass to the inspector. "Why would he leave his rail pass here if he was leaving by train for Hailar or Barim?

It would be a waste of money to purchase a ticket if he could get free passage with this pass," Borya mused.

"Why, indeed," Chinn replied. "Maybe he didn't want to show the pass and tie his name to a trip that ended up in Barim instead of Hailar where he was supposed to be, on the off-chance the ticket seller might remember him. He would only need the money and not his identity to buy a regular ticket. Or maybe he just couldn't find it when it came time to pack... or," and here the inspector allowed a wry smile, "he never really left Harbin alive."

It was Borya's turn to grunt. "Anyway, it's going to take a lot of hours to go through all these papers. And we're going to need a police translator for all the stuff in German."

Chinn waved an arm. "Quite! Find a box and pack it all up. We'll take it back to headquarters. I saw some boxes back in the kitchen."

While Borya headed down the hall towards the back of the house, Officer Galen came stomping down the stairs.

"Find anything upstairs?" Chinn asked.

The young Russian stopped in mid-stride as though thinking of his answer and finishing his descent was too much to do at the same time. "There are drawers left open in all three bedrooms upstairs, but I couldn't really tell if anything is missing. There are still clothes and stuff in the drawers and in the one wardrobe."

"Were there any suitcases or valises? Maybe under the beds?" Chinn asked.

The young officer blushed. "I didn't see any, but I didn't look under the beds. I'll look right away," and without waiting for an answer, turned around and headed back upstairs. Meanwhile, Borya found a large wicker basket in the kitchen and brought it back to the library and filled it with the contents from the desk. He could hear Officer Galen reporting back to Chinn in the parlor on an unsuccessful search for luggage, and he joined the two men there with his burden.

"Good, good," Chinn declared. "Now, I want you two to talk to the neighbors in the houses on either side and across the street. Ask when was the last time they'd seen Geiger. Ask if they've seen anyone in the house in the last three weeks, especially anyone carrying items out of the house. There might have been a houseboy or a cook—there is a room off the kitchen with a cot that looks like it was used recently. Maybe it was a servant who ransacked the house when Herr Geiger didn't show back up when he was supposed to. Talk to the neighbor's servants, too, they usually talk across the fence with each other and might know more. I'll be taking a last look around inside."

Borya left his basket in the parlor, and he and the young Russian paused on the wide front porch outside.

"I'll take the house on the left, the one across from it, and the one directly across the street if you take the two on the right," Borya offered.

Officer Galen nodded. "Sure," and then dropped his voice to a quiet tone, "I'll bet the old detective is in there right now seeing if there's anything left worth taking for himself. Did you see how quickly he jimmied the back door open?"

Borya returned him a frosty stare. "I doubt it. He's got an impeccable reputation at police headquarters, and I trust him. And if he hears you badmouth him, he'll skin you alive." Borya did not know why he made an immediate endorsement of Chinn's honesty, after all he had only known the inspector for a few days, but even as he was saying it, he believed it himself.

The young Russian returned a frosty stare and stomped off the porch to visit the neighboring house on the right. Borya knew what the stare meant—you Asiatics all stick together. Lie together.

The house next door on the left was only one-story but built with brick and painted yellow and roofed with red tiles. Borya twisted the key that rang a bell inside. In less than a minute, the door was opened by a Chinese maid, a woman in her twenties or thirties in a white uniform, startled to see a city policeman on the doorstep.

"I have some questions about your next-door neighbor, Herr . . ." Borya began in Mandarin, but the maid quickly disappeared into the interior of the house, leaving the door hanging open. Another half-minute passed, and another woman appeared at the doorway, this one middle-aged with dark hair in a flowered housedress, not startled like the maid but with wary eyes. Borya guessed her to be Jewish and addressed her in Russian.

"I am with the Special District Police," he restarted, and the woman nodded her understanding. "We are making enquiries regarding your next-door neighbor, Herr Geiger." He produced his notebook and pen to reinforce his intent.

Her eyes softened, and her stance relaxed. "How can I help?"

Borya explained Geiger's disappearance, but did not mention his murder. No, she hadn't seen him lately, maybe three or four weeks ago. Yes, he had a houseboy who she had occasionally seen coming and going since then, but not for at least a week. No, he hadn't been carrying anything from the house the times she had seen him. He was maybe in his twenties, short, and with very short hair, but she didn't know his name. No, she had not seen anyone else at the house in that time. He took down her name and answers in his notebook.

"Did Herr Geiger have many visitors?" he finally asked.

The woman made a face. "No, not many. Mostly young women, but it might have been the same one. I couldn't say, I try not to be nosy."

"Of course. Did you talk with him much?"

She made another face and brushed a loose strand of dark hair from her face. "Not me. My husband would sometimes talk with him in the backyard across the fence, our Yiddish and his German being close enough they could generally understand each other. Mostly just comments about the weather or our gardens. He was not the most friendly of neighbors."

"Thank you very much. Now, I'd like to talk to your servants too." There was just the one, a combination maid and cook. She brought back the Chinese maid/cook to the doorway and stood behind her. Borya wasn't sure if she stood there to ensure her servant's cooperation or give her moral support, or both. He switched back to Mandarin. No, she hadn't seen Herr Geiger for about a month. The last time was in his backyard smoking a cigar, an especially smelly one. Yes, she knew the houseboy and talked to him occasionally. No, she hadn't seen him recently or anyone else or anyone carrying things from the house. "About a week ago, he told me that his master was missing, that a foreigner from his company had come by and told him that he was missing and they were trying to find him. After another week passed, he said he had to move back to his family home in Fujiadian because he was not getting paid. I have not seen or heard from him since."

"What is his name? And do you have his address?" He made his tone firm but not menacing. Nevertheless, he could see the woman stiffen up, and her eyes focused downward to the welcome mat in front of the doorway. Her employer must have placed a steadying hand on her back because the maid flinched slightly.

"His name is Lao Cheng. I don't know his address, only that it's somewhere in Fujiadian."

The name went into the notebook. "Thank you both for your assistance," he announced in Russian and repeated it in Mandarin, closing his notebook and following it with a sincere smile.

The house directly across the street from Geiger's was another two-storey, clapboard and tiled house, but with a Chinese-style gate and fence rather than another white picket fence. There was no answer to his knocks, and he saw no one appear at any of the windows. Likewise, there was no answer at the house across from the Jewish woman's brick home, another one-storey brick house. He returned to Geiger's house where Officer Galen already waited on the porch, still wearing his surly frown. Wordlessly, he led the way inside, where they found Chinn in the parlor in one of the red velvet armchairs next to the basket of papers, the ashtray on the side table now half full of his cigarette butts.

"Ahh, good, I just finished up here," he declared. "What did you two find out?" Borya went through his notes and detailed his results, including striking out at the two houses across the street.

"Well, we need to find this Lao Cheng. I suspect he took out his outstanding pay and maybe more with what is missing from the house. He certainly would have had a key. I can ask the precinct commander in Fujiadian if he knows him. Did you feel the maid was being truthful when she said she hadn't heard from him since?"

Borya replayed the conversation in his head and shrugged. "I can't be certain, but I think so."

Next Galen provided his report. He had gotten no answer at the house to the right. A man answered in the house directly across the street from it. He was home with a bad head cold.

He last saw Geiger when a motorcar, but not a taxi, picked him up early one morning. He was carrying a suitcase and a leather valise. Chinn and Borya exchanged glances. It had been about a month ago, he couldn't remember the date or day, except it wasn't a weekend. He had seen the houseboy a few times since, but not recently. The man had also a Chinese cook, but he was out at the market shopping.

"Good, good," Chinn remarked and included a nod. "Officer Melnikov and I have other leads to follow, so perhaps you can revisit the three houses where no one answered later today and send me a report. I will thank your precinct commander for your assistance, and please ask him keep an eye on the property so hopefully nobody else takes anything away."

"Yes, Inspector," Galen answered, "and were you able to find anything we missed inside?" he added, offering an expression of pure innocence.

"Yes, I did, as a matter of fact." Chinn looked up at him with an equally innocent smile. "There was 100 Yuan in bank notes taped behind a painting in one of the bedrooms upstairs," and then turning to Borya, "and a few more papers in a secret compartment of the desk. I wouldn't have expected you to find it, but I've seen this particular model of desk before. It's all in that basket ready to go." Borya shot a knowing glance at Galen, who now stood stone-faced. He wasn't sure whether the other officer was feeling surprised, chastened, or just angry at himself for missing the money and maybe an opportunity to add it to his pocket.

After Officer Galen left, Chinn had Borya stand outside on Geiger's porch and observe the signal lamps while he worked the switches in the entryway that also connected the house to the city's police and fire alarm system. They worked as they were supposed to, and Chinn flashed the signal again to indicate it was a false alarm, so they didn't cause the local precinct to send out another officer or fireman. That done, Borya and Chinn headed back to police headquarters and the detective squad room, locking the front door of the house behind them. While Chinn smoked and walked, Borya bore the laden basket stoically, first holding it out in front of him until his arms got tired, and then transferring it to one shoulder and holding it in place with one arm and occasionally alternating the shoulder.

"So, what did you take away from our search of the house?" Chinn prompted after they had gone a few blocks.

Borya did not answer immediately, gathering his thoughts for more than a few steps before speaking. "Well, it seemed like an awfully nice house and furnishings to belong to someone that's only been here five years and was a first-line supervisor at an abattoir. I mean, it was more than my father could afford when he was working as a supervisor for the Railway."

Chinn grunted and nodded. "Yes, it would appear so. It would seem unlikely he bought it or is renting and still be able to send much money back to his wife solely from his Chicken and Duck Company salary. But I suppose it could be heavily mortgaged or he brought money with him from Germany. Or maybe he came into an inheritance... hopefully, these papers will tell the story. And what else?"

Borya shifted the heavy basket to his other shoulder. "Well, somebody had rifled the house for money and valuables small enough to be easily carried away. But if it was the houseboy, and I were him, I wouldn't have made it appear so obvious. Drawers were left open and papers strewn about. Better to be discrete as I would be the obvious robbery suspect."

Chinn grunted again. "Yes, but maybe I assumed my employer was not ever coming back after his company sent someone around to the house and told me he was missing. I could quickly pawn the items in one or more of the better shops in Pristan and leave the city before anyone returned to the house, so maybe I didn't care about being careful." Borya nodded, but Chinn was not finished. "Or maybe it was someone who *knew* Geiger wasn't coming back and not the houseboy at all. Neither of the neighbors mentioned seeing him carrying anything away."

"No, but what about the locked doors? You said yourself that the houseboy probably had a key," Borya protested.

"Ahh, but we don't know how many keys there are and who all might have had one? If he was renting, then the owner would certainly have keys. Or maybe Geiger was fool enough to hide one outside in case he or the houseboy locked themselves out. And the lock on the back door was not particularly effective. It took me all of a minute to jimmy it open," and he afforded himself a rare complete smile.

When they reached police headquarters and the detective squad room, Borya was happy to lay his heavy burden down on Chinn's desk. First Chinn put the 100 Yuan of bills into an envelope, marked it, and gave it to the senior clerk to put into the squad room's safe. Then he and Borya divided the papers up into two piles, those that were in Russian or Chinese in one pile, and those in German into another. Those in German Chinn gave to an elderly Russian clerk who was a Volga German, an ethnic German who came from the Volga region of Russia and who read and spoke German as well as he did Russian. He would examine them and make notes, and those that interested Chinn he would translate. Those papers only in Russian Chinn gave to Borya to examine, keeping only those in Chinese to himself, taking advantage of their respective strengths. The papers that were in both Russian and Chinese, not an uncommon in Harbin, he split between them. Borya took his pile to a nearby empty desk that belonged to one of the other murder squad detectives.

Among his allotted papers, Borya found the bill of sale for the house, which showed Geiger had bought it four years previously, the year after he had arrived in Harbin, on a mortgage loan with the First Credit Association Bank on Uchastkowaya Street in Pristan. Another document from that same bank showed he had completely paid off the loan just over a year ago in three large lump sum payments when most of the principal was still owed. Each payment was many times more than his monthly salary at the abattoir. A sizable windfall from somewhere! A passbook from the same bank showed deposits of varying amounts on varying dates of the month that often exceeded the regular equal deposits that he assumed were Geiger's monthly paychecks from the abattoir. There were also receipts for furniture, books, and artwork that indicated an expensive lifestyle such as had been reflected in the furnishings of the house. Nothing explained the source of this sudden wealth. Nor was there a will, although that could have been among the papers in German. It all went into his notebook.

When Borya saw Chinn turn over his last paper on his desk, he rejoined the inspector. Borya gave him the highlights of his own findings and then summarized: "Herr Geiger seems to have come into a sizable fortune in the last year and wasn't afraid to spend it on his house and himself."

Chinn puffed on his cigarette and then grunted out a cloud of smoke. "But nothing of where this newfound wealth came from?"

"No, nothing, Inspector."

"Nor in these," Chinn replied, letting his free hand drop onto his own pile of papers. "But I would rule out any inheritance or trust fund coming from Germany. That would likely have come in one lump sum or identical monthly amounts if it had been from a trust."

"Maybe he was receiving monthly checks from a trust fund, but when he cashed them at the bank, he kept out varying portions for expenses and just deposited the balance," Borya offered.

Chinn bobbed his head in thought before answering. "Well, yes, maybe. But then I would have expected them to be wired to him. And were those extra deposits made the same time each month?"

"Well, no," Borya conceded.

"Maybe something will turn up in the German papers. Meanwhile, let's head to Fujiadian and see if we can track down Song, the missing company agent. I called the precinct commander in Fujiadian yesterday, and he sent a patrolman to check on his house there. He called back to say the Harbin wife and children were there, but he didn't find Song. But I still want to talk to her."

"Did she file a missing person report on him?" Borya asked.

"No. And that's another reason I would like to talk to her."

CHAPTER NINE

THEY HOPPED A STREETCAR on Prospect and rode it all the way down to Fujiadian where they walked down Market Street toward the river, a breeze blowing the musky smells of the Sungari and the docks toward them. Borya treated each daytime foray into the large Chinese district as an adventure; in Fujiadian you never knew what you might see or hear around the next corner—jugglers, street musicians, loud hawkers, the animated haggling between buyers and sellers. There was an explosion of colors and a vibrancy that was more muted in staid Pristan or in the insular ethnic neighborhoods of District 8. But there were also more dangers here, especially after dark, and even in uniform, Borya would instinctively employ the street crafts his grandfather taught him: walking the middle of the sidewalk to provide the optimum distance to respond to an attacker coming from the mouth of an alley, around a corner, or from behind a parked cart or motorcar, and if there was no sidewalk, then walk the middle of the street. But Chinn was leading the way by the most direct path, and Borya dutifully followed suit.

They followed a side street and entered a quieter neighborhood where the houses were larger and set back from the street by courtyards and closed off with metal gates that were locked at night.

"Judging from the status of his neighborhood, I would wager that our illustrious Song Nikan was once a well-to-do Peking Manchu," Chinn observed.

"Peking Manchu?"

"A Manchu official who held a position in the imperial government in Peking. Ofttimes, they left their estates back here in Manchuria in the hands of bailiffs. After the 1911 Revolution, many came back here to the homeland only to find their 'trusted' agents had gained control of their estates through backdoor deals with local officials. So maybe he became a merchant and an agent of a foreign company in order to maintain his former lifestyle. But even if he is prosperous now, it's still a big step down from being a high Bannerman." Chinn spoke matter-of-factly and not particularly sympathetic. Borya was aware that many Han Chinese blamed the Manchus and their Qing Dynasty for holding back China from modernization and thus made it unable to stand up against the Western powers and Japan.

They found the address they were looking for; the number was painted on the white-washed brick wall next to a pair of sturdy iron gates. The gates were unlocked, and they let themselves into a courtyard of hard-packed dirt. Outbuildings of white-washed mud brick stood on either side of the courtyard, and at its end was a grand two-storey wooden house with a sweeping tiled roof in the style of traditional Han architecture. A middle-aged Chinese man in rough clothes was standing at an open door to one of the outbuildings, working on a leather harness that hung from a metal hook. He eyed them warily, paying special attention to Borya's police uniform, but made no move to either approach or challenge them and turned back to his work as they passed by him. A face appeared briefly at one of the first-floor windows of the house.

The front door to the house was ornately carved and substantial. Chinn rang the bell next to it, and the door was immediately opened by a young maid, who looked up at them with wide eyes.

"Is Madam Song at home?" Chinn asked. "We're from the Harbin police."

"Yes, yes," she answered in a soft voice and bowed repeatedly. "Please come in, she is expecting you."

They were led through a small foyer into a front room that was bright with sunlight from two windows, despite being filtered through stout wooden shutters. A long, low tea table and heavy wooden chairs, all in the same dark wood, sat in the center of the room. The faint smell of incense and dust hung in the air.

"Please wait here," and the maid disappeared behind an elaborate painted screen that hid from sight another doorway into the room. A minute later, she returned trailing behind an erect middle-aged woman wearing a long-sleeved gown of green with embroidered borders, her graying hair in the swallowtail of a married Manchu lady.

"I am Madam Song," she announced herself in Mandarin, her voice clear and formal.

"I am Inspector Chinn, and this is Officer Melnikov. We're from the Special District Police. We're here to ask a few questions about your husband, Song Nikan."

"Please sit," and she gestured them toward the chairs while she sat across from them. "Tea?" Chinn nodded, and the maid disappeared back behind the screen.

"What do you want to know about my husband? Another officer was here yesterday looking for him, and I already told him he's on a business trip to Hailar."

"Yes, I know that," Chinn answered patiently. "But your husband went to Hailar as an agent of the Chicken and Duck Company with one of their managers. That manager has... gone missing. It was quite some time ago, and it's well past when they were expected to return . . ." Borya kept his eyes on the woman to see if he could detect a response, but the woman remained impassive.

At that moment, the maid returned with a tea tray. They sat silently while she poured green tea into porcelain cups and put one in front of each of them and then bowed and left the room. Chinn took a sip of tea before continuing.

"Madam Song, have you heard at all from your husband since he left for Hailar?"

"No," she replied simply and sipped at her own tea.

"You didn't think it was strange when he didn't return? Did you think about filing a missing person report?" This time, Borya thought he detected a tiny fluttering of her eyelids before she returned her teacup to its saucer.

"He has other... interests in Hailar. Many times, he spends weeks there before returning. I don't always hear from him then." More fluttering.

"Did your husband mention anything beforehand about this particular trip? Anything different or unusual about it?"

"No, nothing," and this time she shook her head too. "He has gone on several trips before for that company. Always the same." But there was a tiny quaver in her voice.

Chinn sat quiet for a long moment and then reached into his pocket to pull out one of his cards. "Please, if you hear from your husband, or any news about him, please give me a phone call or send a message to me at Police Headquarters. We would like to hear from him to know he's safe."

Madam Song took the card wordlessly and nodded her head. Chinn looked over at Borya, who had been busy scribbling in his notebook, his cue to ask any questions he thought to add.

"Madam Song, did your husband mention the name Manfred Geiger to you, the man he was going to Hailar with?"

"No, not the name. Only that it was a man he had not gone on a trip with before. And that he wasn't a particularly nice man. That is all."

They drank down the rest of their tea and said their goodbyes. The maid met them at the front door to see them out, standing quiet and subdued. Outside, the man was still working on the leather harness, and Chinn took a detour to reach him. The man stepped away from the harness and stood blinking with the sun in his eyes, his posture now stiff.

"Hello, sir. I am Inspector Chinn, and this is Officer Melnikov. You work for the Songs?" The man seemed to relax somewhat, not expecting such politeness from policemen.

"Yes, I take care of the upkeep of the house and tend to their horse," nodding his head toward the interior of the outbuilding, "order the coal and whatever else is needed."

"How long have you worked for them?"

The man thought. "Four years now."

"Is Mr. Song a good employer?"

"Yes, fair enough. Doesn't pay well, but always pays. Four years."

"When was the last time you saw Mr. Song?"

He thought again. "Well, it's been weeks."

"Is that unusual?"

The man smiled now, a shy smile. "No, not really. He'd be gone off to the west for weeks at a time."

"And is Mr. Song an honest man?"

The question seemed to catch him by surprise. He looked up at the house before turning back to Chinn. "Yes, leastways, as far as I know."

Chinn looked at Borya, who shook his head. No other questions.

"So, what did you think?" Chinn asked when they returned to the street.

"About Madam Song? I think she's worried about her husband, but I don't think she knows anything."

Chinn grunted. "Yes, I agree."

"And nobody seems to like Geiger, including Song. Won't that make it hard to narrow down suspects?"

Chinn shook his head. "It usually takes a stronger motive to commit murder than just disliking someone. Geiger had a lot of unexplained income; I still put my money on greed as the motive."

"What will happen to Song's wife and family here if he doesn't show up?" Borya asked.

"Do you mean because he has another wife in Hailar?"

"Yes."

Chinn shrugged. "If he turns up dead, or he's declared legally dead, and there's no will, then it can depend on how and when they were married, and even where." That drew a look of puzzlement to Borya's face. "The laws here in Harbin Special District are not the same as in Heilungkiang Province. Nor are the judges. It could get down to which wife gets to a court first. But I would save my sympathy for that maid if this wife runs out of money. My guess is she's a bondservant, and she'll get sold off to someone else, and it might not be as a maid the next time."

"A bondservant... I thought that was illegal now."

Chinn shrugged again. "A lot of things are illegal. But down south fathers still sell their daughters to pay off their debts. At least she is getting meals and a place to sleep alone, which is better than for a lot of girls who end up in Fujiadian."

———◆———

Chinn led the way to a public square a couple of blocks away. It was too small to host a full-size outdoor market but did hold a small number of food stalls. By now, Chinn was hungry, and they each bought some fried bread and watermelon slices. Borya wrapped half of his fried bread in a clean handkerchief and deposited it in his tunic pocket under Chinn's approving eye. The sun had come out from behind puffy clouds, and they ate standing in the shade of one corner of the square.

"Tell me, who do you think is the most attentive here to who comes and goes? Someone who might recognize and remember our Manchu agent?" Chinn asked, and he waved his piece of fried bread to cover the entire square.

Borya looked around at the square's occupants. Not the pedestrians that were walking through, only intent on their destinations. Not the small knots of customers lined up at the food stalls—they would be gone in another few minutes. "One of the food vendors?"

Chinn snorted. "Try again!"

Borya looked around again. A half dozen beggars were camped out where the intersecting streets emptied into the square. They seemed to be the only other semi-permanent residents of the square. "A beggar?"

"Ahh, but which one?"

Borya looked at each one in turn. There was an older man missing one leg, who sat on a straw mat with his battered crutches. There were two mothers in rags with naked children lying listlessly in their laps. An elderly woman with twisted legs rocked back and forth on her mat. A middle-aged man in a tattered military uniform and missing his nose sat on a blanket. Another man in rags sang lustily, accompanying himself with a bamboo clapper. They all called out loudly, begging for pity, and held out bowls or empty cans for alms, but at the same time they all seemed focused on just those passing by their immediate zone.

"Any of them?"

Chinn snorted again. "Look at the man with no nose. Do you see that yellow stick lying next to him?"

Borya squinted across the square. A short staff wrapped in dirty yellow cotton indeed lay next to the nose-less beggar. "Yes..."

"He is 'top of the staff.' He controls all the beggars in this square as the representative of the beggar's guild. All the other beggars in this square are here because he allows it. All alms are given to him for redistribution at the end of the day, and he takes his own cut. Any other beggars that try to come here will feel that staff on their heads. Now watch his eyes."

Borya watched. The man's head moved only a little, but his dark eyes darted about over the whole square and his kingdom, constantly in motion. Borya nodded his understanding.

"Song likely crosses this square whenever he leaves his house. This man will remember when he last saw him in his neighborhood."

Chinn finished his last piece of bread and rubbed the crumbs off his hands and then walked toward the nose-less man. Before they were half-way across the square, the beggar rose to his feet with the aid of his staff. When they reached him, he bowed low to Chinn. "Welcome, Inspector! To what does this humble square owe the honor of your visit."

Chinn pulled the photo of Song Nikan from a pocket of his suit jacket, the one they had gotten from the personnel files of the abattoir. "When did you last see this man around here?" Meanwhile, Borya watched the flow of pedestrians through the square, not trusting himself to not stare at the man's disfigured face.

The beggar king leaned in to look closely at the photo and then leaned back. "A month ago. He is a rich merchant here in Fujiadian, but stingy. Few alms. Haven't seen him since."

"How about a houseboy named Lao Cheng?" Chinn began and then looked over at Borya.

"Twenties. Short stature with short hair," Borya finished from memory without needing to refer to his notebook.

"Many fit that description, but I don't know that name."

Chinn fished a silver one chiao coin from his trouser pocket and tossed it into the beggar's bowl. "Thank you, Top. If you see him again, could you send word to me through the precinct here in Fujiadian?"

"Yes, Inspector, of course. For you, anytime," and he bowed again as they walked away.

Chinn leaned in closer to Borya once they were out of earshot of the beggar king. "I would wager Song is either hiding out with his other wife in Hailar or he is as dead as our Herr Geiger."

They took the streetcar back to Prospect Street the way they had come. The afternoon sun cast their long shadows across the sidewalks. Chinn seemed preoccupied with his own thoughts, and

Borya thought it best not to disturb him. When they reached the bottom of the steps leading to the headquarters entrance, Chinn suddenly stopped, and Borya had to step backwards to face him.

"I have something to ask you . . ." Chinn began, so solemn that Borya was immediately alarmed. Had he done something wrong? Had he been too casual with his superior? Asked too many questions? Perhaps seeing Borya tense up, the older man bent his head to the side and exhibited a disarming smile. "I have told my wife about you and how much time we have spent together. She wants to meet you. I think she is jealous." The smile broadened. "Can you come to dinner at our house tomorrow evening?"

Borya let out his breath, not aware he had been holding it. "Yes, of course! Of course!"

"Good. Well, enough for today, I will see you in the morning. I was only going inside to write some notes in the case file while they are still fresh in my mind."

"Yes, good day Inspector!"

A good day indeed!

"Dinner at the Inspector's house!" his mother declared, astonished. "Is he married? Children? You must bring gifts!"

"Yes, and yes. And why?" Borya tried to keep up with her frenzied stream of words.

"Why! Because he is giving you a great honor by asking you to his home. A subordinate! You want to show him you are grateful. It can pay to have influential friends when it comes time for promotions. I wish your father had listened more closely to me on this!"

Borya remembered some of those arguments. They weren't really arguments as much as his father meeting his mother's admonishments with shrugs. I'm no good at office politics, he would say. I just work my hardest and my bosses can see that. And he did get promotions along the way until the office politics were replaced with real politics when the Soviets squeezed out all Russians that didn't hold a Soviet passport.

From a drawer, his mother retrieved the silk scarf he had brought her back from Changchun, still wrapped in paper. "Here, give this to his wife, and thank her for the meal. Tell her how wonderful it was."

"No, Mama, I bought this for you!" and he tried to return the scarf to the drawer.

"That's okay, you can buy me another after you're promoted to second grade. How many children does he have? Girls? Boys? What are their ages?" Borya recalled he had heard Chinn mention two daughters during a conversation with one of the other murder squad detectives. He didn't know their ages, but he knew they were young.

"Young?... then buy some candy. Separate it, so they each get their own equal share."

"Yes, Mama."

CHAPTER TEN

"LET'S GO CHECK ON the autopsy, it should be done by now," Chinn declared the next morning after he made Borya wait while he went through the paperwork that had accumulated on his desk.

They left police headquarters, and Chinn led the way further uptown. They crossed Prospect Street in the shadow of St. Nicholas Cathedral, which prominently occupies the center of a traffic circle in the heart of the city. To Borya and the Orthodox community, the colossal timbered edifice of gables, spires, and domes was also the spiritual center of the city. He could not recall how many Sundays he had spent inside it with his father and then his aunt, and despite its familiarity, it still drew his appreciative eye, whereas Chinn gave it only a quick glance.

"Where are we going?" Borya asked, expecting that they would be visiting the office of the police surgeon back in the basement of the Municipal building.

"To the Medical School at the Special Municipal Hospital. Professor Hong there is the head of the Pathology Department and agreed to do the autopsy for me. He has done other... *unusual* cases in the past for me, and so I had the body sent there instead along with a copy of our report and the translation of Ota's."

Borya couldn't argue that this autopsy certainly had to fit the description of "unusual."

Chinn set an ambling pace that Borya's short legs could match comfortably. They soon passed the majestic CER Headquarters, the locomotive repair yard at Machiakow where Borya's father had worked for years, and then the wireless telegraph station. After twenty minutes, they reached the hospital suburb and the Harbin Special Municipal Hospital. Neither man was winded, but both their hats showed perspiration marks from the muggy summer heat. The three-storey hospital loomed over them, a utilitarian concrete edifice with the windows of the first two stories in rectangles, but the windows of the top floor arched at the top.

From the hospital entrance and lobby, Chinn led the way directly to a stairway that took them down two flights to the building's basement. "Of course, the doctor in charge of deaths is banished to the basement," Chinn noted drily. At the bottom of the stairs, corridors ran off in all four directions, and huge pipes and brass light fixtures decorated the grey ceilings. Signs were painted on the walls, but Chinn knew his way without looking, taking the corridor straight ahead and almost to the end of the hallway before stopping at a glass-paneled door with "Dr. Hong Gui, Pathology" painted on it in black letters.

Chinn tapped on the door and heard a barking "Enter!" in Mandarin. Borya followed into a large office made smaller by a cluster of bookcases crammed with hundreds of books and a long row of filing cabinets. Loose stacks of files and papers covered the tops of all the cabinets and bookcases, piled high onto two chairs, and most of the top of a wooden desk behind which sat a small-framed Chinese man in a white lab coat. Professor Hong was easily in his sixties, white-haired, and frail looking, with wire-rimmed spectacles perched near the end of his nose, where they looked ready to slide off his face at any moment. Borya was surprised that the brisk, deep voice he had heard outside the door had come from this frail figure.

"Did we come too soon, Professor?"

"No, no, not at all Inspector," came the booming voice. "I just finished an hour ago, and my report is being typed upstairs as we speak." The doctor turned his eyes on Borya, and he could see the old man's eyes were clear and full of intelligence, with a hint of mirth. "And who is your young policeman friend?"

"This is Officer Melnikov. He is assisting me on this case. He is who wrote up the case report."

"Ahh, I thought it was too precise and organized to be your work, Inspector," the doctor said and ended with a bellow of laughter. Chinn grunted but smiled in reply in a way that belied a longtime familiarity and friendship.

"Come, let's retire to my surgery, and I'll walk you through what I found." With that, the elderly man sprang to his feet with remarkable energy and ushered them out into the hallway and then through an adjacent door marked simply as "Pathology." Immediately, Borya felt physically assailed by the overwhelming odor of corruption and began breathing through his mouth like he had in the cattle barn at the abattoir.

Within was a large square room, the walls covered in white tiles and lined with white enameled cabinets. Several electric light fixtures reflected bright light back from the white walls and ceiling. In the center of the room was a stainless steel table on which lay the familiar dark, leathery form of Herr Geiger, only now without clothes and cut open from his throat down to his groin, exposing a grisly, murky cavity. Here, there was no refrigeration to dampen the smell of death.

"You're not going to throw up, are you, officer?" Hong cheerily confronted Borya. "My assistant has just finished cleaning up." Borya noticed for the first time the young man in a long white lab coat standing against the wall in the far corner, trying to look serious and deferential at the same time.

Borya stared into the corpse. He wasn't repelled by the sight, after all he was seeing it for the second time, but the smell of decay was much stronger now. "I don't think so . . ." He gulped strongly, praying he would not vomit in front of Inspector Chinn.

"Good! But if you feel the urge, please do it in the sink," and the doctor waved a hand at a steel sink in one corner of the room before he spun back around to face Chinn, "So let us begin!" and he moved to the end of the table nearest Geiger's head. "Firstly, I examined the head wound, and it does appear to be from a small caliber bullet, as your Nipponese friends surmised." Here Chinn snorted, as if to ensure everyone present that he was not a friend of the Japanese or their Kwantung government. "The bullet entered at the left temple and exited just below the right ear. I probed the path just to be sure . . ."

"Was the shot in close proximity?" Chinn interrupted.

"Not immediately close—there were no burn or scorch marks on the skin or hair."

Well, that eliminated his suicide-and-offloading the body theory, Borya thought. But at least he would have the satisfaction of crossing it out in his notebook. Fewer threads to pull.

"And from the angle, I would say the shooter was above our victim, aiming down. And when he had his legs," and Hong smiled as though he was telling a joke, "he would have been taller than most men, about like your young friend here. It would be unlikely the shooter was an even taller man in order to be holding a gun leveled downward at him. So the victim might have been kneeling."

"Or the shooter was standing on a higher spot?" Borya offered.

Dr. Hong bowed slightly with a smile, "Or yes, if he had claimed the higher ground."

"Were there any ligature marks on the wrists or neck?" Chinn asked.

"No, unless there were some on the ankles." Another smile. "Now, for the rest of the body, you have certainly brought me a...*challenge* as you promised, or as my assistant offered, a 'mess.'" Borya stole a glance at the young assistant, but he still maintained his blank face and kept his post in the corner.

The professor continued, "I confirmed that the exterior of the body was treated with quicklime after death, presumably to delay putrefaction while the body was being transported in the crate. It is commonly used in the burial of diseased animals and animal parts by farmers, stockyards, and abattoirs to prevent the spread of diseases. But when applied only externally, as was done here, it successfully halts putrefaction only to the outside of the body but does little to prevent the breakdown of internal organs and soft tissues inside. Consequently, I was not able to ascertain the state of his overall health beyond, of course, the fatal gunshot wound." Another smile.

And no doubt the opening of the body had contributed considerably to the intensity of the smell, Borya thought, but it didn't seem to be bothering the professor, his assistant, or Chinn, who actually moved in closer for a better view.

"Any other wounds? Bruises?" Chinn asked.

"Not discernible."

Chinn raised an eyebrow toward Borya as a prompt.

"Then probably not a crime of passion or revenge..." Borya ventured. And so maybe greed, he thought to himself. Chinn favored him with a slight nod.

"Date of death?" Chinn continued.

Professor Hong shook his head back and forth with a grin. "The quicklime complicates making an estimate with any accuracy, but I would guess it corresponds to the reported time of his disappearance, or not many days afterwards."

"Anything else on the body or the clothes?"

"Nothing, with the exception of what appears to be recent chancres in the groin area, indicating the primary stage of syphilis."

"Revenge by a wronged lover?" Borya offered. Chinn shrugged.

Hong continued. "My assistant went through the clothes, including all the pockets and seams. He only found the coin mentioned in the reports and some mud in one of the pockets of his suit jacket. Maybe his hand was muddy, or it might have had something in that pocket that was muddy at the time—Wei..."

The assistant came to life, moving away from the wall and revealing a small beige envelope in his hand that he had been holding behind him and handed it to Chinn. The inspector opened the flap to look inside, snorted, nodded, and stuffed the envelope in his own suit pocket. Then the assistant retrieved a bundle wrapped in brown paper and tied up in twine from a metal table near the sink. "The clothing," the professor explained. The assistant moved to hand this also to Chinn, but Chinn pointed in turn to Borya. Borya took the package and noticed it exuded the same smell of decay. Of course, the lowly patrolman gets to carry the smelly evidence.

"Thank you so much for your services, Professor Hong," Chinn proclaimed, nodding his head to the elderly doctor.

"Certainly. It also provided a good learning experience for my assistant. Why don't you join me in my office for some tea while we wait for my typed report to get finished and then you can take it with you." Chinn nodded again.

They returned to Hong's office where the assistant removed the stacks of files from the two chairs to allow Chinn and Borya to sit and then left to prepare the tea. Chinn and the professor exchanged pleasantries and the health of their respective families. From this, Borya was able to confirm that Chinn was indeed married and had two young daughters and that his elderly father lived with them all in a house in Fujiadian. The tea arrived, and the talk got more serious.

"I am going to guess that Geiger's killer took him by surprise since he wasn't bound and the shot came from the side, whereas executions are usually close up and to the forehead or the back of the neck," Chinn mused. Borya wrote furiously in his notebook to capture it all. Was Chinn's familiarity with executions from investigating the occasional gangland slayings in Harbin? The professor agreed with the theory and the assistant, who without a chair had been left standing, merely nodded and tried to look thoughtful.

"So if taken by surprise, the shooter could have been his travel partner Song," Borya offered.

"Possibly. All the more reason we need to find him," Chinn responded.

At that moment, a clerk entered the office, the door having been left open, holding two copies of the professor's typed report. The professor kept the original, adding it to one of the stacks on his desk, and put the carbon copy into a manila folder for

Chinn and Borya to take back to the police station. They made their farewells with bows all around and left the professor and his assistant to their macabre work. Borya was silently thankful that the autopsy report had been delivered after their arrival, otherwise it might have disappeared within the mounds of all the other files heaped around the professor's office.

They returned to Prospect Street and police headquarters, Borya carrying the pungent bundle of clothes and Chinn the brown envelope containing Geiger's few personal effects and the folder holding the autopsy report. Once inside, Borya took the clothing and personal effects to the evidence storage room to get them logged in, while Chinn updated the case file at his desk. They had now checked all the boxes in the list of tasks Superintendent Liu had given them, and so together, they headed to his office to give him a progress report, the case file in hand. Would Liu decide there was enough evidence now to let them continue their investigation or, Borya wondered, would he put an end to his short career with the murder squad?

CHAPTER ELEVEN

SUPERINTENDENT LIU WAS IN his office, standing by his desk and holding a cup of tea in one hand while looking out the window at Prospect Street. Borya surmised he was either on his way to or had just returned from some public ceremony because this time wore a uniform holding a sprinkling of ribbons over the breast pocket along with a police sword and belt buckle, both adorned with the Chinese plum blossom emblem. This time, Liu waved them into the empty chairs and then sat down in his own chair behind the large desk. His sword tangled with the arm of his chair, and he made an embarrassed face and removed the sword from its belt hanger and laid it on top of his desk while muttering a quiet curse.

"Well?"

Chinn sat forward and in his precise tone went through the details of their visit to the British Chicken and Duck Company, their interview with the company head, the visits to the personnel and Geiger's offices and that of his assistant. Liu listened without interrupting, his piercing eyes focused on Chinn. "And so Herr Geiger went missing after he and the company agent were supposed to have taken the train to Hailar," Chinn summarized before pausing. Again, Liu did not speak but nodded for him to continue.

Next, Chinn went through the search of Geiger's house, what they discovered there, and the interviews with the neighbors. When Chinn described the extent of Geiger's property and wealth, Liu still did not speak, but raised a single eyebrow. "And one neighbor reported seeing him leave his house in a motorcar with a suitcase on a morning around the day of his departure, presumably heading for the train station."

Liu nodded again. After that, Chinn described their search for the missing Manchu agent and Geiger's houseboy in Fujiadian, and then finally, the results of the autopsy. "And that's where we are today. We can't say with any certainty yet where Geiger was killed or why or the fate of the contract agent, Song Nikan. I'm not sure there is much more we can learn here in Harbin. I believe the next steps are to find out whether Geiger or Song ever made it to Hailar, and if so, why they didn't complete their company business there. And also to track down who shipped the body from Barim. Barim could have been a planned stop on their way to or from Hailar for some reason we don't yet know. Perhaps he was lured off the train there and killed." Borya was impressed by the amount of detail Chinn had retained without once having to open the case file on his lap. He also noticed that he had graciously used the term "we" instead of just "I" despite being the one in charge of the investigation.

Liu sat back in his chair slowly. His eyes flicked to Borya, who wondered if the man was looking for him to corroborate or add to Chinn's report. Borya only nodded slightly, and the dark eyes flicked back to Chinn.

"Well, I agree there is something suspicious about Geiger's activities," Liu began. "Why volunteer for this particular trip?

Why leave behind the rail pass? Was he trying to hide another itinerary, as you suggest, or did he just forget to bring it along?" and here added a shrug. "But the man's sudden wealth suggests he is involved in something more than just the buying and cutting up of cattle. Leave me the case file, and I will review it and decide what to do next. Normally, I would not rely on the provincial police in Barim and Hailar to conduct a local investigation for us, but right now Hailar is not the safest place in the Northeast Provinces to be sending someone. The talks in Berlin with the Soviets are not going well, and full-scale fighting could still break out at the borders. I will let you know what I decide in the morning."

Liu stood and returned his sword to its belt hanger, and they knew the meeting was over. They stood and bowed their way out of the office and returned to the detective squad room and Chinn's desk. "I know it's still a little early to go off duty, but I would like to go home and wash up and change my clothes before coming to dinner," Borya asked with a sheepish smile. "Geiger's clothes were a little...fragrant, and I can still smell it on my uniform."

That earned him a dry chuckle from Chinn. "Yes, of course. I'm sure my wife would appreciate the change of clothes," and he gave Borya the address and directions to his house in Fujiadian.

CHAPTER TWELVE

Borya found the inspector's home easily by the address, two blocks into Fujiadian from its border with District 8. It was a square-built, one-storey house painted green with a hipped roof of terra-cotta roof tiles and a red door. It was a Western-style family home of the type his parents had talked many times about buying when Borya was a boy, but in truth, they had never left the sanctuary of their neighborhood in Pristan while his father was alive. His father was always holding out for a house in New Town or Old Harbin, and his mother, the realist, knew those were places where she and her children would never fit in. And so the dream never happened, and then it couldn't happen after that fateful day when the somber man from the Flour Mill came to their door and ended his happy childhood forever. Now, standing on the porch of this solid house with its cheery colors, Borya couldn't help feeling he was on the outside looking into a life that could have been... should have been...

Before he had gathered the courage to knock, he saw the gauze curtain over the adjacent window part, and then the door swung open, revealing the Inspector himself, still in his suit pants and vest but now minus the suit jacket and the leather Mauser holster. His mouth was in an uncharacteristicly broad smile. The older man's eyes were also bright and not the dark caverns that seemed to swallow all light when they were focused on police business.

"Come in, come in," Chinn insisted and grabbed Borya's arm and pulled him into the warm living room within. He was twirled around to face an attractive but diminutive Chinese woman in a flowered dress, barely as tall as his own mother but looked to be years younger than her husband. "This is my wife, Chunhua."

Spring Flowers. Borya thought the name fitting when her face lit up with a warm, welcoming smile.

"So nice to meet you, Borya. I have been wanting to meet the young man who has been spending more time lately with my husband than he has with me," she said in a teasing voice, extending her hand to Borya to shake.

Before Borya could reply, he was twirled around to face an elderly man in a long blue silk robe, sitting in a high-backed chair in the corner of the room next to an iron wood stove. "My father, Chinn Wenyan. This is Borya . . ."

"Sergeevich . . ." Borya filled in with a bow to the elderly man.

" . . . Melnikov. He has been assisting me in the investigation of the dead German found in Changchun."

The old man squinted up at Borya with watery eyes. "You are Russian?" he asked. Borya took no offense, as it was framed as an innocent question and not as a challenge.

"On my father's side. My mother is Korean."

"Ahh," and the old man nodded sagely.

At that moment, two streaks of motion shot into the room from a side door and coalesced into two adorable young girls on either side of their mother, wearing short dresses of the same flowered pattern and wearing identical ribbons in their hair. Borya judged them to be around three and five years old and reminded him of his own sisters at that age.

"And this is Chao-xing and Chenguang. They are actually demons that came here and took the places of my well-mannered daughters." Instead of being cowed by this admonishment, the two girls giggled. Borya bowed low and handed each of them in turn small sacks of haw flake candy he had just bought on his way from a neighborhood shop. Their mother insisted they save the treats for after dinner. Then he presented Chunhua with the silk scarf, still wrapped in tissue paper, which she politely made a fuss over. Both Chinn men smiled appreciatively.

"Please, sit," Chunhua said. "Have some tea, and I will bring in the food. After all, we invited you to a dinner."

Following this whirlwind of introductions, Borya was finally able to take stock of the surroundings. The front room included a contemporary dining table surrounded by straight-backed chairs like the grandfather sat in. A leather armchair with an ottoman and a small side table occupied a corner by the front windows, which he supposed was the Inspector's sanctuary. A corner curio cabinet occupied the other front corner, and a small family shrine sat atop a table in yet another corner. An electric light fixture hung from the center of the ceiling, illuminating soft yellow walls that opened onto three doorways, two of which had their doors closed, and the third leading onto a hallway to where Chunhua had retreated to the kitchen. Borya had expected to find a more conventional Chinese home, but instead, found modern and western furnishings predominated. Borya could imagine his own father sitting in the leather armchair and hearing his own mother's voice calling from the kitchen.

They sat down at the long table, with Chinn helping his elderly father to a seat at its head. Chunhua swept into the room bearing two platters of food and had no sooner laid them down on the table before she left to bring in two more. Borya was assailed by a cacophony of wonderful odors rising with the steam from meat dumplings in a brown broth, spicy bok choy, pickled vegetables, and steamed buns and felt his salivary glands respond. They passed around the dishes in no particular order or status, and although his stomach rumbled, Borya took only small portions of each dish to ensure no one among his hosts would be left out.

"So, what did your father do?" the elder Chinn addressed Borya when everyone had something on their plate and had begun eating. Borya had expected this as the common enquiry into family background and status, but he noted that the question asked what his father "did" rather than "does." His father's premature death was common knowledge in police circles and would have been known to the younger Chinn. He described his father's work on the railroad and then at the flour mill and threw in his grandfather's medicine shop and his aunt's tearoom. At each mention, the elderly man nodded sagely and without comment except for polite noises.

"My father was a judge for the Heilungkiang provincial government in Tsitsihar," the inspector Chinn offered in exchange. "He allowed me to bring him here to Harbin after his retirement." From his age, Borya guessed the man had performed the role under both the Republic and the ending days of the Imperial government, no easy feat.

"Many changes since then," the older Chinn admitted. "And much different than the courts here in Harbin." His son allowed a tight smile that indicated this was far from being a new topic of discussion.

"Have you always wanted to be a policeman?" Chunhua asked Borya. The question startled him for its openness in coming from the wife, although it reminded him of his own mother's forthright manner, and one for which he didn't have a ready answer.

"Not really," he finally admitted. "My father always expected me to train at the Technical Institute and to work for the Railway like he had, and so that's what I thought would happen. After he… had his accident, I had to find any kind of employment, and there were openings for police cadets who could speak multiple languages… so I applied." He noticed the girls' eyes go wide when he mentioned his father's accident.

"Do you like doing police work?" she asked.

Here, Borya could be more forthright. "To begin with, I just wanted a job, but then I found I really enjoy it. There's something satisfying about seeing justice fulfilled and not leaving a crime go unpunished." That drew a smile from the retired judge. "And especially working for your husband. I am learning much of how the investigative side of police work operates, he knows so much!"

That drew a pleased laugh from the wife and an embarrassed smile from her husband. "Well, you are a quick learner. And you have natural investigative skills," Chinn replied. Borya's face glowed, and he could not remember having ever spent a more enjoyable evening away from his family.

When the meal was done, Chunhua swept away the empty platters and enlisted the girls to help carry the dishes to the kitchen. The Inspector helped resettle his father into his chair in the corner and then left to the back of the house to get more wood for the wood stove. The evenings were beginning to get cooler, and although Borya was comfortable, he imagined that the thin, older gentleman appreciated the warmth of the fire more than the rest of them.

Borya wandered over by the leather armchair to glance at a book that lay on the side table, curious. It was a book of Chinese classics, one that Borya had attempted to tackle while still in school. Then he wandered over to the curio cabinet and peered at the objects behind the glass. There were small porcelain figurines, and a few pieces made from jade as well as a medal with a ribbon sitting on a piece of blue velvet. The medal was of a gilded sunburst in the middle of which was a white swastika inside a red circle in turn surrounded by a blue circle with Chinese characters, too small for Borya to read through the glass.

"That is an award from the Hongwanzihui, the Red Swastika Society," Borya heard Chunhua's voice suddenly behind him, having not heard her reenter the room. "Do you know what that is?"

"It's like the Red Cross . . ." Borya ventured. He had, of course, heard of the philanthropic society before but was more familiar with the charities run by the Orthodox fathers.

"Yes. My husband received it for raising a lot of money in donations from the local Chinese merchants and leaders for the widows and orphanages here in Harbin. Even many Russian businessmen contributed. We were all very proud of him and attended the ceremony when he was presented with it. Of course, that was before the Kuomintang's anti-superstitious movement reached Harbin. Now, he no longer wears it in public, but the fact that he helped the widows and orphans is more important to him than the medal. Many of those donations still continue today."

The object of their conversation returned with an armful of wood and smelling of cigarette smoke, followed by the girls, each bearing a single log. He thanked them for their assistance, "And now I think it is late and time for you two to head to bed."

"Story! Story!" they both chimed together.

"Not tonight, we still have company."

Borya raised a hand. "Please allow me. They have been very patient tonight. I think I have a story to tell them."

"Yes! Yes!" came the answering chorus.

Mother and father surrendered under this onslaught. "Let me get them into bed first or they will never get to sleep tonight," Chunhua announced, and led the two girls through one of the side doors. A few minutes later, she returned and waved Borya into the bedroom with a warm smile.

The two girls lay in identical beds on either side of the small bedroom. "In the chair, sit in the chair!" the older girl ordered, pointing to a wooden rocking chair that stood equal distance from the two beds.

Once seated, Borya began. "Okay, have you ever heard the story of the Tiger and the Dried Persimmon?" He hoped they hadn't since it was a Korean fable rather than Chinese, and one that had been a favorite of his own two sisters when they were that young. Two heads shook in denial. So he told them the story of the fussy child whose mother told him that he must stop crying because a tiger was coming, not knowing there was a real tiger outside the house listening. When the child wouldn't stop crying after this threat, the tiger thought the child must not be afraid of tigers. When the mother promised some dried persimmons as a treat, then the child stopped crying. Ahh, this "persimmon" must be a creature scarier than himself to make the child stop crying, the tiger thought. At that moment, a thief who had come to steal the farmer's cow jumped on the tiger, thinking this was the cow he had come to steal. The tiger thought the thief was this terrible "persimmon" and took off running with the thief hanging on for dear life. It did not end well for the thief or the tiger, which managed to elicit peals of laughter from the girls. He was sure he had made friends for life.

Borya emerged from the bedroom to find the adults with smiles on all their faces. "Well, I should probably be getting home to bed myself, as I suppose we have an early start in the morning?"

"Yes, as usual," Chinn replied, his eyes still bright.

Borya thanked the Inspector for his hospitality, the father for his company, and the wife for the wonderful meal.

"Watch out for this young man on the streets," Chunhua chided her husband for Borya's benefit.

"And I will for him," Borya assured her. And he meant it.

PART TWO

CHAPTER THIRTEEN

BORYA REPORTED, AS USUAL, to Chinn's desk in the squad room the next morning, but uncharacteristically there was no Chinn. Instead, there was a note left for him on the desk written by the Inspector, explaining that the investigation had been put on hold, and he had been temporarily assigned to lead a squad charged with arresting newly identified Soviet saboteurs in the city. Borya was to report back to his old precinct commander until the investigation could be resumed. Borya reread the note three times before he allowed himself to accept that it was real. He felt deflated at having to return so soon to his old patrol duties in District 8. But there was nothing to be done about it. At least the note inferred he might be returning to the investigation when the Inspector's emergency duty was over.

Borya trudged over to his precinct station and found Commander Cho in his office. He was just hanging up the phone on his desk and waved Borya inside. Before Borya could explain his prodigal return, Cho scowled and waved him into silence.

"There was a raid last night at the Railway Telegraph building, and they captured several Soviet agents along with a radio set that was being used to communicate with the GPU," Cho related. Everyone in the police department, and most of the city, knew who the GPU were—the Soviet State Political Directorate, Stalin's secret army that was orchestrating the wave of sabotage and dissension in Harbin and all across the Northeast Provinces.

"These agents yielded up the names of other traitors and some of their intended targets. Everything is in chaos," which Cho depicted by waving both hands out to his sides. "The Railway Guards want police reinforcements in order to defend every possible target. You are one of five patrolmen I am sending to them from this precinct, the other four are already on their way. Report to Commander Chu-Kewen of the Guards . . ."

Before Cho could finish or Borya could ask any questions, the phone on Cho's desk rang, and the commander lunged at it and waved Borya out of his office with one hand while bringing the receiver up to his good ear with the other. Borya retreated quickly and soon was standing alone outside the precinct entrance in the cool morning air. He assumed that Commander Chu Ke-wen was stationed in the "Moscow Barracks," the Guards barracks just west of the city's main rail yards near Ostroumoff Suburb. He began heading that way in no particular hurry, giving himself time to ponder how quickly fate and circumstances had changed—one day the assistant to one of the most respected detectives in the Special District police, and the next day, just another patrolman guarding against saboteurs. And, no surprise, Cho had managed to assign him outside his precinct again. Borya no longer held doubts that his precinct commander would be just as happy to see him gone for good. Because he was part Russian and that made him untrustworthy in Cho's eyes? Or maybe just because he wasn't Chinese? It had to be one or the other, as Cho didn't know him well enough to dislike him for himself.

SPECIAL DISTRICT: HARBIN

He contemplated how he could tell his mother and sisters about his sudden descent after the euphoria he felt and just shared with them after the dinner at the Inspector's home only the night before. And finally, he wondered how much ordinary crime would increase while all this attention was being diverted to hunting Soviet spies and sympathizers. But at the same time, another part of him relished taking on the Bolsheviks. Borya had no place in his life or heart for them. They had taken over the Russian share of the partnership in the railroad with the Chinese government in 1924, following the final defeat of the White Russian forces in Siberia and the conclusion of the Russian Civil War. Only a year later, four years ago now, his father was part of the purge of White Russian employees at the CER by the Soviets. Never mind that he had worked for the railroad for almost twenty years, starting long before the Revolution. He became one of the many stateless Russians who had neither a Soviet nor Chinese passport—not that his father would have accepted a Soviet passport, being a diehard monarchist. And not that the Soviets would have given him one anyway since his father's brother had fought and died in the Nechaev Brigade, a body of White Russian mercenaries from Harbin who went to fight the Chinese communists in China's Shantung province.

It was almost two years after their firing, and only after hunger strikes and the attention of the world press, that the CER finally gave his father and the other fired White Russian workers a pittance of the pensions they had earned. Long before that happened, his parents savings had been depleted, and his father was forced to take a job as a shift supervisor at the Tianxingfu No. 4 Flour Mill in Harbin's Fujiadian district at a fraction of the pay he had earned at the railroad where he overseen all shifts that inspected and repaired the steam boilers of the railway's locomotives. It was at the flour mill that his father died when one of their steam boilers exploded, the result of slipshod maintenance done in a shift prior to his. Borya blamed the flour mill owners for putting profit before maintenance, but even more, he blamed the Soviets for leaving his father no option other than taking such a dangerous position in the first place. After, the flour mill provided only token death benefits, then once again the family quickly ran out of savings. His mother moved Borya and his two sisters from their spacious apartment in Pristan to a cramped two-room apartment in District 8, partly for the cheaper rent, but also to be closer to her own father's herbal medicine shop and the Korean community there.

Only a teenager, when he had lost his father, Borya had had a hard time reconciling himself to his death. The funeral had been at the St. Nicolas Cathedral and was well attended by former co-workers from the railroad and from the Russian and Korean communities. Borya remembered little of that ceremony, except the crying of his mother and sisters and the closed casket. He was told there could be no viewing of the body because the catastrophic nature of the death had prevented any restoration efforts. But that allowed Borya to imagine that there could have been a case of mistaken identity; somehow in the chaos of the accident another body had been misidentified as his father. Maybe his father was actually in hiding, targeted by the malicious Soviet CER managers that hadn't been satisfied with merely firing him. For months afterwards, Borya refused to sit at the family dinner table unless there was also a place set for his father. But as the years passed, he wondered why his father hadn't at least gotten word to him, until finally time dissolved all hope. Still, on the streets of the city, his heart would still leap whenever he saw from afar a man with hunched shoulders or a bald patch, only to catch up to them to find they were only a stranger.

It took him almost an hour to cross the southern boundaries of District 8 and Pristan and then past the railroad's central fuel yard and the long rows of rail cars in the car park below the bluff of New Town, before he arrived at the imposing brick building that was the Guards barracks. No doubt had he been headed in the other direction and returning to the detective squad room, his pace would have been faster, but now each step forward felt like he was taking a step further away from his life at the murder squad.

A guardsman at the barracks gate gave him directions to Commander Chu's office. Borya found the officer just outside his office haranguing a Guards corporal. Commander Chu Ke-wen was a hatchet-faced man of maybe fifty, trim, and with a Railway Guards uniform that looked clean and starched but worn at the collar and sleeves and with a parade sword hanging from his belt. Borya waited politely at a distance and tried not to listen to the dressing down but caught the gist of it. The corporal's patrol had been seen spending more time drinking tea and talking to the waitresses at a shop in Pristan than doing active patrolling. Finally, the one-way conversation ended with the curt dismissal of the corporal, to the latter's relief, and Borya approached and drew a fresh scowl from Chu.

"I am Officer Melnikov. I was sent here by Commander Cho of the District 8 Precinct."

"You took your time," the officer said after snorting like an enraged bull, "your fellow patrolmen were here over an hour ago." Borya hoped the man's anger had more to do with the retreating corporal than himself but nevertheless held himself at his most rigid attention.

"I was at Police Headquarters on special assignment when I received orders to report back my precinct commander in District 8. It was only then that I received directions to report to you here, Commander."

The man stared silently at Borya for a half-minute, eye to eye, looking him up and down before finally speaking. "Report to Sergeant Chao in the Equipment Room." Borya had barely opened his mouth to ask for directions before the Commander cut him off, pointing toward a side door before stalking off, one hand holding the scabbard of his sword as though he were looking for an excuse to draw the blade on the next man who displeased him.

Sergeant Chao Yoh-wen sat on a bench alone in the Equipment Room, scribbling on a clipboard. Sergeant Chao was almost as old as his commander and a stout, grizzled man who reminded Borya somewhat of Inspector Chinn. Around them, along the walls, dozens of raincoats and packs hung from hooks along with belts festooned with leather ammo pouches.

Borya came to stiff attention again and announced himself. The sergeant looked up on hearing the Russian surname and scrutinized Borya's face a long minute before consulting his clipboard. "From District 8," the sergeant finally spoke. It was a statement rather than a question.

"Yes, Sergeant."

Looking down at the clipboard once more, the sergeant spoke again. "Are you familiar with the Mosin rifle?" The Mosin-Nagant rifle was one of the main firearms of the current Railway Guards after hundreds of the older model bolt-action weapons had been seized from their Russian predecessors after having been disarmed in 1917 for siding with the Bolsheviks.

"I trained with it at the Police Academy here in Harbin."

This time, the sergeant looked back up from his clipboard. "Any good at it?"

"Fair, Sergeant. I am better on the pistol."

The sergeant sniffed, paused, and then blew his nose at the floor by Borya's shoe, missing it by inches. Borya's nostrils flared. Well, what had he expected? The Guards were almost completely Chinese after the purge of the Bolshevik sympathizers. At least the Special District police had retained a modicum of Russians... and half-Russians.

"Daytime patrols have already gone out. Come back at six p.m. *sharp,* and you'll be on night patrol with me. Now go home and get some rest."

"Yes, sergeant."

There was nothing left to do but return to District 8, and the family apartment, to try and get some sleep before returning for the night shift, now only about eight hours away. Retracing the way he had come, his feet did not seem in any greater hurry on this return trip. He wondered if Chinn was at that moment leading a squad of other detectives, or maybe even patrolmen, to hunt down terrorists in the city, which had to be more exciting than boring night patrols. He knew he hadn't been paying much attention to his surroundings when he found himself in front of his aunt's tearoom in Pristan instead of on the main road to District 8. He had time to kill, so he entered and took his seat at his table by the window. The carefully arranged place setting felt reassuring.

"Borya Sergeevich! I have not seen you in days!" he heard his aunt's voice beside him and felt her warmth. "You look so sad. Are your mother and sisters all right? Your grandfather?"

"Yes, they are all fine... it's just that I have been on special duty with the detective squad for the last week, but now I have been reassigned to night patrols with the Guards because of the emergency. From special duty to guard duty," he added with a touch of irony. He realized he had not visited the tearoom or seen his aunt since he had been assigned to Inspector Chinn. He told her briefly about their trip to Changchun and their investigation upon returning.

"Well, you have been busy! And I know of this Inspector Chinn. They say he is a good man, an honest man," his aunt reflected. "But you must be careful if you are going to be out at night now. They say the Reds are everywhere after dark. Have some tea and sweets to keep up your energy." And then she turned her smile on him, "At least if you are working nights again you can come with me to St. Nicholas' on Sunday morning?"

"Yes, of course, Auntie."

His mother was disappointed but rallied quickly. "So he said you will return to the investigation after the current emergency?"

"That's what he wrote in his note."

"How long will you be on these night patrols? Won't that be dangerous? The Reds just blew up a train near Suifenho."

"That's way out on the eastern border. Besides, we don't patrol alone—I will be part of a whole squad of guardsmen."

Borya retreated to his bedroom and napped until the late afternoon. By then, Min was home from school and was sulking, like Borya's temporary setback was a blow to her own personal fortunes. Hei-rin was still away at her job at the clothiers in Pristan. His mother fixed Borya and Min an early dinner of Bibimpap, a mixture of rice and vegetables fortified with some slivers of fish, and he set off for the Moscow Barracks with plenty of time to reach it before six o'clock.

Borya arrived ten minutes early and found Sergeant Chao in the same equipment room where they had met earlier in the day. The sergeant handed him a leather belt with two leather ammo pouches and then took him to the armory room and issued him a Mosin-Nagant rifle with a sling and enough five-round clips to fill the two ammo pouches. Borya took off his patrolmen's belt and put on the ammo belt and adjusted the straps that went over his shoulders that kept the heavy pouches from dragging the belt off his hips. Then he transferred the holster of his revolver from his police belt to the ammo belt—he might as well carry both weapons since he had bothered to bring the revolver along. Chao watched and frowned but made no comment.

By then the rest of their night patrol arrived—three Chinese Guardsmen and a White Russian patrolman named Puzyrev from the Pristan precinct whom Borya recognized but did not know well as he had graduated from the Police Academy two years before Borya. When they were all armed and ready, the sergeant split them up into two three-man teams, the sergeant leading one consisting of Borya and one of the Guardsmen, the other led by a Guards corporal and including the Russian patrolman and the remaining Guardsman. The sergeant and corporal both carried electric torches for use after the sun went down. Borya would have preferred to team up with the other policeman, but he knew better than to question the sergeant's plan.

"Tonight, we patrol in the main rail yards," Chao announced. "Corporal Ke and his team will patrol the Wood Yard and the adjacent riverbank. My team will patrol the Main Workshops. Be vigilant—we have intelligence that Red terrorists are planning strikes against the railroad sometime in the next weeks, just not where and when. Other teams will be next to us in the Fuel Yard and the car park and along the riverfront below Pristan. Try not to shoot them or get shot yourself." Borya and Puzyrev chuckled and were rewarded with a cold stare from the sergeant. The mask went up.

Through the evening and ensuing dark night, Borya's team walked around and through the huge workshops of the great Harbin rail yard. The sergeant led the way with the electric torch at ready, and Borya and the other guardsman, whose name was Hsu, followed with their rifles at ready, a bullet in the chamber and the tricky Mosin safety in the off position. For hours, they snaked through the alleyways and heaps of material and half-broken cars and locomotives. Sometimes they entered the workshop buildings and walked through them. Some were deserted, while others contained night crews working on repairs, busy and paying scant attention to the intrusion. Borya noticed the younger Guardsman staring at the bellowing machinery and the huge cranes in wonderment, but to him, it was all familiar from tours led by his father when he was a boy. Tours that always ended with his father's assurance he would attend Harbin's Russo-Chinese Technical Institute and work for the CER as an engineer like him. Now, instead, here he was an entry-level policeman carrying a rifle and only guarding over these wonders of modern industry and science.

Every two hours they were allowed a fifteen minute break in the rail yard's guard post, where they took lukewarm tea from a samovar there. The only excitement that night was when one of the night-shift workers who had left his machine shop to use the outhouse didn't immediately answer Sergeant Chao's challenge and was only seconds away from being shot by Borya and Hsu. After that, Borya kept the safety of his Mosin on just to make sure he did not fire it accidentally.

After twelve hours, the sergeant marched them back to the barracks where they turned in their rifles and equipment and were dismissed until the following night. The guardsmen stayed in the barracks while Borya and the other police "reinforcements" were allowed to return to their homes. Before they left, they met Corporal Ke's team returning from the Wood Yard. Their only excitement had been when Puzyrev slipped on a path along the riverbank and ended up getting wet up to his thighs and leaving his white puttees a sodden, muddy brown. He spent the next hours being cold and wet and feeling sheepish.

The following five nights, they followed the same routine—Sergeant Chao's team among the workshops and the corporal's team in the Wood Yard and along the riverfront. Mostly it was a dull, grinding routine following the same routes and timetable. There was only the occasional stray dog or scuttling rats to generate a short adrenalin rush. Some nights, they heard the noises or challenges from other teams off in their adjacent assigned zones. Once they found a sleeping drunk who had wandered into the rail yard despite the night curfew and marched him to the nearest police precinct in Pristan.

There were no nights off, and after the five nights in the rail yards, they spent the next eight on patrol along the railroad tracks that led east out of the city, checking for bombs or missing track. Back in August, saboteurs had managed to pry several rails free along this stretch, but their damage had been discovered before it could result in a derailment. They marched along either side of the rail ties all the way from the flag station above the

Moscow barracks, down through New Town, and for miles past the Old Harbin freight yard and the soybean oil mills. When the sky was clear and the moon was out, it wasn't too bad, but when it was pitch dark, Hsu and Borya had only the faint beam from Sergeant Chao's electric torch to keep them from tripping over the occasional rock or branch. They saw nothing and no one, but one night, they heard distant gunshots coming from somewhere back in the city. Later, they learned the shots had come from another team patrolling the rail line above Fujiadian that had spotted several men who fled when challenged. They were fired upon, but no one was hit, but it wasn't certain they had come across saboteurs or just thieves risking the curfew.

Borya and Hsu would talk together as they walked once they discovered the silent Chao did not seem to mind. They talked mostly of what they would do when their shift was over, the foods they would eat, the new movies that were playing in the city's cinemas, and their favorite parks. Hsu was from a small village near a town north of Harbin, the youngest son of a poor tenant farmer. With no future at home, he had been a prime candidate for recruiters from the Railway Guards. The Guards provided him meals and a home in the barracks, but didn't pay enough for him to accumulate the savings necessary to afford marrying and starting a family. Borya could sympathize. "Be vigilant, and maybe one day you will make corporal, or even sergeant," Chao offered in one of the rare times he joined their conversations.

After each night, Borya would stumble wearily to his aunt's tearoom in the morning sunshine for a bracing glass of tea, pastries, and sympathy before continuing on to the family apartment. There he would retreat to his bedroom to sleep for a few hours before it was time to get up again, grab a quick meal, and head back to the Barracks. One morning, he came home to find out he had forgotten Hei-rin's birthday the previous day. He apologized profusely and gave her some yuan from his small allowance for her to buy herself a present. Hei-rin was understanding, knowing the demanding schedule he was working. Min would not have been as understanding.

Finally, after his fourteenth straight night of patrols, he was given two whole nights off. Borya spent the first night just sleeping for thirteen hours straight, wakened only by a full bladder. The next day, he checked in with Commander Cho at his local precinct. Cho had no news for when Borya and his other men would be returned to their police duties, nor did he pretend to care. Later that afternoon, he saw Inspector Chinn from a distance on the street that separated Pristan from District 8, walking briskly and followed closely behind by two policemen carrying rifles, their faces all set in grim determination. Chinn saw him also and gave a brief nod and a wave of recognition before disappearing around a street corner. Borya stood still for a full minute, treasuring even that brief gesture of acknowledgement. Would he ever work with the inspector again? After more than two weeks assigned to the Railway Guards, it felt a lot more remote than ever. For that matter, would he ever return to any police duties?

CHAPTER FOURTEEN

AFTER THIS BRIEF RESPITE, Borya returned to the Guards Barracks to continue his nightly patrols where Sergeant Chao led them back to the rail yards for another week. At the end of that week, Sergeant Chao addressed both his teams together. "Tonight, and for the next few nights, we will take our turn guarding the Sungari Bridge. Both our two teams will be guarding the north end of the bridge across the river. Commander Chu himself will be commanding the unit at the south end. As you know, the Sungari bridge is a top target for GPU agents, and we must be especially vigilant. Just because there hasn't been a successful major attack in Harbin since the terrorists' radio was seized doesn't mean they're done trying."

They marched under a drizzling sky across the enormous railway bridge that spanned the wide Sungari River. Borya's father had proudly touted it as one of the major engineering feats in the world, stretching over 900 meters and included eight long trussed iron spans. Finished in 1900, now twenty-nine years ago and ten years before Borya was born, it was the linchpin of the whole CER and why Harbin had become the center of the railway's development and operation. Walking through the trusses was like traversing a row of immense iron cages hanging above the swirling water. Wooden planks bordered both sides of the iron rails to provide space for walking, even when trains were passing through. They had been issued raincoats for this night, and the tiny drops clung to the rubberized canvas material like dew.

Finally, they reached the far end of the bridge, past the trusses and where the rails met the rising ground. The day shift of guardsmen were huddled in two revetments formed from sandbags on either side of the rail bed, looking outward into the gathering dusk. On seeing their relief party approach, they quickly rose and happily made their way back across to Harbin to find warmth and dry clothes and sleep in the barracks. Chao assigned each of his three-man teams to one of the revetments, Borya still paired with Hsu and the sergeant himself. They sat down in the wet dirt and tried to tuck the tails of their raincoats under them, but in minutes their wool pants were soaked through anyway.

Dusk came early under the cloudy skies, and when it became too dark to see the far end of the bridge, Sergeant Chao began sentry patrols. Each team would take turns marching down the bridge on their righthand side to the halfway point between the fourth and fifth trussed spans, where they would be met by a like patrol from the south end, then turn around and march back. Borya began looking forward to the sentry walks as the exercise helped to keep him warm. Soon, it was pitch dark, and the only light was from the bobbing flashlights of their own team and their fellow team from the far end and the distant city glow beyond from Harbin's lights. Twice, trains crossed the bridge, and even though they slowed for the crossing and the men hugged the outer ironwork, they were still buffeted by the wind from the passing cars.

"I don't understand why the stupid Soviets would want to blow up the bridge," Borya thought out loud. "They claim they want their share of the railroad back, then why destroy the most important part of it?"

"Because, you fool, they could stop our supplies and reinforcements to the western and northern fronts all at once," Chao interjected. "Everything would have to be unloaded from the trains coming from Mukden and ferried across the river and reloaded again. Then, when the war is over, whoever wins can quickly fix it back the way it was."

Borya didn't bristle at being called a fool; that was the way seniority worked in the world. He did take umbrage that the sergeant didn't automatically believe the Young Marshal would win the war. How could he not with his numbers and the support of the Three Provinces behind him! But he had to concede that a sergeant of the Railway Guards probably knew more of military matters than himself and kept silent on the subject after that.

Nothing happened that night, and they returned to the same duty on the bridge the next night. Again, they were given the northern post, and Commander Chu commanded the southern post. This night, the precipitation came down as a steady light rain, soaking their pants and boots, or shoes as that was the footwear Borya and the other policeman still wore. The bottom of their little fortifications became mud, and they ended up either standing or sat atop the sandbag walls when it wasn't their turn to walk the bridge.

Around two o'clock in the morning, Sergeant Chao was once more leading Borya and Hsu by electric torchlight down the plank walkway. They were about halfway to the midpoint of the bridge when they heard a yell from the far patrol calling out to someone to halt. Chao tried to direct his torch light in that direction, but the distance was too far for the little beam of light to carry. Suddenly, a flurry of shots rang out in the distant darkness—it was the bark of pistols, and they were answered with screams and the louder bang of rifles. Then came the sound of hurried feet tramping on the wooden bridge planks.

"Quick, fire! They're coming this way!" Sergeant Chao hissed, drawing his automatic pistol from his holster with his free hand, a large broom-handle Mauser like Inspector Chinn's. Borya could feel his heart pounding in his chest. He couldn't see a thing in the darkness or within the small cone of torchlight. Chao began firing, and tiny sparks of flame answered and then Borya heard Chao groan, and the torch fell to the planks, and now the darkness was complete. Borya dropped to one knee to steady his aim and to make a smaller target. Aim at what? He pulled the trigger of his rifle. Nothing! The safety was still on, and he fumbled with the wet knob of the Mosin safety before it slid over. Now the rifle banged against his shoulder, but he still had nothing to aim at. Another shot, this time coming from Hsu, who was standing upright next to him. Borya worked the bolt of his rifle and fired again blindly into the darkness. Again. And again. More twinkles of flame appeared, this time brighter.

Bullets were clanging now off the ironworks of the bridge, both in front of him and behind. He tried to fire again, but the firing pin clicked on an empty chamber. He hadn't been counting and wasn't aware he had fired off all five bullets! He fumbled a fresh clip from the ammo pouch on his belt, despite the raincoat being in the way, but when he tried to feed the clip into the Mosin in the darkness, he couldn't see the groove to feed it through the chamber. Now the approaching muzzle flashes were close and brighter, and he could hear running feet coming at them. He dropped the rifle and pulled his revolver from its holster, but his hand was shaking.

Stop it, Borya thought fiercely to himself. In the excitement, he was forgetting everything his grandfather had taught him. He centered his breathing in his abdomen and directed all his energies out through his arm and hand. Time slowed, and his grip on the revolver became rigid. He calmly took aim and fired at each approaching muzzle flash until there weren't any. He clearly heard answering cries of pain in between the sound of his revolver and Hsu's rifle.

Silence, and then there was the sound of running feet behind him, and Corporal Ke and his team appeared, shining their electric torch past Borya and Hsu. The thin beam illuminated two men sprawled barely three meters in front of them, a third man was leaning back against the iron framework, one hand in the air and the other hand holding the upright elbow from which blood was dripping down his arm, crying "Don't shoot, don't shoot!" in Russian.

Borya used the faint torchlight to finish feeding the bullets from the stripper clip into his rifle before he returned his empty revolver to its holster.

"Sergeant Chao is wounded!" Hsu cried out, and Borya looked over to see the old sergeant sitting upright, his raincoat open and holding both his hands tightly to his right hip against a growing red stain, a look of both pain and resolve frozen on his face. Then, from in front, came more bobbing electric torches as men from southern end of the bridge arrived. In minutes, all the terrorists were under the watch of several rifles, and one of the guardsmen was improvising a bandage around Chao's middle. Borya finally stood up from his kneeling position and made the sign of the cross and muttered a quiet prayer of thanks.

It took two hours for everything to get unraveled. Commander Chu and the sentry party from the south had happened upon five men armed with pistols and in the process of setting a bomb onto one of the near bridge spans. Instead of accessing the bridge from its guarded ends, they had reached the deck of the bridge by using a ladder at one of the concrete footings where the bridge was still over land on the Harbin side, ascending while both sentry teams were just starting out from the ends. Commander Chu had come upon them first and was shot in the face and killed instantly. The guardsmen with him returned fire and killed one and wounded another of the terrorists. The remaining three fled north up the bridge, not knowing they were headed straight toward Sergeant Chao, Hsu, and Borya before it was too late and then hoped to blast their way through with their pistols and make their escape. Together Chao, Hsu, and Borya had killed another two of the intruders and wounded the third. Borya did not ask, nor did he want to know, how many of their wounds came from a pistol or from a rifle, and anyway, Chao had fired his own pistol more than once. Mainly, he was just relieved that none of his squad's bullets had hit any of the men from the southern post in all the wild shooting. For the first time, he felt cold rain dripping off his cap and down the back of his raincoat collar and into his uniform beneath, sending a chill down his spine, although it must have been doing that for some time.

Reinforcements arrived quickly from Harbin, including medics to tend to Chao and the wounded terrorists, along with two engineers to disarm the bomb. It was said there had been enough dynamite to drop at least one and maybe two spans of the bridge into the river. Chao had lost a lot of blood, and his right pelvis was shattered, but the medics thought he would still recover.

Borya was happy when the officer in charge of the reinforcements released the night-time squads two hours early from their guard duty. Corporal Ke led them back to the barracks but instead of being dismissed for the night, they all were made to sit through interviews with a Guards lieutenant and report their individual actions and observations as a clerk laboriously wrote down their answers. It took hours before Borya's turn came, leaving him plenty of time to think about his wounded sergeant and the less fortunate Commander Chu. He said a silent prayer for Chao's recovery, and then felt guilty that he hadn't thought to also pray for the soul of the ill-tempered Chu. By the time he was called for his interview, he felt cold and numb, answering the questions in flat monotones. As soon as he was released, he could not remember a single question or any of his answers.

It was the middle of the morning by the time Borya could head toward home to get some much needed rest. The trek back to District 8 seemed longer than ever. He decided to skip his usual stop at his aunt's tearoom on the way, knowing his mother would already be worried by his late return, especially if news of the firefight had reached their neighborhood. Had the sounds of the gunfire reached as far as District 8? Or had rumors reached his mother's ears? Sometimes the neighborhood gossip seemed to travel as fast as gunshots.

He did pause on the Syoko Bridge on the way, the broad concrete span that allowed vehicle and pedestrian traffic to cross over the railway tracks unimpeded. Its sidewalks also afforded a remarkable view out across all parts of the city below the bluff—Ostroumoff Suburb, the Railway yards, Pristan, the wharfs, District 8, and Fujiadian. The morning sunlight shone back from a hundred glass windows like they were on fire. Suddenly, the numbness that had descended upon him after the firefight melted away. It wasn't like the shrugging off an exhaustion but more like emerging from a thick fog. He suddenly began shaking like he was standing naked in a blizzard. The sight of the bodies on the other bridge came flooding back to him vividly, intensely. So quickly had living men become an empty husk, one minute alive and fearful, the next minute devoid of consciousness and their soul. How close he had come to being one of them! If he had died, where would his soul be now? Still here? In Heaven? On its way? He repeated again a prayer of thanks that he recalled from church catechism.

But he *was* alive! He had survived to see another brilliant morning in his city, his world. The edges of the buildings and outlines of boats on the river looked sharper than he remembered them. And inside those buildings and on those boats and in the streets, many thousands were working or begging, eating or hungry, laughing or crying—a whole different world from the one he left behind on the Sungari Bridge. And luck—or fate?—had left him in this world of the living. He concentrated on controlling his breathing, and his shivering subsided. He felt tears on his cheeks, and he brushed them away, looking around to make sure no passersby had seen them before he continued his homeward trek.

When he did arrive home, his mother and both his sisters were waiting out on the sidewalk in front of their tenement. Their sudden smiles upon seeing him told him that the news of the previous night had indeed reached them. The dark circles under his eyes told them everything, and they silently enfolded him in a tight knot of embraces and led him upstairs to home.

CHAPTER FIFTEEN

THAT EVENING, BORYA HEADED back down the familiar route to the Moscow Barracks. Surely they did not expect him to return again so soon, his mother had pleaded, but when he had been dismissed that morning, no one had told him otherwise. He found his squad waiting in the equipment room. Everyone was present except for Corporal Ke and, of course, Sergeant Chao. Corporal Ke, they hold him, was receiving their orders from the new acting Guards commander. No one had heard any news of Sergeant Chao's status since he had been taken to Harbin's Railway Hospital in Pristan.

Borya had grown close to these men over the weeks, especially guardsman Hsu and Sergeant Chao, with whom he had spent the most time, and they to him. There had been subtle divisions to begin with between the Chinese guardsmen and the Russian, and half-Russian, policemen. But they had borne the hardships and boredom equally, and any differences had faded away over long nights sharing stories and snacks and arguing over movies and books. Even Sergeant Chao had mellowed towards Borya and Puzyrev after his initial misgivings of integrating city policemen into his small Guards unit. And now, having gone through danger and the risk of death together, there was even a stronger bond, strong and open enough that as they now each took turns describing what they had seen and heard during the brief battle of the previous night, they could all admit to having felt fear.

Finally, Corporal Ke appeared. With him was a new face—Officer He from Borya's own District 8 precinct with whom he had sometimes shared police watch duties. Ke pointed at Borya. "Melnikov, you are to see the acting commander. He is in his... Commander Chu's old office." A flash of pain crossed the corporal's face upon mentioning his fallen commander, indicating the old man had garnered the respect of some of his men despite his gruff demeanor.

A Guards senior lieutenant now occupied Chu's office, a different lieutenant than the one who had taken his after-action statement the previous night. This man was older with a small, well-trimmed mustache and sat with an erect posture, but behind wire-framed glasses, the eyes were friendly.

"Ahh, Officer Melnikov! Your police commander has sent a replacement for you, and you are to report to a Superintendent Liu tomorrow morning. Do you know where to find this Superintendent Liu?"

Borya's heart leaped. "Yes, I do, sir!"

And then, to Borya's surprise, the officer rose from behind the desk and extended his hand to shake his own. "I understand you were among those being singled out for outstanding performance last night on the Sungari Bridge. On behalf of the Guards, I wish to say we appreciate your service with us during this emergency. I will be sending a letter of commendation to your commander."

Borya shook the hand vigorously. "Thank you, sir! And if I may ask, Senior Lieutenant, do you have any news on Sergeant Chao's condition?"

The officer smiled warmly. "Yes, he had a successful surgery yesterday. He will be a long time recovering and in rehabilitation but is expected to fully recover."

"That's wonderful news, sir. Wonderful!"

In the earliest hours of daylight, Borya hurried to meet Chinn at the latter's desk in the detective squad room, assuming they would meet with Superintendent Liu together. He detoured around the counter and its vanguard of clerks without challenge, a good sign. Even some of the detectives nodded his way as he passed. But, Borya wondered, what would be the state of his relationship with Chinn after weeks of absence? Would his mentor again be the detached senior inspector from the beginning of their shared investigation, or would it be the warmer human side his mentor had shown in the surroundings of his own home? Or maybe both—perhaps the dedicated detective kept his professional and social lives completely separate. Borya did not have long to wait as Chinn looked up from his desktop and greeted him with a smile. His eyes showed tiredness as much as they revealed anything else.

"Did anything new develop in the case while I was away?" Borya asked, hoping he hadn't missed out on anything important.

"No, not really. The clerk finished the translation of those papers from Geiger's house that were in German. Mostly letters from his wife and a brother in Germany. Nothing that indicated a new source of income—in fact, his wife was continuously asking him to send her more money, so he obviously wasn't receiving any large sums of money through her. There was also a copy of a will leaving everything to his wife and children back in Germany, filed with a German attorney here in Pristan. It's a couple years old, but I have to assume it's the latest one. Aside from that, I've been busy chasing after Soviet agents, but most of them seemed to have already left the city. Anyway, let's not keep Superintendent Liu waiting..."

Together, they went upstairs to Liu's office and were immediately ushered inside by another new police cadet. Inside, Liu sat behind his desk, and in one of the guest chairs sat a heavy European with a short beard that failed to hide three chins and a large stomach that strained at his trousers and waistcoat.

"Inspector Chinn, Officer Melnikov, this is Herr Schessler, the German honorary consul in Harbin," Liu began in Russian. The "honorary" prologue to the title meant that the consulship of the German Weimar Republic in Harbin was only a part-time assignment. The German consulate on Arteilreliskaya Street was a small office, and Herr Schessler's primary profession was probably as one of the city's many European businessmen. The fact that Liu bothered to include the "honorary" title probably had to do with the Superintendent's barely concealed impatience. The consul remained seated and waved his hand in lieu of shaking theirs. Borya saw cold but intelligent eyes that scanned their faces with an appraising glance. Since there was only one empty chair remaining, Liu waved Chinn into it while Borya remained standing behind and to the side, although he took a relaxed stance.

Liu continued, "Herr Schessler came to get a progress report on the case of the death of Manfred Geiger, who is one of his local citizens. I was just explaining to him how the current emergency had... temporarily distracted our investigation. Will you please bring Herr Schessler up-to-date with what you were able to learn prior to the... interruptions."

Chinn proceeded to give a short summary of their enquiries after their return from Changchun: the visit to the Chicken and

Duck Company, the search of Geiger's home, the disappearance of Song Nikan, and the autopsy—much the same summary as he had provided to the Superintendent before the investigation had been interrupted. Schessler nodded periodically and smiled positively when Chinn explained how he had arranged for a special autopsy with Professor Hong.

"Could this Chinese company agent have been responsible for Geiger's death?" the German asked.

"That is one line of enquiry. We won't know until we find him," Chinn replied, and then he turned the tables on the consul. "Do you know whether Herr Geiger had any enemies in the Northeast?"

The German smiled back politely. "Not that I am aware of. Herr Geiger was a successful businessman here in Harbin, and an upstanding member of our community."

"Did you know him personally?"

The consul shrugged. "No, I did not have that pleasure, I have only resided in Harbin myself the last six months. I am relying on the testimony of some of my colleagues."

Chinn nodded to signal his questions were at an end, and Borya politely kept his peace.

"And the next steps?" the consul asked, this time addressing Liu.

Liu gave a barely suppressed sigh. "I will send these two to Barim to see if they can determine if Herr Geiger was killed there and then his body shipped, and by whom. If the answers cannot be found there, they will continue to Hailar to see if he or the company agent ever made it to there, along with any contacts they may have made."

"Excellent! And I will get another report upon their return?"

Liu smiled politely. "Of course, Herr Schessler." With that, the heavy man heaved himself to his feet and leaned across Liu's desk to shake his hand, and then bowed briefly to Chinn and Borya before he left the room.

Liu now sighed audibly. "The consul has put considerable pressure on the Chief of Police to close this case, which, of course, he passed down to me. Never mind that we are still in the midst of fighting a terrorist campaign in the city. Draw funds for a trip to both Barim and Hailar. Obviously, you don't need to continue on to Hailar if you find what you need to know in Barim first. But," and here he raised a single stiff finger in emphasis, "do *not* continue on to Hailar if there is fighting anywhere close to that city or if there is a chance your return trip by rail is in jeopardy. I think you have seen enough of war already . . ." and his glance took in Borya as well as the veteran inspector.

CHAPTER SIXTEEN

BORYA MET CHINN AT the train station in the early morning hours. He was happy to have slipped out of the apartment before his mother awoke. She had spent most of the evening wringing her hands over his trip to a "war zone" and reminding him he was no soldier, and Borya, in turn, trying to reassure her that Hailar was far from any fighting, and they weren't even certain they would be going that far. He made quick stops along the way to the station at his grandfather's shop and aunt's tearoom to let them know he would be out of town for a few days. His grandfather gave him a remedy for sleep, as "travel can upset your sleep rhythms," and his aunt filled his travel case with sweet rolls.

Chinn wore his police uniform again and was armed as he had been on their trip to Changchun. Likewise, Borya was in his usual uniform and wore his revolver. It was still an hour before their train was scheduled to depart.

"Herr Geiger supposedly took the train westward from here, at least as far as Barim. We know he didn't use his rail pass, unless he had another pass under an assumed name, but it would be easier just to buy a ticket anonymously. So while we're waiting for our train, I want to question the ticket agents to see if any remember him." Borya looked skeptical. "Yes, it's been weeks, but you never know... *sometimes the smallest seed can bear fruit.*"

There were two ticket windows open serving the westbound trains, one manned by a Russian and the other a Chinese. "You take the one on the left, I'll take the other. If the agent remembers him, ask if he remembers whether he bought a ticket to Barim or to Hailar. We still don't know if he ended up in Barim by design or accident, or whether he was going or coming back for that matter. Maybe someone or something lured him off the train there, or maybe he just got off to stretch his legs and was waylaid." He handed Borya the rail pass with its photo of Geiger and kept for himself the photo that came from the abattoir's missing person report.

"And ask if he was alone?" Borya suggested.

That yielded a smile. "Yes... and ask if he was alone."

Borya waited in line at the left-hand ticket window until it was his turn to face the elderly Russian man in a CER uniform that sat behind it. The spectacled, white-bearded man appeared bored and then unhappy when Borya held up a rail pass below the metal grill that covered the upper part of his window, a photo that in no way resembled the young policeman holding it.

"Do you remember selling a ticket to this man about six weeks ago?"

The old man rolled his eyes dramatically. "Why would he purchase a ticket if he already has a rail pass?"

"We don't know. He might not have wanted anyone to know his destination."

The ticket-seller barely glanced at the photo. "No." And then he pointedly looked past Borya's shoulder at the line growing behind him.

His face assumed the mask. He was on official police business, helping investigate a most serious crime, and this surly old man was not taking him seriously. He guessed the old man's reaction wouldn't have been the same if facing the gruff, hard-eyed Chinn instead of a young "half-breed." How was he supposed to be of any help in the investigation if he couldn't perform even this simple task?

"Look harder, or maybe I need to shut down your window until you can take the time to really look."

This time, the old man looked him in the eye, and his shoulders slumped, and he seemed to deflate as if Borya had caught him in a lie. He took the pink rail pass from Borya's hand and held it up close to his eyes, squinting hard at the oval photograph with its stamp. After a long pause, he handed it back.

"No, I don't recall him, but then I see dozens of Europeans here every day, and hundreds in six weeks. I am sorry, but I don't pay that much attention to faces, just the money and the tickets. My eyes are not what they used to be."

"Thank you, grandfather." Borya took back the pass and relinquished the head of the line. Chinn had already finished his enquiry, and Borya wandered over to rejoin him.

"No luck," he reported.

"Nor me," Chinn replied, "… *but don't fear going slow, just fear standing still,*" he added with a wink.

They boarded a second-class sleeper car, and it wasn't long after the train left the city that they left behind most signs of civilization, save for the occasional village or town that hugged the railway line. It was a beautiful fall day, no longer the sultry heat or summer rains of August, and they had yet to feel the cold winds that swept down from Siberia in October. The treeless steppes of the huge Manchurian Plain stretched out on both sides of the train, occasionally split by gullies bearing creeks and small rivers that were tributaries of the Sungari. Borya watched low rain clouds move across the sky, trailing dark tendrils from their black underbellies. Sometimes the tendrils reached the ground and seemed to boil atop the grasses. Once one of these clouds intersected the train, and huge drops of rain pelted the window of their car so loudly it woke Chinn up from his nap.

Their first major stop was Anda, the infamous "City of Cows." Anda had become the site of a Russian experimental dairy farm, started by the Russian managers of the CER who employed a broad interpretation of their rights and scope under the railway zone treaties, including cancelling the leases of the local Chinese grain farmers. The displaced Chinese farmers took matters into their own hands and invaded the dairy farm, determined to displace the "wasteful cows" and return the land to growing grain again. Negotiations restored many of the Chinese leases, but the dairy farm still remained. Borya remembered his own father's militant stand in favor of protecting the dairy and its Russian crew as a symbol of Russia's effort to modernize the Northeast, just as the railroad had. He wondered which side Chinn would have taken, but thought better than to bring up the subject. From the train windows, the sleepy-looking town looked peaceful enough now, and a mix of Chinese and Russians mingled on the railway platform.

The next major stop was Tsitsihar, or rather what the CER called Tsitsihar Station. The actual old city and provincial capital had been purposefully bypassed by the Russian planners of the CER in order to build their own town eighteen miles to its south. Rejecting this "oversight," the provincial government then built their own light railway with its own station to connect Tsitsihar with the CER station. Chinn and Borya got out to walk the station platform to stretch their legs. The CER station here was a pretentious structure of tiled gables and rows of columns supporting an overhanging veranda in a modern Russian style. Like its train station, the small town beyond reflected its Russian roots and could pass for blocks of Pristan back in Harbin. Chinn bought a small bag of sunflower seeds from a vendor and shared them with Borya, who was careful not to eat more than his share.

Before the train could set off again, there was a delay while an infantry unit of Marshal Chang's Northeast Frontier Defense Force arrived by a train from the old city and boarded their train, bound for the western front where there had been recent skirmishing with Soviet forces in front of the frontier city of Manchouli, beyond Hailar. The grey-clad Chinese soldiers tramped onto their second-class car and squeezed into every available compartment, two to a berth. The existing passengers were forced to double up, and Chinn and Borya ended up sharing a berth, along with civilians from another compartment, who were moved into theirs until its occupancy of four had now become eight. They could hear the grumblings of the displaced in the corridor, but nobody protested too loudly for fear of being called out as unpatriotic.

Just when they thought they were getting underway again, there was another delay as their train was shunted onto a siding in order to marry up with an armored train car being inserted between the locomotive with its tender and the rest of the train. Borya was intrigued and wanted to disembark from their car to see the steel behemoth up close. Chinn declined, saying he had seen enough armored trains during his stint in the old Marshal's army. Although the soldiers were kept on the train by their officers, Borya's distinctive black uniform got him past the sentry at the door of the car. He walked on the railbed until he reached the front of the train, where railway signalmen were switching the tracks to allow the locomotive to push the armored car back toward the first rail car. The steel-clad car looked like it belonged to the top of a warship. Steel plates curved from the sides to form a smooth dome over two gun ports on each side that sported menacing-looking machine guns. Round steel gun turrets rose from each end of the car like shiny silos, each carrying a medium cannon that could rotate in all directions. Borya felt reassured that this monster would be protecting their train, although he supposed the Soviets had armored trains of their own. He watched in fascination as the armored car slowly moved toward the passenger car like it was in a runaway crash in slow motion. Finally, it met the front of the train, engaging in a screeching coupling and a jolting of the smaller, lighter passenger car.

"We'll be leaving now?" Borya asked one of the nearby Chinese signalmen in Mandarin.

"Not yet, we still have to add a second locomotive to the back of the train," he answered.

"I'm not surprised," Borya mused, "that armored car must weigh a lot."

The signalman smiled deferentially. "No, we always have a second locomotive to trains going over the mountains. You'll see."

Borya was ready to return to his own car when a heavy steel door opened at the end of the armored car, and three Russians emerged to disembark and stretch their legs. They wore the old Tsarist uniforms but had armbands identifying them as belonging to the Young Marshal's army. Borya guessed they were White Russian mercenaries who had fled across the border into the Northeast Provinces after the fall of the short-lived Far East Republic at the end of the civil war or else were stragglers from the famed Czech Legion who had crisscrossed Siberia in stolen armored trains in their own exodus to Vladivostok. Some had elected to stay in Manchuria and hired out their stolen armored cars and expertise to whoever had the most money, which up here in northern Manchuria was the Young Marshal.

One of the crew members, with the shoulder bars of an officer, was standing at the foot of the car's steps and lighting a cigarette, a man of about forty with a short beard and tired eyes. Borya approached him.

"That is some weapon," Borya offered his admiration in Russian. "I'm glad you're joining our train. I doubt any Bolshevik bandits will dare attack us now."

The man blew out a cloud of smoke, politely turning his head so that it did not blow directly at Borya. "Yes, we should be okay, at least until Manchouli," he responded matter-of-factly in a clear Russian accent, not Czech.

"Still, you must be pretty safe inside," Borya encouraged. Here was a man with an obvious tie to the past. His father's past.

Another inhale, another cloud of smoke. "Yes, safe as long as the tracks are clear and the locomotives don't get ventilated with bullets. But it can be a real sweatbox in the summer when we're all buttoned up." Another polite smile. He looked up and down at Borya's uniform. "You a Railway guard? Going all the way to Manchouli?"

"No, I am Special District police from Harbin. Going to Barim. Maybe as far as Hailar."

The man nodded, and they both turned as they heard the metallic crash of the second locomotive engaging the rear of the train. "Well, good luck, policeman from Harbin. Personally, I wouldn't go beyond Hailar if I were you." And he took a last drag on the cigarette before tossing it onto the gravel of the railbed and turning to remount the stairs of the armored car with his comrades.

"Good luck to you too!" Borya called back to him as he hurried to return to his own second-class car halfway down the train before it started moving again. He just reached his car as the train began to shudder into motion. Chinn was still inside, sitting on their hard wooden berth, eating the last of the sunflower seeds and spitting the husks into the compartment's spittoon. Chinn and Borya had agreed to switch their conversation to Korean, as it gave them a better chance of keeping their conversations private from their new companions in the compartment. Russian was used less out here in the hinterlands as compared to Harbin, and they had no wish to be suspected of being Soviet agents. Chinn's Korean was passable, but he occasionally fell back into Mandarin for words he didn't know in Korean. Borya told him excitedly about how impressive and formidable the armored car was, and how now they should be safe in the journey ahead, but did include the officer's warning against going beyond Hailar.

Chinn laid his head over onto one shoulder and yielded a half-smile. "And did this armored car have machine guns on top for protection against enemy warplanes?"

"No..."

"Did you see any atop any of the other cars?"

"Well, no. But doesn't the Young Marshal have warplanes of his own?"

Chinn smiled again. "Yes, he does...somewhere. Maybe he has some out near Manchouli, or maybe they're all out on the eastern border. But if I had to guess, I would say they're all sitting in Mukden safely out of reach of Soviet planes. And yes, it would be wise not to go beyond Hailar."

Non-plussed, Borya tried a different tact. "I read in the *Yuandong bao* before we left that General Liang repulsed another Soviet raid on Manchouli without any losses of his own," Borya said.

Chinn snorted. "Of course a Harbin newspaper would say that."

"You don't believe it?" The *Yuandong bao* was considered by many as the most respectable newspaper in Harbin.

Chinn shook his head slowly now, as if it had become a heavy burden to his neck. "Maybe it is true. I would like to believe it's true. But Chang's people will keep any Harbin and foreign correspondents a long way from the front and feed them reports of their own making."

"But aren't the Bolsheviks at the end of a long supply line just like the Tsar's army was in the Japanese War in 1905?"

"Sure, but this is not 1905, and the railroad back to Moscow is no longer single-tracked," Chinn stated matter-of-factly.

"Well, the Young Marshal's soldiers here on our train sound like they are in high spirits. And they seem to believe in the Young Marshal and his stand against Bolshevism."

Chinn allowed a sad smile. "Let me tell you a story. In 1918, I joined the Old Marshal's army when he marched south to Peking to join Tuan and the so-called 'national unification army.' I was all of twenty-three, but I was educated, and so they made me an officer. We, too, were in high spirits because we were part of a great noble cause—we were going to defeat all the warlords and the Canton government and unite all China and make us a great power again. And remember, this was ten years before Chiang Kai-shek and the Northern Expedition. But high spirits didn't mean a thing—in six months, the war was a stalemate, and the grand crusade fell apart, and the Marshal was back in Mukden.

Meanwhile, I took a bullet in my leg in Hunan, and they sent me back north to a hospital in Harbin. I was no longer of any value to the Army, but I was one of the lucky ones because they found me a posting with the city police in Harbin after I got out of the hospital. High spirits and a righteous cause won't stop a bullet or a cannon shell."

Borya offered nothing in reply. What could he say to that? Still, he hoped this time would be different. Wasn't the cause different this time—to root out the Bolsheviks once and for all from the Northeast Provinces? Maybe drive them all the way out past Mongolia! Hadn't the Young Marshal already expelled the Soviets from the entire CER zone and Harbin, with the exception of a few terrorists and agents? If only his father had been alive to see this.

He tried changing the subject again. "Don't you think it strange that Geiger was killed about the same time the Red Terror started?"

Another sad smile. "Murders happen all the time...in Harbin, outside Harbin. No, I think we will find that greed is behind his killing, not politics. Just remember...*A suspicious mind creates ghosts in the dark.*" A wink turned into closed eyes. "And now I am going to take a nap, while I still can."

CHAPTER SEVENTEEN

FROM TSITSIHAR, THE TRAIN crossed the River Nonni on a bridge that paled in comparison to Harbin's long railway bridge over the Sungari, but Borya could still admire it as another example of modern Russian engineering. Soon the ground began to rise as they entered the foothills of the Great Khingan mountain range, leaving the steppe lands behind. Occasionally, towns nestled up against the rail line, surrounded by bare hillsides where the pine trees had been shorn for timber. They stopped at some of these towns so the locomotive could take on more water and sometimes coal, but most of the time they were surrounded by undulating hills and ridges of thick pine forest that made it feel like they were going back in time. It made Borya appreciative of Harbin, which truly stood out in the north of Manchuria like an oasis of modernity and culture. True, they had not seen the real Tsitsihar, but he knew it lacked the number of monumental public buildings of New Town or the number of bright lights in Pristan.

They passed by Tchingis-Khan, named after Ghengis Khan, the Mongol leader, and after that, the tracks began climbing the steadily rising mountains in a zigzag pattern like the switchbacks of a mountain hiking trail. First, the train would labor up each long slope until it reached a level stretch where it would gather speed before tackling the next rise in the opposite direction, both locomotives belching thick clouds of black smoke. Borya now knew what the signalman meant about the need for a second locomotive.

The next stop was Djalantoun and its fairy-land train station of painted brick with elaborately decorated windowsills and entranceway and roofed in black corrugated iron. It looked exactly as Borya remembered it from his childhood. One glorious, hot summer, Borya's father had secured a week's vacation for the family at the CER's celebrated health station here, high up in the cooler mountains above the sweltering summer heat of Harbin. That had been before his youngest sister, Min, had been born, so he figured he had to have been six or seven at the time. They had walked the short distance from the station, trailed by porters carrying their luggage to the grand Railway Club, a stately edifice fronted with stone columns. Inside, the young Borya marveled at the carved railings and dazzling chandeliers in the lobby, while his father checked them in at the reception desk. He also remembered his father's angry tone, although he couldn't hear the words. When his father rejoined them, his face was bright red, and his voice deliberate, but strained. There had been a mix-up, he said, and their reservation was at the health station's boardinghouse nearby. The procession of family and porters all trooped back out of the gleaming lobby and walked the few blocks to the two-storey stone lodge. Borya's mother claimed this location was much better, being closer to the river and most of the recreational features. It was years later before Borya puzzled out that the "mix-up" had only occurred after the Club's staff had caught sight of his father's Korean wife and his mixed-race children.

Borya didn't know that then, nor would have cared. He only knew that for seven days, there was boating and fishing and swimming in the nearby cool river. He met a Jewish boy his own age who lived in Djalantoun and showed him the sights of the town as well as his secret camp in the forest beyond. By the end of the week, Borya wasn't ready to go home. Even his parents had enjoyed themselves, his father trying to teach his mother tennis, at which she failed miserably, and croquet, which she enjoyed immensely. They all tried out the health-station's fabled sun treatments. But all such wondrous things must come to an end, and in every year following, his parents talked about returning, but one thing or the other always derailed their plans. Now, more than twelve years later, Borya couldn't remember the name of the Jewish boy that befriended him, but he could still recall his face.

They stepped out onto the station platform, Chinn to peruse the offerings of the local food vendors and Borya to see what could be seen from the platform of the sites from his childhood visit, not willing to leave the vicinity of the station for fear of being left behind when the train departed. He could see only the upper floors of the Russian Club, but nothing of the boardinghouse or the health station itself. Nevertheless, he felt a pang of sadness for the loss of a different time, a different world that was closed off from him now.

Nobody was leaving the platform, and only a handful of men were boarding their train, and most of them wore the Marshal's grey uniform. Granted, it was past the peak season for visitors to the health station, but he suspected that their proximity to the western war front was putting a damper on recreational travel, despite the optimism displayed in the newspapers. Looking across at the eastbound platform, he could see there were plenty of couples and families there waiting for the next train back to

Harbin to arrive, surrounded by piles of luggage. Most appeared to be Russian or European, with the men decked out in tailored suits, and the women wearing fur or fur-trimmed coats. The adults looked anxious and talked close together in quiet tones, while the children, being children, chased each other around the deadpan porters and their luggage trolleys.

Chinn joined him, holding a paper sack. "Melon seeds. Have some."

"They must share your skepticism of the newspaper reports," Borya noted, pointing to the crowd on the far platform with his chin. "Everyone here is leaving for Harbin."

Chinn grunted. *"The wind may arise and clouds appear in the sky without warning; people's fortunes may change between dawn and dusk of the same day."* Wink. "Let us hope our own fortunes stay good."

The train's whistle and the shouts of the train conductor called them back to their car. Minutes later, the train inched its way out of the station and built up speed for the next set of rises ahead. Next stop was Barim! Now that they were getting closer to their destination, Borya's sense of wonder and adventure was replaced by a different excitement, the possibility of finding new clues to solve their case. For the first time in their journey, he wished the train would move faster.

CHAPTER EIGHTEEN

CHINN ADDRESSED BORYA IN the last miles before the Barim station. "I asked around at Railway Guards headquarters in Harbin about their Barim unit before we left. The captain in charge of the Guards unit at Barim is a man named Lash Minchur. He used to be a high official in the local Mongol Banner until the Republic disbanded the Banner units. Some say he rode with Semenov until the breakup of the provisional Daurian government, and then returned to the Hailar area. After General Tao kicked all the Russians out of the Guards in 1917, he was enlisted because of his ties to the local Daghur clans. He's got to be at least in his fifties or sixties by now."

Borya nodded. He knew all about Semenov, who had been a hero to Harbin's White Russian community when Borya had been a child. Half-Russian, half-Mongol, and more than half-crazy, he had led a mixed army of White Russians and Mongols successfully against the Bolsheviks. Borya idolized him for being anti-Bolshevik, but also for being mixed-race like himself. But then, Semenov tried to establish an independent pan-Mongolian state, and most of the Mongols, like Lash Minchur, deserted him after he tried to subordinate their new government to the White Russian cause. At the same time, he was competing with the

Mongolian lamas who were trying create a theocratic Buddhist state. In the end, the Bolsheviks won out, and the Mongol tribes ended up split between the Bolsheviks in Siberia and their puppet government of Outer Mongolia or, like this Guards' captain, under Chinese rule in Inner Mongolia or the Northeast Provinces.

They disembarked from the train with their traveling cases in hand at the Barim station, a modest structure with a white-painted facade behind rows of wooden columns. It was a far cry from Harbin's Central Station or Tsitsihar, but it did boast its own health station like Djalantoun, this one centered around a Sanitarium for the treatment of consumption and other respiratory illnesses. At this brief stop, they, and a family of five in Mongol dress, were the only ones to step off the train. A couple of Han Chinese porters stirred but then reclaimed their bench when they saw how meager their luggage was. On the opposite platform, only a small knot of Russians waited for the next train eastbound towards Harbin. A Chinese sergeant and four privates of the railway guards lounged by the station door, probably twice the normal contingent for this sleepy railway town before the GPU sabotage threats up and down the railway lines. Noticing their Special District uniforms, the sergeant wandered over to greet them.

"You're a long ways from home," the sergeant began in Mandarin to Chinn, casual in addressing another man of rank.

"Yes, we are on a murder investigation of a Harbin foreign resident," Chinn replied with a nod.

"We have heard of night attacks in and around Harbin—I would have thought that would be enough to keep you Special District men busy at home."

Chinn gave a wry smile. "Well, you know how the foreign consulates can get riled up when one of their own precious citizens gets killed. We have business in the station here first, Sergeant, but then afterwards, can you direct us to your local Guards commander?"

"Of course. Our post is just nearby, but I will send one of my men to show you the way when you are ready." Then, finally looking at Borya, he frowned before turning back to Chinn. "Please keep your officer here close to you, our patrols are somewhat trigger-happy right now. I would not want him to be mistaken for a Bolshevik agent."

Borya wasn't pleased that the sergeant was talking about him as if he wasn't there or didn't understand Mandarin. His face took on the mask. Chinn merely grunted in reply.

Chinn led the way into the train station. "Check with the ticketmaster if he recalls seeing either Geiger or Song. After that, try the rest of the station personnel and the porters. And maybe some of the railway guards were posted here back then. Meanwhile, I will check with the freight office on the shipment of the crate."

The man behind the single ticket window was a middle-aged Russian, completely bald without a trace of stubble on top but sporting a formidable mustache, as though compensating for his lack of hair on top of his head. He greeted Borya with a jovial expression, as though he sat there all day just waiting for the chance to make people happy, a smile that Borya found infectious.

Borya showed him the rail pass with Geiger's photo, although he doubted he would have seen him. Geiger wouldn't have needed to visit the ticket window when he arrived, and he certainly didn't buy a ticket to leave if he was dead and stuffed in a crate. "He might have gotten off the train here."

"Nyet. You said he would have been here over a month ago? I am usually good with faces, but I don't remember him. But he could have gotten off when my second shift replacement was here instead of me. He will be here after five o'clock. Did this man have business here in Barim or visiting the Sanitarium?"

Borya shrugged. Why indeed would Geiger get off the train at Barim on his way to or from Hailar? Was he here for some secret liaison, and that was why he hadn't used his rail pass? Or did he just get off to stretch his legs and got lured away from the station and killed nearby? If so, why? And what about Song Nikan? Why hadn't he come forward to report Geiger missing or dead, unless he was the killer... or also killed.

Borya next showed him the photograph of Song Nikan but only got another "Nyet" and an apologetic smile. Borya entered the name of the ticketmaster and his replacement in his notebook, while marveling that a man so good with dealing with the public had actually been matched to such a suitable position, recalling the dour attitude of the elderly ticketmaster back in Harbin.

Once outside, Borya noted the train had only moved past the platform in order to take on more coal and water. He watched briefly and then turned to interview the other station employees and the Railway guards. The Russian station conductor was sitting on a bench in the sun, smoking a cigarette. He was a heavy-set man, bordering on the obese, and well into his forties. He looked up at Borya with a bored expression as he was shown the photos. Nyet, he had not seen the German nor the Manchu. The two porters were more attentive, both younger men in threadbare coats and worn caps. One shook his head apologetically, but the other nodded an eager affirmative at the little photo on Geiger's rail pass.

"Yes, I think so."

Borya's heart skipped a beat. "When?" he asked.

"Maybe a week ago."

Borya's heart sank again. Geiger had been dead for weeks. Probably the porter was just saying what he thought Borya wanted to hear. Or maybe he thought the right answer might bring him a tip.

"Are you sure?"

"Not sure," the porter smiled again, more hesitant this time.

"Was he arriving or departing?"

Another smile. "Yes."

Borya took down the porter's name in his notebook anyway. The Railway guard sergeant took each photo from Borya in turn and looked at them closely, but shook his head no. The four privates with him gave the same answer.

Borya paced the length of the station platform under the cool gaze of the conductor and the bored glances of the sergeant and his men until Chinn exited the station office and joined him. Together, they walked to the far end of the platform to talk privately.

"Any luck?" Chinn asked first.

"Not really," and Borya detailed the ambiguous "sighting" by the one porter.

Chinn grunted and nodded sagely. "The freight clerk did not recognize Geiger's photo either, which doesn't surprise me. I doubt he would have been in the freight office to order a shipment of his own body," and he chuckled. "But I will take Song's photo from you to show it also. He does not recognize the name on the shipping document either, nor does he recall any crate with a destination of Changchun around that time, but it appears they do enough shipping from here that it's reasonable he just doesn't remember a specific crate. What I found troubling is that he couldn't find a record of the crate being shipped from here. That is worrisome, but I also don't have a lot of faith in his organizational skills. He said he would check all his files from this year in case the station's original copy had been 'misfiled' and we can check with him before we leave here." Borya nodded.

"I did ask him if he sees a lot of deliveries of quicklime to Barim," Chinn continued. "He said there were the occasional orders by local contractors for the making of cement. And the bakery here uses some for leavening bread or something. So the quicklime used in the crate could have been acquired here." Borya nodded again and wondered if he would have thought to ask that question on his own.

After Chinn smoked a cigarette, they returned together to the freight office, where Chinn showed their sole photo of Song Nikan to the freight clerk. The clerk was an elderly Russian, a frail man with wispy white hair and beard and thick spectacles. He squinted at the photo and finally shook his head. Nyet. Borya noticed tall stacks of papers covered his entire desk, and more were stacked atop the three wooden filing cabinets behind his desk and, like Chinn, wondered if the original to their shipping document could be buried somewhere in one of those stacks. But going through them all could take days, a task neither of them dared to suggest out loud.

The Guards sergeant sent a young Han Chinese private, that looked like he barely met the age requirement, as their guide to the local Railway Guards station. With his rifle slung over his shoulder, the soldier led the way through the small town. The shops and houses nearest the train station were clapboard structures in the Russian style, but as they got further from the station, the houses were of the Daghur style, thatched roofs and mudbrick walls surrounded by wickerwork fences. Near the edge of town, but still near the railway tracks, they reached an open square where there was a one-storey brick structure painted yellow with an adjoining wooden stable holding half a dozen horses. The blue and white Nationalist flag flapped listlessly from a flagpole in front of the building. Gone was the CER flag that was a hodgepodge of both the Nanking and Soviet flags that was meant to represent the past "partnership." Borya wondered how soon the CER flag had come down. When the Young Marshal first seized the railway offices in Harbin? Or maybe after the hostilities had started on the borders? Another Guard soldier sat in the shade on a chair by the door, his arms draped loosely over his rifle, and watched two Daghur boys knock around a round wooden ball with bent sticks in some sort of native game. The guard came to attention when they drew near.

"We are here to see your captain," Chinn declared, and gave him their names and ranks. The young guardsman who had accompanied them, his mission complete, sauntered back to his post at the train station.

"Wait here, I will announce you," the second man declared, and disappeared inside. He reappeared a minute later.

"The captain will see you."

The captain's office was in the back of the building, through what appeared to be an assembly room filled with benches and equipment and overcoats hanging from pegs on the wall. The office was small: a desk, two wooden chairs, and another Nationalist flag on a pole standing in a holder in a corner.

Captain Lash Minchur was a formidable-looking man in his fifties, a square head covered with jet black hair sprinkled with grey atop a long, but muscled neck. He looked fit for his age, and his uniform was spotless but lacked the sharp creases of Superintendent Liu's uniforms. Borya could easily picture him atop a steppe pony with a sword in one hand and a carbine slung over his back.

"Yes, inspector, how can I help you?" His tone was friendly, and his dark eyes showed both intelligence and humor. Chinn showed him the photos of Geiger and Song and then the name on the shipping document.

"I have not seen either of these two men, but I know this woman whose name is on your document," the captain began with a frown. "Bolormaa... means Crystal Lady... I don't know if that was always her name. She is a shaman, an *otoshi*," and he scanned Chinn's and Borya's faces for recognition, but on finding none, he waved a hand in apology. "An *otoshi* is a Mongolian healer who treats sick children and women for fertility problems and the such."

"Like a mid-wife?" Chinn asked.

"No, that is a *bariyachi*," and here the captain smiled patiently. "I know it can be confusing, but among the Daghur here, there is a strict specialization among shamans."

"You allow her to practice healing despite last year's law outlawing shamanism?" Borya interjected. He was referring to the 1928 *Standards for retaining or abolishing gods and shrines* that had come up from Nanking the previous year.

The captain waved his hand again, but this time without the smile. "I am a captain of the Railway Guards, not the provincial police. And a lot of the Daghur here still believe in their shamans and the rituals, especially those who live deeper in the Reservoir and away from town," using the old place-name from the late Qing Dynasty when the Manchus allocated reservations to the Mongol clans as a "reservoir" for their Banner recruits. "And the local provincial police here have more important things to do than try to track down and arrest shamans and stir up trouble with the clans. And anyway, she left Barim and lives in the forest alone with her daughter since the law was passed. But you have not explained why you want to see her—you certainly have not come all this way from Harbin to complain about a wayward *otoshi* in the Reservoir."

Chinn explained briefly about the murdered German, the crate, and the paperwork leading back to this woman and his town.

This raised both of the captain's eyebrows. "That all took place after she moved out of the town. I imagine she or her daughter have been back to town occasionally since then to pick up supplies, but that doesn't sound like the kind of trouble she would be involved in. And she certainly would avoid anything having to do with foreigners."

"What kind of trouble *does* she get involved in?" Borya asked, picking up on the subtle innuendo.

The captain sighed. "This is a little hard to explain...we Daghur people are a very superstitious and traditional people. When Chinese settlers began pushing into the Reservoir and the railways and the Russians came through, it was very disruptive to our way of life. The breakup of the Banners was the last straw for many. A lot of Daghurs felt that the old religions and ways had let them down and left them powerless, especially those who ended up in towns and settlements along the tracks. They wanted an explanation for all the change, and many felt it must be coming from 'bad spirits' that were stronger than the old rituals."

Here, the captain spread out both his hands like a gesture of apology. "Along about that same time, this cult of 'were-spirits' cropped up. It gave the superstitious something to explain their misfortune and something tangible to fight against, or at least placate. I have heard...rumors...that this woman was passing off her daughter as a *kianchi*, one who was been touched by the fox spirit, Auli Barkan. Together, they perform ceremonies to purge families of his bad spirit. Expensive ceremonies."

Borya snorted derisively, drawing a disparaging glance from Chinn. "So this girl can change herself into a fox?"

"No, no. The *kianchi* only 'connects' with Auli Barkan and counteracts his bad spells . . ." and here the captain smiled mischievously, "... however, Auli Barkan himself can change into a beautiful girl...or so it goes. Anyway, if you want to talk to this *otoshi,* you will need to go to her camp in the forest. My sergeant can give you directions."

"Do you have a motorcar and driver that can take us there?" Chinn asked.

The captain laughed. "Did you see any motorcars parked outside? I can lend you two horses, but not any of my men; they are all busy guarding the train station or out patrolling the rails in both directions day and night for saboteurs—I can spare none of them. Besides, where you will be going, there is no road."

Chinn thanked the captain for his kindness and assistance, and they left their travel bags in the captain's care.

"My pleasure. Oh, and watch out...they say if a fox runs alongside you, it is Auli Barkan, and he may turn you into an evil spirt!" His laughter followed them out of the office.

Outside, the guardsman who had manned the barracks door took them to the stockade and separated out two sturdy steppe ponies, then saddled and bridled them. Borya watched dubiously. By then, a Guards sergeant, but not the one from the train station, appeared and told them which road leading out of town became the forest trail that would lead them to the shaman's camp, and then wished them luck in a somber tone. Borya wasn't sure if their luck was needed to find her camp or luck to return from it.

"I have never ridden a horse before, except for pony rides at festivals as a child," Borya confided when they were alone again.

Chinn looked surprised. "That's all right, I can lead your horse by the reins. But wait, first, I want to use the privy before we go," and headed to the outhouse behind the Guards' station. He emerged several minutes later and motioned Borya over.

"Take a look inside," Chinn said in a stage whisper.

What could be there that was worth seeing in an outhouse, let alone smelling? But Borya obliged by entering into the dark interior. As his eyes adjusted, he saw a small wooden shrine on a sidewall, and as he looked closer, he saw that at its center was a picture of a fox with the head of a woman. Chinn was waiting for him outside.

"So, what is that?" Borya asked.

"That is Auli Barkan, the fox spirit. Why do you suppose a man who thinks were-animals are a hoax allows a shrine to Auli Barkan?"

Borya shrugged. "Maybe some of his men are believers, and he wants to keep peace with them? Or maybe he is just hedging his bets? Don't tell me you believe in all that were-animal stuff... Inspector." He quickly added the older man's honorific to ensure Chinn knew he wasn't trying to make fun of him, but Chinn only looked thoughtful and not offended.

"No, I don't. But I do believe that there are supernatural things in this world, and just because I haven't seen them with my own eyes, doesn't mean they don't exist."

"Yes, Inspector, there are many mysteries in the world, but eventually science can explain them. But I doubt science will ever find a real were-animal, only hoaxes or the hallucinations of the mentally ill."

Chinn allowed a half-smile. "Didn't your Jesus and Mary perform miracles? Can science explain those?"

Borya opened his mouth, but then quickly shut it again. He was about to explain how that was different, but really, was it? And certainly not for the sake of an argument with his mentor. Instead, he returned the smile and added a nod of submission.

They mounted their ponies, albeit Borya with less grace, and he made no complaint when Chinn took the reins of his mount along with his own and led both their horses out of the yard.

At the edge of town, the road soon petered out and became a forest trail. Borya was disquieted, immediately missing the straight and orderly lines of the lanes and houses of the town, now replaced by the chaos of the thick pine forest that closed in around them. After two hours, they came to a clearing, a meadow about sixty meters across. A small stream gurgled its way through green grasses, beside which stood a white tent. It was a round yurt that Borya knew from picture books were common among the Mongol tribes that still practiced a nomadic lifestyle. It was about three meters in diameter, composed of layers of felt fastened over a lattice of willows and wood with a flap of felt that hung over a low doorway. It looked like it could be easily disassembled and transported by pack-horse, and then easily reassembled in a short time. This one looked like it had been here for a while as there were the remnants of a small vegetable garden behind it. Beyond the tent, three ponies were tethered to stakes and eating the grass within their restricted reach. The late afternoon sun slanted across the meadow, leaving half of it in the shadows of the surrounding pines.

Respectfully, Chinn stopped his pony at the edge of the meadow and dismounted, giving anyone in the tent or nearby time to see their approach. The last thing they wanted to do was to startle someone with a rifle, who might mistake them for bandits, after all, their Special District uniforms were seldom seen this far west or this far from the railway zone. Borya gratefully slid off his own pony, his inner thighs burning from this unaccustomed mode of transport.

There was a flicker of movement at the flap that covered the entrance to the tent.

"Hello!" Chinn called out in Mandarin. A hand pushed back the door flap, and a figure stepped out and unfolded into a thin, middle-aged woman with stern Mongol features. She was taller than Chinn, but not Borya, and appeared even taller by a black crowned headpiece hung with colored ribbons that sat above her hair, which was shot with gray. Below that, she wore a green waistcoat over a red and yellow skirt, and three sashes of the same three colors were wound around her neck. A bronze mirror hung from her waist, and she held a tall wooden staff in one hand, holding it out upright in front of her as though it was a token of authority.

Chinn had just drawn a breath to explain their mission but stopped when she raised her hand for silence. Immediately, both their ponies snorted nervously and would have stepped back to the forest path had not Chinn held them tightly by the reins. Had they caught the scent of a tiger or wolves nearby? Borya checked for movement in the branches of the trees nearest them, but the wind, and any scent, was blowing away from them toward the meadow and not behind them the way they had come. Nor could he hear anything unusual but noted the ponies tethered next to the tent were not agitated. Still, he was far from the city, and he knew little of this forest world, and he felt the hair on the back of his neck rise. Instinctively, he crossed himself.

Another woman emerged from the tent, this one shorter than the first and maybe in her thirties. This woman wore a traditional Mongol dress of blue with a front panel of embroidered cloth and her hair on the top of her head in the swallowtail of a married woman. The first woman, whom Borya surmised was the shaman from her more elaborate dress, talked to the younger one in what seemed some kind of instructions. Borya could only make out an occasional word because of their distance and that she was speaking in Mongol, of which he knew only a smattering. It had something to do with the harmony of spirits and either phases of the moon or menstrual cycles, he wasn't quite sure which. The younger woman bowed deeply and thanked her and then untethered and mounted one of the ponies and rode away on a different path that entered the woods on the far side of the clearing. Only when the rider had disappeared completely from sight did the shaman turn back to them and motioned them forward. At that instant, their mounts stopped fighting the reins and allowed themselves to be led docilely into the center of the clearing.

They stopped a few paces from the shaman, and Borya felt her dark eyes boring into his own. Her eyes were deep, black, and cold and yet held a trace of amusement. He found it a challenge to meet her gaze and then flustered as it took an effort to lock his eyes onto hers. Meanwhile, Chinn spread his feet apart and leaned his hand on the holster of his heavy Mauser pistol, his own display of authority. The gesture seemed to have no effect on the shaman.

"Do you speak Mandarin?" Chinn started in that language. His Mongolian was better than Borya's, but not by a lot.

She nodded assent, but kept her eyes stayed locked on Borya.

"I am Inspector Chinn and this is Officer Melnikov. We are from the Special District Police of Harbin. You are Bolormaa?"

"I am."

"We are tracing a crate that was shipped by you. It is evidence in a murder investigation."

"Shipped by me? From here in the forest?" She finally turned her eyes to Chinn, a tone of derision in her voice. Borya heard no trace of tremor or hesitation in her voice that he might have expected from a woman of her age.

Chinn pulled an oilskin pouch from the side pocket of his uniform tunic and extracted the shipping document that had come from the crate in Changchun. He stepped forward until he was close enough to hold out the document for her to read, but did not offer to hand it to her. "Can you also read Mandarin?"

"Yes."

"Is that not your name?"

She bent forward to look closer. "Yes."

"And you shipped this crate from the Barim station?"

"I shipped no crate or anything else."

"Then how can you explain that your name is on this manifest?"

The shaman snorted through her nose. "Anyone can put my name on a piece of paper. That does not give it powers. I have enemies—any one of them could have put my name on that piece of paper."

Chinn next pulled the photograph of Herr Geiger from the pouch and held this up before her face. "Have you ever met this man or seen him?"

"Never," she replied, barely glancing at the photograph.

"Heard the name Manfred Geiger?"

"We don't get many *laomaoz*i… or *ermaozi* out here in the Reservoir." Her eyes flickered back to Borya, but returned to Chinn.

"That means 'No,' you have not heard the name?"

"I have not."

Next, he produced the photograph of Song Nikan and spoke his name.

"No."

Chinn sighed and returned the document and photos to the oilskin pouch and returned the pouch to his tunic pocket in slow, purposeful movements as if he were disdainful of the progress and direction of the interview. Returning his gaze to the woman, he asked, "Do you own any firearms? A pistol? Rifle?"

"No, I have no need of them."

"No? Even with bandits and tigers here in the forest?"

"They do not bother me. They know who I am."

"Then you won't mind if I check your tent? Is anyone else here?"

"There is no one else here."

Chinn returned his hand to resting on his holster and smiled acidly. "You know, of course, about the law the Kuomintang passed last year, the *Standards for retaining or abolishing gods and shrines*? Anyone performing as a shaman or pretending to be a fortune teller or a healer or a medium or performing an exorcism is breaking the law. That applies also to the Northeast Provinces."

The shaman smiled back as coldly. "Here you are in the Bannerlands of the Jerim League. Here the Prince of Jalait is the law. You are not in Harbin or Nanking or other Han lands. And

I do not *pretend* to be a healer. But go ahead and look," and her smile disappeared, "but be mindful of what you touch."

"Wait outside here," Chinn said to both Borya and Bolormaa, and bent to enter the tent.

Left alone outside with the woman, Borya felt the full attention of her gaze on him. He started to speak but found a knot in his throat that took several coughs to clear.

"You have a daughter... she isn't here? I see two ponies."

The eyes became like black ice. "She isn't here. She went to find ginseng in the forest. She will not be back today."

"She's out there by herself?"

The shaman refound her icy smile. "She will be fine. I have taught her myself."

They stood the next few minutes in silence while waiting for Chinn to finish his search of the tent. Borya finally broke away from her gaze to scan the meadow and the tree line. Chinn emerged a minute later and shook his head at Borya. Nothing.

"We will be investigating further," Chinn announced. "If we find you have been lying or concealing anything, you will be charged with far worse than practicing as a shaman."

The witch smiled back and bowed with the barest motion of her head. "And now you should return to Barim if you don't want to be in the forest after dark. As you said, there are bandits and tigers out there . . ."

Chinn and Borya mounted their ponies and turned them back toward the forest trail. At that moment, Borya saw a flicker of shadow in the corner of his right eye. He turned in that direction, but the sun was close to the horizon now and was dazzling in intensity, shining directly into his eyes. He tried to shade his eyes with his hand but in the glare could only make out the black silhouettes of the nearest row of pine trees twenty meters away.

But then, there was another shadow, this one moving between the pine trees and then disappearing again as it merged with each tree. He thought he could make out the shadow of a slim figure and just the curve of a face in partial profile, then it changed shape like the face was turning toward him, but by this time his vision was swimming with spots, and his eyes filling with water from the glare. He blinked away the tears and thought he caught the barest glimpse of the outline of a cheek and brow, that was all, and something drove the breath from him instantly, and he barely caught himself from swaying out of his saddle. It wasn't a feeling of alarm, instead, it felt like a powerful wave or a warm wind had passed through him. The only other times he remembered feeling like that was practicing the tapping into his inner force during Danjeon breathing exercises with his grandfather, but that came from within him and not from outside like this! A sudden breeze stirred the pines, and somewhere close by, he heard wind chimes tinkling like a girl's laughter. Then all movement ended beyond the last tree. It hadn't merge with the last tree, it just...faded abruptly, as if in turning, the shape had suddenly lost all form and angles.

"What?" he heard Chinn at his side. He turned to find his companion staring at him curiously. "Did you see something? You went pale like you just saw a ghost."

"I thought I saw a girl just past those trees," and Borya pointed to where the figure had disappeared. But this time, instead, he saw a small shadow moving between the trees, a shadow way too small to be human, more the size of...a fox. It had a funny, hopping gait and then it, too, disappeared abruptly. This was what he must have seen earlier, he thought; the glare and shadows together had tricked his eyes.

Chinn stared to where Borya pointed until he too had to turn away from the sun's glare. "I don't see anything."

"There is nothing there," the shaman spoke. She had come over to stand beside them after they had stopped. She looked up into Borya's eyes once more with her dark, cold eyes. "Nothing."

They rode out of the clearing, and the dark forest immediately enveloped them. They had gone no more than fifty meters when suddenly Chinn yanked back hard on his reins, and Borya's mount almost ran into the other's rear and came close to throwing him from the saddle. Borya followed Chinn's line of sight and saw through the trees an all-black fox running past them in a hopping gait parallel to the path, agile despite missing one front leg. Chinn looked back at Borya but said nothing, just staring wide-eyed. It was the first time Borya had seen the older man anything but calm and controlled, save for the time when he had gotten into the tug-of-war with the Japanese police inspector in Changchun.

"Maybe it's the old woman's or her daughter's pet," Borya suggested, but was thinking back to the Guard captain's parting words.

"These people don't keep foxes for pets," Chinn replied in a hollow tone before he took up the reins again. Once the older man's eyes were turned forward again, Borya made the sign of the cross. Twice. Neither of them spoke again the rest of the way back into town. Both were thankful to see the lights at the edge of town ahead of them just as the last glimmers of dusk faded into twilight. It was far from Harbin, but Borya was thankful for even this little bit of civilization and order.

CHAPTER NINETEEN

CHINN AND BORYA RETURNED their mounts to the guardsman in charge of the post stockade and entered the barracks to report the results of their visit with Bolormaa as a courtesy to Captain Lash. However, the captain had already gone home for the day, and they found instead a bored lieutenant seated in his place behind the desk, a pinch-faced Han with spectacles. Even so, Chinn gave a brief summary of their findings, or rather the lack thereof, but leaving out any mention of their encounter with the three-legged fox.

The officer took no notes and his only response was, "Will you be returning to Harbin now?"

Chinn paused. "That is what I have to decide tonight. We might go on to Hailar."

The lieutenant raised an eyebrow in response. "Well, I would certainly not go beyond Hailar. There have been Soviet bombing raids on our side of the border and reports of parties of Bolshevik-led Mongol bandits attacking White Russian farming villages."

"Thank you for your advice. Either way, we won't be catching a train before morning," Chinn replied. "Can you find sleeping accommodations for us here in town?"

"I believe there is plenty of room at the health station boarding house due to the war scare," he answered with a wry smile. "I will telephone over there and let them know you are coming." Since it was dark now, and well past the time meals were served at the boardinghouse, the lieutenant also recommended a restaurant near the train station that he thought might still be open.

They retrieved their travel bags, which Captain Lash had passed along to the lieutenant for safe-keeping, and walked the dark streets back to the center of town. They easily found the restaurant, which was still open with the bright lights inside spilling out through the windows into the street. Inside, there were a few tables occupied by Russian couples or families, probably waiting for the next eastbound train out tomorrow. A sign inside the door said the food served was both Russian and Chinese. The Chinese waitress brought them tea, but rather than give them menus, she just told them what dishes they still had available. "It has been a busy day," she apologized. Chinn ordered them dishes of beef stroganoff, meat dumplings, and pickled vegetables and lit the first of several cigarettes.

Chinn sat quietly smoking and drinking his tea, while Borya carefully rearranged his silverware. Finally, he looked across the table to Borya. "Barim appears to be a dead end. We found no credible witnesses who remembered seeing either Geiger or Song stopping here. I am also bothered that there is no apparent record of the crate's shipping out from here to Changchun. And I tend to believe Captain Lash, that Bolormaa makes an unlikely suspect as she stays away from town. Nor can I see a reason Geiger would make the trek up to her camp; he's hardly the type to be seeking the services of a Mongol shaman. Right now, I am leaning towards continuing on to Hailar to see if we can find any signs that Geiger or Song made it there and maybe what happened. We might even find Song there, holed up there with his second wife."

"But? . . ." was Borya only reply, feeling there was more that Chinn left unsaid.

"But there is danger in getting even that close to the border. Military situations can become rather . . . fluid, rather quickly," and the older man's eyes showed their inky depth in the bright restaurant lighting before he hid them behind his teacup.

"But the Guards lieutenant thought we would be okay as far as Hailar. And we've come this far, after all . . ." and then he switched to Russian, " . . . *He who fears wolves will never go into the woods.*" Chinn responded with a puzzled look. "It's an old Russian proverb," Borya explained weakly.

Chinn looked Borya in the eyes and suddenly erupted into a deep belly laugh, shaking so violently that his mouthful of tea spilled down his chin. Borya was totally taken by surprise at the violence of Chinn's response but soon found he couldn't help laughing along. The other customers stared over at them, wondering whether the two policemen had gone completely mad. Finally, Chinn calmed and wiped his chin with his napkin.

"Okay, okay, you got me. We will catch the train to Hailar in the morning, but we will make it a quick stop. We'll check with the wholesaler who sent the telegram, the company's bank contacts, and Song's residence, and then head straight back to Harbin." Borya couldn't help smiling, happy that the investigation, *their* investigation, would continue.

They walked the short distance to the boardinghouse where they found a sleepy Russian woman behind the lobby desk. Yes, the Guards officer had called ahead and authorized their stay in the railway facility. Could they carry their own bags up to their rooms?—a lot of the staff had already gone to bed for the night.

The lobby here looked very similar to the boardinghouse in Djalantoun, as Borya remembered it from his boyhood stay. They tiredly trudged up the tall stairway to their adjoining rooms, steps that Borya had would have taken at a run and two steps at a time in those earlier years. Even the room looked similar to the rooms in the Dajalatoun boardinghouse, down to the scent of lavender in the curtains and bedding. Exhausted from the long day, his legs and back sore from his unfamiliar equestrian experience, Borya removed his shoes, hat, and belt and lay down on the bed, still fully clothed and quickly fell asleep.

Borya awoke to Chinn knocking on his door. They took breakfast in the boardinghouse dining room, empty except for two Russian couples, one young and the other in their middle years. They ate heartily of fried eggs, bacon, porridge, and bread fried in more eggs and sugar, and Borya felt guilty at eating so much. What were his mother and sisters eating now? But then, it wasn't like he could put leftovers in his travel bag.

Chinn indulged in more than one cigarette, so by the time they had finished, they were the last guests in the dining room. Although they were guests of the railway company, Chinn still left a generous tip for the cook and staff. Stuffed, and Borya still stiff from his horse ride of the previous day, they walked at a leisurely pace to the train station where they were the lone passengers waiting for the next westbound train. Across the platform, there were about a dozen Russians waiting for the next eastbound train heading toward Harbin and safety, including the two couples from breakfast at the boardinghouse.

Their westbound train came first. This one also had an armored car behind the front locomotive and was pulling several passenger cars instead of sleeper cars, along with three flatbed cars that held artillery pieces and caissons held down by chains. The passenger cars were packed full of grey-clad soldiers heading to the front, many of them with the insignia of artillerymen indicating they belonged to the tethered fieldpieces. Borya noted there were no freight cars carrying horses to pull the cannon.

"They're probably going to pick up draft horses along the way. There are always plenty of horses in the stockyards at Hailar to conscript," Chinn surmised. "Leaves more room for other supplies."

They climbed aboard one of the passenger cars, but every seat was filled. They tried the next car and found a couple seats taken up by backpacks along the aisle that friendly soldiers moved so they could sit down.

Later, when they approached the top of the pass of the Great Khingan mountain range, Borya left a snoring Chinn and exited the passenger compartment to stand on the small platform in the rear, joining a couple of Chinese sergeants smoking cigarettes. Like a small child, he watched thrilled as the train entered the famous Hingan Railway Loop, where instead of yet another back and forth, the tracks ascended in a huge circle, crossing over itself on a viaduct before reaching the even more famous Hingan Tunnel.

He had heard details about the Hingan tunnel from his father since before he could remember, but his own train excursions had never come this far west. Another marvel of Russian engineering, the tunnel cut through the top of the last mountain of the range that stood in their path before the descent beyond to Hailar, avoiding the sheer slopes before the summit. At over 3000 meters, the tunnel was one of the longest in the world and had taken railway workers years to blast and dig. They passed by a small station before day suddenly turned to night as the train cautiously entered the tunnel, the eclipse into darkness punctuated by occasional lanterns glowing in recesses in the tunnel walls, their light shining on the chiseled sandstone. After what seemed like the longest interval, but was probably only ten or fifteen minutes, they erupted back into bright sunshine. The long climb finally over, the train passed another small station at the western end and then swept down the gentler western slopes. Now the train's engineer backed off the steam, and the brakemen worked to slow the train from building up too much speed. After more stops at Khingan, Mianduhe, and Yakeshi, the train finally pulled into the station at Hailar in the brilliant light of an autumn morning.

The Hailar train station was a simple two-storey building, nothing like the majestic stations at Harbin or Changchun. The name of the station was spelled out in large Chinese characters, but there were the faint outlines of additional characters. Chinn took pains to point this out to Borya. "You Russians originally spelled out 'hailang' instead of Hailar."

Of course, Borya knew "hailang" meant ocean waves, but he could laugh at this joke at the expense of his Russian half. "Maybe they were just hoping they were closer to Vladivostok and the Pacific than they were."

Hailar was far from the ocean and in the heart of the Mongol Reservoir, specifically the Barga Mongols, although there were still also many Daghur in the area. It was an ancient Chinese frontier city that became a market center and a river port for trade between China and the Mongol lands and points beyond. Much of the livestock that fed the processing plants of the Northeast, like the British Chicken and Duck Company, came from the horse and livestock auctions of Hailar, supplied by herders from hundreds of miles around. A new western-style city had grown up around the CER railway station, separate from the old, walled city of Hulun, but the trade in livestock and hides and horses here remained the principal commerce.

They crossed the street from the train station to the Popov Hotel, as western as the name implied, and the grandest hotel in Hailar. There, they reserved rooms for the night and left their travel bags with the front desk. "Expensive, but we saved money by staying for free at the CER boardinghouse in Barim," Chinn explained. He then asked the desk clerk to see the hotel register for the week that Geiger and Song were supposed to have arrived in Hailar. Neither man was recorded there, at least under their own names. Borya showed the hotel clerk the photos of both men anyway, also with negative results. Chinn had expected Geiger would have stayed at the grand Popov Hotel since he was on his company's per diem, but Song would likely have stayed at his own house. They found an unoccupied sofa in the lobby and sat down to strategize.

"First, I want to check in with the local police, both as a courtesy and to find out what they know about Song," Chinn began. "Does he have a record here? Any rumors or unidentified bodies? Then afterwards, we'll split up to cover more ground. I'll talk to the livestock agent who had the appointment with Geiger and Song and see if anything developed after he sent the telegram to the Chicken and Duck Company. Meanwhile, you go to the branch here of the Russo-Asiatic Bank where the Company has their letters of credit for their auction purchases."

"But Mr. MacKenzie said no one drew any money out," Borya recalled.

"Yes, but did he bother to ask if anyone *tried* to draw money out and were denied? Like Geiger or somebody pretending to be him? The bank might not have bothered to send a wire in that circumstance." Borya couldn't argue with the importance of the distinction.

The police station was only a few blocks from the hotel. The street bustled with traffic, but it was almost all horse or donkey carts, missing the added rattle of streetcars and the many motorized vehicles of Harbin. There were plenty of Russian faces and western clothes among the pedestrians, but the numbers of men and women in Mongol tunics and dress far outnumbered the Han Chinese here. The two-storey sandstone building of the police station looked more familiar to Borya's eyes.

Inside, Chinn explained their mission, and they were directed to the door of the duty officer, who they were told was a Lieutenant Enebish. Inside, they found a heavy-built man in this thirties, clean-shaven with thick, black hair, in the uniform of the provincial police, his hat resting on the corner of the desk. From his name and features, Borya figured him to be Mongolian.

Chinn introduced them and briefly explained their mission.

The lieutenant smiled politely. "Yes, Inspector, we already received a message from your Superintendent Liu saying you might be coming here on a murder investigation. How can I help you?" He seemed genuinely open and friendly, one policeman to another.

"Well, we are trying to find out whether our murder victim, Manfred Geiger, a German national, and his agent, Song Nikan, arrived in Hailar as planned to buy livestock for their employer in Harbin about six weeks ago. And we're trying to find the current whereabouts of Song, who has a residence here in Hailar as well as in Harbin. We have his address and one of his contacts here, and we'll check them out while we're here. But if you could help us by checking if there are any local police reports relating to either men going back, say three months. Perhaps a missing person report was filed on Song, or if you've had any unidentified victims that might fit either description. And if Song has any history here with the police."

The lieutenant smiled again. "Certainly, I can do that. We did not require foreign nationals to check in with us at the station until the recent troubles, and Mister Song would certainly not have to if he is a resident of the city, so I will not able to verify if they were here at that time. You might want to check the hotels here to see if Mister Geiger reserved a room then, most likely he would have stayed at the Popov. If you could give me time to check our records… say by eight o'clock tomorrow morning? I will be back on duty by then."

Chinn thanked him profusely, not bothering to mention that they had already checked the register at the Popov Hotel. Chinn showed him the photographs of Song and Geiger, and Borya wrote out both Geiger's and Song's names and descriptions in his notebook until he ran out of ink halfway through. Why does it always happen to me right when I'm in the middle of writing, he thought, but then he had to admonish himself—what was the likelihood of it happening at the end of the last stroke of the pen?

"May I?" Borya asked, pointing to an ink bottle on the desk. The lieutenant waved a hand in invitation, and Borya thankfully filled his fountain pen while Chinn smoked a cigarette. Then Borya finished the page and gave it to the lieutenant in exchange for a handshake. In the lobby, the desk sergeant gave Chinn directions to find the address of the local agent and Borya the directions for the bank.

Outside on the sidewalk, Chinn held Borya back. "Let's return to the hotel once we've finished checking these leads out, and then we'll go visit Song's wife number two together."

The bank was only a few blocks from the police station on the main street. It was another two-storey sandstone building, grand for Hailar, but not anywhere as big as its main branch in Harbin. Borya waited in line for one of the tellers, and when it was his turn, he asked to speak to the manager, also showing his Harbin police identity card, since his uniform did not exactly match that of the local provincial police. A minute later, he was escorted to an office in the back, the name Charnov with title "Manager" stenciled on the glass of the door. Inside, an older thick-built Russian with spectacles, white hair, and a drooping white mustache half-rose from his chair, but upon seeing Borya closer, he slumped back into his chair.

"Yes, how may I help you, Officer . . .?" And Borya once again showed his identity card. The manager reached for it and held it close to his eyes before returning it, "... Officer *Melnikov* from Harbin," emphasizing the name like he wasn't quite ready to accept it belonged to Borya.

The mask returned. He took an empty chair without invitation. "I am assisting in the investigation into the death of an employee of the British Chicken and Duck Company, a certain Manfred Geiger..." Borya began, but saw the elderly man's brows knit together. "... Officially known as the Binjiang Products British Import and Export Company of Harbin." That brought an impatient nod of recognition, and Borya continued. "We are trying to trace his whereabouts prior to his death. He was headed here on a livestock buying trip and was authorized to draw upon letters of credit the company has with your branch here."

The manager steepled his two hands together on the top of the desk. "Yes, I remember enquiries from the British Import and Export Company about that. But as I told them already, no draws had been made in the last six months."

"Or since then?"

"No. None at all."

"But did anyone try and were denied? Herr Geiger or his agent Song Nikan or someone else purporting to be from the British Import and Export Company?"

The manager frowned and tapped together the ends of his fingers. "Not that I recall," but then he held up one finger and lifted the phone on his desk. When there was an answering voice, he asked for a Mr. Rusov to join them and returned the receiver to its cradle. "Mr. Rusov is the assistant manager. Just in case there was such an attempt and the authorization or identity was insufficient on a day when I was not present at the bank, then Mr. Rusov would have been the one in charge."

Only a minute later, a slight built man in a dark suit and waistcoat, younger but balding with a dark goatee, entered the room. Borya introduced himself and repeated his questions.

"The British Import and Export Company, you say?" Mr. Rusov asked, already shaking his head.

"Yes, the Binjiang Products British Import and Export Company of Harbin… also known as the British Chicken and Duck Company," Borya clarified.

Again, Mr. Rusov shook his head. "No, not that I recall, and I would certainly remember if someone unauthorized had attempted a draw. But if you can wait a couple minutes, I will double-check the files."

Mr. Charnov re-steepled his hands, and they waited in silence until the older man finally broke the quiet. "I read in the papers that you... police in Harbin have had your share of Red sabotage. Here, they've cut the telephone and telegraph connections several times."

Borya allowed a small smile through the mask. "Yes, I think we've had more than our share. I was on duty on the Sungari Bridge the night they tried to blow it up."

At that moment, Mr. Rusov returned. "I have checked, and there are no notes in the file. No one has tried to draw upon their credit in that time period."

Borya thanked them both for their time. As he rose to leave, the manager rose all the way from his chair this time and reached over to shake his hand. Had the manager been impressed by his role in helping saving the Sungari Bridge?

He returned to the hotel lobby, but Chinn had not yet returned from his own assigned task, the local agent's office having been further from the center of town than the bank. Borya spent the time updating his notes. An hour later, Chinn walked in, a cigarette in his mouth.

"Still no contact from Geiger or Song. Not even rumors. He knows Song from business here in Hailar, but he hasn't run into him for months. You?"

Borya gave the details of his similar lack of success at the bank.

"Well, it's past noon," Chinn replied, looking at the clock on the lobby wall. "Let's find some lunch, and then we'll visit the other Mrs. Song."

A restaurant nearby satisfied their curiosity of the local cuisine. The proprietor recommended the khuushuur, which were large, deep-fried dumplings filled with mutton. He also challenged them to try the airig, a beverage of fermented mare's milk, but they both politely declined and settled on salted milk teas. As Chinn settled their bill, he also got general directions to the address of Song's Hailar residence, which Borya had retrieved from his notebook from their visit to the Chicken and Duck personnel department back in Harbin.

They followed the directions to the outskirts of town. Paved streets quickly gave way to dirt ones, dotted here and there with mud puddles where the traces of recent rains survived. Helped by locals, they found a sizable stone house with a corrugated iron roof sprouting three chimneys, with windows of a second-storey peeking out from under the eaves. It was one of the larger houses on that block, but nowhere as grand as Song's house in Harbin. An adjacent wooden outbuilding and a pen holding a half-dozen goats looked like they belonged to the house, and a girl of about five or six was feeding the goats over the fence with something from a basket. Chinn put on a polite smile and enquired in Mandarin if this was the house of Song Nikan. The girl gave a look that was a mixture of incomprehension and trepidation until he repeated the name, whereupon she nodded her head in understanding and ran into the house, leaving her basket on the ground. Borya picked up the fallen basket, which held some vegetable scraps, and they followed the girl to the door of the house.

A woman of about thirty appeared in the doorway before they reached it. She had a pleasing face despite holding a stern expression. She wore an everyday tunic of brown cotton with a yellow sash at the waist and cloth boots that matched many of the women Borya had already seen on the streets of Hailar. She wore her hair in two braids in front of her shoulders in the Mongol style under a yellow scarf rather than the swallowtail style of married Manchu women. Apparently, Song had married a local girl the second time around. The little girl they had met outside peeked at them from behind her tunic.

"Who are you?" the woman accosted them before Chinn had a chance to speak.

"I am Inspector Chinn, and this is Officer Melnikov. We are with the Harbin Special District police. You are Madam Song?"

"Yes. You have found my husband?"

Chinn, not expecting this question, hesitated. "Actually, we came here looking for him. We believe he was traveling with a European to Hailar from Harbin. The European has died under suspicious circumstances, and your husband is missing, and we are concerned for his safety... is he here?"

Madam Song snorted derisively. "No. You had better come inside," she said and stepped backed into the house, almost knocking over the girl behind her. They followed her into a room furnished with a table, stools, and chests all in a light wood and painted with colorful, intricate designs. She remained standing and did not invite them to sit.

"As I was saying, we are looking for your husband. When was the last time you saw him?" Chinn began again.

"I have not seen him for many months. Four or five months." Her words came out in sharp bites.

"And that was here?"

"Yes, of course. I keep his house and children."

"When was the last time you heard from him?"

"Three months ago. He sent a message from Harbin that he was coming home for the cattle auctions. He never arrived."

"Did you file a missing person report with the police here?"

"If I had filed a police report for every time he was supposed to be here and wasn't, they would have thrown me in their jail for bothering them."

"The message he sent, was it a letter? A telegram?"

"No. His nephew was coming here to Hailar, and he told him to tell me that he would be following in a few days. That was three months ago."

"Have you ever heard the name Manfred Geiger or seen this man?" and he produced Geiger's photograph. She looked closely but shook her head.

"We will need to search the house before we leave . . ."

Her eyes flashed with anger. "Yes, look! Maybe I hid him and forgot where I put him! Look under the rugs! Look in the cupboards!"

Chinn looked away and then at Borya, "You look upstairs, I'll look down here."

They both turned to leave the room, but she wasn't done yet. "Why don't you ask that witch in Harbin, his first wife? She can't stand it when he comes to Hailar, that he might be bringing a single fen into this house. She probably killed him and buried him under the floorboards. Did you search her house?" Chinn did not answer. She took one step forward and pointed a finger at each of them in turn. "You should arrest her! Make her talk! You police are good at that!"

Borya was happy to leave the room and quickly found the stairway leading to the second floor, but found it was one long attic, dimly lit by windows at each end. There were chests and broken furniture, but everything was coated with a layer of fine dust, including the floorboards. He returned to the first floor and the front room where Madam Song now sat on a stool, a small boy now on her lap, and the girl sat on another stool next to her. He tried smiling at the girl, but she looked down timidly at the floor. He could hear Chinn still rummaging through another room. More to break the awkward silence than anything, he addressed the mother. "Madam Song, what is the name of your husband's nephew, the one who brought the message?"

"Alin."

Borya entered it dutifully in his notebook. "Does he live here?"

"No, he lives in the Old City. Above the gunsmith. There is only one."

Chinn returned, shaking his head slightly to Borya.

"What, you did not find him!" she addressed him sarcastically. "Well, then he must still be missing!"

Chinn did not rise to the bait, only bowing slightly to her. "Thank you for your cooperation, Madam Song. If we learn anything about your husband's whereabouts, we will let you know through the Hailar police. Likewise, if he turns up here, please send a message to me through the local police," and he handed her one of his cards. She snorted and thrust the card into a pocket of her tunic.

They let themselves out, and Chinn let out a long breath when they reached the muddy street beyond. "I did not see anything indicating he has been here recently. None of his clothes or personal effects were left out." Borya outlined his equally fruitless results in the attic.

Chinn stopped and lit a cigarette and gave one last glance backwards at the Song house. "I have a growing fear that Mister Song might have met the same fate as our Herr Geiger."

They walked back toward the center of Hailar's Russian town. Chinn believed there was a more direct route back and led the way through some side streets. Along the way, they passed a small Russian church, which to Borya seemed unnecessary as there was a sizable Orthodox Church near the center of town. But then he saw the placard next to the doors identifying it as belonging to a Lipovan denomination. Then he stopped when he noticed that there was a large encampment of tents and wagons in an open field behind the church occupied by men, women, and children in Russian peasant garb. All the adult men had full beards and even the younger ones had some facial hair.

"Russians?" Chinn asked out loud.

"Old Believers," Borya replied. "They do not believe in the church reforms of Tsar Aleksi."

"So they are different than your Russian Orthodox Church?" Chinn asked again.

"Yes, I'm not sure how much different—there aren't many of them in Harbin. I know they follow old rituals and do the sign of the cross with two fingers. Some of them came into the Northeast to escape the pogroms and set up their own farming towns around here on this side of the border in the years before Tsar Nicholas granted religious freedom. But many stayed behind here anyway. But that was many years ago, and these people look like they're new refugees."

They stood and watched for a couple minutes as children played and women cooked over open campfires. Some of the men stared back at them warily, but none of them approached, and they continued on their way back to the center of town and the paved streets.

Daylight was fading by the time they got back. They ate dinner at the same restaurant that served them lunch, both the food and prices having suited them. Then they retreated to the hotel, where they got their room keys and retrieved their travel bags. Borya's room was spacious and had an armchair, a dresser, and even a small writing desk and chair beside the bed. It was many times larger than his small bedroom in the family apartment back in Harbin. The window overlooked the alley behind the hotel, which suited Borya fine, as it was less noisy than the rooms fronting the main street and its traffic.

    Tired, he stripped down to his underwear and lay down on the bed, luxuriating in the soft mattress and pillows. But sleep did not come quickly, as the myriad events and sights of that day and the preceding train trip from Barim flashed through his mind. So much was different from home—the forests and the mountains that had none of the orderly straight lines and angles of Harbin, and now this strange city of Mongols out on the frontier.... Finally, sleep claimed him.

CHAPTER TWENTY

BORYA WAS AWAKENED BY the morning sunlight streaming through the curtains of his hotel room window. He dressed in the spare uniform he had packed, putting the dirty uniform back into his travel bag. He found Chinn down in the lobby already, sitting in one of the large armchairs and smoking a cigarette. Borya watched, amused, as a young hotel porter watched with alarm the growing length of the cigarette's ash before he surreptitiously moved a nearby pedestal ashtray under Chinn's hand. At the front desk, they turned in their rooms keys but left their travel bags with the desk clerk for safekeeping.

They tried a Russian tearoom next door for breakfast. The tea and pastries were good enough, but Borya couldn't help comparing everything with his aunt's establishment back in Pristan down to the décor, and finding it inferior. From there, they walked to the police station where they found Lieutenant Enebish waiting for them in his office and waved them into the two empty chairs.

"Good morning, gentlemen. I hope you made progress on your enquiries yesterday," he remarked with another of his many smiles.

"No, I'm afraid not. We could find no evidence of either Mister Geiger or Mister Song being here in the past few months."

The lieutenant made an appropriate expression of sympathy. "And I am afraid I have not found much to help you either," and opened a file folder before him on the desk. "We have no reports in our files from the last few months that mention either man or anyone that fits their description. Nor any match to unidentified bodies. And there is no missing person report filed on Mister Song." Another expression of sympathy. "But I did take the liberty of asking the judicial police to look in the district court files here on Mister Song, since he is a resident. There are no criminal cases involving him, but he was involved in a couple of civil cases. One was a dispute over a debt with a proprietor of livestock, and another over a claim of inheritance. Neither were substantial sums, nor recent. Just in case, I had them make copies of the case summaries for you." So saying, he closed the file folder and slid it across the desk in Chinn.

"Thank you for your troubles, you have been most helpful," Chinn replied sincerely. "At least it eliminates some angles of our investigation … and after all, *don't fear going slow, just fear standing still*," and added a wink. The lieutenant responded with another smile.

Chinn made ready to stand up when Borya spoke. "Lieutenant, I was curious about the encampment by the Lipovan Church."

The lieutenant's face clouded. "Yes, the Starovary refugees. Old Believers. A sad story. Since the conflict with the Soviets started to the west of here, there have been several incursions by Mongol and Cossack bands across the border. They pretend to be bandits, but we know they are being led by the GPU. They seem to be deliberately targeting the Starovary. I don't know why, except just for the fact they are White Russians and Christians. Just recently, they raided two of their villages and killed every man and boy and burnt down the houses. Many others have left their villages to seek protection in the larger towns and cities like Hailar. At least here they are under some protection of the Railway guards and local army units."

They thanked the lieutenant again and made their way outside, much sobered. Chinn stopped to light a cigarette. "I think we've done about as much here in Hailar as we can," he spoke after exhaling a cloud of smoke. "Hailar seems to be as much of a dead end as Barim, but more dangerous. I think it is about time we returned to Harbin and try to pick back up the threads from there."

Borya nodded in reply, but his mind was still stuck on the story of the massacre of the Old Believers. Wasn't he also a White Russian and a Christian? What would happen if the Soviets broke through the front lines? But that couldn't happen, not with the huge numbers of men and materiel the Young Marshal had sent here to the front, and anyway, they would be starting on their way back to Harbin in a matter of hours. They returned to the Popov to retrieve their travel bags and headed across the street to the train station.

When they reached the train station, there were already two long queues, one of civilians and another of soldiers waiting to board the eastbound train, which was a mixture of passenger and sleeper cars. The majority of the civilians looked prosperous from their dress, and Borya wondered if they came from threatened towns beyond Hailar or were simply trying to return to homes elsewhere and had been caught up in the wartime congestion of rail traffic, as here in Hailar they were safe behind Chinese lines of defense. Among the queue of soldiers were many wounded.

Many appeared only slightly wounded with dirty bandages around limbs or their heads, others leaning on crutches or a fellow soldier. About two dozen more seriously wounded lay on stretchers laid out in two rows on the platform, attended by three busy medics. Borya was startled by the large number of wounded, which exceeded any of the reports of casualties he had read in the newspapers. Had Chinn been right that the bright reports in the newspapers were lies? Did the Soviets have this many casualties or more?

No one was boarding because the front of the line was being held back by a squad of soldiers under a harried-looking lieutenant with the black collar tabs of the military police. The soldiers had their rifles in hand with bayonets mounted, and the lieutenant had his Mauser pistol out of its holster and held by his side. Chinn walked to the front of the line trailed by Borya and was able to get the lieutenant's attention, courtesy of his police uniform and rank.

"What's holding up the boarding, Lieutenant?" Chinn enquired, keeping his voice respectful but as one of equal rank.

The officer frowned, more in frustration than hostility. "This train came into the station almost full already. I have orders to remove any unwounded soldiers or civilians and load these wounded men here so they can be taken on to hospitals in Harbin and Mukden. Only after all of them are aboard, can I load any other soldiers, and only those that have orders to leave this zone. After them come the civilians. I cannot guarantee there will be room for you."

Chinn thanked him and they stood aside, staying separate from both the lines of soldiers and civilians to try and establish their distinction above that of the civilians. They watched as the squad of grey-clad soldiers swept civilians out of the cars and checked the unwounded soldiers for military orders, leaving in place only the wounded, the medics, and those with valid orders or passes. A small knot of nervous soldiers without orders were taken to one end of the platform and made to sit down on the bare concrete, suspected malingerers or deserters. Chinn noted grimly that it appeared the number of wounded on the platform awaiting space on the train exceeded the number of those that had been taken off the train. Borya could only stand silent, transfixed by the scene of so many men in pain and the forlorn faces of the civilians.

Next, the wounded on stretchers were carried onto the train, all except one who had apparently expired during the wait. Four of the suspected malingerers were "recruited" to help the medics carry the other stretchers aboard. Then the squad began inspecting the walking wounded, checking them for wound tags or even lifting bandages to ensure that they were really injured and were not more malingerers before letting them enter the passenger cars. An Army major with an aide arrived, and they climbed aboard unchallenged while the lieutenant could only salute and frown. After that, they checked the waiting unwounded soldiers for orders and passes, and about a dozen of them were allowed to board. Even those Borya could see ended up sitting in the aisles, as all the seats were already taken.

"That is all for this train," the lieutenant announced to the crowd, and the train's whistle blew its intention to depart. A cacophony of shouts and wails rose from the cluster of civilians. Several men and women, both European and Asian, assailed the officer with threats, pleadings, and even offers of bribes, but nothing softened the lieutenant's grim looks, nor could they get past the rifle butts and bayonets of his men. But finally, just as the train began inching forward, the officer allowed a young Chinese mother with a feverish child to board the last car. Chinn gave the officer a smile and a nod of approval at this single humanitarian gesture. He received a tiny nod in return, the man reluctant to openly acknowledge what might be seen as a breach of his orders.

"Well, maybe the next train," Chinn sighed aloud.

They decided to stay in the lobby of the train station, determined not to miss a chance to catch the next eastbound train. They camped out at one of the few open tables along with some of the wounded soldiers who also hadn't made it into the train, their uniforms gaining them priority over the huddled knots of rich and poor civilians desperate to leave the city and its growing proximity to the fighting. Chinn used some of their declining stores of cash to buy food and tea from the few vendors who had anything left to sell and at several times the usual rate.

They had just finished eating when they heard the drone of aircraft and seconds later the mournful wail of an air raid siren.

CHAPTER TWENTY-ONE

SECONDS LATER, THE FIRST bomb fell, and the ground shook under their feet, and the air filled with noise and dust.

"Quick, we need to find shelter!" Chinn cried, while motioning to Borya.

"Won't we be safer here? It's probably the sturdiest building around," Borya replied, but also stood up.

"Not when it's the target!" Chinn shouted back, barely audible over the rising screams of the other occupants of the lobby. Another bomb exploded close by outside, and the windows blew in, raining glass onto them and knocking both of them off their feet. Even before they could get back up, they were being stampeded by panicked civilians and soldiers trying to flee the station.

"There must be a basement," Chinn yelled. Borya could barely make out the words over the ringing in his ears, but nodded his understanding. They ran to the end of the lobby where the train offices were located and found a door that opened onto a stairway leading down. More bombs were falling now in quick succession, and Borya could see the concrete walls wobbling back and forth under the concussions, some hitting close by, and others sounding more distant.

Chinn began waving at the remaining civilians and the wounded soldiers, trying to get their attention and to join them in the basement while Borya held the door open. Some noticed and came their way, running or crawling, but the others were still in a mad panic to get outside. Together, they pushed a knot of people through the doorway and down the dark stairway, hoping no one would trip and fall on their way down. Finally, the lobby was empty except for a few people who had taken refuge under tables or vendor carts and were too frozen in fright to answer their calls. Borya then tried to close the stairway door, but the jamb had been tweaked from the concussions and wouldn't close more than halfway, so he left it that way and followed Chinn in the trek downward. Just as they reached the bottom of the stairway and the basement floor, a huge explosion rocked the walls above and several chunks of concrete bounced down the stairs after them in front of a billowing cloud of dust.

They found the others down an unlit corridor in what looked like a boiler room. There was no light from the electric light fixtures, the bulbs had either broken or the electricity had failed. A few men held up cigarette lighters or had struck matches and were providing a degree of illumination that shone over frightened faces looking upward at the ceiling. The only sounds now were the continuing bomb blasts and the occasional wails of the children and the hysterical screams of an elderly woman. Some among them made the sign of the cross, and Borya joined reflexively.

Finally, the bombs stopped, as did most of the wailing. A couple minutes later, the air raid siren spooled back up, signaling the end of the raid. Chinn led the way back up the stairs, and together with Borya, they levered the door all the way open against a pile of broken concrete. Beyond, they found the lobby barely recognizable. One entire wall had buckled inward, and a large section of the ceiling was open to a dust-filled sky. The floor was littered with chunks of concrete and roofing tiles and pools of red. None of those who had stayed and taken shelter under the tables or food carts were moving. With the help of another man, who said he had some medical training, they checked all the bodies, but all of them were dead. Some were torn apart by shrapnel from the bombs or were crushed by falling concrete. Others appeared to be strangely untouched and yet had no pulse, including a mother with her small son laying in her arms.

"From the concussion," Chinn explained, but had to repeat himself. Borya could barely hear him, and it sounded like he was talking underwater. He nodded back numbly and then pointed to a trickle of blood that was dripping from Chinn's ear. Chinn felt it with his fingers and then pulled a handkerchief from his pocket and placed it on the red patch on his scalp and then put on his uniform hat to hold it in place.

"From the glass," he shouted to Borya, "it's nothing. Scalp wounds bleed freely. You have some cuts on your face too," and he pointed back at Borya, who brushed away some blood from his cheeks. He felt a tiny sliver of glass sticking out next to his nose, and Chinn stepped closer and pulled it out with his thick fingers. Somewhere, Borya had lost his own peaked hat during the scramble out of the lobby, and he briefly looked around for it, but it was probably buried under one of the piles of fallen concrete. He felt a deep panic at the loss of the hat, which he later could neither explain nor understand.

By this time, maybe twenty minutes had passed since the bombing had ended, and they heard more sirens, these the shrill sirens of approaching fire vehicles and ambulances.

"Let's go outside. We can't help anyone in here," Chinn shouted. They found their travel bags near where their table had been, unharmed except for a few small tears and a thick coating of concrete dust. Outside, the roof over the train platforms had mostly collapsed, but fortunately, there had been no trains in the station at the time of the raid. One bomb crater had also displaced some rails of the westbound tracks. Beyond the station, one wing of the Popov hotel had fallen into the street, and a fire had already started to feed on the exposed wooden framework.

Civilians and wounded soldiers, some now with new wounds from the bombing, sat dazed on the rubble or lay in the street, some being helped by others who had rushed to the scene, others beyond help lay where they had fallen. A disemboweled horse, still in harness to an overturned wagon, screamed and thrashed. As they watched, the first of the fire trucks and ambulances pulled up, but they saw no local policemen yet on the scene. Instinct propelled them to step in by directing the fire trucks toward the fire in the hotel and the ambulance attendants to the wounded outside, then they kept a path open for the ambulances to turn around and head back towards the city hospital once they were full. After a few more minutes, local policemen arrived on the scene on foot, and Chinn and Borya relinquished the traffic control duties to them and could finally stand back and absorb the enormity of the damage and suffering.

"Why this? Why bomb a city full of civilians?" Borya cried aloud, covering the panorama of horror and destruction with a sweep of a grimy arm. He felt hot and reached to remove his cap, but remembered he had lost it.

Chinn gave a slow shrug of one shoulder and then spoke directly into Borya's still ringing ear in a sad voice. "They want to shut down the rail-line to the front and cut off any supplies and reinforcements. Also to terrorize the local population and turn them against the Young Marshal." It still made no sense to Borya, who couldn't stop shaking his head back and forth.

"Anyway," Chinn continued, "it will be hours or days before they get all the rubble out of the way and the rails fixed and any trains are moving through here again. And we're certainly not going to get rooms at the Popov. Let's head over to the police station and see if they have any space for us there." In one of life's surreal moments, Borya found himself distracted by the strange striping on Chinn's face where rivulets of sweat had cleared paths through the coating of dust. He wondered whether his own face was similarly streaked.

It feels like everyone is trying to kill me, first in Harbin, and now here in Hailar, Borya thought. He thought he had said this to himself because heard no words through the ringing, but Chinn smiled back at him sympathetically, the focus of his dark eyes far back in his head. "Yes, of course they are trying to kill us," he replied. "That is war. But they are not targeting just you or I. And when we die, it will be when fate has decided it is our time. But it won't be today."

At the police station, they found sympathetic ears, and Lieutenant Enebish directed them to a room in the basement with cots that were used by some of the local officers to sleep between shifts. There, they were able to take more careful stock of their minor wounds and their clothing. Borya found his many cuts were all superficial and had already stopped bleeding, but there were still slivers of glass embedded in his palms from when he had been knocked off his feet. Some came out easily, but some were deeper, and he would have to wait for them to work their way to the surface. He found several tears in his uniform, too, where the thick cotton had saved him from more cuts. Chinn was in a similar condition, and when Borya peeled the handkerchief away from the inspector's head, he found even that scalp wound had stopped bleeding.

They stripped off their dusty uniforms and showered. Borya stood for long minutes with his head under the shower nozzle and watched the clouded water flow off him and down the drain. They dressed in the used uniforms from their travel bags, which were now much cleaner than the uniforms they had just taken off. They laid out their dusty clothes and tried to beat off the dust as best they could before putting them into their travel bags.

"Now what?" Borya asked.

"We figure out how best to use our time toward the investigation while we are stuck in this godforsaken city."

"What's the point? We just saw the murder of dozens of civilians and the maiming of dozens more! Geiger is just one more... and he didn't appear to be particularly nice or well-liked," Borya argued, his voice loud enough to echo off the basement walls.

Chinn sighed. "The point, my young friend? It is that war is not a normal state of society. War bursts in and creates chaos and killing, but when it is over, normal society returns because people crave its return. And in normal society, murder is something to be feared and punished, and every member of society, whether they are good or bad, nice or disagreeable, deserve to live as much as you or I. Do not let war change how you think or feel, or else you will no longer fit into society when war is past. I have known too many people who couldn't leave war behind."

Borya could only look down, silence his assent.

"So, where have we not gone in Hailar that we should now visit?" Chinn prodded.

Borya referred to his notebook, which he was happy to find still in his pocket. "The Old City ... where Song's nephew is."

Chinn nodded. "Yes, that sounds good. And maybe the other hotels in Hailar if we have the time. But first, let's wire Superintendent Liu and explain why we have been delayed and see if he can wire us more funds. We are almost out of money."

They walked to the telegraph station but learned the lines had stopped working immediately after the bombing raid. Then they walked back to the train station to check on the repair work and to find out how soon eastbound trains would be running again. The dead and wounded had all been removed, and the fire in the Popov Hotel had been extinguished. Railway workers and soldiers were already busy working to dismantle the collapsed platform roof and fill the bomb craters. They found the White Russian CER supervisor in charge of repairs sitting on the end of the platform where one portion of the roof still stood, smoking a cigar and yelling out orders. He was ready to shoo them away until he recognized the insignia of their uniforms and saw the cuts on their faces.

"Harbin men, you're a long ways from home! Yeah, we should be getting an eastbound train out through here sometime late tonight. We'll be moving trains in and out in the dark in case those flying Red bastards come back. Come back around midnight."

They thanked the man and returned to the street outside. "Well, let's walk to the Old City. Anyway, food will probably be cheaper there," Chinn declared. After the events of the morning, Borya's last thoughts had been of eating, but his rumbling stomach indicated it had other ideas.

CHAPTER TWENTY-TWO

HAILAR'S OLD CITY LAY a couple of kilometers outside the new town, most of it surrounded by a mud wall that had provided protection for the town and a garrison back in imperial times. The road led to a large wooden gate in the wall, and as they neared it, Borya saw a Mongol leading a large, shaggy brown beast by leather reins.

"A camel! A real live camel!" he cried out and ran forward to see it up close. It was, of course, a two-humped Bactrian camel, a common form of transportation on the Mongolian steppes but not seen in the central plateau around Harbin. Chinn smiled indulgently while Borya engaged the camel herder in Mandarin and got permission to feel the camel's thick coat and pat its neck.

"I've never seen one up close like this!" Borya declared. Somehow, this simple discovery had swept away all the horrors of the morning.

"I would never have guessed," Chinn answered with a laugh.

They passed through the gate and entered a warren of narrow streets that wandered between two-storey houses of mud brick, and Borya immediately felt like he had stepped into the past. Most of those on the street were dressed in traditional Mongol dress with a few in simple Han peasant garb, but few in western clothing. Unfriendly stares greeted them and reminded Borya that Hailar had been at the heart of the aborted pan-Mongolian republic. There appeared to be no love lost here for the central authority represented by Nanking and the Young Marshal.

They reached an open square filled with market stalls selling everything from produce to used clothing, scrap metal, or meat by the slice from hanging slabs of mutton and beef and other meat that Borya couldn't identify. Chinn found a small stall where an older Han woman was roasting kebabs of mutton and vegetables over a firepit, and he bought two for each of them with a few copper coins. They stood as they ate hungrily, savoring the greasy meal. Chinn asked her where the gunsmith shop was, and she pointed with her eyes to another alley that led out of the square, not willing to point with her finger and let her neighbors know she was helping the police. They returned the empty kebab sticks to the old woman and wiped the grease from their fingers on a dirty rag that was shared by all her customers.

They followed the alley only a short block before they came to the gunsmith shop, which, unlike the surrounding houses of mud brick, was a two-story clapboard structure. Song's nephew supposedly lived in an apartment above the shop, and they found a wooden stairway on the side of the building that led to a door on the second floor. As they began ascending the stairs, a small knot of Mongol men suddenly gathered at the foot of the stairs. Borya, one step behind Chinn, had not seen where they had appeared from.

"What do you want here, policemen?" one of the men called out in Mandarin.

Chinn stopped and turned to look down at the caller. "We are looking for a man . . ."

"Alin," Borya provided.

"…whose uncle is missing. We only want to ask him if he has seen his uncle since he has returned from Harbin."

"I am Alin," another man spoke from the back of the small knot of men. He was a man of about thirty, in traditional Mongol attire like the rest. Borya thought he saw a resemblance to the photograph of Song Nikan, a face that by now had become familiar to him from all the times he had shown it on their journey. Alin came to the bottom of the stairs, and Chinn stepped down around Borya to meet him, but then sat on the steps nearer the bottom, leaving him at eye level with the nephew. Borya noticed that the small crowd around the man seemed to relax somewhat at this gesture of informality, but he still remained in a protective stance behind the inspector.

"We are trying to find your uncle, Song Nikan. He has gone missing along with the foreigner he was traveling with from Harbin. His… wife here said you had seen him in Harbin before you left?"

The man who claimed to be Alin shrugged. "Yes, I saw him in Harbin the week before he was to travel here. He never showed up." Another shrug.

Chinn shook two cigarettes out of its pack of Pearls and offered one to Alin, who accepted it, and Chinn lit them both with a match. "Have you heard from your uncle at all since then? Or have you tried to contact him?"

A shake of his head and an exhale of smoke. "No, I heard nothing. I sent a letter to my aunt in Harbin, but she had not heard from him since he left. And my aunt here has not heard from him either."

"Has anyone else told you that they have seen your uncle or heard from him?"

"No, no one."

"Did he tell you what he was coming to Hailar for?"

"He and this foreigner were going to buy cattle in the auctions here to send back to Harbin. My uncle was going to pay me to help him."

Chinn nodded his head in thanks but turned back to Borya for any final word.

"Where was it you last saw him?"

"At his house in Harbin. That was where he told me he wanted to hire me."

"Was the foreigner there too?"

Alin laughed and shook his head as if Borya had told a joke. "No."

Chinn thanked him and gave him one of his cards and another cigarette. "If you do hear from your uncle, or hear any news about him, please tell the police here in Hailar, and show them my card, and they will pass along your message to me."

The little crowd parted to let them come down the stairs and pass. Just as they passed the last man, Borya felt the slightest touch on his belt. He turned his head in time to see one of the younger Mongols trying to lift his revolver from its holster. His response was immediate and instinctive, employing the Water element striking set—he pivoted to face the man and with his right hand grabbed the other's right wrist and rotated it inwardly. The man released the revolver and cried out in pain and fell to one knee. Instead of following through with a kick, Borya released him and stepped back, shifting his weight back and moving his head to extend his vision all the way around, watching for the slightest hostile movement in the crowd around him, but the other men were already backing away, empty palms held outward. Meanwhile, Chinn had swiveled around, drawing his Mauser pistol halfway from its holster. There was a moment of frozen silence, and then simultaneously, several of the men broke out laughing and helped their injured companion to his feet as if to say 'no harm done.' Chinn smiled back and returned his pistol to its holster but kept his hand on the butt and motioned Borya to follow him back down the alley. The small crowd stayed behind, heckling their injured fellow for his clumsiness.

"He tried to steal my gun!" Borya explained to Chinn in a loud whisper when they had returned to the busy market square.

"So I saw. He's probably a pickpocket who thought he could get away with stealing it without you noticing. Believe me, your response was better than trying to draw it or wrestle him for it. And Superintendent Liu would not have been pleased if you had lost your weapon."

Mollified, Borya followed Chinn out of the square and back to the city gate by the way they had come, although both were more vigilant than on their entry. Borya felt a weight lifted from him once they emerged onto the open road that led back to Hailar's new city.

Not until they were back in the new district did Borya feel in his element. Not that there wouldn't be pickpockets here, too, but at least every passerby didn't consider them foreign intruders. Here also there were a half dozen other hotels and boardinghouses in the downtown district where Geiger could have stayed that were cheaper than the Popov. *Maybe he has chosen one of those in order to save more of his per diem*, Chinn mused. Borya doubted it after having seen the evidence of Geiger's expensive lifestyle back in Harbin, but kept his opinion to himself. Chinn probably felt the same way, but he had learned from the older man it was better to check than to miss a possible lead. The district was bisected by the railway line, and they each took a half. Borya showed Geiger's railway pass photograph at the lobby of each establishment in his half but received only negative shakes of the head and polite apologies. He met back up with Chinn in front of the damaged train station and learned the older man had had no better luck.

With hours to go before midnight and their chance at another outbound train, they revisited the telegraph office, but the lines were still down and the clerk at the desk didn't know when they would be restored. Then they returned to the police station, where they found Lieutenant Enebish once again in the office of the duty officer. Chinn detailed their sojourn to the Old City and the new city's other hotels, and left him one of his cards in case Song's Hailar wife or nephew brought news of Song's whereabouts or status to relay on to them in Harbin.

"I am not surprised by your episode in the Old City," the lieutenant observed. "It is a dangerous place and has only become more dangerous since the troubles with the Soviets started. There are some among the Mongols here who think they would be better off under the Reds across the border in the Ulan Bator puppet state, especially the young ones who have no standing within the clans. If I had known you two were going there, I would have sent some of my men with you. We no longer go in there without at least half a dozen armed officers."

Chinn only nodded in acquiescence after removing the usual cigarette from his mouth. "Thank you for your advice. If I may ask one more favor of you?"

"And what is that, Inspector?"

"In case the military police are there again tonight at the train station filtering out who gets on the eastbound train, could I get a letter from you explaining how important it is to our investigation that we return to Harbin. The word of someone local might have more weight than the word of someone coming from Harbin."

"Certainly, for what it's worth. I hope it will help." And the lieutenant drew some police stationary from his desk and comprised a short note asking for their priority in boarding, signed it, and stamped it. After more thanks and goodbyes, they took their leave and retrieved their travel bags from the station's basement room, where they had left them during the day's outings.

With nothing more they could think of to do in Hailar for their investigation, and little money left to spend on food or entertainment, they returned to the train station to await darkness and hopefully, the return of train service. They skirted the ruined station house and went directly to the platforms. There they saw much progress had been accomplished in their absence—the broken parts of the platform roof had been taken down and hauled away, the bomb craters filled with rubble from the station walls, and railway workers were well along in the process of laying down replacement ties and rails to bridge the gaps. The same elderly CER supervisor was still there, another cigar in his mouth. He waved them over, and they sat with him to watch the repairs as dusk settled into darkness and lanterns were brought to illuminate the worksite, to be extinguished immediately at the first sound of a siren or an approaching plane.

Well before midnight, the last of the temporary repairs were completed, and the railway supervisor and his workers departed into the darkness. A few of the lanterns were left in place as the only light—the station's electric lights had either been turned off as a blackout precaution or else they no longer worked as a result of the bomb damage. Now the only question was ... would a train come, and if so, would there be space on it for two homesick Harbin policemen.

CHAPTER TWENTY-THREE

IN THE LAST HOUR before midnight, some civilians came to the platform, apparently having heard of the possible return of train service and also hoping to find room on the next eastbound train. Then more wounded arrived, again some walking and some borne on stretchers. Chinn smoked his last cigarette but did not want to leave the platform to buy more in town and possibly appear as a late arrival if and when the military police showed up.

Finally, just before midnight, the same lieutenant of military police from the other day arrived with his patrol of eight armed men. Wasting no time, Chinn approached the officer and showed him the letter from Lieutenant Enebish. He took it over to one of the lanterns and read it, frowning.

"Okay, you may board when the train arrives. But do not take any of the sleeping berths or seats needed by the wounded," he finally declared.

"Of course," Chinn replied, bowing slightly.

Exactly at midnight, the eastbound train approached the platform, having been held outside the city until the predetermined time so as to limit its exposure to another bombing attack. Likewise, the next westbound train would only arrive after this eastbound train had left, so there would be no more than one train exposed as a target at a time. The locomotive steamed in slowly, as if gingerly testing the recent repairs. As was the case with the last train, this one, too, was already packed with wounded and a few civilians. Before anyone was allowed to board, seven stretchers were removed from the train, their occupants completely covered in blankets. These were men who had succumbed to their wounds before the train had even made it to Hailar. Then the lieutenant waved Chinn and Borya aboard the train before anyone else. They found empty seats in one of the passenger cars, where they sat quietly while the wounded were carried or helped aboard. All the walking wounded found seats in their car without Chinn or Borya having to relinquish their seats. Next came a sprinkling of civilians, mostly families. Chinn and Borya gave up their seats to a young Chinese woman with two small children, finding instead a space on the floor at the back of the car where they could sit on their travel bags. Almost an hour later, the train jerked into motion and they slowly crept out of the battered station. Borya let out a long breath and heard Chinn do the same, and they exchanged wordless smiles. Homeward bound at last!

The train chugged up the western foothills of the Great Khingan mountains, retracing their recent race down to Hailar from the pass. It had only been days, but after their enforced confinement in the city, and surviving the bombing raid on the train station, it felt to Borya like half his lifetime had passed there. He found the steady rhythm of the train and each mile separating them from Hailar reassuring, but Chinn found the experience agonizing. After running out of cigarettes before boarding, he was forced to beg cigarettes from the surrounding soldiers. By the time they pulled into Yakeshi, the sun was just rising, and Chinn bolted for the platform to find a tobacco vendor. Borya followed, happy to stretch his legs after the uncomfortable seat provided by his flattened travel bag.

Yakeshi was not a large town, being mainly a center for the shipping of timber. At this early hour, there were only two vendors selling food, and no one was selling cigarettes. The train conductor told them there was a tobacconist at the edge of town just past the Russian Orthodox church, and they would have time to reach it and return before the train left, as they would be adding two logging cars to the train. Yes, even though there was a war going on, commerce had to continue or there would be no freight income and taxes coming in to allow the Young Marshal to pay for his army.

They followed a muddy street between clapboard storefronts and houses and were soon out of sight of the station, and ahead of them they could see the wooden dome of the town's Russian Orthodox church. Although it was still early hours, Borya had expected to see at least some pedestrian or cart traffic, but instead, the street was eerily deserted. They turned a bend in the street and came even with the Russian church, a modest timbered structure. Chinn stopped dead in his tracks and his face went pale.

"The fox ... I saw it cross the street just now ahead of us ..."

Borya looked beyond the church where the town's houses petered out, and he didn't see a fox but reflexively crossed himself. What he did see was an encampment of carts and tents like they had seen in the outskirts of Hailar. Starovary. Unlike the camp at Hailar, there was also a mass of armed men on horseback riding between the tents and wagons that were not Russians; they were Mongol riders in khaki coats and conical hats and brandishing rifles. They were herding the Starovary men and boys out of the encampment and into the street leading out of town, amid a rising wail of cries and alarm.

"We need to get back to the station immediately," Chinn whispered to Borya, and they abruptly reversed directions on the muddy street below the steps of the church.

"Who the hell are you?" a rough voice accosted them in Russian from the entrance of the church, rising above the sounds inside of wood breaking and glass being smashed. The voice came from a tall, square-built man with a thick, black mustache that entirely covered his mouth and had just emerged from the dark interior of the church. He wore a Soviet army tunic without any insignia above Mongol leather trousers and a Cossack hat with a pistol holstered to his belt, the flap of the holster left open to leave the weapon ready to draw. The accent was neither Mongol nor Cossack but pure Great Russian. Behind him stood two Mongol riders carrying unslung rifles in front of them.

"We're not from here, we're Special District police from Harbin," Chinn answered quickly, "returning from an investigation in Hailar. We're only passing through."

The man rested his hand on the butt of his pistol and looked at Chinn with hard eyes from under thick eyebrows, then turned to Borya, lingering long on his face as if his next decision would decide their fate. As it did.

"You two stay right here until we leave," the man said finally. He nodded to the two Mongols with rifles who had been standing behind him. They gestured to Chinn and Borya to join them on the wide stone steps with gestures of their rifles, now held at their waists and plainly pointed in the direction of the two policemen.

They watched silently from the steps of the church while Starovary men and boys were herded down the middle of the street toward the outskirts of town between two files of mounted men. One of the men on horseback was loudly chastising them in broken Russian for being "enemies of the people." There were maybe forty of them; old men with long white beards, boys with barely their first signs of facial hair, middle-aged men with dark beards, all with their eyes downcast. One just passing bore a small bald patch on the crown of his head, a head that sat low between hunched shoulders...

Borya began to tremble uncontrollably. "Wait!" he heard a voice cry out, familiar but for its shrill tone. There was a loud buzzing in his ears, and he couldn't be sure if the voice he heard was nearby or if it was coming from inside his own head... or mouth. "Stop!" it cried out again. He could see Chinn staring at him open-mouthed with shock, and then he found himself turning into the open door of the church, seeking the Russian in charge. He could feel Chinn's hand grab desperately at his sleeve, trying to hold him back but only catching air. Before his eyes could adjust to the darker interior, he saw nothing until the flash of sunlight reflecting off the metal butt plate of a rifle coming straight at his head...

PART THREE

CHAPTER TWENTY-FOUR

TIME FLOWED AROUND AND beyond Borya as he lay unconscious in his hospital bed in the Harbin Municipal Hospital. Bright days and smoky nights flickered past on his closed eyelids like the celluloid frames of a cinema movie reel. Like choreographed loops in his movie, serial doctors entered the ward and his curtained sanctuary to check his vitals and inspect the sutured gash in his forehead for infection. Sometimes, they came to prick him with a needle to elicit a response or raise his eyelids before shaking their heads together in a perfunctory ritual before moving on. Other times, nurses in their own vignettes brought fresh bottles of saline or nutrients to drip into his veins or changed the bottle that collected the urine from his catheter, completing the cycle of bodily functions that once were the actions of a now-slumbering brain. Visitors came and went—his mother, siblings, aunt, grandfather, even some of his fellow officers from the Special District police. Some talked to him, trying to penetrate the barrier of his silence, others merely stood in their own respectful silence or touched a hand as if a physical message could succeed where words failed. Even Superintendent Liu came by to stand at the foot of his bed and observe him silently. His presence was noted by the staff, and Borya's level of care and attention increased.

"Will he ever wake up?" his mother would ask each new doctor that entered the room. The answers were different: "He has had a major concussion . . ." or "There has been swelling on the brain . . ." or "It's hard to say in cases like this . . ." but they all ended with a shrug and maybe a consoling look. Meanwhile, the days passed, and his limbs got weaker from their lack of use, while the gash on his forehead healed into a pink line. One day, the elderly chief of neurology brought a covey of student doctors to his bedside to observe and learn.

"Can you hear what is being said when you're in a coma?" one intern asked.

"Sometimes, I've been told," the old sage ruminated. "There are reports that patients have awoken from a coma and could exactly recall the conversations that took place around them. He may remember this very visit."

"Is he dreaming while he's in the coma?" another asked.

"Perhaps. But he's had a long time to dream ... time enough to relive every terror," the sage spoke, as much to the room itself as to the attentive doctors-to-be.

"When he wakes will he remember those dreams?" a third asked.

"*If* he awakes, let's hope he doesn't remember."

Early one morning before visitors were allowed, and two weeks to the day of his attack and eleven days in the hospital, a nurse came in to replace his glass catheter, but before she could, his eyes fluttered open. The Chinese nurse did not notice until she heard a raspy voice ask, "Who are you?" She gasped and looked up to see him staring at her from dark-rimmed, sunken eyes.

"Aiyo!" she exclaimed and ran from the room to fetch a doctor. Soon, his bed was surrounded by several white-coated doctors, some peppering him with questions while another asked him to follow a moving finger with his eyes. Borya could not make out anything in the confusing cacophony of voices. Finally, the oldest doctor, a white-haired Russian with an equally white beard, shushed the others and commanded Borya's attention.

"Borya Sergeevich, I am Doctor Chernov. Do you know where you are?"

Borya's eyes swept the room beyond the circle of doctors. "It looks like I am in a hospital room. Am I in Harbin? May I have a drink of water? My throat is very dry."

"Yes, of course," and a younger doctor handed him a glass from the bedside table. "Yes, you are in Harbin. You are in the Special Municipal Hospital. How do you feel?"

"Umm … tired. I … I felt a strange touch, and then I woke up. And I have a headache."

The old doctor nodded vigorously, as if had just heard a great joke. "I am hardly surprised. Do you know why you are here?"

Borya thought hard, but he could only remember being somewhere outside Harbin. Somewhere far to the west. "No, Doctor. Did I fall ill in the countryside?"

"No, Borya Sergeevich, I was told you were attacked by bandits out near the western border. You suffered a serious brain trauma. Railway Guards found you and sent you back here to Harbin by train. You have been in a coma . . ." and one of the other doctors handed him Borya's chart " … for two weeks."

It was a lot to take in. Two weeks! Why had he been attacked? Where? "Does my family know I'm here? My mother?" He drank more water, but his throat still felt extremely parched.

The doctor smiled now. "Oh, yes! Your mother has been here every day, and I expect she will be here again soon. And you have had many other visitors as well. A lot of people care about you," and then he added with another smile, "and your grandfather has had many suggestions for us on your care. But for right now, rest. We will talk more later. Are you hungry?"

Borya discovered that he was. Like he hadn't eaten in days. Or two weeks.

He was taking spoonfuls of a thin broth from one of the nurses when he heard a commotion outside the doorway right before his mother burst into the room, tears streaming down her face. "You are awake! You are awake!" she cried in her native Korean before jumping onto the bed and laying across him, sobbing hard. Borya could not think of anything to say or do except wrap his weak arms around her.

After two weeks of lying motionless on the train from Hailar, and then in the hospital, and receiving nutrients only through a tube in his arm, Borya had lost considerable weight and muscle mass. He felt incredibly weak, and his limbs felt stiff even though the nurses had manipulated his arms and legs in a twice daily routine. The doctors wanted him to stay another few days in the hospital to be sure his digestive system was working properly, not that they were feeding him anything more than thin soups and broths, but his mother insisted on bringing him home. The nurses helped him pull himself up to a sitting position, and then a standing one, and finally, by the next day, to take his first walking steps with one of them on each side steadying him.

On the day he was to be released from the hospital, Borya was sitting on the side of his bed, still in a hospital gown and waiting for his mother to bring him some clothes from home. He looked up to see Superintendent Liu standing in the doorway, his hat held stiffly to his side under one arm. "Officer Melnikov . . ."

Borya tottered to attention on wobbly legs.

"No, no, sit down. I only came to tell you that you will be on medical leave until you feel well enough to return to duty. The doctors here will tell me when they feel you are ready."

"Certainly, sir. I felt much stronger in the last couple days. I am sure it will not take long. Will I still be assisting Inspector Chinn when I return?" He couldn't keep a note of optimism from his voice.

Liu looked past Borya and said nothing. Borya watched Liu's collar move as he swallowed hard. "I'm afraid that won't be possible," he finally spoke in a tight voice. "Witnesses in the town of Yakeshi told Railway guardsmen that you were attacked by bandits . . . and Inspector Chinn drew his weapon and was shot by several of the bandits and killed. The guardsmen buried Chinn there in the village and put you on one of the hospital trains headed here to Harbin."

Borya collapsed back onto the bed. The floor started spinning, and he felt a sudden heat burning on the back of his neck. Liu stepped forward to grab his shoulder just in time to keep him from falling forward onto the floor, easing him back into an upright sitting position.

"Just rest and build up your strength, Borya Sergeevich. And don't worry, there will be a place for you when you return. Harbin is still under a state of emergency, and we need every man, but not before you are ready and feeling well." Liu gently released his shoulder but stayed close in case Borya swayed forward again. When Borya stayed upright, Liu stepped back and returned his hat to its precise place on his head. "Your doctors will keep me informed of your progress. Until then . . ." and he was out the door and down the hallway, striding swiftly away. Seconds later, a nurse hurried into the room to check on him.

Chinn dead? It did not seem possible. Had not the grizzled inspector survived years of war and deadly street crime? The guardsmen could have buried anyone—they weren't from Harbin and didn't know who Chinn was. Maybe Chinn was really lying in a hospital in Yakeshi or Hailar. And if he is dead, was it his fault? Hadn't he convinced Chinn to go beyond Barim to Hailar? He tried hard to remember that day in Yakeshi, but nothing came back to him. When his mother returned with his street clothes, she found him staring at the floor, trying hard to will his memory back.

CHAPTER TWENTY-FIVE

IN ORDER TO GET him home, a nurse first brought him to the hospital entrance in a wheelchair and then helped him climb into a taxi with his mother. He couldn't remember the last time he had ridden in a motorcar taxi, only a vague memory of some special excursion with his parents when he was a child. Ironically, the memory of that taxi ride itself left a more distinct memory than the event that necessitated it.

When they arrived at the family apartment building in District 8, the driver told them that the fare had already been paid. Both his sisters were waiting for him on the sidewalk with smiles and hugs, and the driver and Hei-rin, together, helped him up the long stairway to the second floor and down the hallway to the apartment. Just that effort alone left him exhausted and drenched in sweat, and he was happy to collapse into the chair nearest the door.

The next few days, his mother was constantly putting bowls of food in front of him and exhorting him to eat. He obliged, but wondered where the money came from for so much food. Grandfather Jung came by every day after he closed his medicine shop and brought strengthening potions and powders. Day by day, he could feel his strength and stamina returning, and soon he was wandering around the apartment at will and down the hallway alone to the common bathroom. But also every day, the headaches would come, knifing through his head and leaving him nauseous and drained so that all he could do was lie in his bed in the dark. And with the headaches came angry outbursts where he lashed out at his mother and sisters until their sad eyes guilted him into silence.

But slowly, the intervals between the headaches grew. On days when the sun was shining, he would descend to the courtyard behind the building. There he would sit and let the direct rays of the sun fight off the cold October air and read his father's books or help his younger sister Min with her homework. Looking back on it, Borya doubted Min really needed the help and was just trying to lift his spirits by feeling useful. But when he was alone, images of Inspector Chinn, and sometimes his father, would creep into his mind, and he would try again to remember that day in Yakeshi, but there was still a dark, foggy barrier that kept him out. Other times, he was haunted by the thought that somewhere out there Geiger's killer could, at that moment, be feeling smug in having eluded justice. Those days he would sit out there in his chair, silent and staring until it grew dark and cold and his mother would send Min or Hei-rin to bring him back inside.

After more than a week had passed, his grandfather came to the apartment as usual, but this time it was to bring Borya back to his shop. There in his grandfather's basement, Borya began a regimen of kikong, akin to t'ai chi. He felt like he had returned to his childhood, reliving the physical training that the old man had first taught him as a precursor to the more demanding martial arts. Once again, it was the slow, artful movements designed to bring back his physical strength and vitality. Here, where it was just the two of them alone in the basement, his grandfather was sparing in his words. He wasn't being cold or aloof, but it was just his nature to economize on his words so that every instruction was meaningful and what mattered was not buried in idle talk. It also made it easier for Borya to reflect on and retain each measured declaration or observation, whether it was about martial arts, philosophy, or life in general. Each day, the sessions grew longer, and each day Borya felt his health and strength return more. His grandfather also helped him to expand his breathing techniques and meditation in specific ways to counteract the crippling headaches, and although they didn't go away entirely, Borya found he could lessen their pain and duration. And just like the headaches, his thoughts of Chinn grew less often and less painful over time, but never completely went away.

After the end of the third week since his release from the hospital, he returned for another evaluation by the doctors, who this time were astonished by his progress. "I am releasing you to return to duty," Doctor Chernov declared triumphantly. Later, when he told his grandfather of the doctor's astonishment, the old man laughed. "Of course, they think only Western medicine helps."

Borya reported to Commander Cho that same day. Borya was startled to be met with a half-smile from his old commander.

"Since your last assignment was with Superintendent Liu, you need to report back to him." His voice was almost friendly. Was he happy to see him sent away again? Or maybe there was a little sympathy after his near-death experience. Or had the commendation letter from the Railways Guards for the Sungari incident softened him?

Once more, Borya came to attention in Superintendent Liu's office. Everything about the room looked the same down to the crooked picture, and yet to Borya, it felt like it had been years since he had last been there. Liu was standing beside his chair in front of the window, looking out over the light motorcar and horse cart traffic on Prospect, but seeing Borya's reflection in the glass, he turned around.

"Please sit down, Officer Melnikov." Borya picked the chair closest to the desk and sat down, while Liu sat down behind his large desk.

"I understand you have been released by the doctors at the Municipal Hospital to return to duty."

"Yes, Superintendent . . ." Borya intoned, but did not meet Liu's eyes, ". . . but I would like to take some personal leave."

"Do you not feel ready to return to duty?"

"Yes, Superintendent, I do feel fit for duty, but I . . . uh, feel that I have a duty to avenge the murder of Inspector Chinn by the Bolsheviks." There, it was out, and he could let his eyes rise to meet Liu's eyes that were staring back at him. "He is dead because of me. I persuaded him to travel to Hailar from Barim . . ." His voice ended in a choke. He had resolved to not let his emotions show, but it welled up in him now like an overwhelming force of nature.

Liu tapped the top of his desk with one forefinger in thought before he spoke. "How is it you intend to avenge the death of Inspector Chinn?"

"You have probably heard about the forming of a Harbin Student Corps of volunteers for the front. It includes the student defense association formed at my old high school. With my police training, I think they will accept me, and I believe I can make a worthy contribution."

Liu gave a wry smile. "Yes, I know all about the Harbin Student Corps. I also saw the message from Marshal Chang telling the students that their duties lie in continuing their studies, and that would be the best way they can support the war effort."

"If the Marshal does not accept the Student Corps, then I will enlist directly in the Northeast Frontier Defense Force."

More tapping on the desk. "Yes, you could. And I have no doubt they would accept you, but first, listen to what I have to say." Borya nodded his assent while still fighting back the tears forming in his eyes.

"Firstly, Inspector Chinn died resisting a vicious attack. Whether his own actions were the wisest under the circumstances, I cannot say because I was not there. But Inspector Chinn was more than capable of making his own decision on the spot, and he alone made it. Secondly, you can make more of a contribution here in Harbin, where the threat from Bolshevik sabotage and terror is still ongoing, and every trained police officer is needed. ... And, you would likely not be through army training and make it to the front before the fighting is over—I have heard there's already efforts underway to negotiate a political settlement. But then, you would still be stuck in Marshal Chang's army for the length of your enlistment." Liu paused and raised one eyebrow, inviting a response from Borya.

"Yes, sir, that could be true . . ."

"And lastly, the only reason you and Inspector Chinn were out on the western frontier was because someone murdered Herr Geiger. His murderer is then the one who is ultimately responsible for the attack on you and the Inspector. If you want to honor his death, then you can do that best by bringing Geiger's murderer to justice. Right now, I cannot spare anyone from the detective squad to finish this case; they are all still busy chasing down spies and saboteurs here in Harbin... a priority the German consul continues to not understand," and here Liu allowed an uncharacteristic roll of his eyes. "But before you two left for Barim and Hailar, Chinn told me you are an intelligent young man, and he believed you had natural investigative instincts. I have talked to Commander Cho about you continuing your temporary assignment to the detective squad in order to complete the murder investigation." Borya's eyes now flooded with tears at these words of praise that came from beyond the grave.

"Yes, Superintendent, I will do it. I will do whatever it takes."

"Good. I will tell the detective squad to provide you with additional resources if they are available, but I'm afraid you will have to work alone as long as the present state of emergency continues. Be especially careful out there; it is still dangerous out on the streets for both the police and Railway guards. Report directly to me if you feel you have found anything significant or if you feel the need to leave the city for any reason, otherwise report to me weekly."

Liu then nodded, and Borya took that for his dismissal. "Thank you Superintendent, I promise I will see this through to the end." And to himself... if it's the last thing I do!

CHAPTER TWENTY-SIX

HE MADE HIS WAY to the detective squad room and found Chinn's desk exactly as he had left it, and nobody else had sought to claim it. The detectives and clerks, even the surly senior clerk, acknowledged him with friendly nods, but they all left him alone, either out of respect or at a loss for what to say.

What to do next? Borya recalled his conversation with Inspector Chinn when they had sat together in the lobby of the Changchun Railway Station, about pulling on the threads until that one tug pulled apart the seam of lies and deception. Together, they had followed the threads of Geiger's and Song's lives in Harbin, and then followed other threads to Barim and the shaman and to Hailar and their contacts there, but learned nothing new. What threads remained? There was still the evidence he and Chinn had had taken from Geiger's office and home and the autopsy, still in Chinn's desk or in evidence storage, except for the 100 Yuan that should still be in the squad room safe. He retrieved the box of evidence from storage and laid everything out onto the desktop: the copper coin, the DVP pin, the mud balls in their paper envelope, the pornographic postcards, the autopsy report, the notes from the personnel files of Geiger and

Song from the abattoir, and the bundle of Geiger's clothes, which fortunately had lost much of its pungent odor.

What he did not find were the papers that he and Chinn had brought from Geiger's house, except for a copy of the translations of what had been in German. He asked the chief clerk of their whereabouts, who told him that an attorney for Geiger's estate had called the squad room and asked for the papers to be released to him. And since at the time Borya had been in the hospital and Chinn was... well, he saw no reason not to release them. Borya reread the translations, and it only reconfirmed Geiger had been living well beyond his public means, with no clues as to where his extra money had come from. The autopsy report revealed nothing more than what Dr. Hong had told them in person at the morgue and in his office.

He laid each item individually on the desk in a neat row, evenly spaced. The pornographic postcards were of German origin, probably brought by Geiger to Harbin from Germany, and nothing was written on any of them. Embarrassed, Borya quickly put them in a desk drawer before anyone in the squad room could see him studying them and draw the wrong conclusions. The one fen copper coin still looked the same, unremarkable without any unusual scratches or wear and of a denomination and series that was widely circulated. The small coin had probably been overlooked by whoever took his wallet and any other contents of his pockets; Borya could not think of how it could provide any clues. He then looked closely at the enameled DVP pin and wondered for the hundredth time what the initials represented. No one in the detective squad had been able to identify its meaning, including the Volga German clerk who had helped him and Chinn with the translation of the German papers. Maybe this was the next thread, and he considered his options. It probably went back to Geiger's German background or his time in Austria, so he would need to find someone with a background in Germanic politics. He could go to the German consul, Herr Schessler, but that might generate embarrassing questions about the lack of progress on the investigation, which so far had not yielded any suspects.

Borya felt the beginning throb of another headache developing. He concentrated his thoughts on the pin, trying to will the headache away. He knew most of the Germans in Harbin attended either the Lutheran Evangelical Church, along with many of the Baltic refugees, or, if they were Catholic, at one of the two Polish Catholic churches. Since the Lutheran church and the oldest of the two Polish churches in Harbin were both up in New Town, and Geiger had lived in New Town, he figured he would start there first with the clergy of those two churches.

He was, of course, familiar with the location of both churches, having walked past them hundreds of times along the broad boulevard that was Prospect Street. He had never been inside either one, but thought he knew generally what different views each represented. He had found all the spiritual support he needed within his father's Russian Orthodox Church. His father, having been an engineer, had held a strong belief in the sanctity of Science and Reason, and believed that all things in nature and the world at large, even the universe, could be explained by natural forces. Or if not explained, then the science that could explain it had just not been discovered yet. But his father's one exception to this worship of reason was his faith in the mystical power of God and His true representation through the Russian Orthodox Church. Borya remembered as a child asking his father how he could he believe in a God that he couldn't see. Had he witnessed miracles with his own eyes? No, his father replied, but how can there be matter in the universe without God? Or else wouldn't there be just nothingness? His words made sense to Borya, so Reason and Science reigned for him except when God and the Church came into the equation, and that still made sense to him now. His only deviation from his father's beliefs was a polite deference to the ancestor worship of his mother and grandfather Jung, but he found no contradiction in that. Did not the Church preach respect for your parents and all your family? He could even respect the other Christian churches for their beliefs; they just hadn't fit all the parts together as correctly as the Orthodox Church.

He returned all the other evidence but the pin to the drawers of Chinn's desk, but when he rose from the chair, he felt a renewed wave of pain emanating from his forehead. This would not do, he thought fiercely. He had work to do, important work! Pain was relative, he would just have to struggle through it. But when he started to walk away from the desk, he felt an echoing wave of nausea rise from his gut, and he knew he couldn't ignore it any longer. Instead of exiting the squad room through the lobby entrance, he exited through the side door into a backroom, stepping gingerly to avoid worsening the pain and nausea. The last thing he wanted to do was to throw up in front of any of the detectives and clerks, and what a waste of the pastry he had eaten that morning in his aunt's tearoom. He knew many still thought he didn't belong there, and he didn't want to give them an excuse to say he wasn't ready to return to duty. He might be sent back home for further medical leave or even dismissal.

The backroom was a windowless rectangle that held metal lockers belonging to the detectives along with two wooden benches. Borya lay down on one of the benches on his back and closed his eyes. He began some Danjeon breathing exercises as his grandfather Jung had taught him, eyes closed and breathing with his belly, inhaling through his nose and exhaling through his mouth. Habit and practice allowed him to visualize his Ki life force entering through the top of his head and flowing outward through his body. Once he heard the door to the room open and then quickly close again, thankfully, someone was giving him the privacy he needed. Slowly, breath by breath, the nausea ebbed away, and the headache retreated back into a dull ache. He stood up slowly, but the nausea did not return. Back to work. The only work that mattered anymore.

The Polish church was closest. It was a towering neo-Gothic edifice, a jagged, sharp style to which to Borya assigned a certain coldness that he didn't find in the rounded wooden spires and domes of his Cathedral of St. Nicholas. The front doors were unlocked, and the inside of the church was empty, silent, and still, except for the dust motes that danced in the sunlight that came through the stained glass side windows. Then he noticed movement, an older Russian or Polish woman at the far end of the nave near the chancel slowly sweeping the floor. On seeing Borya's approach, she stopped sweeping to lean on her broom as if she had been waiting for his entrance to provide an excuse to take a break from her chore.

"Good morning grandmother, I am looking for the pastor . . ."

The woman silently jabbed a finger toward a side door of the nave. Borya confronted a dark wooden door marked as the church "Office" in Polish; that much Polish he knew. Below those letters was a rectangle of darker, unfaded wood below the letters. Had it been a nameplate for the priest? Had there been a recent change of leadership, or was it an attempt at anonymity? He knocked.

There was a response from within in Polish, and when Borya hesitated, the voice repeated the invitation in Russian. "Enter."

Inside was a large office paneled in dark wood and tall bookcases that surrounded a wooden desk that sat just below a high window that took advantage of the morning daylight streaming in. Sitting at the desk was a ruddy-faced, older man in black cassock and white collar staring at an open book until he saw Borya's black uniform and rose to his feet, leaning his hands on the desktop.

"Please, Father, stay seated," Borya began in Russian. "I am Officer Melnikov with the Harbin Police. I came to ask your help on a police investigation." The priest's eyebrows fluttered at the mention of his surname, an all too-common reaction to try and classify his ambiguous ethnic origins.

"Certainly, how can I help?" the priest replied in Russian, nodding his head in little jerks and waving Borya towards a chair that faced the desk. But instead of sitting, Borya advanced and pulled the enameled pin with the DVP letters from his tunic pocket and laid it on the open book between the priest's hands before retreating to the chair.

"Can you tell me what these initials stand for? It could be German or Austrian."

The priest leaned forward and squinted down at the pin but did not pick it up. "I do not recognize it. It is no doubt from a political party or trade union, but it is not of one of the Catholic parties, that much I know. Sorry. Have you asked Reverend Bruhner at the Lutheran church?"

"No, that is probably my next stop," and he picked up the pin and put it back in his pocket. "Can you tell me, was a Manfred Geiger a member of your congregation?"

The priest's forehead creased in thought. "No, I think I have heard the name before, but he wasn't a member of my congregation. Sorry. Again, I would check with Reverend Bruhner. His church has many more of Harbin's Germans than we do here or in St. Joseph's in Pristan." St. Joseph's was the other Polish Catholic church in Harbin. And Borya did not find it surprising that the priest would have heard Geiger's name before, as the Harbin newspapers had printed the news of his murder in the days when Borya had lain unconscious in the hospital... and Chinn in his grave. It was too much to hope that the death of a murdered foreign businessman could be kept out of the newspapers for long.

"Well, thank you, Father, for your time."

"You're welcome, Officer. Good luck on your investigation."

Outside in the nave, the old woman stopped her sweeping to stare at Borya and lean on her broom again. She continued staring even after Borya extended her a nod of his head, and he did not hear the scrape of her broom again until he had retraced his steps all the way to the church entrance. He certainly did not feel as welcome here as he did at St. Nicholas. Still, there was a marked deference shown, or was it caution, from the Catholic priest, a deference that exceeded what was typically extended to him by the Russian community. Perhaps it came from their experience of being a smaller minority within the Harbin exile community, lacking the numbers and influence that the White Russians could bring to the ongoing competition with the Chinese for authority in the city. Did that deference give him more leverage in his enquiries? Not as much as if he had been full Russian or a real detective.

The Harbin Evangelical Lutheran church was just blocks away at the intersection with Mukdenskaia Street. This church was a large, two-storey neo-Gothic structure that also lacked the charm of St. Nicholas. A smaller entrance, separate from the large doors that led to the chapel, looked like a good prospect for leading him directly to the church office. Sure enough, inside the door was a small office where a squarish white woman with dark hair sprinkled with gray sat behind a small desk, pounding away on a typewriter. Behind her was another door inscribed with "Rev. Hans Bruhner" in painted letters leading to yet another office. There was a third door that probably led directly to the chapel.

"May I help you?" the woman asked in broken Russian with a German accent, seeing his uniform.

"Yes, I am Officer Melnikov of the Harbin Police. I would like to speak with Reverend Bruhner."

"Reverend Bruhner... is a baptism in chapel performing. He will shortly return," she intoned, her words in Russian, but her syntax plainly German.

"Thanks, I will wait." There was a wooden armchair in one corner facing the side door to the chapel, and Borya sat down. Before the church secretary recommenced her attack on the typewriter keys, he could hear muffled voices coming through the side door. On the walls of the small office were city certificates, a calendar with what looked like a snowy Alpine scene, and several framed embroidered homilies, but since they were in German, Borya could only guess at their meaning.

After five minutes, the side door from the chapel swung open, and a beaming white male of about fifty, with a shock of white hair and wearing a white vestment over a black cassock, strode into the room. On seeing Borya, he stopped in mid-stride, the smile still on his lips, but it had left his eyes.

"Reverend Bruhner?" Borya rose and introduced himself. "I came to ask your help in a police investigation." The man relaxed visibly.

"Certainly, why don't you come into my office. Actually, my Chinese is better than my Russian. Would that be okay?" Like any resident in Harbin, he knew the Special District police were required to be fluent in both Russian and Mandarin.

"Certainly," Borya replied in Mandarin.

Reverend Bruhner's office was similar but maybe a little larger than that of his Catholic peer, but here all the walls were covered by bookcases crammed with religious texts. Unlike the tidy shelves of the Polish priest's bookcases, some of the books here were heaped at odd angles, and Borya had the urge to rearrange them.

"Please, sit," and Bruhner waved at two armchairs that faced his desk. The man pulled the white vestment off over his head and hung it on a hanger to a coatrack before taking the seat behind his desk. Again, before sitting, Borya retrieved the enameled pin and set it on the desk in front of the Reverend. "Can you tell me what these initials stand for?"

Bruhner picked up a pair of steel-rimmed reading glasses from the top of his desk and held the pin up to his eyes, bunching up two bushy white eyebrows.

"Ahh, yes, Deutsche Volkspartei—the German People's Party. It is a center-right German party. It's party leader, Gustav Stresemann, is, or at least was, the German foreign minister—we do not always get our German newspapers here in a timely manner. They believe in Christian family values, pro-business and anti-union . . ."

"Anti-communist?" Borya advanced. Could Geiger have run afoul of one of the many Bolsheviks still running rampant in the city?

"Most definitely anti-communist. They are against raising general wages and benefits and any socialist ideas. Along with many center-right and right-wing parties, they hope for a return of the monarchy."

"Is there a strong contingent of DVP members among the Harbin German population?"

Bruhner smiled as though harboring a private joke. "No, not really. We Germans are not in huge numbers here in Harbin. Consequently, we cannot afford to split up in parties and fight with each other. Most German associations in Harbin are cultural in nature … and, of course, there is the Church."

Borya nodded. "So, a Harbin German would probably have kept this pin from an earlier association back in Germany?"

"I would expect so."

"Was Manfred Geiger a member of your church?"

Bruhner looked suddenly sad and removed his glasses to wipe a hand across his face. "Yes and no. He was not an active member. He would come to service on the high holidays … Easter, Christmas … but then I wouldn't see him again for months. He wasn't active in any of the Church's men's activities, and I don't recall ever seeing him outside the Church, although I believe he lived somewhere here in New Town. Are you investigating his murder?—I read about his death in the papers. Sad. Did this pin belong to him?"

"Yes, it did. I am assisting in the investigation of his murder. We found the pin among his effects. Do you ever remember seeing him wear it?"

Bruhner tilted his head to one side, as if trying to sift through his memories. "Not that I recall. But he could have, and I just didn't notice. And I don't recall him as being particularly vocal about the politics back home or here."

"Are there many communists among Harbin's Germans?"

Bruhner now tilted his head to the opposite side. "I don't think so. But then I'm not really in a position to know. If they were true communists, they would be atheists, and they wouldn't be coming to my Church."

Borya nodded in acknowledgement. But still, Geiger could have professed an anti-communist stance within the German community and that had caught the attention of the local Bolsheviks, whether they were German Marxists or Bolsheviks. With the conflict with the Soviet Union still festering on the borders of the Three Provinces, the city was still rampant with Soviet agents and their sympathizers despite the crackdown by the Special District Police. Maybe some among them had seen this as an opportunity to eliminate someone they considered a political adversary, and then sought the added bonus of putting the blame on the Japanese, whom nobody liked.

"Do you know of anybody who had a grudge or dislike for Geiger?" Borya tried.

Another tilt of the head. " ... No."

"Anyone he was particularly close to or friendly with in your church?"

This time, Bruhner shook his head for emphasis. "Not that I saw. He mostly kept to himself. Entering or leaving the Church, he might have a few words with me about the sermon or the weather, but never really engaged with me. He seemed to be a moody, solitary person. Maybe he was only close to his family—I heard they are still back in Germany. So sad. If there is anything

I can do to help? Maybe write his family? I would need their address . . ."

Borya thanked him and retrieved the pin from the desktop. In the office outside, the secretary looked up at him only briefly, without pausing in her assault on the typewriter, and he let himself out and back onto the sidewalk of Prospect Street. Well, one minor mystery solved—the identity of the pin, and one possible motive unearthed!

CHAPTER TWENTY-SEVEN

THE FOLLOWING MORNING, BORYA presented himself to the police cadet posted outside Liu's office and requested a meeting with the Superintendent. It had been only a day since they had last spoken and not the week's time as Liu had set for his reports, but Borya felt that the identity of the German party pin fit the exception of "significant" new information. Could he see the Superintendent briefly? The cadet entered Liu's office and quickly returned.

"Come back in an hour."

Borya returned in exactly an hour and was ushered into Liu's office. The Superintendent was seated behind his desk, his head bent over a thick sheaf of papers, every hair atop his head carefully in its place. "Sit down," he spoke to the top of the desk, and Borya sat. After a long minute Liu grunted, scribbled his name at the bottom of the top sheet of paper, and finally looked up. "What have you found?" The voice was curt, but not unfriendly.

Borya explained about his enquiries and findings regarding the political pin, recounting in detail his conversation with Reverend Bruhner. "It proves that Manfred Geiger belonged to an anti-communist German party. That could have made him a target of the Soviet agents operating in the city," he offered.

Liu frowned and stared at Borya for a minute before speaking. "Well, it implies that Herr Geiger at some time belonged to a German anti-communist political party. But I would have to agree with what the Lutheran minister said about the German community in Harbin not being large enough to support a lot of party activity here. And from how you and Inspector Chinn have described him, Geiger wasn't exactly social or the type to draw attention to himself. I doubt the Soviet Embassy here would have known his politics or even cared."

Here Liu paused, and this time permitted a thin smile. "I know you would like to be able to connect Geiger's murder to the Soviets; believe me, I would like it no less myself. But you can't let that stop you from exploring other theories. Besides, what would the Bolsheviks gain by shipping his body to the Japanese zone? They are showing no compunction about killing their enemies in broad daylight right here on the streets of Harbin, even making a point of it," and here Liu's tone darkened, but Borya felt it wasn't directed at him but rather at frustration over the continuing level of violence. "And we still don't know the source of Herr Geiger's unexplained income. That might not be the cause of his murder, but it certainly raises a lot of questions in my mind."

Borya suddenly flashed to another day, another time. He was riding in the train with Chinn westward toward Barim. "*A suspicious mind creates ghosts in the dark*," he repeated quietly, almost inaudibly, while staring into his hands.

Superintendent Liu froze and looked away quickly, elevating his face as if to keep tears from overflowing his eyes. "Yes... indeed," he said after a long pause, then in a voice as quiet as Borya's, "...good words to remember. Many good words to remember." And finally, he turned his face back to focus on Borya. "Keep digging. I think you are getting close. I believe there are just a few remaining pieces of the puzzle missing. Report back to me when you know more."

"Yes, Superintendent."

Back at Chinn's old desk, Borya drew a line in his notebook through his entry for the DVP pin. A thread that appeared to lead nowhere, but then nothing written in ink gets erased either.

The next morning, Borya returned to the squad room and Chinn's desk. Again, he returned the evidence to an orderly row across the top of the desk. This time, he picked up the envelope containing the small clumps of brown mud. He emptied them out onto his palm and examined them, but they still appeared unremarkable, and he doubted it would be possible to trace the composition of the mud to a specific locale. Next, he pulled out the package that contained Geiger's clothing and unwrapped it. He carefully went over the outside of the trousers and suit jacket, but although there were stains, there were no smears of mud that matched the brown of the mud balls. All the pockets had been cut open by the medical examiner's assistant as part of the autopsy, but there was also no residual mud in the suit jacket pockets where the professor had said they had been found. Finally, he did something he had seen his grandfather do a hundred times in his herbal shop—he held one of the mud balls up to his nose and sniffed. Instead of a musty smell of soil, there was a distinct organic odor, but one he did not recognize. He returned the mud balls to the envelope and put the envelope into his tunic pocket instead of returning it to the desk with the clothing and the other items. Maybe he would show them to his grandfather on his way home that afternoon.

That's when a fingernail tapped the top of the desk, commanding his attention. It was one of the senior Russian clerks, this one an elderly man with a pinched face and thinning hair, one of those who always looked disapprovingly at him whenever he entered the exalted squad room. "You are still working the Geiger case?" he asked.

"Yes," Borya replied. Why else would he still be there in the inner sanctum of the Harbin detective squad?

"Then there is a phone call for you."

The phone was on a table in the front of the squad room, its black bakelite receiver lying next to it.

"Hello?" he enquired.

"Yes, is this the detective in charge of the murder investigation of Manfred Geiger?" came a tinny male voice over the line in Russian. Russian but with some sort of other European accent.

"I am Melnikov, I am working on the case. Can I help you?" He didn't think he needed to volunteer that the caller was not talking to a detective.

"Yes, I hope so. My name is Erwin Shaver, and I am the attorney performing the probate on the estate of the unfortunate Manfred Geiger."

"Okay. Again, how can I help you?"

"Well, I wanted to know whether your investigation has further need to access Herr Geiger's house in Harbin and his dacha on Sun Island. His wife back in Germany would like me to sell those properties as soon as possible."

Borya stood in stunned silence. A dacha on Sun Island? Sun Island was across the Sungari from Harbin proper and contained the vacation homes of many of the Russian and Chinese elite of the city. He didn't remember seeing any evidence of a property there in any of the papers that had come from Geiger's house.

And a deed or bill of sale would certainly have been in Mandarin or both Mandarin and Russian, and he or Chinn would have spotted it immediately.

"Are you there, Officer Melnikov?"

"Yes, I'm still here. I wasn't aware of a dacha on Sun Island. How did you find out about it?"

"From a routine check through the property records at city hall. Does that mean I can't put it up for sale?" There was a slight tone of exasperation in the voice. Should I have checked the property records under Geiger's name at city hall myself? Borya thought. Chinn had not brought it up.

"You can proceed on the sale of the house in New Town, but I need to search the dacha on Sun Island before you can sell that property." Borya wrote down the address of the dacha, as well as Shaver's phone number and the address of his Pristan office in his notebook.

"And I have talked to the police in the New Town precinct, and they say that there were papers and valuables removed from that house. They said I should call here. Do you know anything about that?"

Borya explained about the papers that he and Chinn had removed from the house during their search, including the cash. "But I believe you already possess all the papers that we took from the house, and I'm sure the cash can be released to you upon proof of your power of attorney for the estate. We are still holding onto a small number of personal effects as part of our investigation, but nothing of significant value. But yes, it did appear that a number of small valuables were removed from the house prior to our search. We have not recovered any of those so far. And we are only able to identify a few of those missing collectibles from receipts of purchase among Geiger's papers, but should we do recover any of them, I will let you know immediately."

The attorney thanked him, his tone dry. Borya guessed he probably thought it just as likely that he or some other policeman had taken the missing valuables. He knew it happened often enough that many residents of the city immediately thought about all policemen that way, but nevertheless, it rankled him that this attorney might be thinking that way about he and Chinn. And didn't he just volunteer that they were holding a significant amount of cash found in Geiger's house? Why would he have brought that up if he just went around pocketing everything he came across? But then there wasn't much he could do about what others thought except just to continue to follow the straight and narrow path as his parents had taught him and Chinn had demonstrated.

Putting all that aside, he had one more thought. "And Mr. Shaver, were those the only two properties or major assets Herr Geiger owned?"

"The only ones here in the Northeast Provinces. He also owns the house in Germany where his wife and children reside. I was actually hired by an attorney back in Germany to handle those of his assets and debts that are here."

"Thank you, Herr Shaver. I will get back to you soon." Borya returned the receiver of the phone to its cradle. A whole new and unexpected thread!

CHAPTER TWENTY-EIGHT

SUN ISLAND LAY DIRECTLY across the Sungari River from Harbin. It was far enough from the city to provide an escape from the crowded bustle and noise for a day outing or a picnic, yet close enough to easily return to the city when business and obligations called. When Borya was just a boy, his father would rent a boat from one of the many rentals along Harbin's waterfront and row the family across for a summer's day of fun on Sun Island. They would picnic on the shore, and afterwards, Borya and his sisters would play on the sandbars or swim in the island's cove where the water was quieter than the strong current in the river's main channel. He could vividly remember the bounty of those picnics—the fried chicken, hard-boiled eggs, and fish cakes, and still associated those dishes with these earlier, happy outings. Harbin's well-to-do built dachas on the island so they could extend their leisure time. In the winter, when the ice was thick, they would even drive their motorcars there across the frozen river.

It was now late October, and there had been a few nights that dipped down to freezing, but it wasn't anywhere near cold enough yet for the river to freeze over. Most of the boat rentals were closed for the season, and it was too early for the sail-driven iceboats, but Borya was able to find one dealer who was more than happy to rent him a rowboat and a rower for five chiao, or half a yuan. The rower turned out to be an elderly Han Chinese man whose frail appearance made Borya wonder if he had the stamina to survive the trip across and back alive or wondered whether it would be better if he took a turn on the oars himself. However, once they started out, it was apparent the old man was wiry and stronger than he appeared and quickly began to pull their boat with long, powerful strokes, the muscles of his neck showing like thick cords. He aimed the boat upstream to account for the swift river current and yet still land at Sun Island directly across the river.

Borya was sitting on the rear bench of the boat with his back to the city, where he could look ahead to the far shore over the shoulders of this ancient mariner. As the sounds of the city faded away behind him, Harbin suddenly seemed remote, and Borya could recall that same feeling during his long-ago family excursions, pretending he was on an adventure to a far distant world, distant in both time and space. In the middle of the river, a breeze created small waves, and the little boat danced, but the rower perfectly maintained the boat's direction without once turning his head around to check his accuracy. Borya pulled his overcoat tighter around him to ward off the chill in the breeze that foretold of the much colder weather to come and then closed his eyes and inhaled the scent of the river, more muted from its summer odors by the cold air. Should he be enjoying himself this much when he was on an important mission? But he kept his eyes closed until he felt the bow of the boat touch the sand of the island's cove and opened them to see the elderly man staring at him with a blank expression.

"I have business here," Borya explained as he stood up and walked to the bow, stepping around the old man and over one oar. "Wait for me here, and I'll give you another five chiao to take me back." He managed to step onto the beach with getting only one shoe and his puttees wet. And then, as a way to thank the man for his service, he pulled the bow of the boat further up the sand so the slight current would not pull it back into the river's stronger current, sparing the old man of having to do the task himself.

Borya walked the path up to Sun Island's main street where grand two-storey clapboard and stucco homes, some as opulent as houses in New Town, faced down smaller one-storey dachas. There was little foot traffic, as this was the off-season for those that used Sun Island for a summer retreat. Those few passersby stole quick glances at this uniformed policeman who had invaded their idyll island retreat. He only walked a short way, less than three blocks, before he came to a one-storey house whose address matched that supplied by the estate attorney.

Geiger's dacha was a modest one-storey affair, but by no means the smallest one on the block. The front was painted white with stained wood shutters and a small covered porch with a wooden stairway leading up to it. A sunroom to the left of the porch was painted a light green with a separate slanted roof that looked like it was a newer addition. The main roof was covered in red tiles and surmounted by a brick chimney, and Borya could see a shimmering heat haze at the top of the chimney that told him someone was inside tending a fire to keep off the autumn chill. Someone was obviously living in a house that belonged to the deceased man. Another servant or caretaker that Geiger kept just here on Sun Island? But it had been many weeks since Geiger first disappeared, and how likely was it that a servant would continue on unpaid? It was certainly longer than the houseboy in New Town had stayed. Squatters?

Borya had stood there for a minute pondering this before stepping onto the stone pathway that led to the porch. As soon as he stepped onto the porch steps, he heard a door slam in the back of the house. He jumped off the porch and ran quickly around the house just in time to see the back of a man, short and with close-cropped hair, running quickly through a gate that led through the fence of the adjoining property behind. The man was quick enough that Borya presumed him young without actually seeing the man's face, and quick enough that Borya calculated he wasn't going to catch the man in a foot race through a neighborhood whose back alleys and shortcuts he didn't know, so instead he turned back to the house. The back door was closed but not locked and opened freely to Borya's hand. He was facing a hallway that led through the middle of the house, all the way to the front door. A figure appeared from one of the rooms that connected to the hallway, a pretty Chinese woman in a pink silk robe that was tied around her waist, maybe in her early or mid-twenties with long black hair that spilled over one shoulder, her feet bare. She had a startled look on her face at seeing him. "Who...who are you?" the woman asked in Mandarin.

"I am Officer Melnikov of the Special District Police. Who are you, and what are you doing in a house belonging to the estate of Manfred Geiger?"

"Oh, I am Wang Ju, I am...was Manfred's girlfriend. He left this house to me."

"And the man who just ran out through this door?"

"A friend. He has done nothing wrong, he is just afraid of policemen. All policemen. He saw you coming up the walk and...just took off," and she waved a slim hand in a small circle as if to insinuate the flight was an insignificant act and gave Borya a reassuring smile. A pretty smile. "Please come in, and shut the door. You are making the house chilly. I was just fixing tea for my friend and I and ... well, now he is gone." The silk robe clung close to her body as she led the way down the hallway.

"Your friend's name?" Borya asked, but thought he already knew.

"Oh, something Jian."

Borya followed her into the little kitchen, not ready to let her out of his sight and at the same time listening for sounds of anyone else in the house.

"Any more friends here, Miss Wang?" he asked.

"No, it's just you and me." Another smile. "Do you want sugar? I'm afraid I have no cream or milk."

"Sugar, lots."

She handed him his cup and led the way down the hall to the front parlor. Along the way, Borya looked into the other doorways to see two bedrooms, a small dining room, and a smaller study, occupied with furniture but no other persons. The parlor was like a smaller version of the same room in Geiger's Harbin house, even to identical red velvet sofa and chairs. Wang Ju sat on the sofa and curled her legs underneath her. Borya took the chair opposite, and they each put their teacups down on the small table in between them.

Borya took an exploratory sip of his tea. It was hot, but the liquid helped fill the void in his stomach. He had not eaten since that morning. "When was the last time you saw Herr Geiger?"

She tilted her head to one side like that would let the memory slide out. "It was at the end of July."

"And was that here in this house? Or in New Town?"

"It was here. I've only been to the house in New Town a couple times, but he said he would bring me over there before winter because it gets so cold in this drafty little house. He came over here every weekend except the weekend right before he was leaving on a business trip for his company. He said he would only be gone for a week and would bring me back a present. But then weeks passed, and I heard nothing. Then a friend told me he read an article in the Harbin newspaper that said he was…dead." She blotted her eyes with a sleeve of her robe, but Borya wasn't sure he had actually seen any tears.

"The same friend who just ran away?" She nodded wordlessly. "Did Geiger say where he was going on this trip? And what he would be doing there?"

"Just that he was going out towards Mongolia. To the cattle markets, I think. To buy animals for his company."

"Did he say he would be traveling with anyone?"

"No, he didn't say."

"Have you ever heard of a man named Song Nikan?"

"No, who is he?"

"An agent that worked for the same company as Geiger. He is missing." She shook her head. "Is there anything you remember that was different about Herr Geiger that weekend? Was he acting any different? Said anything strange?"

"We didn't talk a lot when he was here." Now a coy smile that Borya pretended not to notice.

"Did he have any visitors when he was here?"

"No, at least not when I was here."

"Any enemies?"

"I don't think so."

"Did he tell you how he made all his money?"

"He was a big, important manager at the English abattoir, the one in Fujiadian."

"Any other income?"

"Not that he told me. He never discussed money matters..."

They both sipped their tea then in silence. "Is that all of your questions?" she asked after a couple minutes' silence.

Borya put down his teacup and sat back in the chair. "Yes, for the moment. But I must tell you that I have seen Herr Geiger's will, and there isn't anything in it about leaving you this house or anything else to anyone except his wife and family back in Germany."

Alarm showed on her face. Genuine alarm? "But he promised me! He said when he left to go back to Germany in a few years, I could have this house. And money to live on!"

"Did you get tired of waiting? Did you and your friend kill Geiger and hide his body?"

The accusation hit her like a physical blow. "No, I wouldn't! Manfred was good to me!"

Borya thought the spontaneity and force of her reaction seemed genuine. "What about your friend?"

"No, he couldn't." Borya raised a questioning eyebrow. "He is very timid... he has this nervous condition. That's why he ran away when you came to the door."

Time to change the subject. "Did Geiger put leaving you this house or money in writing? Did he keep any of his papers here?"

"Yes... it is here!"

"Can you show me?"

More alarm crossed her face, but this time, her response was delayed. "I... I won't be able to find it right away, but if you come back in a couple days, I am sure I will find it."

I'm sure you will given enough time, Borya thought to himself. "I can help you look, perhaps in his study?"

Alarm again. "I don't think I can go through that right now. This has all been very upsetting. You have brought back all my sadness of losing Manfred." She brushed her hair back off her shoulder in a movement that was meant to look casual, but it laid open her robe to display a well-rounded pale breast.

Borya's face turned beet red. She looked down at her exposed breast as if suddenly aware of her exposure but made no move to cover herself. "But, you know, I no longer have a boyfriend. And you are much younger than Manfred. Do you need a girlfriend?"

Borya could feel the flush on his face and couldn't help the stirrings that were growing in his groin. But then, alarms started going off in his head. He remembered Geiger lying on the metal table of the pathology clinic in that hospital basement, the pathologist pointing out the traces of blisters on the desiccated skin of the groin. His stirrings ceased immediately.

"No thanks, I don't need a girlfriend," he declared and abruptly stood up. Disappointment flashed across her face, and she pulled her robe closed again. "But I will let the attorney in Pristan, who is managing Herr Geiger's estate, know you are here in the house and that you have a challenge to his will. Perhaps he needs a girlfriend." He turned toward the front door as if ready to leave, but instead turned and walked back down the hallway and into the small study that he had passed on his way through the house before. He could hear Ju's bare feet on the floor behind him, following closely.

On a wooden desk in the middle of the small room sat a pine crate. It was filled with objects wrapped loosely in brown paper. He unwrapped one and found a small bronze statue and heard Ju gasp. Another held a porcelain figurine. He rewrapped them and put them back in the crate. Ju was standing in the doorway, a hand frozen to her mouth. Borya hefted the box. It was heavy, and he didn't relish lugging it all the way back to police headquarters in New Town.

"These pieces do not belong to you. They came from Geiger's house in New Town, and they belong to his estate. You or your friend... *Lao Cheng*... need to take them to the estate attorney within two days. If they are not there in two days' time, I will have you both arrested. Do you understand?"

At the mention of the name of Geiger's man-servant in Harbin, Ju showed surprise, but offered no denial. He had guessed correctly. This time, the tears in Ju's eyes were real. "Yes, we will. I promise."

Borya scribbled the attorney's name and his Pristan address on a fresh page of his notebook and handed the page to her. "Also tell the attorney you and Lao are owed back wages from the estate. Bring any paperwork you have to support your cases. And now I am going to search the house for any clues that relate to Herr Geiger's murder."

Ju returned to the parlor while Borya searched the rest of the study. There were only a few papers in the desk, mostly having to do with the purchase of the dacha about a year ago and miscellaneous household bills. Nothing that related to his work, his substantial income, or any friends or business associates. A search of the other rooms turned up even less. Obviously, the dacha was just a place to stash his mistress out of sight from his neighbors and coworkers in Harbin. And maybe friends, not that he seemed to have any of those. Finally, he returned to the parlor where Ju sat as before on the sofa.

"Thank you for your cooperation, Miss Wang," he announced in a flat voice. Her reply was a wan smile. He let himself out the front door and retraced his steps to the cove, where his rowboat and rower waited. The old man lay sleeping across the middle bench of the boat but awakened when Borya approached. Borya pushed the boat out into the cove and hopped into the bow and made his way to the stern before the rower could even lay his oars into the oarlocks. But the old man sprang quickly into action, and in seconds, they were flying out of the cove and out into the Sungari's current.

While the trip across to Sun Island was like traveling into the past, the return to Harbin was a catapult back to the present. As the city loomed larger, Borya felt like years and responsibilities were piling back onto his shoulders with each stroke of the oars. He looked back just once at Sun Island, disappearing into the distance and wondered if Wang Ju and Lao Cheng really would show up in Harbin with the art pieces or would they make a run for it with what were probably the only portable things of value in their possession. If they showed up in Pristan with their loot in two days' time, then more the better, he thought. If they didn't show up, he would notify the estate attorney and Special District's robbery division, but by then the pair would have two days' head start. Was that right? No. But a great deal of wealth from Geiger's assets and properties was already leaving the Northeast to go to his widow and family in Germany. Was that fair? No doubt his family would be well enough off without a handful of collectibles.

The afternoon sun cast long shadows, but his wristwatch, his father's old watch, told he still might have time to drop by his grandfather's shop before he closed.

CHAPTER TWENTY-NINE

BORYA PUSHED OPEN THE front door of his grandfather's herbal medicine shop, triggering the tinkle of the bell above the door frame. The heady wave of smells and scents that greeted him at the threshold always triggered a flood of memories of childhood days spent here, or was it the sound of the bell itself like Pavlov's dogs? Either way, his nose could pick out the fresh scent of peppermint, pungent cinnamon, and the earthiness of licorice. There had been days when his mother was ill or just busy and she would ask her father to babysit him. His grandfather never refused, setting him on a stool behind the counter to watch the ebb and flow of customers and sales. When there were no customers, he would mercilessly pursue his grandfather's cat around the shop until it would finally tolerate his hugs and rough petting. And as he got older, there were the evening sessions downstairs in the seclusion of the basement where the old man taught him the discipline and techniques of Taekkyeon. For years he did not understand his grandfather's insistence on keeping their training secret, until his mother explained to him that the Japanese occupiers of Korea had outlawed all the native martial arts, and her father had barely escaped imprisonment for being one of its followers. It had been another of the many reasons his grandfather had moved his trade and Borya's mother from Korea to the frontier lands of Manchuria. It was not illegal here, but old habits and cautions die hard.

Dark wooden cabinets lined the side walls of the shop, each containing scores of small, square wooden drawers that together resembled a huge honeycomb. Every drawer was decorated in faded yellow Korean characters listing its unique contents. Borya knew many of the common names and their applications, but many also remained mysterious, their purpose locked within the mind of the old man. The tops of the cabinets were lined with glass jars filled with colorful liquids or powders. The back wall of the front room was taken up almost entirely by a long glass counter, behind which a curtained doorway led to the back room. Altogether, the front of the shop was no more than four meters across and as many deep but the room in back was larger, containing storage and the tools for preparing the tonics and remedies of his grandfather's trade—mortars and pestles, copper tankards, drying racks, as well as the stairway that led down to the basement and another up to the living quarters on the second floor.

The living quarters were generous for that neighborhood, but his grandfather also shared them with his widowed younger sister and her daughter, who had fled Korea in poverty after her husband's death from consumption barely five years ago. Borya's great-aunt, Eui, was many years younger than his grandfather; he did not know how many. The daughter, Ae-Cha, his first cousin once removed, was closer to his own age than to his mother, and had never married, owing to a lack of dowry. He found his great-aunt to be a bit stiff and aloof, but Ae-Chai always greeted him warmly whenever they met, which was usually when she was helping out in the shop, but apparently not this afternoon or else she was out making deliveries.

Grandfather Jung stood behind the glass counter across from a northern Chinese man in his mid-thirties dressed in coarse hemp trousers and shirt and straw sandals. Borya figured him for a ginseng hunter as several of the whitish lumpy roots were laid out for inspection on a soiled cloth atop the glass counter, and he wasn't dressed well enough to be a trader or middleman. Grandfather was turning the roots over and inspecting each one carefully but glanced up briefly enough to smile at Borya with his eyes. The ginseng trader also turned to see who had entered the shop and gave a small start at Borya's black uniform, but Borya turned to peruse the jars and boxes of remedies in the front window as if he was waiting his turn as just another customer. The ginseng hunter turned back to the counter, but kept Borya in his peripheral vision. After several minutes of haggling back and forth in Mandarin, Grandfather brought his metal cashbox from below the counter and counted out paper money. The ginseng hunter was offered rubles or yuan and chose the latter, another clue he was not a middleman that belonged to the city. The man left the shop, taking a wide circuit around Borya on his way to the front door, eliciting an amused smile from Borya that he shared with his grandfather.

The two now alone in the shop, his grandfather allowed himself a broad smile and switched back to Korean. "Ah, Borya, you are back on duty! Have you had any more headaches or dizziness?"

Borya smiled and waved his hand to deflect the second question. "No, Grandfather, I am fine. Mostly thanks to you. Yes, I have returned to duty. I have not had a headache for a couple days now, but if they come back, I will certainly come to you for help." He regretted lying about the absence of his headaches, so he quickly moved to change the subject, "Actually I came to you about these . . ." and he pulled the small envelope from the chest pocket of his uniform tunic and deposited the two brown lumps from within it onto the glass counter.

His grandfather's eyebrows raised in twin surprise. He rolled each brown ball between his fingers, and then held each up to his nose and smelled them. Then he put them both on the brass scales that sat atop the counter and added small weights until an even balance determined their weight. Then, still wordlessly, he opened the metal cashbox that still sat on the counter and began counting out large ruble notes in an amount that exceeded what Borya was paid for a whole month's wages.

"No, no, Grandfather!" Borya exclaimed and added a nervous laugh. "I just wanted to know what they are. They're part of an investigation."

The older man stopped, chuckled softly, and returned the money to the cashbox. Then he scooped the brown lumps back into the paper envelope and handed it back to Borya. "They are niu-huang... bezoars," and when that elicited a blank response from his grandson, "... they are gallstones from cattle or oxen. Hard to come by, very expensive medicine. Dried and ground up into powder, they work on the meridians of the heart and liver. It treats heart attack, stroke, fevers, diseases of the mouth... a very powerful medicine."

"Where would you get them?"

"Most of the ones you find around here come from the abattoirs of Harbin. They collect them and sell them in bulk to a single supplier who has a contract for all the animal parts that are used in medicine. I get mine from such a supplier... at a hefty mark up," which drew a wry smile, "but occasionally, a trader or butcher from the countryside will bring in a few to sell, and I can bargain. If you don't end up needing them for evidence, I will give you a fair price for them. Better you get the money than those cut-throat merchants get top price in the south," meaning Korea or China proper.

"Thank you, Grandfather. You have helped me very much!"

Abattoirs indeed! Borya's mind whirled as he left his grandfather's shop. Here was a commodity that involved more than enough money to generate greed. He had to smile to himself, it could be that greed was the motive after all as Chinn had prophesied. Involvement in a black market for expensive animal parts used for medicine could be the explanation for Geiger's unexplained wealth. He would have been ideally placed to exploit it as the supervisor of his abattoir's cattle operations. If so, who else was involved, and why had Geiger been killed? Had he finagled the business trip to Hailar to find new buyers, and the bezoars in his pocket were samples? Or were they just two of many that were overlooked in a double-cross or a simple armed robbery? Either way, this could be the missing thread he and Chinn had been looking for all this time. He lined out "mudballs" under the list of personal effects in his notebook and replaced it with "bezoars" and underlined the word.

Wasn't this just the kind of breakthrough that Superintendent Liu wanted brought to his attention? But he was still feeling the sting of disappointment from when Liu had lectured him for jumping to conclusions over the DVP pin. He had first to prove to Liu that he could act like a real detective, that he had learned from Chinn's lessons. Better this time he explore this new thread further before bringing it up. But how? If he marched straight into the British Chicken and Duck Company and demanded they check for missing bezoars, it might alert anyone else involved in the trafficking… and murder. Then he recalled Chinn's method of questioning the lower rungs, like he had with Song's Harbin servants and the beggar chief in Fujiadian. And he thought he knew where to start.

CHAPTER THIRTY

BORYA WAITED WHERE THE road that led from the gate of the British Chicken and Duck Company met Great New Street and the streetcar line. He wore everyday street clothes instead of his uniform and a quilted cotton jacket to shield against the brisk October wind. Although out of uniform, he carried his police revolver in a pocket of his jacket along with his police identity card to comply with the directive that officers be armed at all hours, even when off-duty. The directive was still in force despite a fall-off in sabotage and terrorism in the city following the abortive attack on the Sungari Bridge. He stood nearby the handful of food vendors who were hoping to find customers from among the day shift leaving the abattoir and tried to blend in, feigning interest in each tasty offering but declining them all.

Finally, the shrill whistle of the abattoir split the early evening sky. Only minutes later, the first workers appeared, a mob of shop laborers in their rough clothes sprinkled with the dark suits of the office workers. After a couple minutes, Borya spotted his former schoolmate Boris Mishchenko, bypassing the food vendors and headed toward the streetcar stop, and he walked briskly to intercept him.

"Boris Gregorovich! How are you?"

Boris blinked in surprise, then smiled. "Borya Sergeevich! What are you doing here?"

"Waiting for you. I need to ask you a favor. Do you still live in Ostroumoff Suburb?" Boris nodded, his face reflecting both amusement and confusion. "Good, then Pristan is on your way. Let me buy you tea and sweets at a tearoom I know there."

"Certainly."

The first streetcar had already left, completely full. They waited for the next one and paid their coins. Borya could have flashed his police identity card in lieu of payment, but he did not want to reveal his background to any of Boris' coworkers who might have boarded the electric car. They got off at Kataiskaya Street, and Borya led the way to his aunt's tearoom and then directly to his own reserved table by the window, causing his companion to raise an eyebrow. He did not see his aunt, but at this hour, she might have gone home for the day. The waiter came over immediately, and Borya ordered tea and sweet rolls for them both. "On me!" he insisted.

The tea and pastries came immediately, and Boris raised his eyebrow again at the speedy service. "You have your own reserved table here? Have they promoted you, Borya Sergeevich?"

Borya grinned sheepishly. "No, I wish. This is my aunt's tearoom, and she keeps this table for me." They took turns loading their tea with sugar.

"So what is this favor can I do for you, Borya Sergeevich?" Boris asked after taking an exploratory sip of his tea.

Borya steepled his hands and looked directly into his schoolmate's eyes. "I have been assigned back on the investigation of the death of Manfred Geiger. I have recently learned that when Geiger was killed, he had two bezoars on his person—do you know what those are?"

This time, both of Boris' eyebrows climbed his forehead. "Yes. I don't deal with them directly in my position as a clerk, but occasionally I see the accounts of their numbers and sale as a sideline to our overall sales. It's a hit-or-miss kind of thing, like finding a pearl in an oyster, but altogether a substantial sum of money."

"Do you know any reason why Geiger would be carrying some of them on his person?"

Boris leaned back in his chair and momentarily closed his eyes before reopening them and answering. "No, not really. They are collected from the workers in the cattle barn on a daily basis. The men are recorded a bonus if they find one to discourage just pocketing them and sneaking them out. Then they are kept locked up in the cattle barn until they are sold monthly or quarterly, I don't remember which, to a middleman along with any other animal parts that have medicinal value."

"Always to the same middleman?"

"No, not necessarily. The company takes bids from all the suppliers on an annual basis and rewards the contract to the one who will pay the highest rates. But whoever has the contract for that year is supposed to get all of them."

Borya took a sip of his own tea and nodded. "Could Geiger have been carrying bezoars on him as samples for discussions with other middlemen for the next contract?"

Boris' answer was swift and accompanied with a shake of his head. "No, the contract is not up until the end of the year. And anyway, Geiger is not the one who negotiates that contract; the buyers do that."

Borya found his companion's eyes again. "Could Geiger have set up sales of his own out of the stockpile in the cattle barn?"

Boris stared back as if Borya had just proclaimed some religious blasphemy. "A daily count is made and kept on file in the offices in the cattle barn ... I suppose Geiger could have altered the files, but it would have been hard to keep any large changes hidden forever from his assistant or the foreman."

"What if not all the bezoars made it into the stockpile and the daily count ..."

"Yes, I guess that's possible. But then Geiger would have to have some kind of arrangement with the foreman to siphon off a portion of the bezoars up front because I believe it's the foreman who collects them and takes the tally to the office upstairs. Otherwise, the foreman would notice something funny if there was a big difference between what he has turned in versus the final count at the time of sale to the middleman. So is this the favor ... telling you how it all works?"

Borya smiled. A smile of two former schoolmates. "Actually, what I was hoping is if you could check out the records of bezoar sales for a few years prior to when Geiger came to the company, five years ago, and up until now. I want to see if there was a noticeable decline in the number of bezoars sold after he joined the company or when he became head of the cattle operations. I would go directly to your director, but I don't want to tip off anyone else who might be involved by asking officially. If it does show up anything suspicious, I can always ask for the information later officially. You would be doing me and the police force a great service."

Boris blew out a long breath. "Wow! Well, yeah ... I suppose the director did tell me before to help in the investigation, so I guess it's okay. The number of cattle slaughters is not the same each month, so what you really want is a history of the bezoars recorded compared to the overall cattle numbers ... a percentage.

And then the percentage averaged over the year because, like I said, finding bezoars is a hit-or-miss prospect. It shouldn't be that hard to check out."

Now Borya put on a serious face. "Be careful as you go about it. Someone murdered Geiger, and it could possibly be over some backdoor sales of bezoars. And the local agent he was going to travel with is still missing. Don't let anyone else know what you're doing. You can call me on the telephone at the detective squad at police headquarters with whatever you find, but don't call from your workplace."

Boris' eyes grew wide, but he nodded his head in sober acknowledgement. Borya wrote out the number of one of the squad room telephones from memory on a page of his notebook and tore it out and handed it to Boris. Silent now, they finished their tea and pastries, and Borya left coins enough to cover it and a tip, although he knew his aunt would have refused his payment. He would skip lunch tomorrow.

They parted at the door of the tearoom, Boris to return to the nearby streetcar stop and Borya to head toward home in District 8. "Good night, Boris Gregorovich," he called after his schoolmate through the chilly night air. "And take care!"

CHAPTER THIRTY-ONE

JUST BEFORE DAWN, BORYA lay in bed, suspended in that narrow world between dreams and waking. He could feel the pressure of the pillow under his neck and the lumps in the mattress beneath his back like he was already awake, but he could not move his head or limbs like he was paralyzed. And although it felt like his eyes were wide open, it was not the cracked ceiling of his little room that he was seeing, instead he was looking up at the tops of tall pines coming together to form a shadowy canopy backlit by a grey sky, like the glow that comes just before dawn. In the trees, he could see the minute detail of their branches and needles that was unlike the fuzzy swirl that colored the backdrop of his typical dreams. He could even hear the clear, crisp calls of an unseen bird.

Then a face appeared above him, looking down on him and blocking out the ring of trees. It was a girl, somewhere between child and woman, with the features of the steppe people, Mongol or Manchu. It was a singularly pretty face with a generous mouth with an upper lip that protruded and curled up at the corners into her cheeks and formed a smile of petulant amusement. Large, dark eyes sparkled but were full of knowing and too serious for such a young face. As she was bent over him, he could only see her upper half below her face, which was clothed in a white dress or blouse covered in ribbons of green, yellow, and red. The girl/woman bent down closer to him, and her long black hair spilled down, framing her face and almost brushing his own. He knew had never seen this face before, and he was sure he would have remembered it, but at the same time there was something hauntingly familiar about it. From where? It was tantalizingly out of reach, in the way dreams spin your thoughts away from your control.

"Borya," the girl spoke, saying his name slowly, like she was experimenting with the sound of it. "I find you interesting. You are not like anyone I've met from outside the Reservoir. I sense you have the breathing skills, but you haven't been trained by a shaman." She spoke in Mandarin but with a steppe accent. Most of his dreams that he could remember were in his native Russian or Korean. "I have been thinking about you, but then you disappeared for so many days. Not here... but not gone. So I reached out to wake you."

Borya struggled to speak. He wanted to ask how she knew his name, had they met, and most of all, who was she? But his tongue was as frozen as his limbs.

"Now I am reaching out again, this time to warn you. You are coming close to the end of your search, but that brings with it new dangers. Be careful... I cannot always help you." Her smile turned wistful, and she reached down and kissed his forehead, her hair tickling his face.

He was wrenched suddenly awake. Her touch, her face, the forest all disappeared behind the cracked pattern of his bedroom ceiling and the dangling electric bulb, as if those parts of his world had crashed down over him from out of that grey sky. Her voice and the call of birds were replaced by the street sounds outside that carried through the thin glass of his bedroom window. He tried to pull the dream back before it melted away, but a sudden flood of adrenalin pulled him further awake.

It had felt so real for a dream. But usually, the visitors in his dreams were people he actually knew or had met before. And why would his subconscious have dredged up his Danjeon breathing exercises apart from all his grandfather's other spiritual and physical training? It wasn't something he thought about often; it was just another aspect of his upbringing and a part of who he was. Danjeon allowed him to tap into his inner strength and life force, but was the dream trying to tell him it was more than that? And what dangers was she talking about? That had to have been brought up by his subconscious from the stress of the investigation. Or maybe the beautiful girl was just a subconscious product of his youthful hormones visiting him during the night.

He was wide awake now, and with no chance of getting back to sleep, he rose early and prepared for the coming day. He hoped this would be the day Boris Mischenko telephoned him.

CHAPTER THIRTY-TWO

BORYA GOT TO THE squad room an hour earlier than usual. He remembered that the two-day deadline Borya had imposed on Wang Ju and Lao Cheng to return Geiger's collectibles had elapsed. He was curious as to whether the pair had surrendered the stolen items to the estate lawyer and had petitioned him for back wages, or had they made a run for it with the stolen goods or already pawned them. He looked up the phone number of Erwin Shaver from his notebook and rang it from one of the detective squad's telephones. Herr Shaver answered the phone on the third ring without any connection through a secretary or switchboard that would have indicated he belonged to one of the larger Harbin law firms. Yes, he would be in the office all morning. He had an hour's appointment at ten o'clock but was free the rest of the day after that.

It was a beautiful fall day in Harbin, sunny except for a few wispy high clouds, and everything seemed in sharp detail in the crisp air. The trees that bordered Prospect blazed with autumnal colors or had shed their leaves altogether. Borya headed down to Pristan on foot, disdaining the crowded streetcar. He paused on a footbridge that passed over the rail lines just as a westbound train approached. The immense black locomotive passed slowly beneath him, and he could feel the whole bridge and the very air vibrate from the proximity to the behemoth, and for an instant, he was enveloped in a damp cloud of steam. There was something exhilarating about being that close to an imposing technological marvel that never went away. His father's marvels.

He found the address on a quiet side street and the suite number of Shaver's office from a readerboard on the stairs that led up over a dry goods store. "Erwin Shaver, Attorney at Law" was stenciled on the glass panel of the suite's door in Russian, Mandarin, and German. He opened the door into a tiny reception room that held a desk and a small sofa, but no one was at the desk. An open door led to an adjoining office, from where a voice hailed him in halting Russian.

"Come in, come in! I'm afraid my secretary is on sick leave."

The office beyond was only slightly bigger, holding another desk, a guest chair, filing cabinets, and a bookcase crammed with leather-bound law books. The voice belonged to a thin, pale man of about thirty in a dark suit, with a high forehead, and a broad mustache, whose ends pointed dramatically upward. His head was pitched forward from the plane of his body on a long neck, giving the impression of a man both perpetually eager and attentive.

On seeing Borya, he looked momentarily surprised, a look one Borya was all too familiar with, but he credited the man with a quick recovery. "You must be Officer Melnikov," he said, rising from his chair and extending his hand to shake Borya's. Borya could see the attorney's eyes move inexorably to the scar on his forehead.

"And you must be Erwin Shaver, the estate lawyer for Herr Geiger," Borya countered, and they both sat down.

"Well, yes, I'm handling the Asian interests of Geiger's estate for the primary estate attorney back in Germany," he corrected, a clarification befitting a lawyer. "I'm actually glad you came; I was just about to call you. I received an unusual visit this morning from two former domestic employees of Herr Geiger."

"Indeed."

"But I assume this comes as no surprise to you because they explained they had been counseled by you to come see me to settle the claims they make for back wages during the time Herr Geiger was missing. They also brought some collectible items that had come from his house in Harbin that they say they had been holding for … 'safe keeping,'" and he pointed to a crate on the floor beside his desk. "I assume I have you to thank for their return?" Borya only smiled. It was the same pine crate Borya had seen in the dacha on Sun Island, but it didn't look quite as full as the last time he had seen it. He did not remark on this observation, as he couldn't be sure.

"The young lady also claimed that Herr Geiger, solely out of the goodness of his heart, had promised to leave the Sun Island dacha to her," Shaver deadpanned. "She even asked whether I had seen that in his latest will or any subsequent addendum to his will. I found no mention of any such a promise in Geiger's legal papers filed with the city or were sent over from your police department. She was quite distressed. Did you happen to find any such legal papers when you were at the dacha?"

"No, sorry to say I did not. Only papers on the original purchase of the dacha, which was solely in Geiger's name. And sundry bills."

Shaver pursed his lips. "Too bad for her sake, but I must fulfill Herr Geiger's wishes as they are outlined in his last will. She said she will be vacating the dacha by today. Is it okay for me to go ahead and prepare the dacha and its contents for sale? It is my last piece of business before closing out his affairs here in the Northeast... and these collectibles," he declared, tapping the crate with the toe of a shiny black leather shoe.

Borya thought for a minute. Could Geiger have squirreled away some bezoars in his lovenest on Sun Island? He hadn't made the most thorough search of the dacha when he was there, and at the time he hadn't been looking for mysterious brown lumps. After all, it's easier to spot something when your eye is specifically looking for it. "Just give me just another few days to get back over there and make a last sweep for evidence."

Shaver raised an eyebrow. "So, the investigation is still ongoing? When I called over to your detective department to get Geiger's papers released, I was told no one was currently working the case..."

"No one was working it while the current emergency was going on. I have only just been assigned back on the case. The senior inspector who had been in charge was . . ." Borya felt a lump rise in his throat and had to cough to clear it, "... was killed out near the western border. But I believe we are making progress on the case." Had he said "we"? Well, there was also Superintendent Liu....

Shaver looked embarrassed and nodded his head rapidly. "Of course, of course! Just let me know when you are done at the dacha. And please, let me know when the case is solved... or closed."

"It will be solved," Borya replied with conviction.

Borya returned to the detective squad room and stayed there all through the afternoon, not wanting to be away in case Boris called. He knew he was being impatient—it had only been the evening before when he had approached his former schoolmate with his request. This didn't allow his friend much time to look up the relevant records without arousing suspicion. It might be days before Boris had the opportunity to research them safely alone, but Borya could still be hopeful. This seemed the brightest path in the investigation thus far, so he stayed sitting at Chinn's old desk drinking tea and reading recent police reports.

All through the afternoon telephones rang, and each time Borya's head shot up, but each time the calls had been for someone else. Finally, in the waning hours of daylight, when all the detectives were gone and Borya and only one clerk remained, a telephone rang and this time the clerk motioned him over.

"Officer Melnikov," he answered, trying to keep his voice steady.

"Yes, Borya Sergeevich. It's me, Boris Gregorovich."

"Yes?"

"I was able to look up the records we talked about. It took me until just now because I had to wait until I was alone in the file room and had the time to copy them down. And then I had to find a telephone where I could not be overheard."

"Of course, I understand." Borya answered sympathetically, but really wanted to reach through the telephone and pull the words out from Boris' mouth.

"And you were right, the numbers look odd. I can't really talk about it over the telephone. I can go over the figures with you and explain them, but it has to be where no one can see us together. I could maybe lose my job, and you said I could be in danger."

"Of course, of course!"

"Are you familiar with the railroad workshops next to Ostroumoff Suburb where I live?"

"Yes, quite familiar." Borya didn't bother to explain that he had spent many nights patrolling that very area with the Railway Guards.

"Can you come to Workshop Number 4 at midnight?"

"Yes." He even knew exactly which workshop Number 4 was. "But how will you get into the train yard? It's guarded day and night."

"You forget, I grew up in Ostroumoff. Us kids knew a dozen ways to get into the train yard that are unguarded. No one will see us there. Come alone and make sure you're not followed. I don't think anybody saw me looking in the files, but I think I was getting some funny looks from a couple of my coworkers. Maybe I'm just being paranoid, but I'm not used to this cloak and dagger stuff… I'm not a policeman like you."

"Of course. Midnight, Workshop Number 4. I'll be there."

"Good, I'll see you then, Borya Sergeevich. I hope this helps."

"Yes, thank you, Boris Gregorovich. Thank you very much!"

Borya all but dropped the receiver onto its cradle. The numbers looked odd! He had tugged on this thread, and he could feel the seam unraveling. He thought about checking to see if Superintendent Liu was still in his office and giving him a quick update, but no, this time he would get solid evidence first and let Liu see it with his own eyes.

CHAPTER THIRTY-THREE

B ORYA SET OUT FROM the family apartment on foot an hour before midnight—no streetcars ran this late. He wore his uniform and carried his police identity card just in case he was stopped by any of the night patrols after curfew, as well as an electric torch and his service revolver, as current rules still dictated. Electric streetlights lit the way through District 8 and Pristan; no blackout here as they were way beyond the range of Soviet bombers. Keeping to the promise he had made to Boris, he checked carefully to make sure he wasn't being followed, stopping more than once around a street corner to see if he could spot anyone, and once he even circled the block. There was no one going in his direction, indeed there were very few pedestrians or vehicles at all on the streets.

Boris was right about there being other ways into the yard. Borya had seen some of them himself during his previous night patrols with the Railway Guards, nevertheless Borya presented himself at the main gate to the rail yard. There he showed his identity card to two sleepy guardsmen. Curious about his business in the rail yard at that hour, he explained he was just checking up on the ongoing police sweeps. Yes, it was a lie, but a lot simpler story than the longer one of meeting an informant and explaining why it was taking place in the railyard.

"Good luck," one of the guards told him after scanning Borya's identity card under an electric torch. "It's quiet in there tonight. The only shifts on tonight are in Workshops One and Two."

Borya easily found his way to Workshop Number Four. At the end of the workshop were huge doors that allowed railcars to be pushed into the building when open, but at midnight they were now shut. Next to these huge doors was a smaller door that was illuminated by an overhead electric light next to the police and fire signal lights that were installed on all the major yard buildings. He tried the knob and found it unlocked. He entered and quietly closed the door behind him. Inside, just a couple of overhead bulbs lit the near end of the cavernous interior, but the rest of the building was bathed in shadows. This workshop was dedicated to repairing freight cars and two of the big boxcars filled the middle of the structure and were flanked by machine tools and undercarriages in various states of assembly or disassembly.

Borya checked his wristwatch, he was five minutes early. Nevertheless, he called out Boris' name in a loud whisper. There was no answer, but he thought he heard a shuffling noise coming from the far dark end of the building.

"Boris?" he called out again, this time in a low voice. No response. Probably rats, he had seen plenty of them both outside and inside the buildings during night patrols. Nevertheless, he turned on his electric torch and tried to shine it past the second boxcar, but its bulk only allowed the beam of light to play over the tools and machinery on one side to the far end and blocked it from the other side. A second scuffing sound came from deep in the shadows, and Borya inched his way forward beside the boxcars, hoping that if they were rats, his presence would chase them out whatever way they had come in.

He made it past the second and last boxcar and was shining his torch at the back doors of the workshop, when a voice suddenly called out to him from within the shadows of a small crane. "Stop right there. Drop the torch." Borya's heart leapt into his throat. It was not Boris' voice, but it was one that sounded familiar. Someone for whom Russian was not their native language. He dropped the electric torch to the concrete floor, and the sound reverberated through the inside of the building, and its beam of light cut out.

A man stepped out of the shadows into the dim light shining past the boxcars, some of it reflecting off a bare pink scalp. It was Entworp, Geiger's English assistant at the cattle barn. He held a small automatic pistol in his right hand pointed at Borya's chest.

"Please be so kind as to sit on the floor facing me with your hands on top of your head," Entworp ordered in accented Russian, his voice calm and almost amused.

Borya complied slowly, watching for any lapse of attention or overconfidence by the Englishman, knowing that once he was down in a sitting position on the floor, he would be at an even greater disadvantage, but the barrel of the pistol stayed aimed on his chest the whole way down.

"You were expecting your friend Mishchenko?... Sorry to disappoint you," Entworp said in a cavalier tone.

"Did you kill him?"

Entworp laughed but kept the pistol trained steadily at Borya's heart, staying within four paces. Borya judged the distance for some kind of response, but the other man was out of reach for any kind of lunging martial arts attack but certainly close enough that it would be hard for Entworp to miss with the pistol. His mind was racing fast; he knew a hundred ways to subdue a man with his bare hands, but none of them, including drawing his own gun or leaping aside, were faster than it would take Entworp to simply pull the trigger. Bereft of a solution within the scope of his Taekkyeon skills, he felt suddenly naked and exposed. He wished his grandfather was there right now. He had a flashback to his younger days in his grandfather's basement. Was this what they meant by your life flashing before your eyes at the end? He was a teenager then and feeling cocky with his increasing skills. "No man, no matter how skilled, is invincible," his grandfather warned him. "But remember, a man who has an ally is twice as capable."

"Aren't you my ally, Grandfather?"

"I can't always be there with you, Borya."

And now he was alone.

"Did you kill Mishchenko?" Borya asked again.

"No, of course not. After you tipped him to the whole bezoar scheme, he figured out it had to be me running the operation after Geiger, since the bezoar counts were still low, and I'm now in charge of the cattle barn. So he came to me with a proposal: that I could take his place at this little meeting for a price. Apparently, he is getting married soon and needs the money. And it was actually a fairly reasonable price," he stated matter-of-factly.

Greed. Again. Borya's pain at his supposed friend's betrayal must have showed on his face because Entworp laughed again.

"And you killed Geiger? Was he your partner, and you got tired of sharing?"

"Sorry, wrong again. He was the one who didn't like sharing. I learned that he and the foreman were skimming a big share of the bezoars from the counts and selling them outside the company for a huge profit. They had gotten greedy and the numbers missing had started to become obvious. When I made a... friendly offer to become another partner, he was most annoyed. Said I could have an accident down on the factory floor. And this, while he and the Chink foreman were making money hand over fist. Quite selfish! He even concocted that whole cattle buying trip to Hailar so he could drum up new buyers outside Harbin. And for the record, I didn't kill him—you wouldn't believe how cheap it is to hire a killer in Fujiadian. He was an odious man that nobody missed. But I do have to say, it would have been much easier for me if you hadn't returned from Barim. But I was pleased to learn that at least my wild goose chase, or should I say scavenger hunt, had you and that fat Chink detective fooled? But unfortunately, your little interference now didn't give me enough time to hire another killer..."

"And the agent, Song Nikan?" Borya interjected, hoping that the longer he could keep the smug Englishman talking, the more time he had to think... to think of what?

"Couldn't have him wandering around Harbin saying that Geiger didn't show up to catch the train... so just another Chink in the Sungari River. Hardly noticeable in these troubled times..."

"B-but why ship Geiger's body to Changchun? Why not just throw his body in the river too?"

"Because the body of a dead white man always draws more attention. And I wanted to keep all eyes focused away from Harbin... but enough prattle. I didn't come here in order to satisfy your curiosity..."

Borya saw Entworp take a step closer and entered the shadow cast by the crane. Now he could only see one side of the man's face, and the arm holding the pistol that was aimed straight at his heart, those the only parts of him still half-lit by the electric light glowing from the far end of the shed. Hopelessness was replaced by another emotion. Not fear, not sadness. Anger. Here he had the final answers to the investigation, but they would die with him. Justice would be thwarted. Chinn's death will have been in vain. Would his notebook be found on his body? For that matter, would his body even be found at all? And would Entworp take his notebook with him? Were there even enough clues written there that could lead anyone to Entworp or Boris? He tried to remember, but his mind wouldn't focus.

Borya tensed as if bunching his muscles could somehow slow the bullet when it hit his flesh. Then the shed resounded with the echo of the shot ringing in his ears. He felt nothing, but then he had heard that sometimes it took a few seconds for the body to register the shock. Or was he already dead, and he was just seeing images through the dying impulses of his brain? He thought it was a trick of the poor light, but he could no longer see the outline of the Entworp's jaw. But then the head turned jerkily towards the light, and Borya could now see that the lower part of the man's face was missing, and blood was spurting from the huge wound. The dark form made a gurgling sound, and then folded in on itself and fell to the floor.

Borya tried to move but felt as if he was pinned to the ground, his muscles refusing to respond. Then another form entered the range of his vision. It was Hsu, his old friend, with whom he had stood side-by-side in the firefight on the Sungari Bridge only months ago. He was holding a rifle before him, and someone from behind played an electric torch across Borya's face.

"Borya!" he heard Hsu exclaim in surprise, now holding his rifle on the collapsed form in front of them. "What are you doing here?" Behind him appeared two other Railway guardsmen, also holding rifles. Hsu helped Borya to his feet and held onto him as he swayed momentarily before finding his balance. "Are you hurt?"

"No, just dazed, I think," Borya answered. One of the guardsmen turned the electric torch directly onto the prone Entworp. He was still alive, thrashing and spraying a bloody foam across the oily concrete floor. There was nothing to be done to help him other than silently watch in morbid fascination until seconds later, he lay still.

"What are you doing here?" Hsu asked again, incredulous.

"I was supposed to be meeting an informant here. Instead, this man showed up, who turns out to be the murder suspect of the case I've been working on. He was just about to shoot me."

"Then you're damn lucky we were right close by," Hsu marveled. "We're on night patrol, as usual, and we saw you flash the police signal light over the door to this train shed. We came inside quietly when I saw this man holding a pistol, so I figured him to be a Soviet agent, and I shot him before he could shoot us. I didn't even see you sitting there on the floor."

Borya stared at him, wide-eyed. "I didn't signal you. But I'm sure glad that you came inside. I'd be been dead otherwise."

"Well, somebody signaled."

They searched every inch of the train shed but found no one else inside. The only other doors besides the front one by which they had all entered were all locked. The switch for the signal light was by that main door, and Hsu swore that they saw no one leave the shed from the time they saw the light go on and when they had entered.

"That's bizarre!" Hsu exclaimed.

"Could it have been a short in the electricity?" one of the other guardsmen suggested.

"Then it has to be the most fortunate of malfunctions I've ever witnessed in my life," Hsu replied as they now all stood in the light of shed entrance. "Well anyway, headquarters will be sending a party to check out the signal, and they can take custody of the body and take down our stories and hopefully let us finish out our patrol. If we're lucky, we won't be tied up all night and past our shift."

It was only then that Borya noticed the extra chevron on Hsu's sleeve. "You made corporal!"

Hsu laughed. "Yes, they promoted me after the Sungari bridge. Just after you returned to police duties. And now I am engaged to a girl in Fujiadian."

"Congratulations, you certainly earned it."

Borya expected he should be feeling alarmed or panicked, but instead only felt a strange serenity. Was he in shock? He didn't think so—his thoughts were still completely lucid. He regretted the death of the Englishman, but only because now there would be no trial. How many brushes with death was this now? First the firefight on the Sungari Bridge, then the bombing at Hailar, the attack at Yakeshi, and now this. Had fate decided again it wasn't his time, as Chinn believed? But it felt like there was more than just fate involved this time. Fate or miracle, Borya made the sign of the cross.

CHAPTER THIRTY-FOUR

BORYA ARRIVED AT THE gate of the Chicken and Duck Company the next morning with an arrest warrant in hand. Coming here felt much different than his previous visit with Chinn. Before, he had felt like an outsider in a European enclave. This time he considered the Binjiang Products British Import and Export Company as an intruder in his city. He was accompanied by two police cadets, one Russian and one Chinese. They weren't that much younger than himself, but to Borya, it felt like there was a gulf of many years since he had been in their position. They had been assigned to him for this task at Superintendent Liu's insistence. "It will be a good learning experience for them, and you might need the backup."

An Indian guard came out of the guardhouse to intercept them, and Borya thrust the arrest warrant at him. It was written in both Russian and Mandarin, but it was plain from the guard's face that he wasn't fluent in either of the two languages, at least in their written forms.

"What is this?"

"It is an arrest warrant for one of your employees," Borya replied, his voice firm but devoid of any emotion behind the mask. A second guard came out of the little guardhouse, and

Borya showed the warrant again and repeated his purpose for being there.

"I will have to call ahead and get permission . . ."

"No, you won't," Borya cut him off and lifted the flap of his holster and put his hand on the butt of his revolver. This time, his voice was icy. The two police cadets also put their hands on their revolvers. The second guard started to protest until he looked at Borya's face, leaving his mouth open but with no words coming out.

"Stay here and make sure neither of them leave or use the phone," Borya directed to the Russian police cadet and then walked around the gate with the Chinese cadet and strode directly for the headquarters building. He ignored the British flag flapping in the autumnal breeze.

Inside the lobby, the prim Mrs. Esibov was sitting as before behind her desk, still guarding the company against all intruders. She rose to her feet at their approach, her mouth opened to protest. Before she could utter a word, Borya slammed the warrant down onto her desk with his open hand, the sound echoing around the lobby like a rifle shot. "Read this." Then he circled around her desk and through into the office bay beyond, the cadet hurrying to keep pace with him. Every clerk's head there had already jerked up at the sound of Borya's hand on the lobby desk and were now staring at him as he entered. Boris Gregorovich was sitting in the next to the last row of desks, and his face went ghostly white when he saw Borya.

"Surprised to see me?" Borya began upon reaching Boris' desk. "Maybe as surprised as I was to see Mr. Entworp last night instead of you."

For several seconds Boris' mouth moved without forming words before he finally found his voice. "H-he, found out I was checking the records. He threatened me . . ." The clerks seated at the surrounding desks watched and listened in astonishment.

"Oh, and so you just forgot to warn me he would be taking your place at our meeting? You couldn't have made another phone call or sent a message to your old friend?"

"He threatened me... to hurt my family . . ." and his head whipped around to face his fellow clerks on either side, seeking understanding but seeing only alarm and confusion.

"Was that before or after you asked him for money to buy your help and silence?" Borya asked, an even darker tone of iciness creeping into his voice. Boris tried to form words, but something from the front of the room distracted him. Borya turned to see the director Mr. MacKenzie enter the room, trailed by a distraught Mrs. Esibov.

Borya waited until they were in earshot before turning back to Boris. "Boris Gregorovich Mischenko, I am arresting you for conspiracy to commit murder."

"But I didn't have anything to do with killing Geiger. I didn't even know Mr. Entworp had him killed until . . ."

"No, not the murder of Manfred Geiger," Borya spoke slowly and deliberately, "the attempted murder of *me*."

Boris now looked all around him wildly, as if seeking an avenue of escape, but Borya and the police cadet stood in his path to the only doorway out of the room. Suddenly, his expression switched from panic to anger. "You were never really one of us, Borya *Sergeevich*," Boris spat out. "Pretending to be Russian when all you ever were was a dirty half-breed *ermaozi!*"

"I'm not one of you? You know, Boris, I think that's the nicest thing you've ever said to me."

Behind him, he heard MacKenzie call out. "Now see here—" but no more words came out when he saw Borya's eyes and how the scar on his forehead now blazed a bright red.

Borya stepped around Boris' desk to stand next to his chair and turned back so he was facing the spluttering British manager. Then he looked him straight in the eye while he put his hand on the high back of Boris' wooden chair and pulled backwards. The chair teetered backwards, and Boris flapped his arms wildly but unsuccessfully to regain balance before falling to the floor in a crash that echoed throughout the room. Every face in the room, including that of Director MacKenzie and Mrs Esibov, were frozen in shock, their mouths agape.

"Take him to Police Headquarters and book him," Borya said in a flat monotone to the Chinese police cadet and then looked down at the stunned Boris. "You know, it's right what you Russians say... *you can never know a man until you've eaten a whole sack of salt together.*" And then he winked. The cadet gave a puzzled look, but Boris understood. Director MacKenzie had to step aside or Borya would have bumped him aside on his way out of the room.

CHAPTER THIRTY-FIVE

BORYA WELCOMED THE SUMMONS to Superintendent Liu's office. It was a week since the death of Peter Entworp and the arrest of Boris Mischenko, and one day after Borya had left a message for Liu that he was prepared to deliver the final summary of the investigation into Manfred Geiger's death. The week had been filled with trying to chase down some remaining loose threads, including a return visit to Geiger's dacha on Sun Island. He found the little house the same as before, save for Wang Ju's personal effects gone and no bezoars or further clues. It bothered him no small bit that there were still gaps in the fabric of the case, but he finally had to conclude that he had taken the investigation as far as he could.

As many times as he had visited that office with Chinn, he could almost feel the presence of the venerable Inspector accompanying him. He found Superintendent Liu seated behind his desk and the German consul, the portly Herr Schessler, sitting in a chair opposite him.

"Herr Schessler, you recall Officer Melnikov from our earlier meeting?"

"Of course, of course," the German replied and extended his hand to Melnikov without standing up. Borya felt the same sweep of those intelligent eyes from their previous encounter, ending on the scar on his forehead. Liu waved Borya toward the one empty chair, and Borya turned it so he could face both men before seating himself, leaving the case folder on his lap.

"Officer Melnikov was able to continue the investigation after the unfortunate death of Inspector Chinn," Liu continued.

"Yes, very unfortunate," Schessler echoed.

"And although I know most of the results of the investigation, I will actually be hearing Officer Melnikov's complete report for the first time with you," Liu explained to Schessler, before turning back to Borya with a nod.

Borya cleared his throat and began the dissertation that he had been carefully practicing throughout the previous day. "As you know, I assisted Inspector Chinn in trying to correlate the days since Herr Geiger went missing, with the plan for his buying trip with his company agent to Hailar, and then with the subsequent shipment of his body from Barim. We were unable to confirm either his or the agent's arrival at either of those locations. I subsequently learned that neither Geiger nor the company agent reached either of those locations."

The German's eyebrows rose in surprise, but Liu raised a single hand to cut off any questions, nodding to Borya to continue.

"We also looked into Herr Geiger's business and personal affairs in order to find a motive for his murder. What was noteworthy was that his expenses far exceeded the income he received from his employment at the abattoir, expenses that included a house in New Town and a mistress and dacha on Sun Island. And we were unable to find any other legitimate sources of income to explain his wealth."

Herr Schessler's eyes suddenly clouded, and he sat up straighter in his chair, but he did not interrupt. Borya thought he saw the slightest hint of a smile on Liu's face at the German's obvious discomfort.

Borya continued after a pause. "Although they were not correctly identified by either the Japanese police in Changchun nor the coroner here in Harbin, two items that were found in Herr Geiger's possession at the time of his death were identified as bezoars. These are gallstones occasionally found in cattle during their slaughter at the abattoir where Geiger worked. They are highly prized for medicinal purposes and consequently bring a high price from producers of natural medicines. Policy in the abattoir is that these bezoars are the property of the company and are collected and sold to the highest bidder as secondary sales. The abattoir has been cooperative in providing me their records to show the numbers and sales of bezoars over the last several years." Here, Borya removed a typed spreadsheet from the folder on his lap and handed it across the desk to Liu. At Borya's request, MacKenzie had ordered a copy of the records made, the director eager to show his cooperation with the police following the embarrassing death of Peter Entworp and arrest of Boris Mischenko, two of his employees. There was no sign in Boris's home or desk at the abattoir that he had even tried to make a copy of the bezoar records for Borya before betraying him, and had stayed stubbornly silent at the direction of his attorney during subsequent interrogation by senior headquarters detectives.

"You can see there was a marked decline in the collection of bezoars starting a year after the arrival of Herr Geiger at the abattoir and his installation as the manager over the cattle processing department in October 1924. He was skimming about half of the bezoars from the cattle barn and selling them outside the company, providing his considerable extra income."

Liu looked at the numbers on the report and then handed the sheet to Herr Schessler, who returned the sheet to Borya after giving it a quick glance. "But Herr Geiger surely wasn't the only one who had access to these... gallstones," the consul argued.

"No, and he wasn't. He had an accomplice on the floor of the cattle barn, his foreman, a man who went missing immediately after we conducted an arrest at the abattoir. The detective squad has put out a bulletin across Harbin and with the provincial authorities for his arrest, however, nobody admits to having seen him in the last week."

"So, the arrest was of Geiger's murderer?" Schessler prompted.

"No, that man was helping to cover up further illegal sales by Geiger's assistant in the cattle processing department, one Peter Entworp. Entworp learned of Geiger's scheme of selling bezoars on the black market and tried to blackmail him into sharing the proceeds. When Geiger refused, Entworp hired a local thug to kill Geiger here in Harbin and took over the racket. He also had the company agent that was to accompany Geiger on his buying trip also killed to try and confuse the investigation."

Schessler shook his head in bewilderment. "But how do you learn all this?"

"Because Entworp told me himself."

"He confessed to all of this?" Schessler asked skeptically.

"Not as a confession, he freely admitted it. You see, he intended to kill me and felt sure his words would die with me. A timely intervention by Railway guards saved me and killed Entworp."

Schessler now stared at Borya speechless, and so Borya turned back to Liu. "Unfortunately, Entworp did not also disclose the name of the killer he hired, only that he came from Fujiadian. Enquiries are being made from that district precinct, but so far they are unsuccessful." Liu responded with a wry smile of understanding. There were always plenty of killers for hire from among the poorer neighborhoods of Fujiadian, where life was cheap and money scarce.

Meanwhile, Schessler had found his voice again. "But how does that explain Geiger's body showing up in Changchun in a crate sent from Barim?"

"That was all a fabrication to make us look outside Harbin for a motive and the location of the two murders. The abattoir's management confirmed that Entworp had easy access to freight shipping forms. Apparently, it was routine for him to ship samples and diseased animals to provincial laboratories for testing and analysis. It wouldn't have been hard to for him to arrange for the killer to pack the body in a crate with quicklime, there was plenty of that to be had at the abattoir, and then ship it from here in Harbin to Changchun on a shipper Entworp forged as having come from Barim. How he came up with a real name from Barim to list as the pretend sender I wasn't able to discover. Perhaps he had heard about her from somewhere. But it explains why we weren't able to find the original paperwork or any witnesses in Barim."

Now it was Liu's turn to speak. "Did you find out which medicine suppliers were buying from Geiger? They had to have known or suspected that sales so large were illegal."

Borya shook his head. "No, sir, I wasn't. All the major suppliers in Harbin know that the abattoir is under contract with just one supplier for all bezoar sales and that in the quantities that Geiger was selling, they had to have known the source was an abattoir and thus illegal. So none would admit to having bought bezoars from Geiger under the table, including the legitimate buyer under contract. But whoever it was always paid in cash because, outside of his salary checks from the abattoir, all of Geiger's deposits at his bank in Pristan were in the form of cash." Borya laid the file folder back onto his lap as a sign he had finished.

Now Liu allowed a complete smile. "Remarkable work! You have shown promising investigative skills that I'm sure will be a future consideration in your career here in the Special District police force. And I trust you now know the value of requesting backup when meeting an informant alone for the first time?"

"Yes, Superintendent," Borya replied seriously, but ebullient in the praise more than he was chastened by the mild criticism.

"And this is your final report?" nodding to the folder.

"Yes, Superintendent," and he handed it across the desk.

"Well, Consul Schessler, as soon as I have reviewed this report and signed off on it, I will send you a copy," Liu announced.

"I thank you, Superintendent Liu… and Officer Melnikov. I will, of course, need it to complete my own report back to my government," replied a chastened Schessler, clearly unhappy with the unsavory image of his deceased fellow citizen. He then rose to his feet and shook the hands of Borya and Liu in turn, and let himself out of the office.

Alone now with Liu, Borya spoke. "I just want to add that I was only completing Inspector Chinn's work. I assisted him in the beginning, and after that, I was applying the techniques he taught me. So he was the one who really solved the case."

"Of course, Officer Melnikov. Of course."

"And I'm sorry I wasn't able to track down the foreman or the illegal buyer."

Liu leaned back in his chair and pointed back over his shoulder at the wall. "Do you see that picture hanging crooked behind me... well, yes, I know you see it because you stare at it every time you're in my office. I leave it crooked on purpose as a reminder to myself that I cannot make everything in my job perfect or complete. There are some things that remain a mystery, and some crimes that go unpunished, but that's just the way it goes. That's real life. Savor the victories, and let go of the losses, and be ready for the next challenge. I meant it when I said you did remarkable work on this case. Go and celebrate. And I will see that a letter of commendation is put in your file."

CHAPTER THIRTY-SIX

RATHER THAN CELEBRATING, BORYA waited at Chinn's old desk in the detective squad room for Superintendent Liu to complete his review and approval of Borya's final report. He knew he didn't need to be there to see that any changes got to the clerks for retyping, but he just wanted to be there to see it through to the last step in person. He felt a certain lightness in his chest at the knowledge that justice had been served and that he and Inspector Chinn had been its instrument. The instigator of the deaths of both Manfred Geiger and Song Nikan had been exposed, and his debt to society paid in full. But Borya's satisfaction was also knowing Chinn's death, as a result of Entworp's deceit, had been avenged. True, he had not found Entworp's hired killer or the foreman, but in the end no one would have been harmed beyond the embezzlement of some abattoir assets had not Entworp's greed set everything in motion. And what counted was the picture, not the crooked frame. And lastly, there was the personal satisfaction of knowing he really did have the investigative skills to solve a murder.

He lined out the final entry in his notebook: Debrief and Final Report. There was a profound sense of satisfaction and finality in that simple act, but also a measure of sadness. The closing of the investigation marked the end of his brief sojourn on the murder squad and his subsequent return to patrol duties under Commander Cho at the District 8 precinct. Which Cho would he find there, the old hostile one or the recent half-friendly one? Somehow, it no longer seemed important—it would be what it would be. There was some consolation in the promised letter of commendation from Liu, and his time spent on the case might someday help him in any consideration of promotion, but he was a long way down the ladder from ever being considered for a detective position.

He passed the time boxing up the evidence from the investigation for placement in storage, including his notebook. He had a brand new blank notebook already in his pocket to start with the next day. With the deaths of both Manfred Geiger and Peter Entworp, he doubted whether any of the evidence would ever be needed by a court procurator. The trial of Boris Mischenko would likely be based on Borya's own testimony alone. Maybe if the missing foreman was found and arrested? Borya touched each piece as if it was a treasured memento. They represented his last material ties to his time with Inspector Chinn.

He came to the small envelope that held the two bezoars, the "mudballs" that had been the key to solving the investigation. So much value in such little innocuous objects! That made him remember the Red Swastika award in Chinn's home and the charity and good it represented. Would Chinn have been comfortable with such objects of value being buried in a dusty evidence room to serve no worldly purpose, maybe even months from now being tossed or rifled by someone less ethical? Maybe by one of the clerks or detectives sitting alongside him in the squad room right now? And were both bezoars really needed as evidence? Wouldn't one be enough? What if that value could be applied to something good? Would Chinn have approved that? What would his Chinese classics have told him? If they were like the Bible, he suspected there was enough variation to allow one to find the answer you wanted to hear. Was this yet another of life's crooked pictures? He rolled the larger of the two bezoars out of the envelope into his hand and then dropped it into a side pocket of his uniform tunic, then pulled his handkerchief from that same pocket and wiped his nose to mask the first motion. He looked around—only one nearby murder desk was occupied, but detective Nika Sergeeva was fully occupied watching the smoke from his cigar rise toward the ceiling through half-closed eyes.

Two hours before the end of the shift, a young police cadet brought the final report down from Liu's office. There were only a few minor corrections, but nothing significant. Borya smiled when he saw that Liu had included his name, along with Chinn's, as one of the investigating officers. He left the report with a clerk for the retyping and filing and left the squad room for the last time. He could have stayed until the end of the shift, but there was nothing left there for him to do. Some eyes followed him out, and even a couple of the clerks smiled his way, and he nodded back in acknowledgement. Did they know this would be the last time they would see him here?

Borya stopped at his grandfather's shop in District 8 along his way home. There was no one in the front of the store, but the tinkle of the bell on the door brought the old man out from the backroom. "Borya!" came his warm greeting. "I have not seen you for many days! You must be very busy!" Borya was relieved by his grandfather's informality, which meant that his recent close brush with death had not reached his ears, nor that of his mother or sisters. There was no point in worrying them unnecessarily.

Borya explained that the investigation was finally over, and he would be returning to his normal police duties. The old man nodded sagely. His eyes showed he understood his grandson's mixed feelings without having to voice it.

"And this is no longer needed as evidence," and Borya produced the larger bezoar from its pocket. His grandfather smiled and immediately placed it on the scales. He then retrieved his money box from below the counter and counted out three ten-yuan notes into Borya's hands. It was more than Borya had expected.

"Can you stay and have some tea? You can tell me all about your latest exploits . . ."

"Sorry, I still have an errand to run today, Grandfather. Can I come by tomorrow after my shift?"

"Of course, of course! Tomorrow!" His grandfather's enthusiasm hid any sign of disappointment.

Borya left the shop and took the nearest street that led eastward to Fujiadian. It was a route that he had made a hundred times in his head since his release from the hospital weeks ago, but a destination he had never made in the real world. To Chinn's house ... or rather, the house of his widow and family.

Walking slowly, he still arrived at the door of the small green house with the red door sooner than he thought possible. Three times he raised his hand to knock on the door, and three times his hand fell back down as if it was too heavy for his arm to bear. Then the curtain at the near window fluttered. Had someone sensed his presence on the porch without his knocking? A second later, the door was flung open and Chunhua, Chinn's widow, was standing before him on the threshold.

"Borya!" she exclaimed with a smile. "Please, come in."

Borya teetered, and then, surprising both Chunhua and himself, he burst into tears. Chunhua's arms folded around him, and she led him inside and to the leather armchair in the corner by the front window to sit. In Chinn's chair. Chinn Wenyan, Chinn's father, sat in his chair by the stove like he had never left it since Borya's last visit, looking puzzled at the intrusion. This was not the entrance Borya had planned, and he furiously wiped his tears away.

"Sorry... sorry. I did not come here to make a scene. I only came to say how sorry I am."

Chunhua sat on the adjacent ottoman and put a warm hand over Borya's. "I know it is hard. It is hard for everyone, but that is part of being the family and friend of a policeman."

Borya felt ashamed now. He had come to apologize and to offer sympathy and comfort to Chinn's widow, but here she was the one consoling him. "But it is my fault... I insisted that we go beyond Barim to Hailar where..."

Chunhua stopped him with a sad smile and a hand on his shoulder. "No, Borya. You should know my husband always made up his own mind. He would not have agreed to go to Hailar unless he had decided himself that it was the right thing to do. You cannot blame yourself. Please, let me fix us some tea. I heard you have solved the case, and I want you to tell me all about it."

Chunhua returned with a tray with a teapot and cups for all three of them, and even a full sugar bowl to satisfy Borya's taste. After they all had had their first sip of tea, Borya told her in detail about all his enquiries and discoveries since he had been released from the hospital and returned to the case, speaking loudly enough that the elder gentleman could also hear him clearly. He emphasized how the techniques and diligence that the younger Chinn had taught him had guided him at every step. Both Chunhua and her father-in-law nodded, and by the time he had finished, all the eyes in the room were glistening with tears.

"Thank you," Chunhua responded sincerely. "I know he is happy now, knowing that justice was fulfilled. He never liked to leave a case unsolved."

"And sorry, I must ask… has there been any issues with his death benefits and pension since he… well, was outside the Special District? Did they try to claim it happened in a war zone?"

"No, not at all. Superintendent Liu took care of everything, the death benefits, and his pension. He explained that you both were still within the CER railway zone at Yakeshi and were working on the investigation when attacked. The pension is not as much as his salary, of course, but we still have his father's pension to help us make ends meet." The old man smiled and nodded. Of course, Borya thought, Liu had made sure the widow and family were taken care of.

At that moment, the door to one of the backrooms opened, and the two young daughters, Chao-xing and Chenguang, entered, rubbing the sleep of a nap from their eyes. The youngest, upon seeing Borya in the room, immediately recognized him and announced, "Story!" Only to be echoed by her older sister.

Borya smiled. "Of course."

After he told the girls another Korean fairy tale, Chunhua asked him to stay for dinner, but Borya politely declined. "My mother will be expecting me home, and she will worry if I am very late. She gets fearful after every attack or crime is reported, even if they happen far outside Harbin."

"Then you must come back and visit us again soon," Chunhua insisted, and her father-in-law nodded in agreement.

"Yes, I will. I am not sure exactly when … I return to normal patrol duties in District 8 tomorrow. I'm only hoping they don't assign me back on night patrols with the Railway guards."

He made his farewells to all in turn. He left behind many smiles and three ten-yuan notes tucked behind the Red Swastika award in the glass cabinet, secreted there when Chunhua had been out of the room preparing their tea and his back had been turned to the grandfather while he pretended to be examining the family heirlooms. He recalled a Chinese proverb, but not from where he had heard it: *Laws control the lesser man; right conduct controls the greater one.*

EPILOGUE

BORYA HAD JUST RETURNED to the District 8 precinct station, from the end of his patrol shift along the waterfront on a cold January day, when he received the summons to report to Commander Cho. He was very glad to be back indoors in the warmth of the station while outside the whole city seemed to be entirely encased in ice, and the roads and sidewalks hidden beneath packed layers of dirty snow. Together, his woolen winter uniform, overcoat, long underwear, hat, and boots hadn't been enough to keep the cold wind from reaching into his bones. At least it had been a quiet night—too cold for the pickpockets and drug dealers to brave it outside. And at least, he wasn't patrolling in Fujiadian, where the patrolmen were the first ones to find the frozen bodies of beggars and addicts in the snowdrifts each morning.

The cold gray day suited his gloomy mood, which seemed to reflect the mood of the whole city. In October, Stalin had instigated a rebellion in the south and forced the national government in Nanking to withdraw their promise to send reinforcements to the Young Marshal. By November, the Soviet armies had cracked the Marshal's lines on both the eastern and western frontiers. In the west, Soviet forces had advanced all the way into Hailar before the Young Marshal was forced to sue for peace. Borya wondered since what had happened to the helpful Lieutenant Enebish of the Hailar police and to Song Nikan's widow and family. And worst of all, as part of the price for peace, the Young Marshal had been forced to accept the return of Soviet leadership to the CER and the civil administration in Harbin. Once again, the obnoxious Bolsheviks in their ill-fitting suits swaggered through the streets of New Town and Pristan, and the communist newspapers reopened to flood the city with lies. Yes, the city had endured but had somehow fallen a step behind, its luster a shade less.

And if that wasn't bad enough, the stock market crash in America at the end of October was already beginning to generate ripple effects across the entire globe. Business in the Northeast Provinces had already been depressed from China's defeat by the Bolsheviks, and now this world-wide depression had begun to dry up the Northeast's export market of soya bean cakes and oil to Europe and Japan. Because the soya bean market underpinned much of the Northeast's economy, the effects were being felt daily in Harbin. Businesses and manufacturers were closing or shedding employees to try and stay solvent, and with rising unemployment came rising crime. The clothing store where his sister Hei-rin worked had already drastically cut her hours. Ironically, the rise in crime made the police one of the very few "growth industries" in the city. The other bright spot had been his promotion to Officer Second-Rank in recognition of his "valuable" service on special assignment to the detective squad and with the Railway Guards. The promotion brought with it a welcomed small increase in pay, and Borya was proud the family dinners now included fish and meat more than once a week. Commander Cho had tried to make it sound like the promotion had been all his idea, but Borya knew it had been initiated from police headquarters. Still, Cho had done nothing to block it and had treated Borya civilly since his return.

Cho's office door was open, and the commander waved him in. Cho sat behind his desk, but his chair was turned sideways to the desk, and he was facing up toward the room's single window, and he was watching the falling flakes of snow over the top of a piece of paper he held out in front of his face.

"You are to report to Superintendent Liu immediately," Cho stated flatly.

At first, Borya's heart leaped. Was he being assigned to assist another detective? Had his success on the investigation of Geiger's murder shown he deserved such promise? But why then was Cho avoiding looking at him and sounding so aloof? Was he in some trouble over the investigation? Had someone discovered the bezoar missing from the evidence box?

"Did they say why I was being summoned?"

"Superintendent Liu will explain."

"Yes, Commander," replied Borya, his heart now in his throat.

Since it was the end of the shift and late in the day, Borya took the streetcar from District 8 up into New Town to police headquarters. It was faster than on foot on the icy sidewalks, and he didn't want to be the cause for the Superintendent to be held late in his office. On the second floor, he found the police cadet that guarded Liu's door already gone and the door open. Liu was standing by the window, watching the setting sun color the snow-laden clouds past Prospect Street, but he caught Borya's presence in his reflection in the glass. On his desk lay the police saber that Liu wore for public ceremonies. Had there been another ceremony up here in New Town today? Sometimes, news of public events didn't always make it down to the city below the bluff.

"Officer Melnikov. Thank you for coming so promptly. Please come in and close the door. Sit down." The voice was somber, like the voices of the priests at St. Nicolas on Sunday, and his mouth formed a smile that did not reach his eyes. He picked up a piece of paper from the top of the desk as though he intended to read it aloud, but instead sent it spinning back onto the desktop to land atop the sword. Then he looked across at Borya directly into his eyes.

"I don't know any other way to say this but just in plain words. As you know, part of the recent peace agreement with the Soviets was their assignment of their own civil officers to the Special District administration. They have now issued an edict releasing all the White Russian officers from the police force, effective immediately. Your name was included in the list they provided . . ."

Borya sat stunned. This was the last thing he had expected. Being a policeman was the only thing he knew how to do. The only thing he wanted to do. And how could his family get by without his pay? He realized Liu was still speaking, and he tried to focus on his words.

". . . having a Russian surname, of course. They might have also have read the commendation in your file about the action against their agents on the Sungari Bridge."

Borya tried to find his voice, but it came out in a croak. "Wha . . . what about an appeal? I am only half-Russian . . ."

"There will be no appeals. It was the first thing I checked into."

Borya slumped and grabbed onto the arms of the chair before he could slide out onto the floor.

"Listen, Borya. Listen to me," Liu raised his voice until Borya finally returned his gaze, his attention caught more by being addressed by his first name than the volume. "I asked Cho that I be the one to give you this news because I knew it would be hard for you to hear. And that I want you to know that I feel it is grossly unfair. But I also wanted to tell you I have come up with an alternative that I think matches your skills and intelligence."

Borya blinked, concentrating hard to listen above the loud buzzing in his ears. "Alternative?"

"I have friends here in the city. Influential friends. I have told them about you, and they have agreed to sponsor a scholarship for you to attend the Law Institute here in Harbin. It will cover tuition and all your fees, including a small stipend to help your family from the loss of your police income. They tell me they can insure your acceptance at the Institute despite the Soviet civil officers."

"But I never finished secondary school," Borya confessed.

"They know that, they have your records. The scholarship will be there when you finish your last semesters."

Now Borya's head swirled faster. As soon as the sun had set and his world grown cold, then the sun rose again. "But why? Why are you... they doing this for me?"

This time, Liu's smile reached his eyes. "First, you proved to me and Inspector Chinn your intelligence and promise during the Geiger murder investigation, and you proved your courage on the Sungari Bridge. But also, my friends and I believe that for China to be strong and once more take its place among the world powers, it must embrace both the traditional and the modern. To embrace the modern, we must look outside China and take the best from the West in science, government, and organizational skills, but at the same time still retain our own culture and virtues.

You, Borya, already have feet in both the East and the West, the old and new. We think you, and others like you, will be needed to build the new China."

For the first time in his life, Borya felt that maybe, actually, there was somewhere he belonged. And to something. Except for his father and aunt, the Russian community had looked at him as that "Asian" boy who was always trying to fit in. Outside of his mother and grandfather, the Korean and Chinese communities had inherently mistrusted him as some kind of interloper. Now he was hearing that Liu and his circle of friends thought those very things that made him an outsider were what they thought were needed to help build a new future for the country.

Borya looked down to hide the tears welling up in his eyes. "Thank you, Superintendent. I will work hard to make you and your friends proud."

Liu smiled again and then stood up behind his desk. He picked up the sword and solemnly handed it across the desk to Borya as if he was commemorating some passing of the guard. "I want you to have this, so you will always have something to remind you of your time here in the police force."

"I cannot, sir!"

"No, you can. Take it. Let it help you to remember what Inspector Chinn taught you, as he taught me. *Whoever is your teacher, even for a day, consider your father your whole life.*"

Borya stood to take the sword in both hands, cradling it. He held it close to his eyes so he could see through the tears there the plum blossom encircled by a wreath of rice stalks on the backstrap of the hilt. A symbol of China.

"Thank you, Superintendent." And then Borya backed out of the room, afraid he would begin sobbing out loud if he stayed any longer.

Downstairs he passed the door to the detective squad room, almost deserted now at this hour except for two of the White Russian detectives who were emptying their desks and putting personal items into boxes, other victims of the Bolshevik purge. One of them was Nika Sergeeva from the murder squad. Borya hurried past before they saw him, not wishing to add to their own hurt and embarrassment. Outside, he took the streetcar that would take him down to District 8 and home, huddling with the other passengers to block the wind-blown snow coming through the open doors, gripping the sword tightly between his legs. He knew he would still have to return to his own precinct to return his uniform and service weapon, but since he had no civilian clothes at the station to change into, it would have to wait until tomorrow. On the bumpy trip down, he thought about how he could break the news to his mother in a way that would let the good news win out over the bad.

His mother stared wide-eyed at the sword in his hands when he entered the apartment. "Wonderful news, mother!" he began. He told her first of his firing from the police force, and it took a while before she listened closely enough to understand the good news part of the story. Finally, after many repetitions and questions answered, she finally understood.

"The Law Institute!" both Hei-rin and Min shouted excitedly that evening when he repeated the day's events, both of them jumping up and down in Borya's arms and then each other's. His mother cried both happy and worried tears all over again.

Borya started the first morning of his new life at his table at his aunt's tearoom. She had already heard of the wholesale firing of the White Russians from the police force but was ecstatic when she learned of Borya's sponsorship and scholarship to the esteemed Harbin Law Institute. She had been disappointed ever since he had quit school to become a police cadet, not because he had become a policeman, but because he hadn't finished his education. Education has always been important in the Melnikov family, she would repeat.

"Your father would be so proud! Did you do know the Marian Fathers have started a new school in Harbin called the Lyceum Saint Nicholas?" she said excitedly. "You could finish your secondary school there! What will you do until the next semester starts?"

"As soon as the snow melts, I want to try and find someone in Barim... to thank them."

"A girl?" his aunt asked with a knowing smile.

"Yes, a girl..."

AFTERWORD

THIS IS A COMING of age story taking place amidst tumultuous times. A young Borya Sergeevich Melnikov was still trying to make sense of his world after the tragic death of his father, amidst the turbulent politics of 1929 Manchuria. Like many of the inhabitants of Manchurian Harbin, he was caught up in the crosscurrents of rising Soviet aggression, awakening Chinese nationalism, and declining White Russian fortunes. And if that wasn't chaos enough, there was the added horror of a full-blown border war and a wave of terrorism that was the Sino-Soviet conflict of 1929. And yet each time he felt lost or defeated, strong figures emerged that showed him that you can still rise above the chaos if you stand by your virtues and beliefs. I believe that is still true today in our own turbulent times.

Although the main characters in this story were fictional or fictionalized, many of the events in this story were real: the undeclared war between the Soviet Union and Nationalist China, the latter represented by Chang Hsueh-liang, the "Young Marshal"; the concurrent wave of Red terror and sabotage in Harbin and across Manchuria; the bombing of Hailar; the massacre of Starovary villages and refugees by GPU "bandits"; and even the attempted sabotage of the Sungari Bridge. I have, however, taken liberty with the timeline of some of these events to help fit them within the narrative of this story.

I have used contemporary romanized spellings for Chinese individuals and place-names to conform to the time-period, perhaps inconsistently but with good intentions. And although many of the Harbin streets and localities had already had their Russian names replaced with Chinese names prior to 1929 by edict of the Chinese civil administration, I have in most cases purposefully retained their original Russian names as these would be how Borya remembered them, and after all, we are seeing the city through his eyes. Likewise, bias and prejudices reflected herein are intentional in order to portray a worldview shaped by someone who would have experienced Borya's life and circumstances.

Finally, I have tried to represent the world of 1929 Harbin and Manchuria as historically accurate as possible within the extent of my personal research of scholarly works and articles, travel books, and guidebooks on the time and subject. I take full responsibility for any errors or misrepresentations, but in the end I hold steadfast in the defense that this is, after all, a work of fiction.